Praise for Maud Hart Lovelace

"There are three authors whose body of work I have reread more than once over my adult life: Charles Dickens, Jane Austen, and Maud Hart Lovelace."
—Anna Quindlen,
New York Times bestselling author

"Slipping into a Betsy book is like slipping into a favorite pair of well-worn slippers: It's always a pleasure to live in Betsy's world for a little while, to experience her simple joys but also her (thankfully short-lived) sorrows."
—Meg Cabot,
New York Times bestselling author

"I reread these books every year, marveling at how a world so quaint—shirtwaists! Pompadours! Merry Widow hats!—can feature a heroine who is undeniably modern."
—Laura Lippman,
New York Times bestselling author

"I read every one of these Betsy-Tacy-Tib books twice. I loved them as a child, as a young adult, and now, reading them with my daughter, as a mother. What a wonderful world it was!"
—Bette Midler, actor and singer

"Some characters become your friends for life. That's how it was for me with Betsy-Tacy."
—Judy Blume, beloved bestselling author

"The Betsy-Tacy books were among my favorites when I was growing up."
—Nora Ephron, Academy Award–nominated writer-director

"I am fairly certain that my independent, high-spirited grandmother must have had a childhood similar to Betsy Ray's. . . . As I read . . . I felt that I was having an unexpected and welcome peek into Granny's childhood—a gift to me from Maud Hart Lovelace."
—Ann M. Martin, creator/author of *The Baby-sitters Club*

"Family loyalty and the devotion of friends to one another . . . for me are the defining characteristics of the Betsy-Tacy stories."
—Esther Hautzig, award-winning author, former director of Children's Book Promotion for Thomas Y. Crowell Co. and publicist for *Betsy's Wedding* in 1955

"I truly consider *Betsy and Tacy Go Downtown* to be the finest novel in the English language! I will never love any other books as much as I love the Betsy-Tacy books."
—Claudia Mills, children's book author

"I grew up thirty miles north of Mankato, and trips to town were filled with mystery and magic because I was walking the same streets that Betsy and Tacy once walked. The Betsy-Tacy books . . . more than any other books, fed my dream of becoming a writer one day."　　　—Jill Kalz, Minnesota Book Awards Readers' Choice Award winner

"At school visits, when kids ask what books I read as a child, I have only one answer: Betsy-Tacy—the entire series. . . . Truthfully, I think those were the only books I read as a child. But they were enough to make me know that characters in books had true and honest feelings and that made all the difference."
　　　—Maryann Weidt, author of the Minnesota Book Award–winning picture book *Daddy Played Music for the Cows*

"As a Minnesota girl, I read the Betsy-Tacy books about a thousand times as a kid. I used to go to sleep at night with one of the books under my pillow whispering to myself about the girls, hoping I'd dream I was playing with them."
　　　—Anne Ursu, award-winning author

The
Betsy-Tacy
Treasury

The Betsy-Tacy Books

Book 1: *Betsy-Tacy*

Book 2: *Betsy-Tacy and Tib*

Book 3: *Betsy and Tacy Go Over the Big Hill*

Book 4: *Betsy and Tacy Go Downtown*

Book 5: *Heaven to Betsy*

Book 6: *Betsy in Spite of Herself*

Book 7: *Betsy Was a Junior*

Book 8: *Betsy and Joe*

Book 9: *Betsy and the Great World*

Book 10: *Betsy's Wedding*

The Deep Valley Books

Winona's Pony Cart

Carney's House Party

Emily of Deep Valley

The Betsy-Tacy Treasury

Betsy-Tacy
Betsy-Tacy and Tib
Betsy and Tacy Go Over the Big Hill
Betsy and Tacy Go Downtown

Maud Hart Lovelace

Illustrated by Lois Lenski

HARPER**PERENNIAL** ● MODERN**CLASSICS**

NEW YORK ● LONDON ● TORONTO ● SYDNEY ● NEW DELHI ● AUCKLAND

Betsy-Tacy

TO
BICK *and* MERIAN

Contents

Contents

Author's Note

Author's Note

I cannot remember back to a year in which I did not consider myself to be a writer, and the younger I was the bigger the capital "W." Back in Mankato I wrote stories in notebooks and illustrated them with pictures cut from magazines. When I was ten my father, I hope at not too great expense, had printed a booklet of my earliest rhymes. Soon after I started bombarding the magazines and sold my first story when I was eighteen.

For a long time now I have been happily absorbed in a succession of books for children, chiefly the Betsy-Tacy series. I began these by pure accident. Earlier, for many years, I wrote historical novels and there was a time when I would have told you I was unlikely ever to write anything else. The field delighted me. Especially, I loved the research involved.

I was well into my fourth novel when our daughter Merian was born—quite unexpectedly, because we had been married fourteen years. I finished that novel and wrote two more in collaboration with my husband. But I found myself less and less interested in inventing plots for adult readers. As Merian grew old enough to listen to stories, I loved to tell them to her and I found that most of them centered about my own happy childhood in Mankato. By the time she was seven, and my writer's (now a small "w") conscience was upbraiding me because I had not done a book for several years, I saw suddenly that I could make a book of the stories I was telling her.

The first of the Betsy-Tacy books resulted and ever since then I have written stories for children, most of them about Betsy who is, in some measure, myself. The Ray family is plainly the Hart family. I meet grandfathers now who tell me that they still remember my father's onion sandwiches. It is a great joy to me to have that dear family between book covers.

I must make clear that these are books of fiction. Plots for them have been invented freely. But many—although not all—of the characters are based on real people.

This situation led me into a new kind of research. Letters began to fly. "Tacy," "Tib," "Carney," and other close friends answered lists of questions from me about themselves and our doings when we were young. They drew diagrams of Mankato streets. (Mankato is the Deep Valley of the stories.) They sent old photographs of themselves and their relatives and their houses which Lois Lenski and Vera Neville enjoyed embodying in their delightful pictures. I dived into my own diaries and kodak books and memory books, while the New York Public Library—and later the Claremont libraries—helped out with old newspapers, old fashion magazines, collections of old popular songs, and Sears and Roebuck catalogues.

As our daughter grew up, so did Betsy, and there are now ten mainline Betsy-Tacy stories and three more in which Betsy appears. The letters from children which began with *Betsy-Tacy* flow into our mailbox and are a constant inducement to continue writing juvenile books.

Maud Lovelace

1961

There was a time when meadow, grove, and stream,
The earth, and every common sight,
    To me did seem
Apparell'd in celestial light,
The glory and the freshness of a dream . . .

—WILLIAM WORDSWORTH

1

Betsy Meets Tacy

IT WAS difficult, later, to think of a time when Betsy and Tacy had not been friends. Hill Street came to regard them almost as one person. Betsy's brown braids went with Tacy's red curls, Betsy's plump legs with Tacy's spindly ones, to school and from school, up hill and down, on errands and in play. So that when Tacy had the mumps and Betsy was obliged to make her journeys alone, saucy boys teased her: "Where's the cheese, apple pie?" "Where's your mush, milk?" As though she didn't feel lonesome enough already! And Hill Street knew when Sunday came, even without listening to the rolling bells, for Betsy Ray and Tacy Kelly (whose parents attended different churches), set off down Hill Street separately, looking uncomfortable and strange.

But on this March afternoon, a month before Betsy's fifth birthday, they did not know each other. They had not even seen each other, unless Betsy had glimpsed Tacy, without knowing her for Tacy, among the children of assorted sizes moving into the house across the street. Betsy had been kept in because of bad weather, and all day she had sat with her nose pasted to the pane. It was exciting beyond words to have a family with children moving into that house.

Hill Street was rightfully named. It ran straight up into a green hill and stopped. The name of the town was Deep Valley, and a town named Deep Valley naturally had plenty of hills. Betsy's house, a small yellow cottage, was the last house on her side of Hill Street, and the rambling white house opposite was the last house on that side. So of course it was very important. And it had been empty ever since Betsy could remember.

"I hope whoever moves in will have children," Betsy's mother had said.

"Well, for Pete's sake!" said Betsy's father. "Hill Street is so full of children now that Old Mag has to watch out where she puts her feet down."

"I know," said Betsy's mother. "There are plenty of children for Julia." (Julia was Betsy's sister, eight years old.) "And there are dozens of babies. But there isn't one little girl just Betsy's age. And that's what I'm hoping will come to the house across the street."

That was what Betsy hoped, too. And that was what she had been watching for all day as she sat at the dining room window. She was certain there must be such a little girl. There were girls of almost every size and boys to match, milling about the moving dray and in and out of the house. But she wasn't sure. She hadn't absolutely seen one.

She had watched all day, and now the dining room was getting dark. Julia had stopped practicing her music lesson, and Mrs. Ray had lighted the lamp in the kitchen.

The March snow lay cold and dirty outside the window, but the wind had died down, and the western sky, behind the house opposite, was stained with red.

The furniture had all been carried in, and the dray was gone. A light was shining in the house. Suddenly the front door opened, and a little girl ran out. She wore a hood beneath which long red ringlets spattered out above her coat. Her legs in their long black stockings were thin.

It was Tacy, although Betsy did not know it!

She ran first to the hitching block, and bounced there on her toes a minute, looking up at the sky and all around. Then she ran up the road to the point where it ended on the hill. Some long-gone person had placed a bench there. It commanded the view down Hill Street. The little girl climbed up on this bench and looked intently into the dusk.

"I know just how she feels," thought Betsy with a throb. "This is her new home. She wants to see what it's like." She ran to her mother.

"Mamma!" she cried. "There's the little girl my age. Please let me go out! Just a minute! Please!"

Mrs. Ray was moved by the entreaty. She looked out at the colored sky.

"It does seem to be clearing up," she said. "But you could only stay a minute. Do you want to go to the bother of putting on your things . . ."

"Oh, yes, yes!"

"Overshoes and mittens and everything?"

"Yes, really!"

Betsy flew to the closet, but she could not find her pussy hood. The mittens were twisted on the string inside her coat.

"Mamma! Help me! Please! She'll be gone."

"Help her, Julia," called Betsy's mother, and Julia helped, and at last the pussy hood was tied, and the coat buttoned, and the overshoes buckled, and the mittens pulled on.

Outside the air was fresh and cold. The street lamp had been lighted. It was exciting just to be out at this hour, even without the prospect of meeting the new little girl. But the new little girl still stood on the bench looking down the street.

Betsy ran toward her. She ran on the sidewalk as far as it went. Then she took to the frozen rutty road, and she had almost reached the bench when the little girl saw her.

"Hello!" called Betsy. "What's your name?"

The other child made no answer. She jumped off the bench.

"Don't go!" cried Betsy. "I'm coming."

But the other child without a word began to run. She brushed past Betsy on her headlong flight down the hill. She ran like a frightened rabbit, and Betsy ran in pursuit.

"Wait! Wait!" Betsy panted as she ran. But the new child would not stop. On fleet, black-stockinged legs she ran, faster than Betsy could follow.

"Wait! Wait!" pleaded Betsy but the child did not turn her head. She gained her own lawn, floundered through the snow to her house.

The entrance to her house was through a storm shed. She ran into this and banged the door. The door had a pane of glass in the front, and through that pane she stared fearfully at Betsy.

Betsy stood still, winking back tears, a mittened finger in her mouth. At last she turned and trudged slowly back through the snowy dark to her house.

She had almost reached her porch when the door of the storm shed opened. The new little girl stuck out her head.

"Tacy!" she shouted.

"You needn't call names!" Betsy shouted back. Tacy was shouting her own name, really. But it was such an odd one, Betsy didn't understand.

She trudged on into the house.

The lamp hanging over the dining room table was lighted now. A delicious smell of fried potatoes floated from the kitchen. "Well," her mother called out cheerfully. "Did you get acquainted?"

"What's her name?" asked Julia.

"I don't know. I don't like her. I'm mad at her," said Betsy. It was all she could do not to cry.

That was as near as Betsy and Tacy ever came to

a quarrel. And of course it didn't count. For they weren't friends yet.

They began to be friends next month, in April, at Betsy's birthday party.

2

Betsy's Birthday Party

THE TIME in between was lost because of bad weather. It was filled with snowing and blowing, raining and sleeting. It seemed as though spring never would come. But up in the hills pasque flowers were lifting their purple heads; and down in the valley beside the frozen river, the willow twigs were yellow. Birds were back from the south, shivering red-winged blackbirds and bluebirds and robins. Betsy and Tacy peeped out their windows at them, and if they saw each other they made faces and pulled down the blinds.

However, when it came time to make out the list for Betsy's birthday party, Betsy's mother included Tacy.

"Of course we'll invite the little girl from across the street," she said. And she spoke to Julia. "Will you find out what her name is?"

For Julia, who was eight years old and went to school, was acquainted now with Tacy's older sister. Katie was her name; she was eight, too.

Julia came home next day at noon and said, "Her name is Tacy."

"Tacy!" said Betsy. "Tacy!"

She felt herself growing warm. She knew then for the first time that Tacy hadn't been calling names when she put her head around the storm shed door, but had meant to say that she wanted to be friends after all.

"It's an odd name," said Mrs. Ray. "What does it stand for?"

"Anastacia. She's Anna Anastacia."

So Mrs. Ray wrote out the invitation, inviting Tacy to Betsy's birthday party. She invited Katie, too, to be company for Julia. She invited fifteen boys and girls in all.

"I hope to goodness it will be nice weather," said Betsy's mother. "Then they can play out of doors."

For the Ray house was small. But the sloping lawn was big, with maples and a butternut tree in front of the house, and behind it fruit trees and berry bushes and a garden, and Old Mag's barn, and the shed where the carriage was kept.

It would be much more fun if they could play out of doors, Betsy thought.

She was excited about the party, for she had never had one before. And she was to wear her first silk dress. It was checked tan and pink, with lace around the neck and sleeves. Her mother had promised to take her hair out of braids for the party. She had promised to dress it in curls.

Sure enough, on the night before the party, after Julia and Betsy had had their baths in the tub set out before the kitchen fire, Betsy's hair was rolled up on rags. There were curl-making bumps all over her head. And either because of the bumps or because the party was getting so near, Betsy could hardly sleep at all. She would wake up and think, "There's going to be ice cream!" And then she'd go to sleep again. And then she'd wake up and think, "I wonder if Tacy will come." And so it went, all night long. When she woke up finally it was morning, and the sun was shining so brightly that it had quite dried off the lawn, which had been free of snow for several days.

Betsy flew downstairs to breakfast.

"Dear me," said her father, shaking his head when he saw her. "Betsy can't have a party. She's sick. Look how red her cheeks are! Look at those bumps that have come out on her head."

Betsy's father loved to joke. Of course there were bumps on her head, because the curls hadn't been unwrapped. They weren't unwrapped for hours, not until almost time for the party. Betsy's hair didn't take kindly to curls.

But her hair was good and curly when the rags were removed. It stood out in a soft brown fluff about her face, which was round with very red cheeks and a smile which showed teeth parted in the middle.

"When Betsy is happy," her mother said, "she is happier than anyone else in the world." Then she added, "And she's almost always happy."

She was happy today . . . although she had little shivers inside her for fear that Tacy wouldn't come. The silk dress rustled beautifully over two starched petticoats which were buttoned to a muslin under-waist over woolen underwear. The legs of the underwear were folded tightly under her white party stockings and into the tops of her shoes. They made her legs look even chunkier than they were. She and Julia had hoped that their winter underwear would come off for the party. But their mother had said, "In April? Certainly not!"

At one minute after half-past two, the children started coming. Each one brought a birthday present which he gave to Betsy at the door. Each one said, "Happy birthday!" and Betsy said, "Thank you!" And one little boy who was named Tom said, "Let'th thppeak pietheth." (He meant to say, "Let's speak pieces," but he couldn't, because he had lost two teeth and the new ones weren't in yet.)

Betsy kept waiting for Tacy to come. At last she saw her crossing the street, hanging on to Katie's hand. Tacy held her head down, so that her long red ringlets almost covered her face. You could hardly see what she looked like.

She handed Betsy a package, looking down all the while. The present was a little glass pitcher with a gold painted rim. She wouldn't look up when Betsy thanked her. She wouldn't say, "Happy birthday!"

"She's bashful," Katie explained.

She certainly was bashful. She hung on to Katie's hand as though she were afraid she would be drowned if she let go. She wouldn't join in any of the games. She wouldn't even try to pin the tail on the donkey.

The sun shone warmly so that they could play their games on the lawn. Betsy's mother gave prizes. To please the little boy named Tom she let them all speak pieces. He knew a piece . . . that was why he had been so anxious to have them spoken.

"Twinkle, twinkle, little thtar," he said, his eyes shining like big brown stars.

But all the while Tacy kept her head snuggled against Katie's arm.

At last Julia formed the children in a line. Betsy's mother would play a march on the piano, she explained. Betsy, because she was the birthday child, could choose a partner and lead the line. They would march into the house for their refreshments.

The music started, and when Tacy heard the music she tossed back her curls a little. Betsy was sorry she had made that mistake about saying, "Don't call names!" so she chose Tacy for her partner. And Betsy and Tacy took hold of hands and marched at the head of the line.

They marched around and around the house and in and out of the parlor and the back parlor. Betsy's mother loved to play the piano; she came down hard and joyously on the keys. Every once in a while Tacy would look at Betsy sidewise through her curls. Her bright blue eyes were dancing in her little freckled face, as though to say, "Isn't this fun?" They marched and they marched, and at last they were told to lead the way to the dining room. There the cake was shining with all its five candles, and a dish of ice cream was set out for every child.

Betsy kept hold of Tacy's hand, and they sat down side by side. From that time on, at almost every party, you found Betsy and Tacy side by side.

Betsy was given beautiful presents at that fifth birthday party. Besides the little glass pitcher, she got colored cups and saucers, a small silk handkerchief embroidered with forget-me-nots, pencils and puzzles and balls. But the nicest present she received was not the usual kind of present. It was the present of a friend. It was Tacy.

3
Supper on the Hill

THAT SUMMER they started having picnics. At first the picnics were not real
picnics; not the kind you take out in a basket. Betsy's father, serving the plates at the head of
the table, would fill Betsy's plate with scrambled
eggs and bread and butter and strawberries, or
whatever they had for supper. Tacy's father would
do the same. Holding the plate in one hand and a

glass of milk in the other, each little girl would walk carefully out of her house and down the porch steps and out to the middle of the road. Then they would walk up the hill to that bench where Tacy had stood the first night she came. And there they would eat supper together.

Betsy always liked what she saw on Tacy's plate. In particular she liked the fresh unfrosted cake which Tacy's mother often stirred up for supper for her big family. Tacy knew that Betsy liked that cake, and she always divided her piece. And if baked beans or corn bread or something that Tacy liked lay on Betsy's plate, Betsy divided that too.

While they ate they watched the sun setting behind Tacy's house. Sometimes the west showed clouds like tiny pink feathers; sometimes it showed purple mountains and green lakes; sometimes the clouds were scarlet with gold around the edges. Betsy liked to make up stories, so she made up stories about the sunset. When she couldn't think what to say next, Tacy helped her.

Betsy always put herself and Tacy in the stories. Like this:

One night two little girls named Betsy and Tacy were eating their supper on the hill. The hill was covered with flowers. They smelled sweet and were pink like the sky. The sky was covered with little pink feathers.

"I wish," said Tacy, "that I had a feather for my hat."

"Do you really?" asked Betsy.

"Certainly I do," said Tacy.

"I'll get you one," said Betsy.

She stood up on the bench. They were through eating their suppers and had put their plates down in the grass. Betsy stood up on the bench and reached her hand out for a feather.

Tacy said, "You can't reach that feather. It's way over our house."

Betsy said, "I can so."

She reached and she reached; and the first thing she knew one of the feathers had come near enough for her to touch it. But when she took hold of it, instead of coming down, it began pulling her up.

Tacy saw what was happening, and she took hold of Betsy's feet. She was just in time too. In another minute Betsy would have been gone. Up, up, up they went on the feather into the sky.

They floated over Tacy's house. The smoke was coming out of the chimney where her mother had cooked supper. Far below were Tacy's pump and barn and buggy shed. They looked strange and small.

Betsy and Tacy could see Betsy's house too. They could look all the way down Hill Street. They could see Mr. Williams milking his cow. And Mr. Benson driving home late to supper.

Betsy said, "Wouldn't our fathers and mothers be surprised, if they could look up here and see us sitting on a feather?" For by this time they had climbed up on the feather and were sitting on it side by side. They put their arms around each other so that they wouldn't fall. It was fun sitting up there.

"I wish Julia and Katie could see us," said Tacy. Julia and Katie were like most big sisters. They were bossy. Of course they were eight, but even if they were eight, they weren't so smart. They didn't know how to float off on a feather like Betsy and Tacy were doing.

"We'd better not let anyone see us, though," Betsy decided. "They'd think it was dangerous. They wouldn't let us do it again, and I'd like to do it every night."

"So would I," said Tacy. "Tomorrow night, let's float down over the town and see Front Street where the stores are."

"And the river," said Betsy.

"And the park," said Tacy. "Page Park with the white fence around it and the picnic benches and the swings."

"We may even go there to eat our supper some night," Betsy said. "Let's go some night when your mother has baked cake."

"Do you suppose we could hold on to our plates?" asked Tacy. "When we were riding on this feather?"

"We'd have to hold tight," Betsy said, and they looked down. It made them dizzy to look down, they were so high up.

Tacy began to laugh. "We'd have to be careful not to spill our milk," she said.

"We might spill our milk on Julia and Katie," Betsy cried.

"I wouldn't care if we did."

"It would make them mad, though."

And at the thought of spilling milk on Julia and Katie and making them mad, they laughed so hard that they tipped their feather over. It went over quick like a paper boat, and they started falling, falling, falling. But they didn't fall too fast. It was delicious the way they fell . . . like a swallow sinking down, down, down . . . to the very bench where they had been sitting.

Only now the sunset had dimmed a little and the grass was cold with dew and down in their dooryards Betsy's mother and one or two of Tacy's brothers and sisters were calling, "Betsy!" "Tacy!" "Betsy!" "Tacy!"

Betsy and Tacy looked at each other with shining eyes.

"Don't forget it's a secret," Betsy said, "that we can go floating off whenever we like."

"I won't forget," said Tacy.

"Tomorrow night we'd better bring jackets, if we're going down to Front Street. I felt a little cold sitting up on that feather, didn't you?"

"Yes," said Tacy, wriggling her bare toes. "I wished I was wearing my shoes."

"Betsy!" called Betsy's mother.

"Tacy!" called four or five of Tacy's brothers and sisters.

"We're coming," called Betsy and Tacy, and they picked up their plates and glasses and came slowly down the hill.

That was the kind of picnic they went on at first. Later, when they grew older, they packed their picnics in baskets.

4
The Piano Box

BETSY AND Tacy soon had places which belonged to them. The bench on the hill was the first one. The second one, and the dearest for several years, was the piano box. This was their headquarters, their playhouse, the center of all their games.

It stood behind Betsy's house, for it had brought that same piano on which Julia practiced her music lesson and which Betsy's mother had played for Betsy's party. It was tall enough to hold a piano; so of course it was tall enough to hold Betsy and Tacy. It wasn't so wide as it was tall; they had to squeeze to get in. But by squeezing just a little, they could get in and sit down.

Julia and Katie couldn't come in unless they were invited. This was Betsy's and Tacy's private corner. Betsy's mother was a great believer in people having private corners, and the piano box was plainly meant to belong to Betsy and Tacy, for it fitted them so snugly. They decorated the walls with pictures cut from magazines. Tacy's mother gave them a bit of rug for the floor. They kept their treasures of stones and moss in a shoe box in one corner.

One side of the piano box was open. As Betsy and Tacy sat in their retreat they had a pleasant view. They looked into the back yard maple, through the garden and the little grove of fruit trees, past the barn and buggy shed, up to the Big Hill. This was not the hill where the picnic bench stood. That was the little hill which ended Hill Street. Hill Street ran north and south, but the road which climbed the Big Hill ran east and west. At the top stood a white house, and the sun rose behind it in the morning.

Sitting in their piano box one day, Betsy and Tacy

looked at the Big Hill. Neither of them had ever climbed it. Julia and Katie climbed it whenever they pleased.

"I think," said Betsy, "that it's time we climbed that hill." So they ran and asked their mothers.

Betsy's mother was canning strawberries. "All right," she said. "But be sure to come when I call."

"All right," said Tacy's mother. "But it's almost dinner time."

Betsy and Tacy took hold of hands and started to climb.

The road ran straight to the white house and the deep blue summer sky. The dust of the road was soft to their bare feet. The sun shone warmly on Betsy's braids and on Tacy's bright red curls.

At first they passed only Betsy's house and her garden and orchard and barn. They had gone that far before. Then they came to a ridge where wild roses bloomed in June. They had gone that far, picking roses. But at last each step took them farther into an unknown country.

The roadside was crowded with mid-summer flowers . . . big white daisies and small fringed daisies, brown-eyed Susans and Queen Anne's lace. On one side of the road, the hill was open. On the other it was fenced, with a wire fence which enclosed a cow pasture. A brindle cow was sleeping under a scrub oak tree.

"Just think!" said Betsy. "We don't even know whose cow pasture that is."

"We don't even know whose cow that is," said Tacy. "Of course it *might* be Mr. Williams' cow."

"Oh, no," said Betsy. "We've come too far for that."

They plodded on again.

The sun seemed warmer and warmer. The dust began to pull at their feet. They turned and looked back. They could look down now on the roofs of their homes, almost as they had done the night they rode the feather.

"We've come a dreadful way," said Tacy. "If we were sitting in our piano box, we could see ourselves up here."

"We would wonder who were those two children climbing the Big Hill."

"Maybe we ought to stop," said Tacy.

"Let's go just a little farther," Betsy said. But in a moment she pointed to a fat thorn apple tree on the

unfenced side of the road. "That would be a nice place to stop," she suggested. And they stopped.

Under the thorn apple tree was a deep, soft nest of grass. The two little girls sat down and drew their knees into their arms. They could see farther now than the treetops of Hill Street. They could see the roof of the big red schoolhouse where Julia and Katie went to school.

A squirrel whisked down the tree to look at them. A phoebe sang, "Phoebe! Phoebe!" over and over again. A hornet buzzed in the noonday heat, but did not come too near.

"Let's live up here," Betsy said suddenly.

Tacy started. "You mean all the time?"

"All the time. Sleep here and everything."

"Just you and me?" Tacy asked.

"I think it would be fun," said Betsy. She jumped up and found a broken branch. "This is the front of our house," she said, laying it down.

Tacy brought a second branch and laid it so that the two ends left a space between. "This is our front door," she said.

"This is our parlor," said Betsy. "Where this stone is. Company can sit on the stone."

"And this is our bedroom," said Tacy. "If your mother will let us have her big brown shawl to sleep on, my mother will give us a pillow, I think."

They worked busily, making their house.

"But Betsy," said Tacy after a time. "What will we have to eat?"

Betsy looked thoughtfully about her. "Why, we'll milk the cow," she said.

"Do you think we could?"

"'Course we could. You hold him and I'll milk him."

"All right," said Tacy. "Only not just yet. I'm not hungry yet."

Betsy rolled her eyes upward. "We can have thorn apples too," she said.

"That's right," said Tacy happily. "We can have thorn apple pie."

They started picking thorn apples. But after a

moment Betsy interrupted the task.

"And I like eggs," she said.

Something firm and determined in her tone made Tacy look around hurriedly. Betsy was looking at a hen. It was a red hen with a red glittery breast. It had wandered up the hill from some back yard in Hill Street, perhaps. Or down the hill from the big white house. Betsy and Tacy could not tell. But Betsy was looking at the hen so firmly, there was no mistaking her intention.

"We'll catch that hen," said Betsy, "and keep him in a box. And whenever we get hungry he can lay us an egg."

"That will be fine," said Tacy.

They began to hunt for a box.

With great good fortune they found one. It was broken and old and water-soaked, but it was a box. It would hold a hen.

"Now," said Betsy, "we have to catch him. I'll say, 'Here chickabiddie, chickabiddie! Here chickabiddie, chickabiddie!' like I've heard my Uncle Edward do, and when he comes right up to my hand, you grab him."

"All right," said Tacy.

So Betsy called, "Here chickabiddie, chickabiddie! Here chickabiddie, chickabiddie!" just as she had heard her Uncle Edward do. And she called so

well and made such inviting motions with her hand (as though she were scattering feed) that the hen came running toward her. And Tacy swooped down on it with two thin arms and Betsy bundled it up in two plump ones. Somehow, although it flapped and clawed, they got it into the box.

But the hen was very angry. It glared at them with furious little eyes and opened and shut its sharp little beak and made the most horrid, terrifying squawks.

"Lay an egg, chickabiddie! Lay an egg, chickabiddie!" said Betsy over and over.

But the hen didn't lay a single egg.

About this time voices rose from Hill Street.

"Betsy!" "Tacy!" "Betsy!" "Tacy!" One voice added, "Dinner's ready."

"I don't believe he's going to lay an egg," said Tacy.

"Neither do I," said Betsy. "He isn't trained yet."

"Maybe," said Tacy, "our piano box is a nicer place to live after all."

Betsy thought it over. The hen kept making that horrid, squawking sound. Probably there would be strawberry jam for dinner, left over from what went into the jars. And the piano box was a beautiful place.

"Our piano box," she agreed, jumping up, "has a roof for when it rains."

So they ran down the Big Hill.

"We climbed the Big Hill," they shouted joyously to Julia and Katie who had been doing the calling.

"Pooh! We climb it often," Julia and Katie said.

5
The First Day of School

WHEN SEPTEMBER came, Betsy and Tacy started going to school. Julia took Betsy and Katie took Tacy, on the opening day. Betsy's mother came out on the steps of the little yellow house to wave good-by, and Tacy's mother came out on her steps, too, along with Tacy's brother Paul and Bee, the baby, who weren't old enough yet to go to school.

Betsy was beaming all over her round rosy face. Her tightly braided pigtails, with new red ribbons

on the ends, stuck out behind her ears. She wore a new plaid dress which her mother had made, and new shoes which felt stiff and queer.

Tacy's mother had brushed the ringlets over her finger 'til they shone. They hung as neat as sausages down Tacy's back. Tacy had a new dress, too; navy blue, it was, because she had red hair. But where Betsy was beaming, Tacy was frowning. She held her head down and dragged from Katie's hand.

She was bashful; that was the trouble. Betsy had almost forgotten how bashful Tacy could be. Tacy wasn't bashful with Betsy any more, but she was very bashful starting to school. "She'll get over it," said Katie, and they set off down Hill Street.

The maples were beginning to turn yellow but the air was soft and warm. It smelled of the smoke from Grandpa Williams' bonfire.

"We're going to school, Grandpa Williams," Betsy called to him.

"That's fine," said Grandpa Williams.

Tacy said nothing.

They went down Hill Street to the vacant lot. It was knee deep with goldenrod and asters. It would have been fun to stop and play there, if they hadn't been going to school. But they cut through by a little path and came out on Pleasant Street.

There on the corner on a big green lawn stood a chocolate-colored house. It had porches all around it, a tower on the side, and a pane of colored glass over the front door. It was a beautiful house but they had no time to look at it. They were busy going to school.

They crossed the street and turned the corner and came to a little store.

"That's Mrs. Chubbock's store," Julia explained. "That's where you go to buy gum drops and chocolate men if anyone's given you a penny."

"I wish that someone had given me a penny. Don't you, Tacy?" Betsy asked.

Tacy didn't answer.

Just beyond Mrs. Chubbock's store, they came to the school yard. They came first to the boys' yard, a big sandy yard with one tree. On the other side of the schoolhouse was the girls' yard which looked much the same. But the girls' yard had more trees. The schoolhouse was built of red brick trimmed with yellow stone. A steep flight of steps led up to the door.

At the top of the steps stood a boy, holding a big bell. When he rang that bell, Julia explained, it was time for school to begin.

"Oh, oh!" said Betsy. "I wish that I could be the one to ring the bell. Don't you, Tacy?"

Tacy didn't say a word.

The girls playing in the school yard came crowding around Julia and Katie to see their little sisters. Tacy shook her long red curls over her face. Between the curls her face was as red as a beet. She wouldn't look up.

She didn't look up until the boy at the head of the steps began to ring the bell. Ding, dong, ding, dong, went the bell. Tacy jumped like a scared rabbit and pulled at Katie's hand. She pulled away from the schoolhouse because she didn't want to go in. But

Katie was stronger than Tacy; besides, she was the kind of person who never gave up. So she pulled harder than Tacy and got her to the Baby Room door.

Julia had already taken Betsy to the door, and had said to Miss Dalton, the teacher: "This is my little sister Betsy."

Now Katie said, "This is my little sister Tacy." And she added, "She's very bashful."

"Never mind," said Miss Dalton, smiling brightly. "I'll take care of that. I'll put her right by me." And she placed a little chair beside her desk and put Tacy into that.

Tacy didn't like it. Betsy could tell from the way she scrunched down and hid herself beneath her curls. She liked it less than ever when Betsy was put far away at a regular desk in one of the rows of desks which filled the room. But Miss Dalton was too busy to notice; Julia and Katie went out; the door closed, and school began.

If it hadn't been for Tacy's looking so forlorn, Betsy would have liked school. The windows were hung with chains made from shiny paper. On the blackboard was a calendar for the month of September drawn with colored chalk. And Miss Dalton was pretty; she looked like a canary. But it was hard for Betsy to be happy with Tacy such a picture of woe.

Instead of looking better, Tacy looked worse and worse. She gazed at Betsy with pleading eyes, and her face was screwed up as though she were going to cry.

"She's going to cry," someone whispered in Betsy's ear. It was the little boy named Tom.

"Oh!" cried Betsy. "You've got your teeth." She knew because now he said "s" as well as she did. Besides, she could see them, two brand-new teeth, right in the front of his mouth.

"Yes, I got them young," said Tom.

He sat at the desk behind Betsy's.

Betsy was glad when recess time came. They formed in two lines and marched out of the room and through the front door and down the stairs. The girls skipped off to the playground at the left, the boys to the one at the right. Now, thought Betsy, she would find Tacy and tell her not to be bashful. But when she looked about for Tacy, Tacy was nowhere to be seen.

Betsy ran to the sidewalk and looked down the street. Flying red ringlets and twinkling thin black legs were almost out of sight.

"Stop, Tacy! Stop!" cried Betsy. She ran in pursuit. But it was no use. Tacy could always run faster than Betsy. She ran faster now. At last, however, she slowed down so that Betsy could catch up.

They had reached Mrs. Chubbock's store.

"Tacy!" cried Betsy. "We're not supposed to leave the yard."

"I'm going home," said Tacy. She was crying.

"But you can't. It's not allowed."

Tacy only cried.

She cried harder than Betsy had ever seen her cry. She wrinkled up her little freckled face. Tears ran over her cheeks and dropped into her mouth and spotted the navy blue dress.

Ding, dong, ding, dong, went the schoolhouse bell. It meant that recess time was over.

"Come on, Tacy. We've *got* to go back."

Tacy cried harder than ever.

The lines of marching children vanished into the schoolhouse. A strange calm settled upon the empty yard. From an open window came the sound of children singing.

"We're supposed to be in there," Betsy said. She felt a queer frightened lump inside.

"You go back if you want to," said Tacy between sobs.

"I won't go back without you," said Betsy. She sat down miserably on Mrs. Chubbock's steps.

The door of the little store opened and Mrs. Chubbock came out. She was large and stout, with a small soft mustache. She leaned on a cane when she walked.

"What's this? What's this?" she asked. "Why aren't you in school?"

"We . . . we . . ." said Betsy. Her lip trembled.

"Aren't you supposed to be in school?"

"Yes, we are. But she . . . she's bashful."

"Runaways, eh?" said Mrs. Chubbock.

At the sound of the dread word, Betsy's eyes filled with tears. That was what they were exactly. Runaways. That was a terrible thing to be. How could she go home from school and tell her mamma? Would they ever be allowed to go to school again? Betsy too began to cry.

Once started, Betsy cried as hard as Tacy. Harder, perhaps. And when Tacy heard Betsy cry, she took a fresh start. They held each other tight and wailed.

"Now, now," said Mrs. Chubbock. She limped back

into her store. When she came out, she opened her two hands and each of them held a little chocolate man.

"Do you eat the head first or the legs first?" Mrs. Chubbock asked.

Betsy ate the head first and Tacy ate the legs first. They couldn't very well eat and cry together. So they were eating and not crying when they saw Miss Dalton hurrying across the schoolhouse yard. The sun was shining on her canary-colored hair. She looked pretty but very worried.

"Oh, there you are!" she cried gladly when she saw them. "You weren't supposed to go home, my dears. That was only recess."

The tears began to trickle again.

"I know," said Betsy. "But Tacy doesn't like school. She's bashful."

"And she won't go if I won't," said Tacy.

"No, I won't go if she won't," said Betsy. They lifted anxious faces, smeared with chocolate and tears.

Miss Dalton stooped down and put an arm around each of them. She smiled up at Mrs. Chubbock.

"Tacy," she said. "How would you like to sit with Betsy? Right in the same seat?"

So they went back to school. Tacy sat with Betsy, right in the same seat. They were crowded, but no more so than they were in the piano box. The little boy named Tom sat right behind them.

And after that Tacy liked school.

Betsy had liked it all the time.

6

The Milkman Story

EVERY MORNING Betsy called for Tacy, so that they could walk to school together.

Betsy came to Tacy's house a little early, usually, to be there when Tacy had her hair combed. There was a painful fascination in this business, for Tacy always cried.

Her ringlets were tangled after her night's sleep. When she washed for breakfast, they were merely tied back with a ribbon. Tacy's mother was busy getting breakfast for thirteen, and Tacy's curls took time. After breakfast the time for curls arrived. Tacy began to cry at sight of the comb.

Betsy's eyes grew round and she swayed back and forth as she watched. "But she cried harder than that, the first day of school, Mrs. Kelly."

"Then she must have cried pretty hard that day," Mrs. Kelly would answer. "Keep still, Tacy. I'm trying not to hurt."

Mrs. Kelly was stout and gentle. She was like a large, anxious dove. She was different from Betsy's mother who was slim and red-headed and gay. Betsy's mother knew how to scold as well as to laugh and sing. But Tacy's mother never scolded.

"If I tried to scold eleven I'd be scolding all the time," she explained to Betsy one day.

After the curls were brushed over Tacy's mother's finger, Betsy and Tacy started off to school. They walked to school together, and they walked home together. Back and forth together, every day.

At first it was autumn; there were red and yellow leaves for Betsy and Tacy to scuffle under foot. Then the leaves were brown, then they were blown away; that was in the gray time named November. Then came the exciting first snow, and this was followed by more snow and more. At last the drifts rising beside the sidewalk were higher than their heads.

Betsy and Tacy lay down in the drifts and spread out their arms to make angels. They rolled the snow into balls and had battles with Julia and Katie. They started a snowman in the vacant lot, and added to him day after day until . . . before a thaw came . . . he was as fat as Mrs. Chubbock.

The snow was fun while there was sun to glitter on it from a sky as bright and blue as Tacy's eyes. But after a time the weather grew cold; it was too cold for Betsy and Tacy to play in the snow any more. Their hands inside mittens ached, and their feet inside overshoes grew numb. The wind nipped their faces in their snugly tied hoods; their breath froze on the bright scarves knotted around their necks.

On days like that, as they walked home from school, Betsy told Tacy the milkman story.

It started one day when a milkman passed them on the corner by the chocolate-colored house. His wagon was running on runners; and it wasn't an ordinary wagon; it looked like a little house. The milkman sat covered with buffalo robes, and from deep in shadows came the glimmer of a fire. It might have come from the milkman's pipe, but Betsy and Tacy thought that it came from a little stove inside the milkman's wagon.

That gave Betsy the idea for a story.

The story went differently on different days, but one day it went like this:

Two little girls named Betsy and Tacy were walking home from school. It was very cold.

"I wish we could catch a ride," said Tacy.

And just at that moment a milkman came riding by. He was riding in a wagon which looked like a little house. He had a little stove inside. He said to Betsy and Tacy:

"Hello, little girls. Wouldn't you like a ride in this wagon? I'm through delivering milk, so you can have it for yourselves."

Betsy and Tacy said, "Thank you very much!" And the milkman jumped out, and they jumped in. And the milkman went away.

But before he went away he said, "You don't need to drive that horse. It's a pretty cold day for keeping hold of reins. Just wind the reins around the whip."

So Betsy and Tacy wound the reins around the whip, and they said to the horse, "Take us home, horse." The milkman's horse was a magic horse, but nobody knew it except the milkman and Betsy and Tacy.

The horse started off over the snow. The sleigh-bells jingled on his back, and the wagon ran so smoothly that it hardly joggled Betsy and Tacy. They were sitting beside the little stove in the very inside of the wagon. They were sitting on two little stools beside the stove.

In just a minute they were as warm as toast. It was cozy sitting there with the wagon sliding along. Only by and by Tacy said, "I'm hungry."

And Betsy said, "That's funny. Look what I see!" And she pointed over to a corner of the wagon, and there were two baskets. One was marked, "Betsy," and one was marked, "Tacy." They were covered with little red cloths.

Betsy and Tacy took off these cloths and spread them on their knees, and they looked into their baskets. Each one found a cup of cocoa there. It was hot. It was steaming. And it hadn't spilled a drop. That was because the milkman's wagon was magic like his horse.

And beside each cup of cocoa were doughnuts. They were hot too. They smelled like Mrs. Ray's doughnuts smell when she lifts them out of the lard on a fork. They smelled good. There were plenty of doughnuts for Betsy and plenty for Tacy.

"Isn't this fun?" Tacy said. "Riding along in the milkman's wagon and eating doughnuts?"

Just then the horse turned his head. "Those doughnuts smell good," he said.

"Oh, excuse me," said Betsy and Tacy. "We didn't know that horses ate doughnuts."

"Well, *I* do," said the horse. "Of course I'm a magic horse."

And Betsy and Tacy put three doughnuts on the whip and they held out the whip and the horse opened his mouth and the doughnuts dropped right in.

"Thank you," said the horse. "I'll take you home every day it's cold. I'll meet you where I met you today, on the corner by the chocolate-colored house."

In a minute he turned his head and said, "Of course it's a secret."

"Oh, yes," said Betsy and Tacy. "We understand that."

They had come so far now that they had come to Hill Street Hill. They were halfway up. They put their cups back in the baskets and covered the baskets with the red cloths, and they climbed out of the wagon.

"Thank you, horse," they said.

"You're welcome," said the horse.

They were almost up Hill Street Hill, and they weren't cold at all, hardly, on account of the ride they'd had.

Julia and Katie were just ahead.

"Hurry up!" they called. "Hurry up so you don't get frost bite."

"Frost bite!" said Betsy and Tacy, and they looked at each other and laughed.

"We're warm as toast," said Betsy, stamping her feet.

"We're hardly cold at all," said Tacy, swinging her arms.

Betsy said to Tacy, "Let's go ask your mamma if you can't bring your paper dolls and come over to my house to play."

"Yes, let's," said Tacy. "I hope we meet that milkman again tomorrow. Don't you, Betsy?"

"Those were good doughnuts," said Betsy. "Maybe my mamma will give us some more."

7
Playing Paper Dolls

UITE OFTEN, after school, Betsy and Tacy went to Betsy's house and played paper dolls.

Betsy and Tacy liked paper dolls better than real dolls. They wanted real dolls too, of course. The most important thing to see on Christmas morning, poking out of a stocking or sitting under a tree, was a big china doll . . . with yellow curls and a blue silk dress and bonnet, or with black curls and a pink silk dress and bonnet . . . it didn't matter which. But after Christmas they put those dolls away and played with their paper dolls.

They cut the paper dolls from fashion magazines. They could hardly wait for their mothers' magazines to grow old. Mrs. Benson didn't have any children, so she saved her fashion magazines for Betsy and Tacy. And when Miss Meade, the sewing woman, came to Betsy's house, she could be depended upon to leave a magazine or two behind.

The chief trouble Betsy and Tacy had was in finding pictures of men and boys. There had to be father dolls and brother dolls, of course. The tailor shops had men's fashion sheets. But those fashion sheets were hard to get. Tacy's brother George worked next door to a tailor shop. He told Mr. Baumgarten, the tailor, that his little sister Tacy liked those fashion sheets. After that Mr. Baumgarten saved all his fashion sheets for Tacy, and Tacy divided them with Betsy.

The dolls were not only cut from magazines; they lived in magazines. Betsy and Tacy each had a doll family living in a magazine. The servant dolls were kept in a pile between the first two pages; a few pages on was the pile of father dolls; then came the mother dolls, and then the sixteen-year-olds, the ten-year-olds, the eight-year-olds, the five-year-olds, and the babies.

Those were the dolls that Betsy and Tacy played with after school.

Betsy and Tacy stopped in at Tacy's house to get her magazine and eat a cookie. Then they went on to Betsy's house, and when Betsy had kissed her mother and both of them had hung their wraps in the little closet off the back parlor, Betsy brought out the magazine in which her doll family lived.

"Shall we play here beside the stove, Mamma?" she asked.

"Yes, that would be a good place to play," said Mrs. Ray; and it was.

The fire glowed red through the isinglass windows of the big hard coal heater. It shone on the wild horses' heads which ran in a procession around the shining nickel trim. Up on the warming ledge the tea kettle was singing. Underneath the stove, on the square metal plate which protected the green flowered carpet, Lady Jane Grey, the cat, was singing too.

She opened one sleepy eye but she kept on purring as Betsy and Tacy opened their magazines.

"What shall we name the five-year-old today?" Tacy asked Betsy.

The five-year-olds were the most important members of the large doll families. Everything pleasant happened to them. They had all the adventures.

The eight-year-olds lived very dull lives; and they were always given very plain names. They were Jane and Martha, usually, or Hannah and Jemima. Sometimes Betsy and Tacy forgot and called them Julia and Katie. But the five-year-olds had beautiful names. They were Lucille and Evelyn, or Madeline and Millicent.

"We'll be Madeline and Millicent today," Betsy decided.

They played that it was morning. The servant dolls got up first. The servant dolls wore caps with long streamers and dainty ruffled aprons. They didn't look at all like the hired girls of Hill Street. But like hired girls they got up bright and early.

The fathers and mothers got up next. Then came the children beginning with the oldest. The five-year-olds came dancing down to breakfast in the fingers of Betsy and Tacy.

"What are you planning to do today, Madeline?" Betsy's father doll asked his five-year-old.

"I'm going to play with Millicent, Papá." (Madeline and Millicent pronounced papa, papá.)

"And I'm going to play with Jemima," said Betsy's eight-year-old who was named Hannah today.

"No, Hannah!" said her father. "You must stay at home and wash the dishes. But Madeline may go. Wouldn't you like to take the carriage, Madeline? You and Millicent could go for a nice ride. Here is a dollar in case you want some candy."

"Oh, thank you, Papá," said Madeline. She gave him an airy kiss.

Meanwhile Tacy's dolls were talking in much the same way. Both father dolls were sent quickly down to work; the mothers went shopping; the babies were taken out in their carriages by the pretty servant dolls; and the older children were shut in the magazines. Then Betsy and Tacy each took her five-year-old in hand, and the fun of the game began.

First they went to the candy store under the patent rocker. Madeline's dollar bought an enormous quantity of gum drops and candy corn. Next they sat down in their carriage which was made of a shoebox. There were two strings attached, and Betsy and Tacy were the horses. Madeline and Millicent took a beautiful ride.

They climbed the back parlor sofa; that was a mountain.

"Let's have a picnic," said Madeline. So they did. They picnicked on top of a pillow which had the head of a girl embroidered on it.

They swished through the dangling bamboo

curtains which separated the back parlor from the front parlor. And in the front parlor they left their carriage again. They climbed the piano stool; that was a merry-go-round, and of course they had a ride.

After calling on Mrs. Vanderbilt, who lived behind the starched lace curtains at the front parlor window, and Mrs. Astor, who lived under an easel which was draped in purple silk, they slipped by way of the dining room into the back parlor again.

And here they met with their greatest adventure!

The Betsy horse began to rear and snort.

"What's the matter?" asked the Tacy horse.

"A tiger! A tiger!" cried the Betsy horse. She jumped and kicked.

The Tacy horse began to jump and kick too, looking about her for the tiger. Lady Jane Grey was awake and washing her face.

"She's getting ready to

eat us!" cried the Betsy horse, leaping.

"Help!" cried the Tacy horse, leaping too.

They leaped so high that they overturned the carriage. Out went Madeline and Millicent on the highway of the green flowered carpet.

"We're running away!" shouted the Betsy horse.

"Whoa! Whoa!" shouted the Tacy horse.

They ran through the rattling bamboo curtains into the front parlor. There they stopped being horses and raced back, out of breath, to be Madeline and Millicent again.

Lady Jane Grey loved to play with paper. She entered obligingly into the game.

"He's biting me!" shrieked Madeline.

"He's scratching me!" shrieked Millicent.

The tiger growled and pounced.

Madeline and Millicent were rescued just in time. The father dolls rushed up and seized them and jumped into the coal scuttle. Lady Jane Grey jumped in too and jumped out looking black instead of gray, and Betsy and Tacy scrambled in the coal scuttle trying to fish out the father dolls before they got too black. There were never enough father dolls, in spite of Mr. Baumgarten.

Julia and Katie came in just then from skating. The opening door brought in a rush of winter cold and dark.

"Well, for goodness' sake!" they cried. *"For goodness' sake!"* They cried it so loud that Betsy's mother came in from the kitchen, where she was getting supper.

"Betsy!" she cried. "Come straight out here and wash! And use soap and a wash cloth and warm water from the kettle! You too, Tacy."

"Yes, ma'am," said Betsy and Tacy.

When they had washed they put their paper dolls back into the magazines. And Katie helped Tacy into her outside wraps and took her by the hand, and they started home.

Right at the door, Tacy turned around to smile at Betsy. "Whoa!" she said, instead of "Good-by!"

"Giddap!" said Betsy, instead of "Come again!"

"Whoa!" "Giddap!" "Whoa!" "Giddap!" they said over and over.

"Whatever are you two talking about?" said Julia and Katie crossly, which was just what Betsy and Tacy had hoped they would say.

8
Easter Eggs

JULIA AND Katie were nice sometimes. They were nice when it came time to color Easter eggs. That happened a few days before Easter.

It seemed to be still winter. There was lots of snow outside, and coal still went rattling into the back parlor stove, but Betsy and Tacy knew that spring was near. All of a sudden they didn't care a bit about sliding down hill on their sleds. All they could think or talk about was coloring Easter eggs.

They colored the eggs in Betsy's kitchen. Tacy's little sister Beatrice was sick. She was Bee, the baby, and she was very sick. Mrs. Ray kept Katie and Tacy over at her house all she could.

Julia and Katie put on big aprons and acted important, but not too important. They let Betsy and Tacy help, coloring the eggs.

First they collected all the cups they could find which had handles missing and cracks along the sides. Then they dissolved the dye in warm water from the kettle, each color in a different cup. The eggs were placed in the cups for a while, and when they were taken out they were red or purple or orange. The colors were so bright . . . it was thrilling to look at them.

On Easter morning everyone ate as many eggs as he could. At Betsy's house, they did.

"I ate three," said Betsy, when Tacy came running over to ask. "And my papa ate five."

"I ate three, too," said Tacy. "And last year my brother George ate ten. But this year nobody paid much attention to eggs at our house, except Katie and Paul and me."

That was because Baby Bee was sick.

They went to church, though, from Tacy's house.

Everyone in the family went, except Tacy's mother who stayed home with Bee. And Tacy had a new hat (navy blue, because she had red hair). It was straw and showed her ears and had stiff gay flowers on the top.

Betsy had a new hat which looked much the same, and she went to church too with her father and mother and Julia. Her mother sang in the choir, and the church smelled of lilies. Betsy liked Easter.

She liked it especially after church, for Katie and Tacy came to dinner. They had chicken, and everyone was very well behaved. After dinner they sat by the back parlor stove and played with their colored eggs.

Katie and Tacy were to stay until they were called for. By and by it grew dark. Mrs. Ray said, wouldn't it be fun if they could stay all night? Katie could sleep with Julia, and Tacy with Betsy. But after supper Mr. Kelly came over.

"Thank you very much," he said. "But Mrs. Kelly wants the children home."

Tacy put her colored eggs into the pocket of her coat. She went home and the next day she didn't come over. She didn't come over the next day, nor the next, for Baby Bee died. Betsy's father and mother went to the funeral.

Betsy was very lonesome for Tacy. The next

morning she went out early before anyone was up. She often went out early in the summer time; Tacy did too. But it was strange going out early at this time of year.

Betsy dressed in all her warm clothes, just as she knew she should. She dressed without waking Julia, and she stole down the stairs without waking her father and mother, and she got her coat and hood and overshoes and mittens out of the back parlor closet and put them on softly and went softly out of the side kitchen door.

The lilac bush stood by that door. It didn't seem to be awake. The snow which had melted yesterday had frozen in the night, and it hadn't come unfrozen yet. Everything in Hill Street seemed to be waiting for the sun. The trees and houses waited in a dim gray light. Behind the white house which stood on the Big Hill, the sky was colored pink.

Betsy walked over to Tacy's house and looked at the upstairs windows.

Tacy must have known that Betsy would come over. After a while she came out of the house. She too had gotten up without waking a soul. She had put on everything warm, the way she knew her mamma would want her to—her coat and hood and overshoes and mittens. She even had her scarf tied around her neck.

She and Betsy looked at each other, and then they started walking.

"What shall we do?" asked Tacy.

"Let's climb a tree," said Betsy.

It wasn't the time of year for climbing trees, but Betsy and Tacy were great tree climbers. So they climbed a tree.

They didn't climb Betsy's backyard maple which was their favorite tree to climb. They went up the Big Hill until they found a tree with branches low enough to reach, and they climbed that and sat there.

Somewhere a bird was singing a little up and down song. They couldn't see him but they could hear him. His busy up and down song was the only sound in the world. Hill Street was still sleeping, but the color in the sky was spreading. Gold sticks in the shape of a fan were sticking up over the hill.

After a while Tacy said, "It smelled like Easter in the church. Bee looked awful pretty. She had candles all around her."

"Did she?" asked Betsy.

"But my mamma felt awful bad," said Tacy.

Betsy said nothing.

"Of course," said Tacy, "you know that Bee has only gone to Heaven."

"Oh, of course," said Betsy.

But Tacy's lip was shaking. That made Betsy feel queer. So she said quickly, "Heaven's awful nice."

"Is it?" asked Tacy, looking toward her. Her eyes were big and full of trouble.

"Yes," said Betsy. "It's like that sunrise. In fact," she added, "that's it. We can't see it during the day, but early in the morning they let us have a peek."

"It's pretty," said Tacy, staring.

"Those gold sticks you see, those are candles," said Betsy. "There's a gold-colored light all the time. And there are harps to play on; they're something like pianos. But you don't need to take any lessons. You just know how to play. Bee's having a good time up there," said Betsy, looking up into the sky.

Tacy looked too. "Can she see us?"

"Of course she can see us. She's looking down right now. And I'll tell you what tickles Bee. She knows all about Heaven, and we don't. She's younger than we are, but she knows something we don't know. Isn't that funny? She's just a baby, and she knows more than we do."

"And more than Julia and Katie do," said Tacy.

"Even more than our fathers and mothers do," said Betsy. "It's funny when you come to think of it."

"She's a long way from home though," said Tacy.

"But she gets all the news," said Betsy. "Do you

know how she gets it? Why, from the birds. They fly up there and tell her how you are and what you're all doing down at your house."

"Do they?" asked Tacy.

And just at that moment, the little up and down song stopped, and there flew past them, going right up the hill, a robin red breast. He was the first robin they had seen that spring, and he was as red as a red Easter egg. He flew up the hill fast, as though he knew where he was going.

"He's going to see Bee, of course," Betsy said. "He'll be back in a minute."

Tacy put her hand in her pocket, and it touched the colored Easter eggs she had brought from Betsy's house.

"Betsy," she said, "do you suppose he'd take one of these Easter eggs to Bee?"

"Of course he would," said Betsy. "The only trouble is how to give it to him."

She looked about her. She looked up, and high up in the tree was a nest. It was a big ragged nest. It looked as though it had been there all winter. But it was a nest; it was a bird's house.

"Give me the egg," she said. "Which one are you sending?"

"The purple one," said Tacy. "It's the prettiest."

"I'll put it in that nest," said Betsy. "The robin

can take it up in his mouth."

So Betsy took the purple egg, and she put it in the pocket of her coat. And she climbed up the tree, higher than she had ever gone before. She didn't look down; she looked up instead. She held on tight with her arms to the rough trunk of the tree, and she felt for the branches with her feet.

She climbed to the very top of the tree, and put the purple egg in the nest.

"There!" she said when she came back to Tacy. "Bee will like that egg."

They scrambled down the tree and skipped down the hill. The sunrise was almost finished. A pale surprised light was spreading over Hill Street. Smoke was coming out of kitchen chimneys here and there.

"Dyeing those Easter eggs was fun," said Tacy.

"Yes," said Betsy, "and I saved the dye. Mamma was going to throw it out, but I teased her, and she let me have it."

"What will we do with it?" asked Tacy.

"I don't know exactly. But something. You'll see."

So they skipped down the Big Hill to breakfast. They were hungry, too. And for once no one was calling "Betsy" and "Tacy." No one was awake to call.

9
The Sand Store

THAT SPRING Betsy's father built a room on their house. He said, "What if our family should grow bigger? There's a bedroom for mother and me, and one for Julia and Betsy. But what about Robert Ray Junior, when he comes along?"

So he hired a mason and a carpenter, and they built another bedroom. It was downstairs, tucked into the corner between the back parlor and the kitchen. It was going to belong to Betsy's father and mother after all. Robert Junior could have one of the upstairs bedrooms, Betsy's father said.

Betsy and Tacy thought it was exciting to have a room built on. They played see-saw on the clean, good-smelling planks. They made curls for their dolls out of the fresh yellow shavings. They dug in the sandpile which the mason had left.

That sand was what started the sand store.

Betsy and Tacy had played store lots of times. The piano box had been first one kind of store and then another, the summer before. It had been a millinery store, full of hats made from maple leaves, and it had been a lemonade store, where they sold lemonade. Now it became a sand store, on account of the fresh new sand.

It happened on the first, good, play-out Saturday in spring. The sun was warm over the earth. Robins and bluebirds and orioles flew in and out of the newly leaved maples, singing as they went. The air smelled sweet from the blooming plum trees in Betsy's father's orchard and the plumy purple lilacs by the side kitchen door. Julia and Katie had gone up on the hill to pick flowers. But Betsy and Tacy had stayed to play in the sand.

The sand was so white and pretty that Betsy got an idea.

"Let's put it in bottles and sell it," she said.

"Where will we get the bottles?" asked Tacy.

"Oh, we'll ask our mammas and Mrs. Benson," said Betsy.

So she and Tacy ran to get the bottles.

Betsy's mother gave them an olive bottle and a pickle bottle and a catsup bottle. And Tacy's mother gave them a pickle bottle and a catsup bottle and a big fat jar. And Mrs. Benson gave them a catsup bottle and a pickle bottle and a perfume bottle with a blue colored stopper. Betsy and Tacy washed all the bottles and took them to the sand pile.

"Now we'll fill them," said Betsy, and they each began on a pickle bottle, putting the sand in with spoons.

Tacy held her bottle up to the sun and looked at it. "I wish that sand was colored like our Easter eggs," she said.

Then Betsy jumped up, and began to jump up and down.

"Tacy!" she cried. "I saved those Easter egg dyes. They're put away in bottles in our piano box."

And sure enough, they were! They were hidden in a corner under a pile of yellow shaving curls, and some Sunday School cards and a box where a turtle had lived. There was green dye and yellow and purple and red and blue.

Betsy and Tacy ran into their houses and got cups (the cups with handles missing and cracks along the sides). They emptied the dye into the cups and put sand into the dye and they left it in the dye until it was colored. Then they spread it out on one of the new planks, each color in a different heap.

While it dried they sang a song which Betsy made up. It went like this:

"Oh, the Easter egg dyes,
The Easter egg dyes,
We could make this sand
Into Easter egg pies.
But we're going to fill beautiful
Bottles instead
With Easter egg yellow
And Easter egg red."

At dinner time Julia and Katie came down from the hill with their hands full of violets and hepaticas, blood roots and Dutchmen's Breeches. They stopped and stared when they saw the colored sand.

"Well, for goodness' sake!" they said. And then they said, "We'll help you fill those bottles after dinner."

Julia and Katie were nice sometimes. Besides it was fun, filling the bottles.

The vanilla bottle and the catsup bottles were

filled with sand of just one color. That was because they were hard to fill; their necks were small. The other bottles had sand in layers . . . purple with yellow, green with red, red with blue.

The jar that Tacy's mother had given them was the prettiest of all. Into that one they had put sand of every color. The mouth of the jar was wide, so that the stripes could be made smooth and even. It made Betsy throb inside to see the shining colors through the glass.

When they had finished, Julia jumped up. "Now I've got to practice my music lesson," she said.

"I've got to take care of Paul," Katie said.

Betsy and Tacy didn't care.

In front of the piano box they put two chunks of wood, the kind that Betsy's mother burned in the kitchen stove. Across those chunks they laid one of the planks from the room Betsy's father had built. They got a cigar box to hold their money, and Tacy sat behind the counter, and Betsy called, "Sand for sale! Sand for sale!" She called it as loud as she could.

At last the children began to come, all the children of Hill Street.

They bought bottles of sand and they paid for them with pins. The bottom of the cigar box was glittery with pins. But Betsy and Tacy wouldn't sell their two best bottles for pins. They wouldn't sell the perfume bottle with the blue colored stopper nor the big fat jar.

"We'll sell them to Mrs. Benson," they said.

So when all the rest of the bottles were gone, they went to Mrs. Benson's house.

She was busy getting supper, but she stopped to admire the bottles.

"What beautiful bottles of sand!" she said. "How much do you ask for them?"

"We don't know," said Betsy and Tacy.

"Would five cents apiece be enough?"

"Five cents apiece!" said Betsy and Tacy. They were astounded.

Mrs. Benson gave them each a nickel, and put the big fat jar on her piano and the perfume bottle on her parlor table.

"Don't they look beautiful!" she said.

Betsy and Tacy thought they did.

Halfway up the hill, Betsy said, "Five cents is a terrible lot of money."

"I know it," Tacy said.

"I'm not sure," said Betsy. "But I *think* that five and five make nine."

"I'm sure they do," said Tacy. "I've heard Katie talking about it."

"It's a lot of money to keep around and not spend," said Betsy.

After a moment Tacy said, "We could go to Mrs. Chubbock's."

"No," said Betsy. "You only need pennies to buy candy. These are *nickels*. We can buy something more important than candy."

She thought and she thought.

"Do you know what I think we'd better buy?" she asked, after she had thought.

"What?" asked Tacy.

"That chocolate-colored house."

"The one we pass when we go to school?" asked Tacy.

"With the tower," said Betsy. "And the pane of colored glass over the door."

"What would we do with it when we got it?" asked Tacy.

"Why, live in it. We'd sleep in the room with the tower."

"We could look through that colored glass whenever we pleased," Tacy said.

So they decided to go and buy the chocolate-colored house.

At the vacant lot they met one of Tacy's brothers. It was George, the one who asked the tailor for fashion sheets for Tacy.

"Aren't you two a long way from home?" he asked.

"We go to school this way every day," Tacy said.

"But this isn't school time. This is supper time," said George. As he spoke the whistle blew for six o'clock.

"Well, it's like this," said Betsy. "Tacy and I earned a lot of money today."

"So you're going to Mrs. Chubbock's."

"No," said Tacy. "We're going to buy a house."

"A house! What house?"

"That house," said Betsy and Tacy, and they pointed through the trees on the vacant lot to the corner of the street beyond. You could see, quite plainly, the tower of the chocolate-colored house.

"How much money have you got?" asked George.

"Nine cents," said Tacy.

"We *think* it's nine cents," said Betsy. They opened their hands and showed him the two nickels.

George pulled his mouth down hard, as though he were thinking.

"It's lots of money, all right," he said. "It isn't quite enough, though, to buy that house. I wouldn't buy it today if I were you. What are we having for supper, Tacy?"

"I don't know," said Tacy. She hung her head in disappointment. Betsy swallowed hard.

"Maybe it's near enough summer," said George,

"so that you two could take your plates up on the hill. Do you remember how you used to do that?"

"Oh, yes!" cried Tacy.

"It was fun," cried Betsy.

They had almost forgotten how they used to eat on the hill.

They looked up Hill Street, and the hill seemed to have been painted with a light green brush. Their little bench was waiting in the rosy sunset light.

"I'll go ask my mamma," said Betsy.

"I'll go ask my mamma, too," said Tacy.

They both started to run.

"And put those nickels in the bank," George called. "Save them! Do you hear?"

But Betsy and Tacy were running too fast to hear.

10

Calling on Mrs. Benson

![W]HEN SUMMER TIME came Betsy and Tacy didn't need to bother with school any more. They could play all day long. They did play all day long, and they never once ran out of things to do.

"The days aren't long enough for those two," Betsy's mother used to say to Betsy's father.

This was true; although it was strange, for a day was very long.

A day filled all the hours which it took the sun to wheel from behind the white house on the Big Hill, across the vast blue spaces of the sky, to the trees down behind Tacy's barn. By the time evening came and Betsy and Tacy were playing games with the other Hill Street children (not made-up games, but real games, like Pom Pom Pullaway and Run, Sheep, Run), they could hardly remember the cool morning hours when they had had the world to themselves. But in all the long golden time in between, they never ran out of games to play.

One of their favorite games was dressing up. They loved to dress up in grown-up clothes and go calling.

One day Betsy's mother let her dress up in her old tan lace dress. It was a beautiful dress with a big pink rose in the front. Betsy poked an old table cloth underneath her skirts behind to make a bustle like her mother's. And she wore an old hat of her mother's, a round hat with a veil.

Tacy wore a striped blue and green silk dress of her grown-up sister Mary's. Her curls were pinned high, and she wore a big hat covered with flowers. And Mary let her carry her parasol, which was pink with ruffles all around it.

When Tacy was given the parasol, she and Betsy raced back to Betsy's house.

"Mamma," Betsy cried, "Tacy has a parasol. May I carry your parasol?"

"No," said Betsy's mother. "But you may carry my cardcase." She got it out of the bureau drawer. One side was filled with cards which said "Mrs. Robert Ray." A little lace-edged handkerchief, smelling of violet perfume, peeked out of the other side. Betsy's mother carried this case when she went calling. She left a card at every house.

Betsy took the cardcase and Tacy opened the parasol, and they started down Hill Street.

"We'll call on Mrs. Benson," Betsy said.

So they called on Mrs. Benson, and she was very glad to see them.

"Come right in," she said. "How are you, Mrs. Ray? How do you do, Mrs. Kelly?"

She pretended that they were their mothers, instead of Betsy and Tacy. Of course that was the right thing to do.

"Sit right down," she said, and they sat down on the sofa. "It's lovely weather we're having."

"Yes, isn't it?" said Betsy in a very grown-up tone. Tacy didn't talk much; she was bashful.

"I hear you bought some sand, Mrs. Benson," said Betsy in the grown-up tone.

"Yes, I did. Would you like to see it?" asked Mrs. Benson, and she went to her desk and brought out the two bottles full of sand which Betsy and Tacy had colored, the perfume bottle with the blue colored stopper and the big fat jar.

"Mercy, what beautiful sand!" said Betsy.

"Isn't it!" cried Mrs. Benson. "I bought it from two little girls named Betsy and Tacy."

Tacy looked up then, her blue eyes dancing into Mrs. Benson's. "I know those little girls," she said.

"I thought maybe you did," said Mrs. Benson.

After a minute Mrs. Benson asked, "Wouldn't

you like some tea?"

"Tea?" asked Betsy, so surprised that she forgot to talk like her mother.

"Afternoon tea," explained Mrs. Benson. "What ladies drink when they go calling."

"Oh, of course," said Betsy. "I'd love some. Wouldn't you, Tacy?"

So Mrs. Benson gave them some tea . . . cambric tea, she called it, and it was delicious. They had cookies with their tea, and Betsy and Tacy nibbled them daintily. But they ate them to the very last crumb.

When the cookies were gone, Betsy said, "Well,

I'm afraid we'll have to be going. Good-by, Mrs. Benson."

"Good-by, Mrs. Ray," Mrs. Benson said.

"Good-by, Mrs. Benson," said Tacy, not bashful any more.

"Good-by, Mrs. Kelly," said Mrs. Benson. "May I help you open your parasol?"

Then Betsy remembered the cardcase.

"And I must leave you a card," she said. "Here's a card for me and one for Tacy."

Betsy and Tacy went on, down Hill Street Hill.

"Who shall we call on next?" asked Tacy.

"I know," said Betsy. "We'll call at the chocolate-colored house."

So they went on down Hill Street Hill to the corner and through the vacant lot. It was farther than they had ever gone before in grown-up clothes. They held their long skirts high so that the weeds and bushes would not tear them, and they came to the chocolate-colored house.

"Tacy," said Betsy, "I never yet saw anybody around this chocolate-colored house."

"Neither did I," said Tacy.

They looked at it a moment before they climbed to the door.

It sat like a big plump chocolate drop on the big square corner lot. There weren't many trees around it; just a green lawn with flower beds on either side of the white cement walk which led to the porch steps.

Betsy and Tacy walked up that walk and climbed the porch steps.

They rang the bell and waited.

While they were waiting they looked around. The tower jutted right out on the porch. It had windows in it, but all the shades were pulled down. The pane of colored glass over the front door shone

ruby red in the sunlight.

No one answered their ring, and Betsy and Tacy rang the bell again. They rang it again and again.

At last the lady next door came out of her house. She looked busy and cross.

"What are you doing on that porch, little girls?" she asked in a sharp voice.

"We're ringing the bell," said Betsy. "We've come to call."

"Tell her about the cardcase," whispered Tacy.

But before Betsy could speak again, the lady said, "Well, the people who live there aren't home. They've gone to Milwaukee."

She went back into her house and shut the door.

"Milwaukee," said Betsy.

"Milwaukee," said Tacy.

They liked the sound of the word.

"I wish I could go to Milwaukee," said Betsy.

"What's it like?" asked Tacy.

"Oh, it's lovely," said Betsy. "Milwaukee. Milwaukee." She said the name over and over.

"While we walk home," she said to Tacy, "I'll make up a poem about it." Betsy liked to make up poems.

"First we must leave a card, though," said Tacy.

"Of course," said Betsy.

They opened the cardcase and took out a card

and put it in the mailbox. Mrs. Robert Ray, it said on the card. They took out another and left that one too. The second one was from Tacy.

While they walked home, Betsy made up the poem about Milwaukee. It went like this:

"There's a place named Milwaukee, Milwaukee,
Milwaukee, Milwauk, MilwaukEE,
There's a place named Milwaukee, Milwaukee,
A beautiful place to be;
I wish I could go to Milwaukee,
With Tacy ahold of my hand,
I wish I could go to Milwaukee,
It sounds like the Beulah Land."

"That's a nice poem," said Tacy. "I like the part about me."

So they sang it together, making up a tune. They sang it all the way through the vacant lot. And just at the edge of the vacant lot they saw Betsy's father who was driving home for supper. He was driving Old Mag and had just slowed down for Hill Street Hill.

"Stop!" "Wait!" "Give us a ride!" cried Betsy and Tacy. They picked up their long skirts and began to run.

"Why, how do you do, Mrs. Vanderbilt?" said

Betsy's father. "And how do you do, Mrs. Astor?"

He stopped Old Mag and cramped the wheel of the buggy, and Betsy and Tacy climbed in.

Betsy took the reins and Tacy held the whip. Julia and Katie were watching from the steps of the Ray house.

"Giddap!" said Betsy.

"Whoa!" said Tacy.

They drove in triumph around the little road which led to Old Mag's barn.

11

The Buggy Shed

ETSY AND Tacy liked to ride home with
Betsy's father, or Tacy's. Along about sunset they would walk to the foot of Hill
Street Hill and wait. Sometimes they rode up the
hill with Mr. Ray and sometimes with Mr. Kelly.
Always they rode around to the barn and helped to
feed and water the horse, and saw straw put down

for his bed and the buggy rolled into the buggy shed.

During the day they liked to play in Betsy's buggy shed. It was dark and smelled of hay and oats from the barn which stood right beside it. When Old Mag was in the barn they could hear her chewing oats and stamping flies, but she wasn't often there. She was gone to the store and so was the buggy. Only the surrey was left in the buggy shed for Betsy and Tacy to play with.

The surrey had two seats and a canopy edged with fringe. There was a pocket in one corner for the whip, and a dust robe to spread on their laps. It was used mostly on Sundays when the family went to church or took a picnic to the river, and on summer evenings when they sometimes went riding while their bedrooms cooled off after the heat of the day.

"Shall we sit in the front seat or the back seat?" asked Tacy now, as she and Betsy climbed in.

"The front seat," said Betsy. For children usually sat in the back seat. So Betsy and Tacy sat in the front seat, and Betsy picked up the whip. Tacy tucked the robe around them, although it was a very warm day.

"Giddap!" said Betsy, cracking the whip.

"Don't go too fast," said Tacy.

"I won't," said Betsy. "I think too much of my horse." That was what her father said, so she knew it was the proper thing to say.

Through the open door of the buggy shed, they could see the Big Hill. It was pleasantly green with an arc of blue above it.

"See things fly past!" said Betsy. "Streets and houses and things."

"Where are we going?" asked Tacy.

"To Milwaukee," said Betsy.

"Goodie!" said Tacy. "That's the place I want most of all to see."

"Well, you're going there now," said Betsy, and she cracked the whip again. "Tuck up good," she said.

"Did we bring a lunch?" asked Tacy.

"Yes," said Betsy. "It's under the seat. There are chicken sandwiches and hard-boiled eggs and potato salad and watermelon and chocolate cake and sweet pickles and sugar cookies and ice cream."

"It ought to be plenty," Tacy said.

They went down Hill Street to Broad Street where the churches and the library and the big houses were; and they turned from Broad Street to Front Street where the stores were. They went past the office where Tacy's father sold sewing machines and past the store where Betsy's father sold shoes.

But they didn't stop.

"We haven't time," said Betsy.

They went on down Front Street to the Big Mill at the end. That Big Mill blew the whistle for six o'clock in the morning and twelve o'clock noon and six o'clock at night. It wasn't blowing any whistles now. Betsy and Tacy rode past it. They rode up Front Street Hill and out of the town of Deep Valley. They were out in the country now.

"I think it's time for our lunch," Tacy said.

"Yes, it is," said Betsy. "We'll stop here beside this lake."

So they stopped beside a lake, and they let Old Mag's check rein down so that she could drink. And Betsy and Tacy sat down in the shade and opened their picnic basket.

"I just love chicken sandwiches," said Betsy.

"This ice cream is good," said Tacy. "It hasn't melted a bit."

"We must be careful not to squirt this water-melon," Betsy said.

"Yes," said Tacy. "We forgot to bring any napkins."

When they had finished eating they climbed back into the surrey and they rode and rode and rode.

"I see Milwaukee," Betsy said after a while.

"Do you?" asked Tacy. "Where?"

"See those towers a way, way off?" Betsy said. And when they had come closer, she said, "It looks like the cities on my Sunday School cards, with that wall and all those towers."

"That's right," said Tacy. "I see palm trees."

"The people will wear red and blue night gowns, like they do on the Sunday School cards, most likely," Betsy said.

"Maybe there will be camels," said Tacy.

"Of course there will be camels. I think I see a camel's head now, sticking around. . . ."

There was a head sticking around the side of the buggy shed door. But it didn't belong to a camel. It belonged to the little boy named Tom.

"Hello," he called out doubtfully.

"What are you doing here?" Betsy asked.

"My mother brought me. She came on an errand."

"Oh! Well, you can play with us if you want to."

"What are you playing?"

"We're going on a trip in this surrey."

"Where to?" he asked, coming in.

Betsy hesitated, and Tacy didn't speak either. They liked Tom; but boys were boys; they didn't always understand. And Milwaukee was no ordinary city. Milwaukee was their secret. They had a song about it.

"Just going on a trip," said Betsy. "Is there anywhere you'd like to go?"

"Sure," said Tom. "I'd like to go to St. Paul. I went there once. Stayed at a hotel. And a man gave me a nickel. We went to St. Paul on a train though. Do you think that horse could make it?" he stared at the empty shafts.

"This is a fine horse," said Betsy. "And you may drive because you're company."

So she and Tacy didn't get to Milwaukee that day, after all. But they had a good time in St. Paul. They stayed in St. Paul until Julia and Katie came to tell them that there were lemonade and cookies for the children under the butternut tree.

12

Margaret

THAT SUMMER Julia and Betsy went for a visit to Uncle Edward's farm. They had a good time too. They saw the cows milked and they helped to gather eggs and they played with chicks and ducklings and they rode on the big farm wagons. But at last the time came to go home, and Betsy was glad. She wanted to tell Tacy all about it.

Betsy's father didn't come to get them. Uncle Edward drove them home. They drove into town and up Hill Street and up to the very end of Hill Street. Betsy was looking everywhere for Tacy; she wanted to tell her all about the farm.

But before she could find Tacy she saw her father. He was standing on the porch waving to them.

"Hurry!" he called. "I've got a surprise." And Uncle Edward began to laugh, and stopped the horse. And Julia and Betsy scrambled over the wheel and out of the buggy and ran up the steps of the little yellow cottage, to the porch where their father was waiting.

He was smiling all over his face, and he hugged them and kissed them and said, "Guess what's waiting for you inside the house."

Betsy thought and thought. And she knew they had a cat, so she was going to say, "A dog!" But Julia cried out, "Robert Ray Junior!"

Her father laughed out loud at that, and he gave her a squeeze. "Guess again," he said. And Julia said, "A little sister!" And Betsy's father said, "That's right. A little sister! And we can't very well call a girl Robert, so you and Betsy have to find a name for her. You can name her all by yourselves."

Betsy's father led the way into the house. For some reason he went on tiptoe. And he led the way into the parlor and into the back parlor and into the new downstairs bedroom, and there was Betsy's mother lying in bed. And resting on her arm was a little red-faced baby. A woman wearing a white apron stood beside the bed.

"Julia! Betsy!" cried their mother. "Come here and kiss me, and see your baby sister."

Julia and Betsy tiptoed toward the bed.

The room smelled of medicine, and the woman with the white apron was strange, and Betsy felt strange, too. And she didn't at all like the looks of her baby sister! But her mother was gazing at them with such shining eyes . . . Betsy couldn't bear to hurt her feelings. So she didn't say a word.

Julia actually liked the baby. You could tell that she did. She "Oh-ed" and she "Ah-ed" and she said, "Oh, let me hold her. *May* I hold her, Papa?" And she lifted up one of the tiny hands and cried, "Isn't she darling?"

Betsy was disgusted with Julia. Julia never did have much sense, she thought to herself. When nobody was looking she slipped into the kitchen and out the back kitchen door.

She had thought that the first thing she would do when she got home would be to run over to Tacy's, but she didn't want to go to Tacy's now. She wanted to get away where nobody could see her, and for a very special reason. She went out past the back-yard maple and through the garden and the little orchard and past the buggy shed and into the barn. Old Mag was there munching hay. And Betsy went into a corner of the barn and sat down and began to cry.

She didn't know why she was crying except that everything was so queer. Her mamma in bed, a strange woman around, the room smelling of medicine and that *unnecessary* baby.

"It's a perfectly *unnecessary* baby," Betsy said aloud. "*I'm* the baby." And the more she thought that, the harder she cried, and the farther she scrunched away into a corner of the barn.

Bye and bye Tacy came in. Tacy hadn't seen Betsy go into the barn. She just seemed to know that Betsy was in that barn, as Betsy had known that Tacy would come outdoors early the morning after Baby Bee's funeral. Tacy came in, and she came straight over to the corner where Betsy was sitting, and she sat down beside her and put her arm around her. She held Betsy tight. Betsy went "sniff, sniff," "sniff, sniff," every two sniffs farther apart, until at last she wasn't crying any more. She was just sitting still inside Tacy's arm.

Then Tacy said, "Most everybody has babies, you know."

"Do they?" asked Betsy.

"Yes. Look at our house," said Tacy. "First I was the baby, and then Paul came. And then Paul was the baby, and then Bee came. And then Bee died so now Paul's the baby again. But I expect there'll be another baby most any time.

"You can't keep on being the baby forever," Tacy said, finishing up.

Somehow that made Betsy feel better, to know that Tacy used to be the baby and now wasn't the baby any more. Tacy got along all right. And if this was something that happened to everybody, having a new baby come to the house now and then, why it just had to happen to her.

"Our baby's funny looking," she said in a low voice.

"All babies are at first," said Tacy. "They get pretty after a while."

"My mamma seems to think it's pretty right now," Betsy said.

"Of course," said Tacy. "Mammas always do."

"Julia," said Betsy slowly, "didn't mind at all. She liked the baby right away."

"Well, but she's the oldest," said Tacy. "The oldest is always different."

Betsy rubbed her fists into her eyes to dry them. She leaned back against Tacy's arm and smelled the smell of the barn.

All of a sudden she thought how odd it was that Tacy should be talking like this. Usually she herself did most of the talking. But now Tacy was doing the talking. She was trying to comfort Betsy just as Betsy had comforted her after little Bee died. And she *had* comforted her. All the sore hurt feeling was gone.

"I'll help you wheel that baby out in the carriage," Tacy said. "We'll wheel her to the chocolate-colored house."

Betsy sat up happily. "That will be fun," she said. "And my papa said that Julia and I could name her."

"*Name the baby?*" cried Tacy.

"That's what he said," said Betsy proudly.

"Why, I never named a baby in my life!" said Tacy. "What will you name her?" she asked.

Betsy thought a moment. "Rosy would be a nice name," she said. "Come on, let's find Papa and tell him."

So Betsy and Tacy took hold of hands and skipped down to the house.

Mr. Ray was looking for Betsy. "I was wondering where you had gone to," he said. "Come on in, we've got to name the baby."

"Tacy and I have thought of a name. It's Rosy," Betsy said.

"Rosy!" said Betsy's father. "Rosy! It's certainly a beautiful name."

And later he and Betsy and Julia sat down in the kitchen. They drew their chairs into a circle and talked importantly in whispers. But the baby wasn't named Rosy after all. For Julia wanted to call her Ginivra.

Betsy wouldn't have Ginivra, and Julia wouldn't have Rosy. Julia wouldn't have Rosy Ginivra, and Betsy wouldn't have Ginivra Rosy.

"See here," said Betsy's father. "How about Margaret?"

Betsy liked Margaret better than Rosy. Julia liked Margaret better than Ginivra. They all thought that Margaret was a beautiful name. So they named the baby Margaret.

And Tacy was right about the baby getting pretty. She grew prettier every day.

13

Mrs. Muller Comes to Call

SOON AFTER Baby Margaret was born, two
things happened to Betsy and Tacy. The first
one was: they climbed the Big Hill, all the
way to the white house which stood on the top. The
second one was: . . . well, that comes after the first.

It was a late summer day. Goldenrod and asters
were coloring the hill. The days were growing
short, the birds were gathering in flocks, and there

was a feeling in the air that school would be starting soon.

Betsy and Tacy were sitting in the backyard
maple, and suddenly Betsy said, "Let's climb the Big
Hill, all the way to the top."

"Let's," Tacy said.

So they ran and asked their mothers.

"All right," said Betsy's mother. "But you'd better take a picnic."

"All right," said Tacy's mother. "What a good
thing it is that I was just baking a cake!"

So they took along a picnic. And this was the first
time that they had taken a picnic in a basket. They
packed their picnic in a brown wicker basket, and
they both took hold of the handle, and they climbed
the Big Hill.

They climbed to the ridge where wild roses grew
in June. They had gone that far before. They passed
the tree where they had left the egg for Bee in a
nest at the very top. They passed the thorn apple
tree where they had planned to make a house.
There was a pasture on one side, and a cow and
a calf were in that pasture; on the other side the
country was open and free. They turned to look
back, there, but they kept on climbing. They
climbed and they climbed, and they came to the top
of the hill.

The land was as flat as a plate, and there were oak trees scattered about, and the white house stood there . . . the one the sun came up behind in the morning. They went to the white house and they peeked all around it. They almost expected to find the sun in a pocket behind that house. But there was only a deep ravine, with the sound of water gurgling, and another hill beyond.

"Goodness!" said Betsy. "The world is big."

They had thought they would be satisfied when once they had climbed the Big Hill. But now they wanted to go down in the ravine, and see this water which sounded so merry, and climb the next hill.

"We will some day, too," Betsy said.

But they thought that for one day they had done enough. So they sat down on the rim of the Big Hill and ate their lunch.

They sat on the rim overlooking Hill Street. And they could look down, along the road they had come, into the maples of Hill Street and down on the roofs of their homes. They could see the trees in the vacant lot. They could see the tower of the chocolate-colored house. They could see the red brick schoolhouse where they went to school.

And they could see farther than that for they could see down to Front Street, where Tacy's father had his office and Betsy's father his store. They could see the towering chimneys of the Big Mill where the whistles blew for morning, noon and night. They could see Page Park with the white fence around it. And beyond that, down in the valley, they could see a silver ribbon. They knew that was the river.

"Mercy!" said Tacy. "There are lots of places to go."

They ate their sandwiches and the cake Tacy's mother had made and started down the hill.

And when they reached Betsy's house a great surprise awaited them. Betsy's mother was sitting on the porch, rocking the baby. She was laughing, and she looked very young and pretty, with her red hair (like Tacy's) flying around her face and the baby in her arms.

"You two little rascals, come here!" she said.

Betsy and Tacy came there.

"Do you remember the day I let you take my cardcase?" Betsy's mother asked.

Betsy and Tacy nodded. Of course they remembered.

"Well, what do you mean by leaving my cards at strange houses?"

"Strange houses?" asked Betsy.

"The houses of people we don't know."

As Betsy and Tacy did not answer, she went on: "You must have left a card at that big new house on the corner of Pleasant Street."

"Why, yes," said Betsy. "We did." But she wondered how her mother knew. She and Tacy had kept that visit a secret.

"The people had gone away," Tacy said. But she didn't say where.

"Well, here is what happened," said Mrs. Ray, still laughing. And Julia and Katie, who were standing by the porch, laughed too.

"This afternoon I was sitting here on the porch, and a carriage drove up. A lady got out, and she came up the steps of the porch and said, 'Mrs. Ray? I am Mrs. Muller. It was so kind of you to call.' And then she explained that she and her husband had moved here from Milwaukee. They had bought that house and settled it, she said, and then they had gone back to Milwaukee. But now they have come here to stay and get their little girl in school."

"Their little girl!" cried Betsy and Tacy together. "Is there a little girl?"

"Of course. Didn't I tell you that the little girl was with her? Julia and Katie entertained her, for I couldn't find you two. But she's just about your age."

"What's she like?" asked Betsy and Tacy breathlessly.

"Oh, she's darling," said Julia and Katie. "She's perfectly sweet."

"She has little yellow curls," said Julia. "Short ones. Like this."

"And big blue eyes," said Katie.

"She wore the prettiest dress," said Julia. "White lace with bows of blue ribbon all over."

"And she dances," said Katie. "She danced for us. All by herself."

Betsy and Tacy looked at each other.

"What's her name?" asked Betsy.

"Her name is Tib." "It's short for Thelma." Julia and Katie explained.

Betsy and Tacy didn't say a word. They started down Hill Street. "Do you suppose we'll like her?" they asked . . . but silently. Down in their hearts they thought they wouldn't.

They took hold of hands when they reached the vacant lot. They walked as though they were walking into danger. The tall trees and the bushes and the brush seemed to wait in breathless excitement as Betsy and Tacy approached the chocolate-colored house.

14
Tib

 THEY APPROACHED the chocolate-colored house from the rear for it faced on Pleasant Street. On the back lawn was an oak tree which stood on a small knoll. On the knoll they saw what looked like a clothes pin, standing prongs up. It was a little girl standing on her head.

She righted herself when they came near and stood on her bare feet. She was dainty and small.

Her arms, legs and face were tanned, which made her blue eyes look even bluer than they were and her short fluff of yellow hair look very yellow. She stared at them silently out of her round blue eyes.

"What were you doing?" asked Betsy.

"Standing on my head."

"What were you doing that for?"

"I was practicing."

"It must be hard," said Betsy.

"Oh, no, it isn't." The little girl looked surprised.

Tacy didn't say a word. She was bashful.

Betsy stared back at the little girl. It was certainly Tib. "But my sister said you had a white lace dress on," she said at last.

"I took it off when I came home," Tib answered. "I'm not allowed to play in my best dress."

"Neither am I," said Betsy. "Neither is Tacy. I wish we could see your dress, though," she added after a moment.

"Do you?" asked Tib, looking surprised again. "I'll show it to you."

She led the way into the chocolate-colored house.

They went in by the back door. "Wipe your feet," said Tib, pausing on the doormat. The kitchen was so clean . . . it shone like a polished pan. It smelled good, of something baking. A hired girl was standing by the stove.

There was a swinging door which led into the dining room and another door which led into a pantry full of glittery china and glass. The third door led up some narrow stairs and up these they followed Tib.

Upstairs was a long hall with doors admitting to the bedrooms.

Tib took them into one of
these, and hanging in a closet
was the white lace dress.

"It's a beautiful dress," said
Betsy.

Tacy touched one of the
pale blue satin bows.

Tib led them down the hall.
There were front stairs as well

as back stairs! They went down the front stairs, and just as the steps turned at a little landing, they came in view of the pane of colored glass. The afternoon sunlight, streaming through it, turned it to ruby red.

"Tacy and I like that colored glass," said Betsy.

"What colored glass?" asked Tib.

"That colored glass over your door."

"Do you. Why?" asked Tib. She looked at it as though she had never noticed it before.

"We like your tower too," said Betsy.

"What tower?" asked Tib. "Do you mean the round room? That's our front parlor."

They crossed the hall and entered it.

It was round and beautiful. Hanging over the piano was a picture of an old man giving a little girl a music lesson. The chairs and sofa were covered with blue velvet and there was a bamboo table draped with a blue silk scarf. The table held two little china dolls, a shepherd and a shepherdess.

Tib led them through blue velvet curtains into the back parlor. This had a window seat from which you could see the red brick schoolhouse. A lady sat there sewing. She was short and chunky and had yellow hair like Tib's and earrings in her ears.

"Is this the little Ray girl?" she asked.

"Yes, ma'am," answered Betsy. "I'm Betsy and this is Tacy."

Tacy held her head down and covered her face with her curls.

"Well, I hope you children will all be good friends," Tib's mother said, smiling.

"Mamma," said Tib. "May we have some coffee cake?"

"Yes," said the lady. "Matilda will give you some. But eat it out on the knoll."

So Matilda—she was the hired girl—gave them some coffee cake. It was hot out of the oven. And they sat down to eat it on the knoll.

Tib kept staring at Betsy and Tacy with her round blue eyes. She looked awed and admiring, which was nice but very strange. For Tib was the one who danced, thought Betsy. She was the one who had a white lace dress. She was the one who had a house with front and back stairs and a tower and a pane of colored glass.

Betsy and Tacy looked at each other. Both of them looked surprised. They hadn't expected to like her, but they did.

Tib didn't say a word and neither did Tacy, so at last Betsy said:

"When you came to our house, we were up on the Big Hill."

"Were you?" asked Tib.

"We climbed to the very top," said Betsy.

"Did you?" Tib replied.

"There's a little hill too," said Betsy. "With a bench on it. We eat our supper there."

"All by yourselves?" asked Tib.

"All by ourselves," said Betsy.

"And Betsy makes up stories," said Tacy. It was the first word she had said.

"Do you mean," asked Tib, "that she tells about Cinderella?"

"No, I make them up," said Betsy.

"But how can you?" Tib asked.

"Why, I just do," said Betsy. "Tacy helps me."

"Will you make one up now?" asked Tib.

"Yes, if you want me to. I'll make one up about you and me and Tacy and that pane of colored glass over your door."

Tib was speechless with astonishment, but Tacy jumped to her feet and said:

"Let's go up to our bench. That's the best place for stories."

So she took one of Tib's hands and Betsy took the other. And they walked through the vacant lot and up Hill Street Hill.

As they walked they were very busy talking.

"We've got a piano box we play in," Betsy said.

"And Betsy's got a baby sister," Tacy said.

"We play paper dolls," said Betsy.

"And store," said Tacy.

"We dress up and go calling."

"And Betsy makes up games."

Tib held their hands tightly. She sighed deeply with content.

"I'm glad I came here," she said. "I like this better than Milwaukee."

Betsy and Tacy stopped still. They looked at each other, their eyes as round as Tib's. She liked Hill Street better than Milwaukee! Well, they had always known it was nice.

After a silent moment they went slowly on toward the bench on the hill.

"We'll have lots of fun," said Betsy. "You and me and Tacy. Lots of things will happen."

And so they did.

THE END

Betsy-Tacy
and Tib

FOR
MIDGE *and* JOAN

Contents

Foreword

I was ten when I discovered the books about Betsy, Tacy, and Tib. This was years and years ago, in 1965, and even then the stories seemed old-fashioned—in a tantalizing way that sent me hurrying to our school library to see just how many books by Maud Hart Lovelace I might find there.

After reading the first few pages of *Betsy-Tacy*, I remember flipping to the front of the book to check the copyright date. It had been published in 1940, and the other books about Betsy and her friends followed soon after. I made some calculations in my head. In the early 1940s my mother had been young, a high-school student. But surely the adventures of Betsy, Tacy, and Tib were supposed to have taken place long before then. I was right. A talk with my mother revealed that the stories were about girls who were growing up at the time my grandmothers were little. In fact, Granny, my grandmother Adele, was nearly the same age as Maud Hart Lovelace, who wrote the stories about her own childhood. Ms. Lovelace was born in 1892; Granny was born in 1893. And I am fairly certain that my independent, high-spirited grandmother must have had a childhood similar to Betsy Ray's. Never mind that Betsy and her friends lived in Minnesota and my grandmother grew up in Arkansas. As I read about the School Entertainment and ice-cream socials, about ladies leaving calling cards and the milkman with his horse-drawn wagon, I felt that I was having an unexpected and welcome peek into Granny's childhood—a gift to me from Maud Hart Lovelace.

As I continued to read about Betsy and Tacy and Tib, I discovered something equally as wonderful as the fact that the books could have been about my beloved granny. Even though they took place at the turn of the twentieth century, the things that happened in the books were very like some of the things that happened to my parents when they were growing up later, in the 1920s and 1930s. The trouble at the School Entertainment in *Betsy and Tacy Go Over the Big Hill* prompted a story from my father about the time he broke his arm during a school play. I told my mother about Betsy and Tacy and the ornery hen in *Betsy-Tacy*, and she told me about getting in trouble in first grade for letting some visiting chickens out of their cage. These were small stories, things that could happen to anyone, but when Maud Hart Lovelace told small stories she made them seem big.

And, I eventually realized, the small stories were stories that could happen at any time. The more I thought about it, the more I discovered that I liked Betsy and Tacy and Tib because although they were growing up a good seventy years before I was, their lives weren't really so different from mine. My friends and my sister and I were active, independent girls. We staged parades and carnivals and plays. We built things, we planned things, we concocted things. We had big ideas and we carried them out. I could be Betsy, I thought, as I read about choosing a Queen of Summer, or making a house in a piano box, or walking along the Secret Lane, or being granted permission to go to the library all alone.

When I grew up and decided that I wanted to be a writer, I remembered how Maud Hart Lovelace had made small stories big. And I remembered that she had written about her childhood. Many of the incidents I have written about are small events from my own childhood—setting up a stand in our front yard to sell strawberries, wildflowers, and lemonade; putting on a carnival to raise money for the Red Cross; going on school field trips. The trick is making those small stories big enough—interesting or funny enough—to merit their places in books. I also found myself creating mostly girl characters—independent girls who operate not quite outside the world of adults, but not quite within it either. They hover somewhere between, with their own plans and big ideas, and friends to help carry them out.

Very much like Betsy, Tacy, and Tib.

—Ann M. Martin

Three can make the planets sing

—MARY CAROLYN DAVIES

1

Begging at Mrs. Ekstrom's

BETSY AND Tacy and Tib were three little
girls who were friends. They never quarreled.
Betsy and Tacy were friends first. They
were good friends, and they never quarreled. When
Tib moved into that neighborhood, and the three of
them started playing together, grown-up people said:

"It's too bad! Betsy Ray and Tacy Kelly always
played so nicely. Two little girls often do play nicely,

but just let a third one come around. . . ." And they stopped, and their silence sounded as though they were saying: "then the trouble begins!"

But although so many people expected it, no trouble began with Betsy, Tacy and Tib. The three of them didn't quarrel, any more than the two of them had. They sometimes quarreled with Julia and Katie, though. Julia and Katie were Betsy's and Tacy's big sisters; they were bossy; and Betsy and Tacy and Tib didn't like to be bossed.

Betsy and Tacy lived on Hill Street, which ran straight up into a green hill and stopped. The small yellow cottage where the Ray family lived was the last house on that side of the street, and the rambling white house opposite where the Kelly family lived was the last house on that side. These two houses ended the street, and after that came the hill.

Tib didn't live on Hill Street. She lived on Pleasant Street. To get to Tib's house from the place where Betsy and Tacy lived you went one block down and one block over. (The second block was through a vacant lot.) Tib lived in a chocolate-colored house which was the most beautiful house Betsy and Tacy had ever been in. It had front stairs and back stairs and a tower and panes of colored glass in the front door.

Tib was the same age as Betsy and Tacy. They

were all eight years old. They were six when Tib came to live in Deep Valley, and now they were eight. Tacy was the tallest. She had long red ringlets and freckles and thin legs. Until she got acquainted with people Tacy was bashful. Tib was the smallest. She was little and dainty with round blue eyes and a fluff of yellow hair. She looked like a picture-book fairy, except, of course, that she didn't have wings. Betsy was the middle-sized one. She had plump legs and short brown braids which stuck out behind her ears. Her smile showed teeth which were parted in the middle, and Betsy was almost always smiling.

When Betsy ran out of doors in the morning, she came with a beam on her face. That was because it was fun to plan what she and Tacy and Tib were going to do. Betsy loved to think up things to do and Tacy and Tib loved to do them.

One morning Betsy ran out of her house and met Tacy who had just run out of hers. They met in the middle of the road and ran up to the bench which stood at the end of Hill Street. From that bench they could look 'way down the street. They often waited there for Tib.

Betsy and Tacy had to wait for Tib because they got ready to play sooner than she did. Betsy's mother was slim and quick; she didn't need much help around the house. And Tacy's mother had ten children besides Tacy, so of course there wasn't much for Tacy to do. Tib's mother had a hired girl to help her, but just the same Tib had to work. Tib's mother believed in children knowing how to work. Tib dusted the legs of the chairs and polished the silver. She was learning to cook and to sew.

Betsy and Tacy didn't mind waiting today. It was June, and the world smelled of roses. The sunshine was like powdered gold over the grassy hillside.

"What shall we do today?" asked Tacy.

"Let's go up on the Big Hill," Betsy answered.

The Big Hill wasn't the hill which ended Hill Street. That was the Hill Street Hill. The Big Hill rose up behind Betsy's house. And a white house stood at the top.

"Shall we take a picnic?" asked Tacy.

"I wish we could," said Betsy. "But it's pretty soon after breakfast to ask for a picnic."

"If I went in the house to ask," said Tacy, "I might have to help with the dishes."

"Better not go," said Betsy. "But we'll be hungry by the time we get to the top." She thought for a moment. "We may have to pretend we're beggars."

"What do you mean by that?" asked Tacy, her blue eyes beginning to sparkle.

"Why, muss up our hair and dirty our clothes and ask for something to eat at the white house."

"Oh! Oh!" cried Tacy. It was all she could say.

Just then Tib ran up. She looked so clean in a starched pink chambray dress that Betsy thought perhaps they had better not be beggars.

"What are we going to do?" asked Tib.

"We're going up on the Big Hill," said Betsy. "Of course, we have to ask."

They were eight years old, but they still couldn't climb the Big Hill without permission; Betsy and Tacy couldn't; Tib's mother always told her that she could go wherever Betsy and Tacy were allowed to go. Tib's house was too far away to run to every time they had to ask permission.

Betsy and Tacy sent Paul, who was Tacy's little brother, into their houses to ask permission now. Paul trotted into Tacy's house and into Betsy's house, and he trotted back with word that they could go. So Betsy and Tacy and Tib started walking up the Big Hill.

Julia was practising her music lesson, and the sound of the scales she was playing flashed out of the house as they passed. It sounded as though Julia were enjoying herself.

"I wouldn't like to be playing the piano today," said Betsy.

"Neither would I," said Tacy.

"Neither would I," said Tib. "Of course," she

added, "we don't know how."

Neither Betsy nor Tacy would have pointed that out. Tib was always pointing such things out. But Betsy and Tacy liked her just the same.

"We could learn quick enough if we wanted to," said Betsy. "I can play chopsticks now."

They came to a ridge where wild roses were in bloom. They stopped to smell them. They passed a thorn apple tree where they would pick thorn apples later. Now the tree was covered with little hard green balls. There were lots of trees on that side of the road and the grass was deep and full of flowers. On the other side was a fenced-in pasture with Mr. Williams' cow in it.

At last they came to the top of the hill. They could look down now on the roofs of Hill Street. They could see the school house where they all went to school and the chocolate-colored house where Tib lived. They could see all over the town of Deep Valley, 'way to the Big Mill. And deep in the valley they could see a silver ribbon. That was the river.

The top of the hill was flat, and there were oak trees scattered about. The white house stood in the middle. It was a small house with a flower garden at the front. Some people named Ekstrom lived there. Behind the Ekstroms' house was a ravine, with a spring of water in it, and a brook. Betsy and

Tacy and Tib had been down in the ravine, but not without Julia and Katie.

"Let's go down in the ravine," said Betsy.

They took hold of hands.

The way to the ravine was through the Ekstroms' back yard. Betsy and Tacy and Tib didn't know the Ekstroms, but they had seen them often going up and down the hill. They didn't see any of the Ekstroms now. They saw a dog who barked at them in a friendly sort of way. They saw some hens who clucked sociably. And through an open barn door they saw a cow. They went past the kitchen garden and came to the edge of the ravine.

A steep twisting path led into the ravine. The hillside was crowded with trees. There were big trees and seedling trees, old graying trees and fresh fine green ones. The grass was full of red and yellow columbine.

Betsy and Tacy and Tib descended carefully, picking flowers as they went.

All the way down they could hear the brook, and when they reached the bottom they could see it, rushing over its stones. There was a spring with four boards around it. When you leaned over to drink, the water smacked your face. They drank from the spring and the water tasted good, but it wasn't as good as something to eat would have been.

"I'm hungry," said Tacy.

"So am I," said Tib.

"Let's suck the honey from our columbine," said Betsy, so they sucked the honey out of all their flowers. But they were still hungry.

Betsy looked around.

"There's syrup in those maple trees," she said. "If we'd brought a knife, we could cut a hole and get some."

"And make a fire and fry pancakes!" cried Tacy. She and Betsy jumped up to hunt for a knife, but Tib stopped them.

"You need flour to make pancakes," Tib said. Tib knew. She could cook.

"Well I'm hungry," said Tacy. "I wonder where we're going to get something to eat." And she looked at Betsy hard.

Betsy knew she was thinking of what Betsy had said about begging, and she almost wished she hadn't said it, but she was getting hungrier every minute. She spoke loudly and importantly.

"We *may* have to beg," she said.

"What's that?" asked Tib.

"Muss up our hair and dirty our dresses and pretend we need something to eat."

"We *do* need something to eat," said Tacy. "No pretend about it."

"My mother wouldn't like me to muss up my dress," said Tib. She meant that her mother wouldn't *like* her to muss up her dress. She didn't mean she wouldn't do it.

"She'd rather have you muss up your dress than starve," said Betsy. "We might starve to death down in this ravine."

"Might we?" asked Tib.

"I feel sort of starved already," said Betsy.

"So do I," said Tacy. "I feel weak."

They listened to the spring bubbling out of the ground.

"If we *all* got mussed up," said Betsy, "maybe our mothers would see that it couldn't be helped." So they began to muss each other up.

It was fun mussing each other up. It was such fun that they almost forgot they were hungry. They loosened Betsy's braids and tangled Tacy's ringlets and ruffled Tib's fluffy hair until she looked like a dandelion gone to seed. Then they put mud on one another. Mud on cheeks and noses, and mud on arms and legs. There was plenty of mud beside the brook and they put on plenty. They put it on their dresses and smooched it down with their hands.

When they had finished they began to climb out of the ravine.

"Who's going to ask for something to eat?" asked Tacy.

"Tib," said Betsy firmly. "Because she's the littlest. But you and I will stand right beside her, so we'll be just as much to blame as she is."

"That's right," said Tib.

They had reached the Ekstroms' kitchen garden, and when the dog saw them he began to bark. He barked differently now from the way he had barked when they went down. He barked as though he didn't like the way they looked.

They went past the henhouse, and the hens clucked. They went past the barn, and the cow mooed. They went up to the back door, and the dog barked harder than ever. He yelped and snapped.

The door was open. Only the screen door was closed to keep out flies. There were strips of paper hanging down it, to flutter and scare flies when the door was opened. Between those strips of paper they could see a woman in the kitchen. Betsy knocked.

Mrs. Ekstrom came to the door. She was small and thin. She had yellow hair pulled into a knob and a thin tired face. She looked at Betsy and Tacy and Tib and said, "Heavens and earth!" Then she said, "What happened? What's the matter?" And she looked at Betsy hard. "You're the little Ray girl," she said.

"We're hungry," said Tib.

"And the little Kelly girl," Mrs. Ekstrom continued, staring now at Tacy.

"We're hungry," said Tib.

"And the little Muller girl, I think. *Aren't* you the little Muller girl?" she asked addressing Tib.

"We're hungry," said Tib.

"Hungry!" said Mrs. Ekstrom. "You're lots besides hungry. What happened to you anyway?"

"We got hungry," said Tib.

Betsy and Tacy didn't say a word, but they tried to act as hungry as they could. Betsy put her hands over her stomach and leaned forward and groaned. Tacy forgot to be bashful and she opened and shut her mouth. She opened and shut her mouth and made queer hungry noises.

Mrs. Ekstrom's face broke into a smile.

She opened the kitchen door to let them come in, and gave them a paper to stand on.

They had come to a good house to be hungry in, Betsy saw at once. Mrs. Ekstrom was baking cookies. They had just come out of the oven, and they smelled delicious. They were sugar cookies. Betsy and Tacy and Tib watched Mrs. Ekstrom while she lifted cookies on a pancake turner and filled a plate.

She put the plateful of cookies down on the table.

"Wait while I get some milk," she said, and she

went into the pantry.

Betsy and Tacy and Tib looked at the cookies. They looked good.

While Mrs. Ekstrom was in the pantry, the dog started to bark. His bark didn't sound angry any more. It was just the friendly sociable kind of bark he had barked when they first went through the dooryard. Steps sounded outside and someone knocked on the kitchen door. Mrs. Ekstrom darted out of the pantry.

"How do you do, Mrs. Ekstrom?" came a voice. It was Julia's voice, sounding very grown-up; and Julia could sound extremely grown-up although she was not yet eleven. "Have you seen Betsy and Tacy and Tib, Mrs. Ekstrom?" Julia asked.

"We're looking for them," Katie's voice added.

Betsy stopped rubbing her stomach, and Tacy shut her mouth. Tib turned her round blue eyes from one to the other for instructions, and Betsy said, "Run!"

There was an open door in the kitchen which led to the front hall. Betsy and Tacy and Tib ran down the hall and out to the porch and jumped three steps into the flower garden. They ran and they ran and they ran, and they ran down the Big Hill.

They ran fast for they thought they heard Julia and Katie behind them. But they were mistaken. It was their own feet they had heard. When they got to the bottom of the hill, Julia and Katie weren't there at all. They weren't even in sight.

"They're up there eating our cookies!" said Betsy.

"They make me mad!" said Tacy.

"They make me mad too!" said Tib.

The three of them sat down to rest, breathless and panting, their legs stuck out before them.

Betsy looked at her mud-streaked legs, and after a moment she began to smile.

"But we were the ones who almost starved," she said. "We were the ones who put mud on ourselves and went begging."

"We had all the fun," said Tacy. "We always do."

"I'd have liked a cookie, though," Tib said matter-of-factly. Tib always said things like that. But Betsy and Tacy liked her just the same.

2

Learning to Fly

ETSY AND Tacy and Tib were scolded for going begging. They weren't surprised that they were scolded, but they were surprised at what they were scolded for. They had expected to be scolded for putting mud on themselves, for mussing up their dresses and tangling their hair. But none of the fathers and mothers seemed to mind that very much. What they minded was their asking for something to eat.

The fathers and mothers tried to explain. It was telling a lie to pretend that they were hungry when they weren't.

"But we were!" cried Betsy and Tacy and Tib.

"Well, even if you were, it was wrong to ask food from Mrs. Ekstrom when you had plenty at home."

"You ought to respect yourselves too much," said Betsy's father, "to ask for help you don't need."

Betsy and Tacy and Tib tried to understand.

They understood that they had been naughty. They understood that they weren't to go begging again. For besides being scolded they were punished. They were forbidden to go up on the Big Hill for a month.

They had never wanted so much to go up on the Big Hill as that month when they weren't allowed to go. From Betsy's backyard maple it looked tall and full of mystery. Julia and Katie went up and came down with their arms full of flowers . . . wild sweet peas and Queen Anne's lace and white and yellow daisies.

Betsy and Tacy took care of Betsy's baby sister, Margaret. And Tib took care of her baby brother, Hobbie; Hobson was his name. Their mothers thought it was a good thing for them to make themselves useful. Besides, they couldn't think of anything else to do.

It was strange . . . when they were allowed to go up on the Big Hill they didn't go often. Almost all their games were played down on Hill Street or up on the Hill Street Hill. Yet now that they weren't allowed to climb the Big Hill they couldn't think of anything else worth doing.

But one day Betsy had an idea.

It was a warm afternoon, and they were sitting under the backyard maple. They were taking care of Hobbie and Margaret, of course. Hobbie was in his carriage, and Margaret was staggering around through the grass the way a two-year-old does. Tacy's little brother Paul was there too. He was playing with a cart. Paul was always playing with carts.

The world was so quiet, you could hear the bees buzzing over Betsy's mother's nasturtiums. The air was full of a nasturtium smell which matched their red and orange colors. Betsy stared up into the backyard maple, and Tib jiggled Hobbie's carriage (hoping he would fall asleep), and Tacy chewed a piece of grass and kept her eyes on Margaret, who wasn't supposed to go too near the terrace for fear of tumbling down.

"There ought to be *some*thing we can do," said Betsy, staring into the tree.

"Well, what is it, I'd like to know?" asked Tacy, jumping up to pull Margaret back from the terrace.

"It will have to be something with babies in it," said Tib, jiggling the carriage.

Betsy watched a bluebird take off from the maple on a voyage through the sunlit air.

"What *can* we do?" she murmured, watching him; and just as the bluebird melted into the sky, somewhere above Tacy's roof, she sat up with very bright eyes.

"I know!" she said. "We'll learn to fly."

"To fly!" cried Tacy and Tib.

"To fly!" answered Betsy positively. "Birds can fly. Why can't we? We're just as smart as birds." Tacy and Tib didn't answer, and Betsy went on: "Smarter! Did you ever hear of birds going into the Third Grade the way we're going to do this fall? We can fly just as well as the birds, only we have to learn how, of course. And that's what we're going to do right now."

"How?" asked Tacy.

"We'll start jumping off things. First we'll jump off something low. And then something higher. And then something lots higher. And so on. We'll jump off the house at last, but we prob'ly won't get to that today."

"What will we use for wings?" asked Tib.

"Our arms," said Betsy. "We'll wave them like this." And she began to run and wave her arms, and

Tacy and Tib ran after her and waved their arms too, and Paul stopped playing with his cart and ran and waved his arms.

"No, Paul," said Betsy. "You're too young to fly. It's dangerous. But you can watch us, and so can Margaret and Hobbie."

So Paul sat down in the grass and watched, and they put Margaret into her gocart and she watched too. Hobbie had fallen asleep.

"We'll begin with our hitching block," said Betsy, and she ran out to the hitching block and jumped off, waving her arms. "It's easy!" she cried.

"I'll go next," said Tacy, and she jumped off, waving her arms. She waved them beautifully.

Tib went last. She went as lightly as a puff of wind, but she called out, "I'm afraid I only jumped."

"Jumping and flying are a good deal the same, just at first," Betsy explained.

Next they tried the porch railing. And again Betsy went off first. She waved her arms, but she landed on the ground with a pretty hard thump. "It takes time to learn, of course," she said, rubbing her feet.

Tacy went next, and she didn't fly quite so nicely this time. Her waving wasn't so good.

Tib stood on the railing and smiled before she flew. Tib had had dancing lessons, and besides she was light as a feather. She waved her arms as she came down

and she landed on the tips of her toes.

"Tib," said Betsy, "you're learning how to fly just fine. I think you'll be the first one of us to learn."

"It feels just like jumping," answered Tib.

"Well, it isn't," said Betsy. "It's beginning to be flying. Next we'll try the backyard maple."

Now the backyard maple was a very big tree. Of course they could climb it; they were all good tree climbers. But the lowest branch was a long way from the ground.

"It's pretty high to jump from," Tacy pointed out.

"It isn't as high as the house will be," said Betsy. "We'll be flying off the house tomorrow, prob'ly."

"I'll go first," said Tib, "because I fly the best."

"All right," said Betsy and Tacy.

Tib went up the tree in a flash. She climbed out on the lowest branch, but there wasn't room to stand up; she had to squat. She waved her arms, though, and kept her balance too.

"What kind of a bird am I?" she called, waving her arms.

"You're a Tibbin," answered Betsy. "You're a Tibbin bird."

"Here comes the Tibbin!" cried Tib, and she waved her arms and came down. She fell on her knees, but she laughed as she dusted them off. "I like this flying game, Betsy," she said.

"I'll go next," said Tacy, because Betsy didn't say a word about going next. "That is, if Paul is all right. Are you all right, Paul?"

Paul said he was all right.

"Of course I'm sort of looking after Paul," said Tacy. "But I'll go next, unless you want to, Betsy."

"Oh, you can go next if you want to," said Betsy. So Tacy went next.

She climbed out on the lowest branch. But she sat on it; she didn't squat. She didn't even try to wave.

"What kind of a bird am I?" she asked. But you could see it was only to pass the time. She didn't look happy as Tib had looked; she looked scared.

"You're a Tacin," answered Betsy. "You're a Tacin bird."

"Oh," said Tacy.

She waited a long time before she flew, but at last she flew. She let herself down, holding tight to the branch with her hands; then she loosened her hold and dropped.

"That's good," Betsy said. "That's fine, Tacy. Well, I suppose it's my turn."

Nobody said it wasn't.

Betsy got to the lowest branch and sat on it. She held on tight and swung her legs. She didn't fly though.

"When are you going to fly?" asked Tib.

"In a minute," answered Betsy. She sat there and swung her legs.

"What kind of a bird are you, Betsy?" Tacy asked.

"I'm a Betsin," answered Betsy. "I'm a Betsin bird."

She looked up into the leafy world above her, and she looked down at the ground. The ground was a long way off.

"Don't Betsin birds like to fly?" asked Tib.

"Oh, yes," said Betsy. "They love to fly." But still she didn't fly. She looked up again into the cool green branches.

"They like to fly so well," she said at last, "that

it's a wonder they ever stopped doing it. But they did. Do you want to know why?"

"Why?" asked Tacy and Tib.

"Sit down and I'll tell you," said Betsy. "It's very interesting. Maybe Paul would like to hear too."

So Tacy and Tib sat down in the grass to listen. Paul put aside his cart and leaned against Tacy, and Tib jiggled Margaret's gocart. Hobbie was still asleep.

"Once upon a time," said Betsy, "there were three little birds named Tibbin, Tacin, and Betsin.

"There was something funny about these birds. They used to be little girls.

"They turned into birds one day when they were trying to learn to fly. It was only sort of a game at first, but they learned to fly just fine, and so they got turned into birds.

"Tib got turned first. She took dancing lessons and she learned to fly awfully quick. The real birds saw how pretty she flew and one of them . . . it was a bluebird . . . said, 'Mercy, that little girl flies so pretty she ought to be a bird.' So he turned her into a Tibbin. A Tibbin is yellow like a wild canary; and Tib had yellow curls.

"Tacy got turned next. She had long red ringlets so she got turned into a Tacin. That's red like a robin.

"Betsy got turned last. She got turned into a Betsin, because a Betsin is brown like a wren and

Betsy had brown hair.

"Betsin, Tacin and Tibbin just loved being birds. They had all kinds of fun. They made themselves a nest right here in the backyard maple, and they lived in it together. They found wild strawberries to eat, and Julia and Katie (they were Betsy's and Tacy's big sisters) put out cake crumbs for them. Julia and Katie never dreamed they were giving their cake crumbs to Betsy and Tacy and Tib. You put out cake crumbs too, Paul. You put out delicious crumbs.

"Betsin and Tacin and Tibbin flew in and out of the branches; those green branches up there. They flew up to the roofs of their houses and even up to the clouds. They liked the sunset clouds, and at sunset time they each used to pick out a cloud and sit on it. The Betsin bird took a pink cloud and the Tacin bird took a purple one and the Tibbin bird took a yellow one, most always.

"One night they were sitting on their sunset clouds and Betsin heard someone crying. She said to Tacin and Tibbin, 'Who's that I hear crying?' And Tacin and Tibbin said, 'We don't hear anything.' And Betsin said, 'Listen! Listen hard!' So they listened hard, and sure enough they heard somebody crying. 'We'd better fly down and find out who that is,' said Betsin. So they all flew down to Hill Street.

"And when they got there, they found out that it was their mothers crying. Their mothers were crying hard like this: 'Ooh! Ooh! Ooh!' 'Ooh! Ooh! Ooh!' 'Where are Betsy and Tacy and Tib?' 'Where are Betsy and Tacy and Tib?' So then Betsin and Tacin and Tibbin knew why their mothers were crying. They knew it was on account of them. And it made them feel funny."

Tacy interrupted.

"It makes me feel funny now," she said, and her voice sounded all choked up.

"It makes me feel funny too," said Tib, winking her eyes. "I never heard my mamma cry."

"Oh, their fathers were crying too," said Betsy. "At least they would have been crying if they hadn't been fathers. They were feeling awfully bad. And Julia and Katie were crying. Julia said, 'Boo! hoo! I'm sorry I used to be bossy to Betsy!' And Katie said, 'Boo! hoo! I'm sorry I used to be bossy to Tacy too.' And they cried, and they cried, and they cried . . ."

"And *I* cried!" cried Paul, interrupting. "I cried!" And no sooner had he said it than he began to cry in earnest. He put his curly head into Tacy's lap and wailed.

"But Paul!" cried Betsy. "It's going to come out all right."

Paul kept on crying.

And when Margaret heard Paul cry, she began to cry. She had been almost asleep with all Tib's jiggling, but now she woke up and began to cry. And Hobbie woke up and began to cry too. But Paul cried hardest of all.

"Stop, Paul!" cried Betsy from the maple. "Hear how it's going to come out!"

Paul lifted a streaming face and sniffed.

"Betsin and Tacin and Tibbin felt bad just the way you do."

"Did they?" asked Paul, sniffing.

"Certainly they did. They didn't want to keep on being birds after they knew how everybody felt. And Betsin said, 'I don't believe we'd better be birds any more. We've had lots of fun being birds, but I think it's time we stopped.' And Tacin and Tibbin said that was exactly how they felt. So Tibbin changed herself out of a bird, and she climbed down the maple. And Tacin changed *her*self out of a bird, and *she* climbed down the maple. And Betsin changed *her*self out of a bird, and *she* climbed down the maple. Like this," said Betsy.

And she climbed down the maple.

Just then Betsy's mother came out the kitchen door with some gingerbread. Paul had stopped crying, but Margaret and Hobbie were still crying hard, and Betsy's mother thought that perhaps some gingerbread would help. So she brought out enough for everybody.

Julia and Katie came down from the Big Hill and they had some too. Then Julia went into the house to practise her music lesson and Katie took Paul home to wash him up for supper. Mrs. Ray had already taken Margaret in, and Tib thought that perhaps she had better wheel Hobbie home.

Betsy and Tacy walked a piece with her. They always did. They always walked as far as the middle of the vacant lot. They were talking as they walked, about what they would do up on the Big Hill after they were allowed to go up there again. All of a sudden Tib interrupted.

"Betsy," she said. "I know a joke on you."

"Do you?" asked Betsy.

"You didn't ever fly down out of the maple."

"*Didn't* I?" asked Betsy, sounding surprised.

"No," said Tib. "You didn't. I did. And Tacy did. But you got to telling that story and forgot all about it. It's a joke on you," said Tib, laughing.

Betsy looked at Tacy but Tacy was looking the other way. She was looking the other way hard.

"Oh," said Betsy. "Well here's the middle of the vacant lot. We'll see you in the morning."

3
The Flying Lady

STRANGELY ENOUGH, soon after they tried to learn to fly, Betsy and Tacy and Tib saw a Flying Lady. It happened this way:

A Street Fair came to Deep Valley. A carnival, some people called it. It was a little like a circus, but it lasted for a week. And instead of being held out on the circus ground, it was held on Front Street.

Front Street was decorated with bunting and flags. There were tents and booths at every corner. The air was filled with excitement from the music of the merry-go-round and the voices of men who shouted in front of the tents, urging people to come in.

There were plenty of people to go into all the tents, for the sidewalks were crowded. Men and women and children walked up and down, up and down Front Street, buying whips and balloons and lemonade and popcorn and peanuts and ice cream. There were open booths where you could shoot at dolls, and if you hit a doll you won it. Tacy's brother George won a doll, and he gave it to Tacy.

Betsy and Tacy and Tib went to the Street Fair with their fathers and mothers. They rode on the merry-go-round and they rode on the Ferris Wheel, rising high into the quiet air above the dust and glitter. The Street Fair was full of wonders, but one surpassed all others, and that was the Flying Lady.

Mrs. Muller invited Betsy and Tacy to go with Tib to see the Flying Lady. It was fun to go to the Street Fair all together. They wore their best dimity dresses, trimmed with lace and insertion, and their best summer hats with flowers and ribbons on them. Mrs. Muller looked nice too. She wore a shirt waist and skirt and a round straw hat. She bought each one a bag of popcorn; it was hot and buttery.

Before they went into the show they stood in front of the tent eating popcorn and listening to the man on the platform.

"Right this way!" he shouted through a megaphone, pacing up and down, dripping sweat. "Right this way to the one and only Flying Lady! She's beautiful! She's marvelous! She flies! Come right in and see for yourself, folks! It's the wonder of two continents. It's the thrill of a lifetime! And all for one dime . . . two small nickels!"

Betsy touched Mrs. Muller's sleeve.

"Is it time to go in, Mrs. Muller?"

"Not yet," Mrs. Muller answered.

"Right this way," the man kept on shouting, "to the one and only Flying Lady. She's beautiful! She's marvelous! She flies! The show's beginning, folks. Step right up and get your tickets. You can't afford to miss a moment of this beautiful, educational, inspiring, astounding, spectacular exhibition. . . ."

Tacy poked Betsy, and Betsy looked at Mrs. Muller sideways. She hated to ask again. But she knew Tacy was worried, and she was worried too. Maybe Mrs. Muller wasn't listening? Maybe she hadn't heard what the man had said about the show beginning?

"Do you s'pose we ought to go in, Mrs. Muller?" she asked.

"There's plenty of time," Mrs. Muller answered.

The man was pacing up and down now like a lion in a cage.

"Right this way," he shouted, "to the one and only Flying Lady! She's beautiful! She's marvelous! She flies! Don't run, folks! But hurry just a little! Hurry just a————"

Tacy poked Betsy again, a hard jab this time. Betsy knew it wouldn't be polite to keep on asking Mrs. Muller to go in, so she poked Tib, as a hint that Tib might ask her. Tib said right out loud, "What do you want, Betsy? What are you poking me for?" That was just like Tib. Fortunately Mrs. Muller was ready to go in anyway. She said, "Well, come along, children!"

She bought the tickets from a lady with golden hair. The lady had three golden teeth too; they were right in front, and they showed when she smiled. She smiled at them all, but especially at Tib, and she said to Mrs. Muller, "She looks as though she could fly herself." At that Tacy poked Betsy, and Betsy poked Tib, and this time Tib understood what the poke meant, and they all began to laugh.

There were plenty of seats empty. In fact there were only three or four seats filled. But Betsy and Tacy didn't mind that. It was fun to be able to choose the seats they wanted. They tried seats in the back of the tent, and they tried seats in the middle, and they tried seats in the very front row.

"We ought to sit close," Betsy whispered, "because we're trying to learn to fly ourselves. We ought to see how she does it."

"That's right," said Tacy. And Tib thought so too. So they sat down in the very front row.

The tent was darker than most tents. There were heavy curtains hung all around to make it extra dark. And of course there were curtains concealing the stage. They looked like black velvet.

Out in front the man was still shouting: "She's beautiful! She's marvelous! She flies!" Sometimes he said that the show was just beginning. But it didn't begin. More people came in though; and more, and more.

Betsy and Tacy and Tib finished their popcorn and wiped their fingers on the handkerchiefs which their mothers had pinned to their dresses. They looked around until they had seen everything there was to see. Still the show didn't begin.

"When do you think it will begin, Mamma?" asked Tib.

"Pretty soon," Mrs. Muller answered.

And pretty soon it did.

It began with music which came from behind the curtains. And the music changed everything. It brought magic into the dark tent. The piece being played was a piece Julia played. It was named *Narcissus*.

"Dee, *dee*, dee, *dee*, dee dee dee dee dee dee *dee*."

Betsy and Tacy and Tib took hold of hands.

The curtains concealing the stage were drawn aside, but the stage was as dark as a cave. It was hung with black draperies, and the music made things mysterious.

"Dee, *dee*, dee, *dee*, dee dee dee dee dee dee *dee*."

Just as Julia played it.

"Dee, *dee*

"Dee, *dee*. . . ."

And then something white appeared, parting the black draperies which mistily filled the stage. The something white was rising slowly up. Wings (or arms) were waving in time to the music.

Betsy and Tacy and Tib leaned forward, staring. Their eyes grew accustomed to the darkness, and they saw that the floating figure was indeed that of a lady. She was dressed in white robes which covered her arms (or wings). Red ringlets like Tacy's hung down across her shoulders. A bright light shone on her face, but the rest of her was in shadow.

"Dee, *dee*, dee, *dee*, dee dee dee dee dee dee *dee*."

She smiled at the people as she flew.

"Dee, *dee*, dee, *dee*, dee dee dee dee dee dee *dee*."

Up and down she went, in time to the music.

And not only up and down, but from side to side of the stage. Betsy squeezed Tacy's hands, and Tib's, and Tacy and Tib squeezed back. Their eyes strained through the darkness in order not to miss a movement of the glowing airy figure flying up and down, back and across, to that tune which Julia could play.

They could have watched for hours, but the show did not last very long. In no time at all the curtains were drawn, the music had stopped, and people were clapping their hands and pushing out of the tent. Mrs. Muller, with Betsy, Tacy and Tib, came out last of all.

"Did you like it?" Mrs. Muller asked.

"Oh, yes!" said Betsy and Tacy and Tib. At first that was all they could say.

Mrs. Muller took them across the street to Heinz's Restaurant, and each one had a dish of ice cream. It was vanilla ice cream, and they had vanilla wafers with it. They talked about the Flying Lady as they ate.

"She looked like Tacy, Mamma," Tib said.

"Yes, she did," said Mrs. Muller.

That made Tacy bashful.

"I wish it hadn't been quite so dark," Betsy said.

"I think they made it dark on purpose," Mrs. Muller answered, smiling.

"I wish they hadn't," Betsy said. But she didn't say why.

Of course the reason was that if it hadn't been so dark she and Tacy and Tib could have learned more about flying. Tacy and Tib were thinking the very same thing. But they didn't discuss that with Mrs. Muller. They doubted that a grown-up would understand.

They told Mrs. Muller that they had had a nice time, and she took Betsy to her father's shoe store and Tacy to the office where her father sold sewing machines. Betsy and Tacy and Tib all rode home with their fathers, and they didn't have a chance to discuss the show with each other, until after supper. Then they met on the bench at the top of Hill Street.

They had changed out of their best dresses and taken off their shoes and stockings. It was pleasant to sit with their feet in the dewy grass and talk about the Flying Lady.

"If we look hard," said Betsy, "maybe we'll see her flying through the sky."

"I'll bet we will," said Tacy. "If I could fly, I wouldn't fly just in a dark old tent."

"Neither would I," said Tib. "I'd go up in the sky and do tricks."

They looked all over the sky, but they didn't see a sign of her. There were no white draperies floating among the pink clouds in the west.

"That's funny," said Betsy, "for a sunset would be such fun to fly in."

The Flying Lady did not come, and the sunset faded. It was almost time to go home when they noticed color in the northern sky, far down over the town. Faint music drifted from the same direction. They knew that it came from the Street Fair.

"My papa and mamma are going there tonight," Tib said. "My mamma wants my papa to see the Flying Lady."

Betsy and Tacy looked at each other in sudden understanding. They spoke almost at once.

"Of course!" cried Betsy.

"She's down there making money!" cried Tacy.

"She couldn't be flying up here on the hill," they explained to Tib, "when she's flying down there in the tent."

"That's right," said Tib. "Well, maybe she'll fly in the sky tomorrow morning."

"Let's come up here early to look," Betsy said.

And they all ran home.

Betsy and Tacy met on the bench right after breakfast and started looking for the Flying Lady. It was a sunshiny sweet-smelling morning, just the kind of a day it would be fun to fly in. The sky was full of little fat chunks of cloud.

"Marshmallows probably," said Betsy, "in case she gets hungry."

"Or cushions in case she gets tired," said Tacy.

They stared faithfully upward.

They were staring upward so hard that they didn't see Tib until she called out to them. Then they looked and saw her running up the street. As soon as they saw her, they saw that something was wrong. And sure enough, as she sat down, she said:

"I know something terrible."

"What is it?" Betsy asked.

"That Flying Lady," said Tib, "she doesn't really fly."

"I don't believe it," said Tacy.

"My papa said so," said Tib. "He was explaining it at breakfast."

And Tib explained it to them.

The lady was sitting on one end of an iron bar, she said. The bar was like a see-saw. The lady sat on one end and something heavy sat on the other and moved her up and down, over and across.

"That's why they kept the tent so dark," Tib said. "So we couldn't see the see-saw."

There was a moment's stricken silence.

But then Betsy jumped up and began to jump up and down.

"That gives me an idea!" she cried.

"A show!" cried Tacy, reading her mind.

"In our buggy shed!" cried Betsy. "We'll ask my papa to wheel the surrey out, and we'll cover the window with a gunny sack, to make the buggy shed as dark as that tent was. And we'll put a see-saw inside . . ."

"I know where there's a lovely plank," Tacy interrupted.

"We'll have a curtain across the middle," Betsy hurried on. "And we'll put out chunks of wood for seats. And we'll ask admission, five pins admission and a penny for the grown-ups. Julia could play *Narcissus*, but the piano's too far away."

"We could hum it," Tacy said.

But Tib had a better plan than that.

"Tom can play it on his violin," she said.

They knew a little boy named Tom who could play the violin. He could play *Narcissus*.

"Yes, Tom can play his violin," said Betsy. "And I'll stand out in front and shout for people to come. 'Right this way to the one and only Flying Lady! She's beautiful! She's marvelous! She flies!'"

"What will I do?" asked Tib.

"You'll sell tickets," said Betsy. "We'll paste a strip of gold paper over your front teeth."

"Who'll be the Flying Lady?" Tacy asked nervously.

"You," said Betsy. "Because you look just like her. Do you s'pose you can wear one of your sister Mary's night gowns? After I get through calling out about the show, and Tib gets through selling tickets, we'll go inside behind the curtain. We'll sit on the back end of the see-saw, to make you go up and down."

Tacy didn't like the idea any too well.

But that was what they did, that very day. They gave a Flying Lady show in Betsy's father's buggy shed. All the children of Hill Street came, and a few grown-ups. Mrs. Benson, who didn't have any children of her own, came and paid a nickel.

And Betsy shouted out in front, "Right this way to the one and only Flying Lady. She's beautiful! She's marvelous! She flies." And Tib took tickets, showing her gold teeth all she could. And the little boy named Tom played *Narcissus* on his violin. He played it beautifully.

They gave a wonderful show but there was one unfortunate incident. Betsy and Tib made Tacy's

end of the see-saw go so high that Tacy got scared. She clutched the plank and cried, "Stop! Stop! I'm falling!" And of course a few rude children laughed, but most of them applauded.

After that show Betsy and Tacy and Tib stopped trying to fly. They never tried to fly again.

4
The House in Tib's Basement

BETSY, TACY and Tib didn't always play on Hill Street. Sometimes they played at Tib's house, over on Pleasant Street.

They loved to play at Tib's house for they thought it very beautiful with its chocolate color and its tower and the panes of colored glass in the front door.

They loved especially to play in Tib's basement.

At Betsy's house there wasn't any basement. There was only a cellar. Her father opened a trap door in the kitchen and took a stub of candle and went down and came back with apples which were kept there in a barrel, or perhaps a jug of cider. At Tacy's house it was much the same. But at Tib's house there was a basement.

It was floored with cement, and it was warm and dry and sunny. In the center was a strange contrivance called a furnace, which heated Tib's house. This was the only furnace in Deep Valley. In the basement also there were tubs for washing clothes. There were closets where glass jars full of pickles and jellies were stored. And there was a great open space where wood was piled, stacked in long orderly rows.

One day just before school began Betsy and Tacy came over to play with Tib. They wiped their feet hard on the mat at Tib's back door, for Tib's house was very clean. After they had wiped their feet hard, they rapped and the hired girl came to the door.

"Hello," said Betsy. "We came over to play with Tib."

"Hello," said the hired girl. Her name was Matilda. She was old and wore glasses and had graying yellow braids wound round and round her head. "Have you wiped your feet?" she asked, looking down at their shoes.

"Yes, we have," said Betsy.

"Well, it doesn't matter anyway," said Matilda, "for Tib is down in the basement. And there's such a mess there; it couldn't be worse."

"What kind of a mess?" Betsy asked eagerly, and Tacy's blue eyes began to dance. A mess! That sounded like fun.

"Go see for yourselves," said Matilda. "You can go down the outside way."

The two sloping doors which admitted from the outside of the house to the basement were flung open. Betsy and Tacy scampered down the stairs. And down in the basement they did indeed find a mess. A beautiful mess!

The winter's supply of wood had been thrown into the basement but it had not yet been piled; it had just been thrown in helter skelter. There seemed to be an ocean of wood, and rising like islands were two small yellow heads, belonging to Tib and her little brother Freddie.

Tib had two brothers, but the one named Hobbie was hardly more than a baby. Frederick was Paul's age; he was old enough to play with; and like Tib he was good natured and easy to play with.

"We're building a house out of wood," he shouted now, as Betsy and Tacy waded joyfully in.

"Come on and help!" cried Tib.

Betsy and Tacy took off their hats and helped.

They piled the wood just the way Tib and Freddie told them to. For Tib and Freddie were good at building houses; their father was an architect. This house they were building was like a real house. It was wonderful.

It was big enough to sit down in. It was even big enough to stand up in, if you didn't stand too straight. It had a window, and a doorway you could walk through, if you stooped only a little.

They found some boards and laid them across the top for a roof.

"Now it can't rain in," Betsy said.

They worked so hard that they grew warm and sticky and dirty and very tired. But it was such fun that they were amazed when they heard the whistles blowing for twelve o'clock.

"Oh, dear, we must go home for dinner," Betsy said. "But we'll hurry back."

"We'll eat fast," Tacy said.

"We'll eat fast too," said Tib, and she and Freddie hurried up the stairs.

Betsy and Tacy ran all the way home to their dinners.

"Mercy goodness, what's the matter?" asked Betsy's mother when Betsy ran into the house. "Your cheeks are like fire."

"Oh, Mamma!" cried Betsy. "We're having such fun. We're building a house in Tib's basement."

"When can we move in?" asked Betsy's father, who was already eating his dinner with Margaret in the high chair beside him. Betsy's father loved to joke.

Betsy washed her hands and face and sat down opposite Julia. She thought she ate her dinner quicker than a wink but she wasn't quite through when she heard Tacy yoo-hooing from her hitching block. Tacy's mother wouldn't let her come over to the Rays' house when they were eating a meal. She didn't think it was polite. So Tacy always waited on the hitching block. But she yoo-hooed once in a while.

Betsy gobbled her peach pie and gulped her milk.

"It's Julia's turn to wipe the dishes. 'xcuse me?" she asked, jumping up.

Her braids flew out behind her as she vanished through the door. She and Tacy took hold of hands and ran down Hill Street.

As fast as they had been, Tib and Freddie were in the basement before them.

"We have to hurry," Tib explained, "for a man is coming at four o'clock to pile this wood."

"And we won't have a house any more," Freddie said, as though he didn't like it.

"It's a long time 'til four o'clock," Betsy said.

"Where'd you get the carpet?" Tacy asked.

"Our mamma gave it to us," Tib and Freddie answered proudly.

It was a beautiful carpet. It was red with yellow roses in it. They spread it down inside their house and placed chunks of wood for chairs.

When they had finished they sat down inside their house. There was room for all, although it was crowded. Tib didn't mind if Freddie put his feet in her lap. Betsy and Tacy didn't mind being squeezed against each other.

"Has your funny paper come?" Betsy asked.

Tib's father's paper came all the way from Milwaukee. There was a Sunday edition, and that had a funny paper in it.

"Yes, it came today," said Tib, and she ran upstairs to get it.

They squeezed into their little house again, and Betsy read the funny paper out loud, all about Buster Brown and Alphonse and Gaston and the Katzenjammer Kids. Matilda came down to visit them, bringing some coffee cake. (Butter and sugar and cinnamon were pleasantly mixed on the top.)

It was fun to eat coffee cake and read the funny paper in their own crowded little house.

"I wish it would never get to be four o'clock," said Freddie. Betsy and Tacy and Tib wished so too.

But bye and bye it got to be four o'clock.

A strange man came down the stairs in his shirt sleeves, and behind him came Mr. Muller. He had come down to see the house, he said. The children all scrambled out so that he could see it better, and he walked around it smiling.

"That's a good little house," he said, patting

Freddie on the shoulder. "Freddie, when he grows up, shall be an architect like Papa."

"What about me, Papa? Will I be an architect too?" asked Tib.

"*Nein*, you will be a little housewife," said her father.

Betsy and Tacy thought that was strange, for Tib had done as much as Freddie toward building the house. But it didn't matter much, for in their hearts they were sure that Tib was going to be a dancer.

"And now," said Mr. Muller, "we must take this nice house down."

Nobody answered, and Mr. Muller looked around the circle. Betsy's face was very red, Tacy was hanging her head and Tib's round blue eyes were fixed on her father pleadingly. Freddie walked over to a corner of the basement. He pretended to be hunting for something.

Mr. Muller rubbed his mustache.

"Do you remember," he asked after a moment, "the story of the three little pigs?"

"Oh, yes," cried Betsy and Tacy and Tib.

"They built three little houses," said Tib's father, "and the Wolf knocked them down."

"That's right," said Betsy and Tacy and Tib all together.

"Very good," said Mr. Muller. "Well, you, Betsy and Tacy and Tib, are three little pigs. Only you have built just one house between you, just one little house, and this is it. And you, Freddie, are the Wolf, and you must knock it down."

"All right," cried Freddie, running back, forgetting to cry.

"I'm Whitey!" cried Tib, ruffling up her curls.

"I'm Blackie!" cried Betsy.

"I'm Reddie!" cried Tacy. (She couldn't be Brownie, because her hair was red.)

They rushed back inside the little house and

started pretending they were pigs.

Freddie came loping up to the doorway. He made his voice very sweet and soft.

"Little pig, little pig, let me come in."

Betsy and Tacy and Tib roared together.

"Not by the hair of my chinny-chin-chin."

Freddie roared back in the loudest voice he could find.

"Then I'll puff, and I'll huff, and I'll blow your house in."

He jumped around outside the little house, puffing and huffing, and Betsy and Tacy and Tib clung to each other and screamed.

"Watch out!" cried Mr. Muller. "Don't get hurt, anyone!"

Freddie puffed, and he huffed, and he huffed, and he puffed. At last he jumped straight into the little house and down it fell in chunks of wood around Betsy and Tacy and Tib. And he chased them through the basement, and he chased them up the stairs, and he chased them out to the knoll on the back lawn which was one of their favorite places to play. There they all fell down laughing underneath the oak tree.

But after they got rested they went on with the game. They pretended to do all the things the three little pigs in the story had done. They hunted for turnips, and they hunted for apples, and they went to the Fair.

It was a lovely game, and it lasted all afternoon. It lasted until Julia and Katie came hunting for Betsy and Tacy.

5
Everything Pudding

WHEN SCHOOL began Betsy and Tacy
stopped every morning to call for
Tib. At noon they all walked home
together. And after dinner, when they went back to
school, Betsy and Tacy called for Tib again. And
after school at night they walked home together.
But then they did not separate and go to their own

homes; they usually went to one house to play.

Sometimes it was Tib's house, and sometimes it was Tacy's, and sometimes it was Betsy's. The place they went depended upon several things . . . upon the weather, upon whether they were playing outside or in, upon what the game required and upon what their mothers were doing. If a mother was cleaning house or having company, another mother's house was a better place to play. There wasn't any special invitation given. Not usually, that is.

But one day Betsy's mother said:

"Betsy, will you ask Mrs. Kelly and Mrs. Muller whether Tacy and Tib may come to play with you tomorrow after school? I am going to a party and I wish that Tacy and Tib could come and help you keep house."

"Will Julia be here?" asked Betsy.

"No," said her mother. "Julia will be taking her music lesson, and she is going to stay late to practise for the recital. Aunt Eva is going to look after Margaret for me, and Julia, Margaret and I will all come home with Papa."

"What time?" asked Betsy.

"About half-past five," said Mrs. Ray.

Betsy rushed out of the house to ask Mrs. Kelly if Tacy might come. Mrs. Kelly said she might. Then Betsy rushed to ask Mrs. Muller if Tib might come.

Mrs. Muller said she might. Betsy and Tacy and Tib thought it would be glorious to keep house all alone. They could hardly wait for the next day to come.

Next day after school Betsy came home alone, for Tacy and Tib . . . feeling something very special about the occasion . . . went home to clean up. They arrived about ten minutes later, by way of the front door, ringing the bell as though they were company.

Mrs. Ray was waiting for them, smelling of violet perfume. She was wearing a new tan dress with a high collar and wide yoke of brown velvet and bands of brown velvet around the billowy skirt. Her big hat was trimmed with brown velvet roses. She looked pretty.

"Now children," she said, "you know that you are not to touch the fires."

Of course they knew that; they had known that since they were babies.

"The back parlor stove and the kitchen range have both been fixed for the afternoon," she said. "Don't open a door or lift a lid."

They promised that they wouldn't.

"I've made some cocoa for you," Mrs. Ray said. "You'll find the pan on the back of the range. Just heat it up when you get hungry. There's a plateful of cupcakes to go with it. You may have a little party."

And Mrs. Ray put on her coat and her fur boa. (That smelled of violets too.) She kissed Betsy and said good-by to Tacy and Tib and went smiling out the door.

When the door had closed behind her the house seemed very still. It was so still that they felt they wanted to tiptoe when they walked. Tacy tiptoed to the piano and touched it. And Tib tiptoed over to Lady Jane Grey, the cat, and picked her up. And Betsy tiptoed to the window to look out.

It was snowing, and that made keeping house together all the nicer. Fleecy curtains of snow shut them into their warm, neat, quiet nest.

"What shall we do?" asked Tib.

"I think," said Betsy, "that we had better have our party."

Tacy and Tib thought so too.

They went out to the kitchen and Tib pulled the pan with cocoa in it to the warmest part of the stove. The fire was making small sociable noises. The tall clock on the kitchen shelf was ticking cheerfully. The table was set with a blue and white cloth and three blue and white napkins.

When the cocoa was hot they filled their cups and sat down at the table. They sipped their cocoa and ate their cupcakes with beautiful manners.

"We're getting pretty old when we can be left

alone like this," Betsy said.

"And warm up our own cocoa," said Tacy.

"Of course," said Tib, "I could have made the cocoa myself if your mamma had wanted me to. I know how to cook. I like to cook."

"I don't know how to cook," said Betsy. "But I think it's time I learned." She looked around the kitchen. "Do you know what I'd like to cook first?" she asked.

"What?" asked Tacy and Tib.

"It's called Everything," said Betsy. "It's called Everything because it's got everything in it." Tacy and Tib looked puzzled and Betsy explained. "A little bit of everything there is, cooked up in one pan. I think it would be delicious."

"I think it would be queer," said Tib.

"It *sounds* queer," said Tacy. "What would it be like, I wonder?"

"Well," said Betsy, looking at the ceiling. "I've never tasted it, of course. Nobody's ever tasted it, because nobody ever cooked it. We're inventing it right now. But I imagine that it would taste like everything good mixed together. Ice cream and blueberry pie and chicken with dumplings and lemonade and coffee cake . . ."

"Coffee cake is baked," said Tib.

"This wouldn't be baked," said Betsy, "because

Mamma said we weren't to open the oven door. But we could mix it in a pan and heat it on top of the stove the way we did the cocoa."

Tacy's blue eyes were sparkling.

"Why don't we?" she asked.

"Let's!" said Betsy.

So they put on aprons. Each one tied one of Betsy's mother's aprons around her neck, and Betsy got out a frying pan, the biggest one she could find.

"Now we mustn't put in much of any one thing," she warned. "Or else there won't be room. For we're going to put in *some* of *every thing*, absolutely everything there is. What shall we put in first?" she asked. She had never cooked before, and she didn't know how to begin.

"Bacon grease would be good," answered Tib. "Lots of things begin with bacon grease."

"Bacon grease then," said Betsy.

Tib went to the ice box and got a spoonful of bacon grease. It melted in the pan. Betsy added some sugar and Tacy poured in milk. They stirred it together well. Then Tib brought an egg and boldly broke it. Betsy and Tacy stared with admiration as it sloshed into the pan. Tacy put in flour and Betsy got some raisins.

"They ought to be washed first," said Tib. So Betsy washed them carefully and dropped them in.

Beside the big can of flour stood the cans of coffee and tea.

"Coffee ought to be boiled in a pot," objected Tib as Betsy approached them.

"Everything goes in together," said Betsy firmly. "Everything."

So coffee and tea were dumped into the pan.

"Here's tapioca," cried Tacy from the cupboard.

"Fine! Put it in!" cried Betsy.

"And cornstarch."

"Put it in."

"And gelatine. Gelatine's good," said Tacy.

"This is going to be good too, you bet," said Betsy, stirring.

"It doesn't look good yet," said Tib. "I believe it needs some soda." So she put in some soda.

They took turns stirring, and all three of them rummaged. Betsy put in cinnamon, and while the spices were out Tacy added ginger and allspice and cloves.

"Nutmeg needs to be grated," said Tib, so she grated nutmeg and sprinkled it in.

Tacy put in salt, and Tib put in pepper, and Betsy put in red pepper.

"I didn't know red pepper . . . kerchew! . . . made you sneeze so much . . . kerchew! kerchew! . . ." said Betsy, sneezing.

"I didn't know molasses was so sticky," said Tacy, pouring.

"I'll put in some bay leaves," said Tib. "Matilda often uses bay leaves."

The bay leaves floated strangely on the surface of the sticky mass.

They found the cruets of vinegar and olive oil. Betsy poured in vinegar and Tacy poured in olive oil. Tib added mustard and they stirred again.

They put in oatmeal, and cornmeal, and farina.

Tib was enjoying herself now. She was up on a chair poking into the upper shelves.

"Here's cocoanut. That's good."

"Hand it down," said Tacy.

"And chocolate and cocoa."

"Chocolate and cocoa," said Betsy, "is just what this needs."

They added butter and lard and an onion.

"My mother says an onion improves anything," said Betsy as she tossed it in.

They put in syrup and saleratus and baking powder. They put in rice and macaroni and citron. At last Tib said:

"Now it's time for flavoring, because we've put in everything there is, and flavoring always comes at the end. What kind shall we use?"

"Why, every kind," said Betsy. "Every kind there is."

"But Betsy, nobody uses more than one kind of flavoring."

"Nobody ever made this recipe before," said Betsy.

"What's the name of it?" asked Tib.

"Oh, its name is . . . let's see . . ." said Betsy.

"Everything Pudding would be good," said Tacy.

"That's right," said Betsy. "Its name is Everything Pudding."

And somehow that sounded like the first line of a song, and she began to hum it. She added a second line, and Tacy added a third, and Betsy chimed in with a fourth, and so on. They hummed it together, while Tib poured in the flavorings . . . vanilla and lemon and almond and rose. And Tib began to hum while she stirred, and pretty soon they were all singing together. The song went like this:

> "Oh, its name is Everything Pudding,
>   Its name is Everything Stew,
>   Its name is Everything Cake or Pie,
> 'Most any old name will do.
>   It's better than strawberry shortcake,
>   It's better than apple pie,
>   It's better than chicken or ice cream or
>   dumplings,
>   We'll eat it bye and bye."

They liked that song. And while the mixture sim-
mered on the stove, and Tib stirred, they sang it
lustily:

*"Oh, its name is Everything Pudding,
    Its name is Everything Stew . . ."*

And when they came to the part where they
named the things it was better than, they put in all
the things they liked best . . . peach cobbler and
sauerkraut and gingerbread and potato salad . . .
but they always left apple pie at the end of one line
for the sake of the rhyme.

They sang so loud that Lady Jane Grey began to
yowl. She wasn't a very musical cat. Then Tib who
was sniffing at the mixture said, "I'm sure it's
done." And Betsy said, "All right. We'll eat." She
brought three plates, and Tib spooned out some of
the Everything Pudding (if that was what it was).
And they sat down to eat it.

Betsy took a generous mouthful.

"It's perfectly delicious," she said. But she made
a queer face.

Tacy took a mouthful, and when she had swallowed it she said, "It's lovely. But we put in just a
little too much of something. Don't you think so,
Betsy?"

"Yes," said Betsy. "I do."

Tib didn't say a thing. But before they had half finished what was on their plates, she put down her spoon and said, "I'm not going to eat any more."

"I don't care for any more either," said Betsy. "Let's give it to Lady Jane Grey."

The cat had been mewing and brushing against their legs, and she purred loudly as they put the Everything Pudding down on the floor. But when she had smelled it delicately, she walked away.

"Oh, well," said Betsy. "We'll just throw it out."

And she went out through the woodshed and scraped the Everything Something or Other into the pail.

"Now," said Tib, "we must clean up." And she took charge of things, for she was good at house work.

First she washed all the dishes, and Betsy and Tacy wiped them. Then she washed the pan and scrubbed off the stove and table. She even swept the floor. The broom was taller than Tib but she knew how to use it. She swept into every nook and corner.

It was growing dark and the kitchen looked as clean, almost, as it had been when they began.

The front door opened and Mr. and Mrs. Ray and Julia and Margaret came in. Mrs. Ray was smiling and looked pretty; she smelled of violet perfume.

"Did you have a good time, darlings?" she asked.

"Yes ma'am, we did," said Betsy, Tacy and Tib.

"Did you warm up your cocoa?" asked Julia, putting down her music roll.

"Yes, we did, and we ate up the cupcakes," Betsy answered.

"You left a nice clean kitchen," Mrs. Ray said. She walked around sniffing. "There's an odd smell though," she said.

Betsy and Tacy and Tib looked at each other. They were glad when Mr. Ray said, "Hop into your coats, T and T. I'll take you both home."

In the middle of the night that night, Tib had a stomach ache. She got up and went down to the kitchen and took a little soda. Tib knew that soda was good for stomach aches.

And Tacy had a stomach ache, and Katie took

care of her. Katie was bossy sometimes, but she was nice to have around when you felt sick.

And Betsy had a stomach ache, a bad one, and Julia was good to her too. But after Julia had given her peppermint and tucked her in, she said:

"Did you and Tacy and Tib have anything to eat besides those cupcakes and that cocoa?"

"Let's see!" said Betsy. "Did we or didn't we?"

After a moment she said, "Julia! Do you know what it would make if you took everything there is in the cupboard and cooked it up together?"

"Goodness!" said Julia. "You must be sick to think of such a thing!"

6

The Mirror Palace

ONE DAY that winter, when Tib's mother was going shopping, Betsy and Tacy and Tib kept house alone at Tib's house. That is, they were almost alone. Matilda was there but she was taking care of Hobbie; and Freddie was there, but he was out coasting on the knoll. Mrs. Muller said that they could have the run of the house. For Mrs. Ray had told her what good children they were when they kept house alone at Betsy's house.

"She said that you left the most spic and span kitchen!" Mrs. Muller said. "Well, good-by, my dears. Matilda has some nice fresh apple cake for you."

And Mrs. Muller went away downtown.

It was fun to have Tib's house all to themselves. Betsy and Tacy knew it well by now, but it still charmed them . . . the colored glass in the front door, the tower room with its blue velvet draperies, the back parlor with its broad window seat where they loved to sit and look at pictures of beautiful ladies in *Munsey's Magazine*.

The day they were left alone they found the most beautiful lady of all but she wasn't in a magazine.

Tib had taken them up to her mother's room to show them the new curtains. They were made of white lace over pale pink silk, threaded with pink satin ribbon and tied back with pink satin bows. The large room stretched across the front of the house, with an alcove beside it where Hobbie's bed was placed. Betsy and Tacy were roving about, admiring the curtains and the bureau with its bottles of perfume and the silver-backed mirrors and brushes, when Betsy picked up a framed photograph.

"Tib!" she cried. "Come here! Tell me who this is."

Her tone was so excited that Tacy came running

to look at the picture. Tib glanced at it and said:

"Why, that's Aunt Dolly."

"Your *aunt*?" asked Betsy. "Really? Did you ever actually *see* her?"

"Of course," said Tib. "I saw her every day when we lived in Milwaukee."

"Is she as beautiful as this?" asked Betsy.

Tib examined the photograph earnestly.

"Well, that looks just like her," she answered.

Betsy gazed, and Tacy gazed too. This was certainly a most beautiful lady. She was leaning against a marble pillar on which her elbow rested while her hand supported daintily her small exquisite head. A long train curled about her feet, making her slender rounded figure look as though it had been carved. She had masses of soft blonde hair and a doll-like face.

"She looks like Tib," said Tacy.

"Yes, she does," said Betsy.

"I'm supposed to look like her," said Tib. "But I don't expect I'll ever be that pretty."

Betsy and Tacy turned to look at her.

"You're quite pretty now, Tib," Betsy said.

"Especially when you're dressed up," said Tacy.

"I'm too tanned," said Tib.

She picked up her mother's mirror and inspected her small tanned face while Betsy and Tacy gazed at the photograph, heaving great sighs of admiration.

But they couldn't look at the photograph forever, so at last they put it down. Tib was still gazing into the mirror.

"I'm not looking at myself any more," she explained. "I'm looking at the ceiling. It looks different in the mirror. See?"

She handed the mirror to Betsy and Tacy and they peered in. Sure enough, the ceiling did look different. It didn't look like a ceiling. It looked like the floor of a new mysterious room.

"It's a Mirror Room," Betsy said.

The Mirror Room was carpeted with tiny pink flowers, for the ceiling wall paper was covered with tiny pink flowers. They matched the big pink flowers which twined around silver poles on the walls of the room. At the top of the wall, next to the ceiling, was a border with silver leaves and large and small pink flowers all together. If you tilted the mirror just a little, you could see that border.

Holding the mirror between them, and looking down into its depths, Betsy and Tacy started to walk. They walked around the room and into the alcove, bumping a bit, but that didn't matter; Hobbie wasn't in his bed; he was down in the kitchen watching Matilda iron.

"It's fun walking through this Mirror Room. You try it," said Betsy, offering the mirror to Tib.

"I'll go get mirrors for us all," said Tib. And she did. She brought her father's shaving mirror for Tacy and Matilda's mirror for herself. Matilda's mirror was a big square mirror in a dark brown frame. It was heavy. But Tib didn't mind.

They walked out into the hall, looking in their mirrors as they went.

"We'll explore this whole Mirror Palace," Betsy said. "That's what it is . . . a Mirror Palace."

"Who lives in it?" asked Tacy.

"Aunt Dolly," said Betsy. "She's the Queen."

Tib was so surprised that she almost dropped Matilda's mirror. She stared at Betsy with her round blue eyes.

"Why, Betsy!" she cried. "My Aunt Dolly lives in a flat in Milwaukee."

"She used to, maybe," Betsy said.

"But I'd know if she lived in this house," said Tib.

"The Mirror Palace has no connection with this house," said Betsy.

"Oh," said Tib. She still looked surprised, but she was beginning to get used to Betsy. She had played with her for two whole years. So when Tacy said, "Come on! Let's explore the Mirror Palace," Tib said, "All right." They formed a line and descended the stairs, each holding fast to her mirror with one hand and grasping the rail with the other.

In the downstairs hall the floor of the Palace was leathery brown. That was because the ceiling wall paper was leathery brown. In the front and back parlors, the floor became delicately blue, with darker blue scrolls visible when you tilted the mirror just a little. The dining room was the nicest of all. There the floor was thrillingly red and gold.

"This is the Throne Room," Betsy said, and they walked around the Throne Room. "Now," she continued, "we'll inspect the Royal Kitchens."

They started toward the kitchen but Tib checked them.

"We'd better not go out there," she said. "Matilda's ironing. Maybe she wouldn't like this walking around with mirrors. Especially when one of them's hers."

"Maybe not," Betsy and Tacy agreed.

"Anyway," said Tacy, looking around the dining room with its rich red and gold walls, the sideboard laden with silver and the long table spread with a heavy woven cloth and a silver dish filled with oranges, "Anyway I think it would be fun to play right here in the Throne Room."

"Oh yes!" cried Betsy. "We'll make a throne for Aunt Dolly."

"But where *is* Aunt Dolly?" asked Tib.

"When you look in the mirror," said Betsy, "that makes Aunt Dolly."

Betsy pulled out Tib's father's armchair which sat at the head of the table, and Tib ran to get her mother's paisley shawl. It was old; she was allowed to play with it. They draped it over the chair and pushed the chair up against the window. The window's red draperies made a majestic background.

Tacy was inspecting the sideboard.

"Some of this silver would come in handy around a throne," she said. "But maybe we shouldn't touch it."

"We'll put it all back," Betsy said.

"You decorate while I get something," said Tib. She ran away and came back wearing her mother's feather boa.

At the right of the throne Betsy and Tacy had put the silver coffee urn; at the left, the silver teapot.

"She can use this big ladle for a sceptre," said Betsy. "But what will we do for a crown?"

"The sugar bowl's a good shape," said Tacy. "But it's full of sugar lumps."

"The spoon holder," said Betsy, "is just the thing."

So they dumped out the tea spoons and clamped the spoon holder upside down upon Tib's head. Her little yellow curls sprang out beneath the silver bowl. With the fluffy feather boa she looked supremely queenlike.

"Now look into your mirror and you'll turn into Queen Dolly," Betsy cried.

Tib looked into the mirror and Betsy took the silver fruit dish and went down upon one knee.

"Will your Majesty deign to eat an orange?" she asked.

Tacy began to giggle as she seized the sugar bowl and bowed.

"Some sugar, I prithee, Queen," she said.

Queen Dolly crooked her little finger and accepted an orange and a sugar lump.

Just then Freddie burst in through the swinging door. He had left his sled outside, of course, and his rubbers beside the kitchen door, and his coat and cap and muffler in the kitchen closet, but his pink cheeks brought in the out-of-doors.

"Whatcha playing?" he asked.

"We're playing Mirror Palace," Betsy answered. "Tib's playing she's Aunt Dolly."

"And Aunt Dolly's the Queen," Tacy explained.

Freddie looked puzzled. He knew how to play that someone was another person, but he hadn't ever played that someone was *two* other persons. He thought he had better change the subject.

"We're not supposed to play in the dining room," he said.

"Why, Freddie!" Betsy cried. "We're not playing in the dining room. This is the Throne Room." And she explained about the Mirror Palace. Freddie looked down into the mirror Tib was holding, and he could see for himself what a shining mysterious room the mirror held.

"But Tib ought to be upside down," he remarked.

"What?" exclaimed Betsy and Tacy.

"Her feet ought to be on the Mirror Palace floor."

Betsy and Tacy looked dismayed. It was perfectly true. If the ceiling of the dining room, reflected in the mirror, was the floor of the Mirror Palace, then Tib's reflected feet ought to be where her head was.

"You ought to be standing on your head," said Betsy.

"That's easy," said Tib.

For Tib was a dancer. It wasn't a bit of trouble for Tib to stand on her head. She took off her spoonholder crown and put Matilda's mirror carefully on the seat of the throne. She jumped to the arms of the chair and went upside down, her head upon the mirror, her legs stretching straight and true into the air.

Betsy and Tacy and Freddie, looking down into the mirror, had a fleeting dazzling vision . . . Queen Dolly with her dainty feet pointing toward the floor. But the vision was fleeting, indeed!

The kitchen door swung open and Matilda, her arms full of freshly ironed linen, entered the dining room.

"*Gott im Himmel!*" cried Matilda, and table-cloths and napkins fell in a snowy shower.

Tib came rightside up in a hurry. She came in such a hurry that she tumbled to the floor. The coffee urn crashed, and so did the teapot . . . they were silver, so they didn't break. Oranges rolled in all directions.

But Matilda was looking at the mirror.

"Whose mirror is that?" she demanded.

"It's yours, Matilda," said Tib. "I borrowed it for this game we were playing."

"We were going to put everything back, Matilda," Betsy said.

Tacy was already picking up the linen and Freddie was pursuing oranges.

Matilda examined the mirror.

"It isn't broken. No thanks to you," she said.

"We're glad it isn't broken, Matilda," Betsy said. And she and Tacy folded the linen so neatly, you would not have known it had fallen, hardly. Freddie had found all the oranges, so now he was picking up silver. Tib put the feather boa and the paisley shawl away.

Matilda stalked back to the kitchen.

Working silently and swiftly, Betsy and Tacy and Tib and Freddie put the dining room to rights. It looked so tidy when they had finished that no one would dream it had ever been mussed up. Then they went to the window seat and sat down softly.

"I wonder if we'll get the apple cake," asked Freddie in a whisper.

"Probably not," said Tib.

"Never mind," said Betsy. "I'll tell you a story about Aunt Dolly and how she happens to live in a mirror."

So she told them the story while twilight spread purple gauze over the drifts outside.

But before she had finished Matilda brought them the apple cake. They could hardly believe their eyes when she stalked in with the tray.

"Thank you, Matilda," said Tib. "I'm glad your mirror wasn't broken."

"So'm I," Tacy murmured.

"The dining room looks all right now," Betsy added. "Doesn't it, Matilda?"

Matilda looked at the tidy dining room. She swept it with a stony glance.

"I hear," she said meaningly, "that Mrs. Ray's kitchen looked nice *too* after you kept house for *her* one day."

And she stalked back into the kitchen.

7

Red Hair, Yellow Hair, and Brown

THAT SPRING Tacy had diphtheria.

Betsy and Tacy and Tib had always thought that spring was the nicest part of the year; but it wasn't much fun that year; it wasn't much fun without Tacy.

The snow melted up on the Big Hill and came rushing down the slopes in foaming torrents. And Betsy and Tib made boats and sent them bobbing down the stream to the Atlantic and the Pacific. They did it every year; it was one of their favorite things to do; but it wasn't much fun without Tacy.

May Day came, and of course they made baskets. They made them out of tissue paper in all the colors of the rainbow; beautiful baskets with fringed paper trimming and braided paper handles. And they filled the baskets with spring flowers from the chilly snow-patched hills, and hung them on people's door knobs; and rang the bells and ran away. But it wasn't much fun without Tacy.

The trees on the hill turned slowly green and the wild plum was dazzlingly white and fragrant, and gardens were planted, and birds came back, and the last day of school arrived. Betsy and Tib emptied their desks. . . . Betsy emptied Tacy's desk too . . . and she brought home Tacy's books as well as her own. She and Tib marched home with their arms full of books singing loudly:

> *"No more Latin,*
> *No more French,*
> *No more sitting on a*
> *Hardwood bench. . . ."*

But it wasn't much fun without Tacy. At least not so much fun as it would have been *with* Tacy. Betsy and Tib would forget and have fun, and then they would remember that Tacy had diphtheria.

Fortunately, by that time she was almost well. People had stopped looking sober when you mentioned Tacy's name. Tacy's father and her big brother George and her grown-up sister Mary called out jokes when they saw Betsy and Tib, and the other brothers and sisters laughed and played on the lawn. They couldn't leave the yard for they were quarantined with Tacy. "Quarantined" meant that they had to stay at home in order not to give anybody diphtheria. While Tacy was so sick they had to play quiet games, but now they could make all the noise they liked.

Tacy got so well that she could come to the window. She would hold up that doll George had given her at the Street Fair and make it wave its hands. Betsy and Tib sent her gifts on the end of a fish pole. They would tie the gift on the end of a pole and poke the pole over into Tacy's yard and Katie would untie it and take it to Tacy. They sent notes and stories and pieces of cake and bouquets of flowers and a turtle.

At last Tacy got well, as well as anybody, but she was still in quarantine. She sat on the porch and she walked around the yard, and Betsy and Tib could shout at her but they couldn't play with her. They stood on the hitching block and shouted, and she came as near them as she was allowed to come. They could see how tall she had grown and how pale. Her freckles were almost gone, and the paleness made her eyes look big and blue.

"Tacy's pretty," Betsy said to Tib. "She's almost as pretty as you are."

"Yes, she is," Tib agreed.

One day over at Tacy's house there was a great deal of sweeping and scrubbing. Piles of trash were burned in the back yard and a man came to fumigate. That meant that he filled the house with a cleansing smoke. The next day the quarantine ended.

The minute it was ended Betsy and Tib ran over to see Tacy. The three of them ran around the yard and jumped over Mrs. Kelly's peony bed and ran down to the pump and pumped water and splashed and yelled with joy. Mrs. Kelly came out on the porch and watched them, and she was smiling but she looked as though she wanted to cry. That trembling look she had on her face made Betsy feel funny. It gave her an idea.

She didn't mention her idea for a while, there were so many things to do. Tacy could leave her own yard now; she didn't need to stay there any more; so Betsy took hold of one of her hands and Tib took hold of the other and they went to all their favorite places. They went to the bench at the top of Hill Street, and they went to Betsy's backyard maple, and they went to the ridge where wild roses were in bloom.

They were sitting down on the ridge resting and smelling the roses when Betsy mentioned her idea.

"I've been thinking," she said. "I've been thinking a lot this morning. I've got an idea."

"What is it?" asked Tacy and Tib.

"I've been thinking," said Betsy, "that Tacy was pretty sick. And if she had died we wouldn't have had a thing to remember her by."

"I'd've remembered her," said Tib.

"And anyhow I didn't die," said Tacy. "But I was certainly pretty sick. I was so sick the doctor came every day. I was so sick it's all mixed up, like a dream. What's your idea, Betsy? I'll bet it's a good one."

"It's this," said Betsy. "We three ought to have something to remember each other by. You got sick, Tacy, and I might get sick too, any day. I might get sick and die."

"I hope you won't," said Tib, looking worried.

"You might yourself," answered Betsy. "You might get sick just the same as Tacy did, and you might die. We certainly ought to have something to remember each other by."

"I think I'd remember you, Betsy," said Tib. "I'm sure I would. Wouldn't you remember me?"

"Well," said Betsy, "it wouldn't hurt to have

some special thing to help me. Like my Grandma's got something to remember my Grandpa by."

"What's she got?" asked Tacy.

"It's a piece of his hair," said Betsy. "It was cut off his head, and she wears it in a locket."

Tacy and Tib looked impressed.

"We'll get us some lockets," said Betsy. "And we'll put in our lockets a piece of all our hairs. We could sort of braid them together. They'd look nice because Tacy's is red, and yours, Tib, is yellow, and mine is brown."

"They'd certainly look nice," said Tacy.

"But we haven't got any lockets," said Tib.

"No," said Betsy. "But we could cut off the hair. We could get that much done right away. I'll run down and ask my mamma for some scissors."

"And we'll try to think what we can use for lockets," Tacy said.

Betsy jumped up and ran down the hill to her house. Her mother was in the kitchen making a cake, and she was pretty busy. She was beating eggs as fast as she could.

"How's Tacy?" she called out over the noise of the egg beater. "Is she glad to be out?"

"Yes," said Betsy. "And we need some scissors for something we're doing. May I take the scissors, please?"

"Yes," said her mother. "You may take the blunt pair I let you cut paper dolls with. Hold the points down, and don't run."

And she finished beating her eggs and began sifting flour. Betsy took the scissors and went out the kitchen door.

Tacy and Tib called out as she came near.

"We've been thinking," Tacy said, "what we could use for lockets. We won't be able to afford lockets for a while. But do you know what we could use?"

"Pill boxes," said Tib without waiting for Betsy to answer. "They're just the right shape."

"While I was sick," said Tacy, "our house was full of pill boxes, but my mother burned them all up yesterday."

"We have a few pill boxes at our house," Betsy said. "Maybe some of them are empty."

"And Mrs. Benson would have some pill boxes, I imagine," Tacy said. "Tib and I will go and ask her while you ask your mother."

Tacy and Tib ran down the street to Mrs. Benson's and Betsy ran into the house to her mother again. Her mother had finished sifting flour now. She was beating the cake hard.

"Mamma," said Betsy. "Have you any old empty pill boxes Tacy and Tib and I could have?"

"What do you want pill boxes for?" her mother

asked, sounding surprised.

"To make lockets of," said Betsy. "We're going to punch holes and run strings through and hang them around our necks."

"Oh," said Mrs. Ray. "Well, I think I've got a pill box somewhere. Just wait a minute, and I'll see." And she scraped the cake into the pan and popped the pan into the oven and went into the bedroom. Before Betsy had finished cleaning out the bowl and Margaret had finished licking the spoon, she was back with one pill box.

"That's all I could find," she said. "There's some string on the clock shelf."

Betsy took the pill box and the ball of string and ran back to the ridge. Tacy and Tib had just come back from Mrs. Benson's, and they had two pill boxes, beautiful ones.

"We told her we were going to make lockets," Tacy said. "She thought it was a fine idea."

So they took the scissors and punched holes in the pill boxes, and they ran string through them and tied them around each other's necks. They made lovely lockets.

"Now," said Betsy, "it's time to cut off the hair."

And she picked up the scissors.

"Who'll cut it?" asked Tacy. "I think we should take turns, because cutting hair will be fun."

"That's right," said Betsy. "Well, I'll cut yours, and you can cut Tib's, and Tib can cut mine."

She walked around Tacy looking at her hair and trying to decide where to begin. Tacy's hair, as usual, was dressed in ringlets. There were ten long red ringlets, as neat as sausages.

"I'll begin on this one," said Betsy, and she lifted up a ringlet right next to Tacy's face. She cut it off close to the head.

The shimmering long red ringlet looked beautiful on the grass.

"I think I'll cut off another one," Betsy said. And she did.

"It makes her look funny," Tib said, staring at Tacy.

"That's right," said Betsy. "I'd better cut off exactly half. Then it will look neater."

So she cut off three more ringlets, one after another. Exactly half were gone. And one side of Tacy's head had five short stubs of curls while the other side had five long ringlets.

"Well, that's done," said Betsy, and she handed the scissors to Tacy.

Tacy walked around Tib looking at her hair. The short yellow curls would not be so easy to cut.

"They're not so regular," said Tacy. "But I'll try to cut off exactly half."

She began at Tib's left ear and cut off all the curls on the left side of her head. Shining yellow rings showered the ground.

Then Tib took the scissors and walked around Betsy.

"Betsy's easy," she said. "She's got two braids, and I'll cut off one."

She unbraided one braid and cut off the hair which had made it. Unbraided, Betsy's hair looked crinkly; it was almost as curly as Tacy's and Tib's.

They put all the hair they had cut in a row on the grass. Red ringlets, short yellow curls, crinkly brown hair. They divided it into three equal piles, and each one took a pile. But the piles were much too big to stuff into a pill box. The pill boxes wouldn't hold a fraction of what they had cut. They filled them as full as they could, and they spread the rest of the hair on the wild rose bushes.

"The birds can use that hair in their nests," Tacy said. "I once saw a bird carrying hair."

They played around the rose bushes a while but the more they looked at each other, the funnier each one thought the other two looked. They began to be a little worried about going home.

"Let's go all together," said Betsy. "Three can explain things better than one."

So they took hold of hands, very tightly, and went down the hill.

They went to Betsy's house first. And when Betsy's mother saw them she shrieked. Grown-ups don't often shriek, but that was what Betsy's mother did.

"Betsy!" she cried. "Tacy! Tib! Whatever have you done to yourselves!"

"We've cut off our hair," said Betsy.

"But why? What for?" cried Betsy's mother.

"To remember each other by," said Betsy.

"That's nonsense!" cried Betsy's mother. And she put down her knife . . . she had been frosting the cake . . . but she didn't offer a speck of the frosting to anybody. She took off her apron and lifted up

Margaret, who was staring at Betsy with eyes like saucers. "You come along with me," she said, and Mrs. Ray and Margaret and Betsy and Tacy and Tib went across the street to Mrs. Kelly's.

Mrs. Kelly was sweeping the walk. She saw them coming, and after she had looked at them hard she threw her apron over her head. When she took down the apron she was crying. She ran her hand over Tacy's head and said, "Oh those beautiful long red ringlets! Those beautiful long red ringlets!" She felt bad.

"I'm so sorry, Mrs. Kelly," Mrs. Ray said. "I'm sure it was Betsy's idea."

"We did it to remember each other by," said Tacy.

But nobody seemed to pay any attention.

Julia and Katie had been playing hop scotch. They ran to see what was the matter.

"Well, for goodness' sake!" they cried. "For *goodness' sake!*"

Paul had been racing two carts down the terrace. He ran to see what was the matter too.

Mrs. Kelly wiped her eyes and took off her apron.

"I'll go along with you to Mrs. Muller's," she said to Mrs. Ray.

And Mrs. Ray and Mrs. Kelly and Julia and Katie and Paul and Margaret and Betsy and Tacy and Tib went down the street and through the vacant lot to Mrs. Muller's.

"I'm glad you're all coming along," said Tib.

And it was a good thing that there were plenty of people on hand to explain to Mrs. Muller. For Mrs. Muller didn't like it at all that half of Tib's hair was cut off. Mrs. Muller was proud of Tib. She was proud of how pretty and dainty she was, and of

how she could dance. She was proud of her yellow curls.

At sight of those shorn yellow curls Mrs. Muller turned white. She stood up . . . she had been embroidering a dress for Tib under the oak tree on the knoll.

"Tib," she said. "Go to your room. You are going to be punished."

"Mrs. Muller," said Mrs. Ray, "I am so afraid this is one of Betsy's ideas. Let's talk it all over."

"Let's find out what they did it for," Mrs. Kelly said.

"All right," said Mrs. Muller.

Betsy swallowed. She swallowed hard.

"I thought," she said, "that we ought to have some of each other's hair to remember each other by."

"It's because I was so sick," said Tacy.

"And I might get sick too," said Tib, "and so might Betsy."

"So we cut off a little of each other's hair to put in our lockets," explained Betsy.

And they showed their mothers their pill boxes full of brown and red and yellow hair.

Mrs. Ray looked at the pill boxes and she began to laugh. She had been very angry, but she could get over being angry fast. Mr. Ray said it was on account of her hair, which was red like Tacy's. Mrs. Kelly began to laugh too, although she was wiping her eyes again. And at last Mrs. Muller began to laugh. She called Freddie.

"Freddie," she said, "will you ask Matilda to bring me the scissors, please?"

And Matilda brought the scissors, and Mrs. Muller cut off what was left of Tacy's long red ringlets and of Tib's short yellow curls and she cut off Betsy's one remaining braid.

"At least," she said as she clipped, "it is summer time. And short hair will be cool. But just the same," she said to Tib, "you are going to be punished."

"And so is Betsy," said Mrs. Ray, "very severely too."

"And so is Tacy," Mrs. Kelly added.

But Mrs. Kelly hated to punish Tacy because she had had the diphtheria. She took Tacy's long red ringlets and put them in a candy box and kept them in a bureau drawer.

8

Being Good

T WAS strange that Betsy and Tacy and Tib ever did things which grown-ups thought were naughty, for they tried so hard to be good. They were very religious. Betsy was a Baptist, and Tacy was a Catholic, and Tib was an Episcopalian.

They loved to sit on Tacy's back fence and talk about God.

Tacy's back fence was a very good place for such talk. There wasn't a soul around to listen except the cow, and sometimes the horse, munching and stamping behind them. And above the crowding treetops there was a fine view of sky, the place where God lived.

Betsy and Tacy and Tib were talking about Him one morning. They were looking up at the great fleecy clouds sailing across the sky.

"It will be fun living up there after we die," Betsy said. "We'll all be so beautiful . . . we'll look like Aunt Dolly."

"Tib looks like her already," Tacy said.

"Not since I got my hair cut," said Tib. "I'm not very pretty since I got my hair cut."

There was a pause.

"Well, you'll have long hair in Heaven," Betsy said. "All of us will. We'll all be beautiful. And we'll sail around with palm leaves in our hands. They have good things to eat in Heaven, I imagine. They have ice cream and cake for breakfast even."

"I'd like that," said Tib.

"We have to be good though," Tacy said, "or else we won't go there."

"We're pretty good already," Betsy said. "We're lots better than Julia and Katie. Getting up a Club and not inviting us!"

"The stuck-up things!" Tacy said.

Betsy and Tacy and Tib all covered their mouths with their hands and stuck out their tongues three times. They had made an agreement to do this, in public or in private, whenever Julia's and Katie's Club was mentioned. Julia's and Katie's Club was called the B.H.M. Club. No one under ten years of age had been invited to join. The meetings were held on the Big Hill every Tuesday afternoon. And this was Tuesday morning.

"I know what let's do!" cried Betsy. "Let's get up a Club ourselves."

"Let's get up a Club about being good," suggested Tacy.

"That doesn't sound like fun," said Tib.

"Well, we can't think about fun all the time if we want to go to Heaven," said Betsy.

"That's right," said Tacy. "The saints didn't have much fun; I'll tell you that. They used to wear hair shirts."

"Did they?" asked Betsy. "What for?"

"To punish themselves. To make themselves gooder. And if they did anything bad they put pebbles in their shoes."

"What else did they do?" Betsy asked.

Tacy looked at her suspiciously.

"You're not thinking about doing things like that

❧236❧

in our Club, are you, Betsy?" she asked.

"Not exactly," said Betsy. She sat thinking, her bare toes curled around a wooden bar of the fence.

"My mamma wouldn't let me wear any different kind of shirt," said Tib. She sounded as though she didn't like the Club.

"Don't worry," said Betsy. "We wouldn't know where to buy hair shirts, even. Besides, we haven't got any money. What would be a good name for our Club, do you suppose?"

They all thought hard.

Betsy suggested The Christian Kindness Club. And they liked that name because it made such nice initials. Clubs were called by their initials, for their names were kept secret. T.C.K.C. sounded fine.

"What shall we do in our Club?" asked Tib. She still sounded as though she didn't like it. But Tib always did what Betsy and Tacy wanted to do. She was very pleasant to play with. "Will we have refreshments?" she asked, cheering up.

"No," said Betsy. "This is a pretty serious Club, this T.C.K.C."

"It's about being good," said Tacy.

"And we'll never get to be good if we don't punish ourselves for being bad. A child could see that," said Betsy. "So in our Club we'll punish ourselves for being bad."

"But we haven't been bad yet," said Tib. "I wasn't even intending to be bad."

"We were born bad," said Tacy. "Everyone is. Go on, Betsy."

"The pebbles gave me the idea," said Betsy. "We'll take our marble bags and empty out the marbles and pin the bags inside our dresses."

Tib looked uncomfortable. "Doesn't that remind you of those pill boxes?" she asked. "There isn't any cutting off hair in this Club, is there, Betsy?"

"Of course not," said Betsy. "This is a Being Good Club. We're going to put stones in those bags around our necks."

"Oh," said Tib.

"Every time we do anything bad," continued Betsy, "we'll put a stone in. If we're very bad, we'll have to put in two stones, or three. By tonight those bags will be bulging full, I imagine . . ."

"I wouldn't wonder," said Tacy, her eyes sparkling.

"I don't see why," said Tib. "I thought we were going to be *good*."

Just then the whistles blew for twelve o'clock. And Betsy and Tacy and Tib flew in three directions.

"We'll meet on my hitching block right after dinner. Bring your bags," cried Betsy, as she flew.

Betsy hurried through her dinner. Julia was hurrying too, for the B.H.M. Club, so she said, met that afternoon. When Julia said that, Betsy lifted her napkin and poked out her tongue three times.

"Did you choke on something, Betsy?" her father asked.

"No sir," said Betsy. "Mamma, it's Julia's turn to wipe the dishes."

"Yes," said her mother, "and you may look after Margaret for me until it's time for her nap."

While Julia was wiping the dishes, Betsy hunted up her marbles bag. She emptied the marbles into a box, and pinned the bag inside her red plaid dress. It made a bump on her chest. Taking Margaret's chubby hand, she ran out to the hitching block as fast as Margaret's chubby legs would go.

Tacy was already there, and Tib was in sight, wheeling Hobbie's gocart up the hill.

There was a bump on Tib's chest beneath her yellow dimity dress; and there was a bump on Tacy's chest too beneath her striped blue and brown gingham. While they were admiring one another's bumps Julia and Katie started up the hill, carrying lunch baskets, and a stick and a square flat package which they always took to their Club.

Betsy made a face at them. It was a regular monkey

face, the kind her mother had said she should not make for fear her face would freeze that way.

"Oh dear!" she said. "Now I've been bad. I must put a stone in my bag."

And she found a pebble and put it into her bag.

"I think I'd better put a stone in my bag too," said Tacy. "Because when Katie told me she was going to her Club I called her stuck up."

So Tacy put a pebble in *her* bag.

Tib ran to the foot of the hill and called loudly after Julia and Katie.

"You're stuck up! You're stuck up!"

And *she* put a pebble in *her* bag.

Margaret and Hobbie began shouting too. "'tuck up! 'tuck up!" But they didn't understand about the pebbles.

Betsy's mother came to the door of the little yellow cottage.

"Betsy! Betsy! What are you playing?"

"This is our Club, Mamma. We've got a Club too. This is our T.C.K.C. Club."

"What do you do in your Club?" asked Mrs. Ray.

"Oh," said Betsy. "We see how good we can be."

"Well, there's certainly no harm in that," said her mother. She went back into the house.

But the Club didn't work out exactly as they had expected. The little bags didn't make them want to be good; it was too much fun putting in the stones.

Tib climbed up on the rain barrel and drabbled the skirts of her yellow dimity dress . . . two stones.

Tacy climbed the backyard maple and swung by her knees from a branch; her mother had said this was dangerous . . . one stone.

Betsy ran into the kitchen and got cookies without asking . . . one stone.

Margaret ran happily screaming in a circle. Hobbie bounced up and down in the gocart and yelled.

"'tone! 'tone!" cried Margaret and Hobbie. For even Margaret and Hobbie knew now that stones were part of the game. But Betsy, Tacy and Tib didn't give them any stones. They didn't pay any attention to them.

Betsy's mother came to the door again.

"A little less noise would be *very* good," she said.

"Yes, ma'am," said Betsy.

But it was such fun putting stones in their bags. They grew naughtier and naughtier.

Tacy picked a bouquet of her mother's zinnias. Betsy filled the pockets of her red plaid dress with mud. Tib jumped into the seat of the baker's wagon, which was standing in front of Mrs. Benson's house while the baker's boy offered his tray of jelly rolls and doughnuts at Mrs. Benson's back door. She took up the reins and took up the whip and pretended she was going to drive off. She scared the baker's boy almost to death.

Betsy's mother came to the door again and said that she thought they were possessed. Tacy's mother came to *her* door and told Tacy to be a good girl. And Tib's mother would have come to *her* door too, only Tib's house was so far away that her mother didn't know a thing about what was going on.

The bags on their chests grew bigger and bigger. At last they were almost full.

Tacy sat down on the hitching block, red-faced from laughing.

"Gol darn!" she said distinctly.

"*Tacy!*" cried Betsy. "That's *swearing*. That earns you three stones."

Tacy was proud to be the first to get three stones. The three stones filled her bag.

Betsy looked around for something she could do to earn three stones. She saw her mother's golf cape airing on the line, and she took it down and put it on and walked to the corner and back.

"That earns me three stones too," she said, taking it off quickly.

"I know how I can earn three stones," cried Tib. "Just watch me!"

She ran out into Betsy's father's garden and began to pick tomatoes.

"That's three stones all right," said Betsy, when Tib returned with the red tomatoes in her skirt.

Now all this time Margaret and Hobbie had been just as bad as they knew how. They had screamed and yelled and kicked and jumped, but no one had given them a single stone. Perhaps Margaret and Hobbie thought that they hadn't been bad enough. Or perhaps they just liked the looks of the ripe red tomatoes. At any rate Hobbie took a tomato and threw it at Margaret.

Margaret was delighted when the soft tomato broke in a big red splotch on her dress. She threw one at Hobbie. Hobbie threw one at Tacy and Margaret

threw one at Betsy and they both threw one at Tib.

"'tone! 'tone!" cried Hobbie, smearing tomato into his pale yellow hair.

"'tone! 'tone!" shrieked Margaret, rubbing the red juice into her chubby cheeks.

"Oh! Oh! Oh!" cried Betsy and Tacy and Tib.

Betsy's mother came out just then. And after that the Club wasn't much fun for a while. Betsy and Margaret were motioned into the house in a terrible silence, and the door closed behind them. Tacy was called home, and the door closed behind her too. And Tib took Hobbie home, but she cleaned him up first, the best she could, at Tacy's pump.

Down on the back fence behind Tacy's barn that night, Betsy, Tacy and Tib counted their stones. Tib had the most. But when they were counted she threw them away.

"I think," she said, "that we'd better use these bags for marbles again. We seem to get into trouble when we tie things around our necks."

"That's right. We do," said Tacy. And she threw away her stones too.

"Maybe we'd better change our Club a little," Tacy said, "have our meetings up on the Big Hill."

"Have refreshments," said Tib.

"Take lunch baskets up," said Tacy.

"And a stick and a package, maybe," said Tib.

"What do you think, Betsy?" Tacy asked. For Betsy had not yet thrown away her stones. She was looking up at the western sky where a pale green lake was surrounded by peach-colored mountains, distant and mysterious.

"All right," said Betsy, and she threw away her stones. "But of course we must keep on being good."

"Oh, of course!" said Tacy.

"That's what our Club is for," added Betsy.

"It's a Being Good Club," Tacy said.

"Well, it didn't make us good today," said Tib. "It made us bad."

Neither Betsy nor Tacy would have mentioned that. But they didn't mind Tib's mentioning it. They understood Tib.

In silence the three of them looked at the sunset and thought about God.

9
The Secret Lane

ROM THAT time on T.C.K.C. meetings were held on the Big Hill. Every Tuesday Julia and Katie went up on the Big Hill for a meeting of their B.H.M. Club. And every Tuesday Betsy and Tacy and Tib climbed the hill for T.C.K.C. meetings. Yet not once had Betsy and Tacy and Tib caught a glimpse of Julia and Katie. That shows how big the Big Hill was.

Betsy and Tacy and Tib did different things at their meetings. . . . They always took a picnic lunch, of course; but they didn't take a stick and a package, for they didn't know what Julia and Katie did at their Club with a stick and a package. They couldn't imagine. Sometimes Betsy and Tacy and Tib called on Mrs. Ekstrom and laughed about that day when they had pretended they were beggars. And sometimes they turned left at the top of the hill and walked to that lofty rim from which they had a view over the town and the river. But one day they turned right.

Here the Big Hill stretched away to the south. Flat and grassy and dotted with trees, the top of the Big Hill stretched to they didn't know where. Betsy and Tacy and Tib decided to walk in that direction. They walked and they walked and they walked.

They were carrying a picnic basket; and although they took turns carrying it, it grew heavy at last. The day was warm and they were almost ready to stop and eat their lunch beneath the shade of the trees when Tib made a discovery.

"Look!" she said. "These trees aren't just scattered every which way any more."

"They're going in two rows," said Tacy.

"It's a lane!" cried Betsy. She stopped still. They all

stopped, and they looked before and behind them.

Sure enough, it was a lane. The trees were no longer scattered oaks and elms and maples; they were all beech trees and they were planted in two rows. The rows ran as straight as though they had been laid down with a ruler. They ran like two lines of marching soldiers . . . where?

"Where do you suppose this lane leads to?" Tacy asked.

"There isn't any house up on the Big Hill, except the Ekstroms'," Tib said.

Betsy peered down the mysterious shadowy lane.

"Maybe Aunt Dolly lives up here," she said.

"Oh no," said Tib. "She lives in Milwaukee."

"She *used* to live in Milwaukee," said Tacy. "That doesn't mean she will live there forever."

"Well, she lives in Milwaukee now," said Tib. "Because my mamma had a letter from her. She's coming to visit us."

"What?" cried Betsy.

"You never told us!" cried Tacy.

"I was going to tell you," said Tib. "But this Aunt Dolly who's coming to visit us . . . she's just Aunt Dolly. She doesn't live in a mirror or up in the sky or here in this lane or anything. Does she, Betsy?" Tib looked puzzled.

"Wait and see," said Betsy. "When's she coming?"

"Next week," said Tib.

"Tib!" cried Betsy and Tacy.

They could hardly believe their good luck.

"We can see her!" cried Betsy.

"We'll come over and peek," said Tacy.

"Oh, I'll invite you in," said Tib. "You can come in and talk to her."

"I'd be scared to," said Tacy.

"Why, she's very nice," said Tib. "Would you be scared, Betsy?"

"Yes, a little," Betsy said.

"I don't see why," said Tib.

"Well," said Betsy. "Let's investigate this lane. And then we can talk some more."

The lane was like a tunnel, green and dim. No clover or butter-and-eggs or daisies grew beneath the beeches. Tacy found some clammy Indian pipes but mostly the grass was empty now. There were traces of a path.

"There's a path here," Betsy said.

"There used to be," said Tib. "But nobody uses it much any more."

"I wonder why not," said Tacy. She said it in a whisper.

"It's leading to something," said Tib excitedly.

"It's so stately," said Betsy looking overhead. "It seems as though it should lead to a Palace."

"It's scary," whispered Tacy. "I'm almost scared to go on."

Betsy was scared too, but she wouldn't admit it. Tib wasn't scared though. Tib was tiny but she was never scared.

"Come on," she said. "There's nothing to be afraid of." And she flew ahead like a little yellow feather. Betsy and Tacy followed, and they came to the end of the lane.

At the end of the lane was the beginning of a house. Just the foundation walls of a house, and it seemed to have been built a long time ago. Tall woolly mullein stalks and blue vervain and sunflowers crowded around the low stone wall which was crumbling and falling away.

"Who do you suppose started that house?" asked Betsy, staring at it.

"And why didn't they finish it?" asked Tacy.

"I'll ask my father," said Tib. "He knows all about houses."

"Oh, no!" cried Betsy. "Let's have this for a secret. We'll call it the Secret Lane."

"We'll say S.L.," said Tacy, "so no one will know what we mean."

"If anyone asks us where we've been today, we'll say we've been to the S.L.," said Tib, dancing about in delight.

"And sometimes we'll say, 'Let's go up to the S.L.,'" said Tacy.

"We'll drive Julia and Katie nearly crazy," Betsy said.

And they all began to laugh, and they scrambled up on the wall. Tib started to walk around it.

"Don't do that, Tib," said Betsy. "These stones are pretty wiggly."

"And this cellar's deep," said Tacy, looking down into the weed-grown soggy place.

But Tib didn't listen to them, and she didn't fall either. She ran on light toes to the back of the cellar wall. When she got there she turned around and came back, so swiftly, so eagerly, that Betsy and Tacy knew she had news.

"Ssh! Ssh!" she said as they drew near.

"What is it?" whispered Betsy and Tacy.

"Just wait 'til you see," Tib replied.

"Do we have to walk on the wall?" asked Betsy.

"No," said Tib. "We can go this way." And she took hold of their hands.

She led them softly around to the back of the house. Reddening sumac bushes crowded close, almost concealing the wall. Tib motioned Betsy and Tacy to pause. They hid themselves in the bushes.

At the back of the house a wing jutted out. A plum tree shaded a little square of ground. And there beneath the plum tree, which was covered with small red balls, sat Julia and Katie.

A fringed blue and white cloth was spread out on the grass. And each girl had a hard-boiled egg in front of her, and a sandwich, and a chunk of cake. Stuck up beside them was a stick and on the stick was a big square card, the same size and shape as that package they always carried to their meetings. It was lettered in large red letters:

BIG HILL MYSTERY CLUB

"Big Hill Mystery! That's B.H.M." Betsy whispered. Tacy and Tib nodded excitedly.

Julia and Katie peeled and salted their eggs. They were having a very serious conversation. They were talking about what they would be when they grew up. Julia thought she would be an opera singer, and Katie thought she would be a nurse.

"Either a nurse or a . . ." began Katie. But just then Betsy moved, and a branch crackled.

"Ssh!" said Julia. "What's that I hear?"

She and Katie looked around.

Behind the sumac bushes Betsy and Tacy and Tib hardly dared to breathe. They scrunched down and waited until Julia and Katie had turned back to their lunch. Then they put their fingers to their lips and pointed to the front of the house. Saying "Ssh! Ssh! Ssh!" and lifting their feet very high, they crept away.

Back in the Secret Lane they hugged one another for joy.

"We know their secret," Betsy said.

"We know where their Club meets," Tacy added.

"We know what B.H.M. means," cried Tib.

They jumped and danced . . . but softly.

"Where shall we eat our lunch?" asked Tacy.

"Right here," said Betsy. "And when they come out from their Club they will see us, and they'll know that we know where their Club meets."

So they sat down and spread out a red and white fringed cloth; and a hard-boiled egg apiece, and a sandwich apiece, and a chunk of cake apiece.

"What's that noise I hear?" asked Tacy as they peeled and salted their eggs.

"Nothing," said Betsy. "They wouldn't be through with their lunch. Let's print the name of our Club on a card and stick it up whenever we meet."

"The Christian Kindness Club! It would look fine," Tacy said.

"I'll print it," said Tib.

While they ate their lunch they had a very serious conversation.

"What shall we do when we grow up?" asked Betsy.

"I'm going to get married and have babies," said Tacy without even thinking.

"I'm going to be a dancer," said Tib, "or else an architect. I haven't made up my mind."

"I'm going to be an author," said Betsy. "And I'm going to look exactly like Aunt Dolly."

"You'll have to get different colored hair," said Tib.

"I know it," said Betsy. "But people do."

"Ssh! Ssh! I hear something," Tacy said.

This time Betsy and Tib heard it too. And they caught the flash of red and blue dresses around the corner of the wall.

"We see you!" they cried, jumping up.

Julia and Katie started to run, and Betsy and Tacy and Tib started to chase them. Tib remembered, though, to pick up the basket and the red and white fringed cloth.

They chased Julia and Katie through the Secret Lane and past Mrs. Ekstrom's house and down the Big Hill. Nobody caught anybody but it was very exciting. Shouting, feet pounding, skirts flying, they ran into Betsy's yard.

Betsy's mother was sitting there with Margaret playing beside her.

"Mercy! What's the matter?" she asked, as they dropped in a heap of waving arms and legs.

"We know where your B.H.M. Club meets!" shouted Betsy, Tacy and Tib.

"We know where your T.C.K.C. meets," Julia and Katie shouted back.

"Big Hill Mystery!" yelled Betsy, Tacy and Tib.

"The Christian Kindness Club!" yelled Julia and Katie.

"You see," said Tacy to Betsy and Tib, "I *told* you someone was there."

Betsy's mother took Margaret on her lap to be out of the way of the waving arms and legs.

"I have a suggestion to make," she said, smiling.

"Since you know all about one another's clubs, and since they both meet up on the Big Hill, why don't you have your meetings together?"

"Together!" cried Julia and Katie and Betsy and Tacy and Tib.

"Go up on the Big Hill together and eat your picnics together. I think it would be fun," Betsy's mother said.

Julia and Katie looked at each other in horror, and Betsy and Tacy and Tib exchanged horrified glances too.

Wasn't that just like a grown-up, thought Betsy, to think that that would be fun?

"You think it over," said Betsy's mother, smiling.

"Yes ma'am," said Julia and Katie and Betsy and Tacy and Tib.

And they thought it over. But the B.H.M. and the T.C.K.C. never met together. Not once.

10
Aunt Dolly

AUNT DOLLY'S train was to reach Deep Valley at night. Betsy and Tacy would be in bed and asleep when she arrived. They wanted to be at Tib's house early the next morning. So they worked out a plan.

That night when Tacy went to bed, she was to tie a string to her big toe. She was to let the string hang out the window. In the morning Betsy would come over and pull the string to wake her up.

"But maybe you won't wake up first, Betsy," Tacy said as she and Betsy climbed the stairs to the little room Tacy shared with Katie.

"That's right," said Betsy. "Maybe I won't. Maybe we'd better tie a string to my toe too."

So after they had poked a string . . . with a stone on one end to make it fall to the ground . . . through a hole in the screen, and tied the other end of the string to the bedpost, awaiting night and Tacy's toe, they crossed the street to Betsy's house. They climbed the stairs to the little room Betsy shared with Julia and poked a string through a hole in *that* screen and tied the other end to a post of *that* bed, awaiting night and *Betsy's* toe. And that night Julia and Katie helped them tie the strings to their big toes. (Julia and Katie were nice sometimes.)

But, as it happened, neither string got pulled.

Tacy had bad dreams and twisted and turned in the night so that the string was wound around her leg and Betsy would have had to stand on stilts to reach it. And Betsy's string came off her toe in the night. But both of them woke up early just the same. They met in the middle of the road.

It was very early; the sky was the color of Betsy's mother's opal ring. The air was cold, and up on the

Hill Street Hill where Betsy and Tacy went to pick flowers for Aunt Dolly, the grass was wet with dew. When their arms were full of goldenrod and bright purple asters, they went down to Hill Street and sat on Tacy's hitching block. It was too early yet to go to Tib's.

"I imagine she'll be beautiful," said Tacy.

"Of course she will," said Betsy. "Remember how her picture looked?"

"It looked like a grown-up doll," said Tacy.

The sun came up higher and higher, and the sky turned a bright gay blue. Smoke began to pour from chimneys, and Grandpa Williams came out to mow his lawn.

"I think we could go to Tib's now," said Betsy.

"We'd better," said Tacy, "or we'll be called to breakfast."

So they skipped down Hill Street and through the vacant lot and rapped at Tib's back door.

Matilda came to the door. She had on an apron and she held a long fork in her hand. She looked busy.

"Tib can't come out yet. She's eating breakfast. There's company," Matilda said.

Betsy and Tacy looked at each other. There was company! Then there hadn't been any mistake.

"It's the company we've come to see," said Betsy.

"We've brought her these flowers," said Tacy.

"We've wiped our feet," said Betsy, and she wiped them again, hard, and so did Tacy.

"Well, wait a minute," Matilda said.

She went through the swinging door into the dining room. Betsy and Tacy waited.

"You can come in," Matilda said when she returned.

They followed her into the dining room. The family was at breakfast there. Tib's father sat at the head of the table with Hobbie in a high chair beside him. Tib's mother sat at the foot. Tib and Freddie sat on one side of the table; and on the other side, facing them, sat Aunt Dolly.

She was more beautiful than her picture. She was more beautiful even than they had imagined her to be. She had blue eyes like Tib's and a pink and white face like a doll's. Her blonde hair was piled in curls on the top of her head.

When Betsy and Tacy entered the room, Tib's face turned red.

"Come in," said Tib's mother in her brisk kind voice. "Matilda says you came to see Aunt Dolly."

"Yes, ma'am," said Betsy. Her face was shining with excitement.

Tacy didn't say a word. She was bashful. Tacy wasn't bashful with Mr. and Mrs. Muller any more, but she was very bashful with Aunt Dolly.

Betsy wasn't bashful exactly, but she felt queer inside.

"We brought her some flowers," she said, nodding toward Aunt Dolly.

Aunt Dolly threw back her head and laughed. She had a little tinkling laugh; it sounded like those bells made of glass and painted with strange flowers which hung on the porch at Betsy's house and chimed when the wind blew.

"Why do you bring flowers to me?" she asked in a tone which showed that she knew the reason perfectly well.

"Because you're so pretty," said Betsy, and everyone laughed.

"That's because I had a grandmother who came from Vienna," Aunt Dolly said, pushing her soft light curls into place.

"Frederick," said Mr. Muller. "Where are your manners? Won't you draw up some chairs for these ladies?"

"Oh," said Betsy. "We didn't come to breakfast."

"Have some coffee cake at least," said Mrs. Muller. "Matilda will put the flowers in a vase."

So Matilda put the flowers in a vase, and Freddie brought chairs, and Betsy and Tacy ate coffee cake and looked at Aunt Dolly. Tib and Freddie looked at Betsy and Tacy. The grown-ups talked about Aunt Dolly's visit, and presently they all finished breakfast and Aunt Dolly stood up.

Betsy and Tacy could see her better then. She was wearing a teagown of pleated white silk, and beneath her small bosom pale blue ribbons were tied.

"I must go to unpack," she said, patting back a yawn with polished fingertips. "Would you children like to come along and see my clothes?"

"Oh, yes," said Betsy and Tacy.

"Freddie can tell your mothers where you are," said Mrs. Muller. "He is going to play with Paul."

So Freddie went off to tell Mrs. Ray and Mrs. Kelly that Betsy and Tacy would be home after a while, and Betsy and Tacy and Tib followed Aunt Dolly to her room.

Her big trunk stood open, and while Betsy and Tacy and Tib watched, entranced, she lifted out her dresses. She certainly had plenty of dresses! There were morning dresses and afternoon dresses; a dress just for horseback riding and a dress just for bicycle riding and lots of ball gowns.

"Dolly!" said Tib's mother, laughing. "Did you forget that you were coming to visit in a small Minnesota town?"

"Oh, I knew you'd like to see them," said Aunt Dolly. "And I like to show them." And she went off to the bureau and moistened her fingers with perfume and touched the lobes of her ears. "Thank you for the flowers, children," she said in a tone which showed that she was ready for them to go.

"You're welcome," said Betsy and Tacy.

"May I go out to play?" asked Tib.

And Betsy and Tacy and Tib went out to the knoll.

"Well," asked Tib when they were seated beneath the oak tree. "What do you think?"

"She's beautiful," said Betsy.

"Do you think she lives in all those crazy places?" asked Tib. "In the Mirror Palace or up in our S.L.?"

"That's what I've been wondering," said Tacy.

Betsy did not answer right away.

"Not any more she doesn't," she said at last.

"What do you mean . . . 'not any more'? I don't understand," said Tib.

Betsy hesitated. It was hard to explain. The truth was that Aunt Dolly was more thrilling being just what she was, than she would be being anything that Betsy could invent. Was that because she was grown-up?

Tacy knew what Betsy was thinking.

"I wonder what it will be like to be grown-up," she said.

"I don't think it will be as nice as being children," said Tib.

"Neither do I," said Tacy. "You don't want to be grown-up, do you, Betsy? At least, not right away."

Betsy sat still for a long moment and thought. She thought about the fun it was being a child. She thought about the Hill Street Hill, and their bench. She thought about the Big Hill and the ravine and the Secret Lane. She looked up into the green shade of the oak tree and thought about the backyard maple.

"No," she answered slowly, "I don't want to be grown-up yet. But I want to be just a little older."

"You're nine already," said Tacy.

"Next year," said Tib, "we'll all be ten."

Betsy jumped up joyfully.

"That's what I'd like to be . . . ten. You have two numbers in your age when you are ten. It's the beginning of growing up, to get two numbers in your age."

Tacy and Tib jumped up too, and they started through the vacant lot.

"But what will we do when we are ten?" asked Tib as they climbed Hill Street Hill.

"I suppose we'll be going to balls," said Betsy. "I'm planning to have a pale pink satin ball gown."

"I'll have a blue one," said Tacy.

"Mine will have a long train," said Betsy.

"I'll carry a big feather fan," said Tacy.

"But we won't be going to balls when we are only ten years old," said Tib.

Tib always said things like that. But Betsy and Tacy liked her just the same.

"We won't be going to balls, maybe," said Betsy. "But we'll have lots of fun, you and me and Tacy."

And so they did.

THE END

Betsy and Tacy
Go Over the Big Hill

*For KATHLEEN and TESS,
the villains of the piece*

Contents

Contents

Foreword

When I was about nine my mother saw an ad in the paper for a series of books by Maud Hart Lovelace. She showed it to me and asked if I would be interested. She wanted some assurance, I guess, that if she ordered these books I would read them. The ad, from Bambergers department store in Newark, New Jersey, was intriguing. It promised stories about two girls, Betsy and Tacy, who are best friends. So I told my mother, yes, I would like to read them. I understood that this was different than taking books out of the library. If I started a library book and didn't like it, I could take it back. This was a commitment. We didn't just go to the bookstore to buy children's books then, though I was proud of the shelves of grown-up books in our living room. My mother was always reading, usually the latest best-sellers, and my father unwound at night with mysteries. A neat stack of books sat on each of their bedside tables.

Though I owned all the Oz books (and would eventually buy a Nancy Drew mystery each Saturday), I loved our weekly trips downtown to the main branch of the public library, where I climbed a set of rickety outside stairs to get to the children's room. Once there, I would sit on the floor, sniff the books, and browse. At home, I waited anxiously for the Betsy-Tacy books to arrive. And when they did, I sniffed them to see if they smelled as good as the books I borrowed from the public library. They did. Even better.

I'd always liked to read, but until the Betsy-Tacy books I'd never found stories about girls who were anything like me and my friends. Even though I knew from the start the books took place in the olden days, the characters felt so real it didn't matter what they wore, or how they fixed their hair, or that they thought a dollar was a lot of money. In fact, I found these details fascinating. I couldn't wait to read the next book or the one after that, following Betsy Ray's life. Betsy sometimes made mistakes, she sometimes talked too much. She could be stubborn, or angry, or sad. Best of all, she had a lot of imagination. I totally identified with her. She was a girl who'd been making up stories all her life, just like me. Until then I was sure I was the only one. But unlike Betsy, I never told anyone about my stories. And I never wrote them down, either.

I'd think about Betsy and her friends as I went to bed

at night, wondering what would happen next. I didn't care that they were only five years old at the beginning of the first book. I never felt that I was reading a *baby* book. Besides, I knew that Betsy, Tacy, and Tib were going to grow older in each book. I knew that they'd soon be older than me. And I didn't want to miss a minute. I needed to know as much about them as I possibly could. I longed to know them as well as they knew each other.

The following year my mother surprised me with the next three books in the series. Now Betsy was a teenager. Given the chance, I'd have jumped right into the pages of those books to share the famous "Sunday Night Lunches" at Betsy's house. And afterward, to gather around the piano with Betsy and her friends, singing for hours. It seemed to me that Betsy had a perfect life—good friends and a warm, secure, and loving family, where she knew someone was always on her side.

While I didn't feel the darker undercurrents I sometimes felt in my own family, or even in my own friendships, I still believed in Betsy. I laughed and cried and dreamed with her. I loved those books too much to ever do a book report on them. They weren't for sharing. They were for keeping deep inside.

Did Betsy inspire me to become a writer? After all, she knew when she was very young that's exactly what she was going to be when she grew up, and she never changed her mind. But writing wasn't on my mind when I was reading about her, so I would have to answer, *probably not*, although who can say where inspiration really comes from?

I don't know why I didn't get to read the last three books in the series (*Betsy and Joe, Betsy and the Great World*, and *Betsy's Wedding*) when I was growing up. Surely I would have, if only I'd known about them. I read them recently for the first time. I was nervous as I opened to the first page. What if the stories didn't hold up well? What if I couldn't imagine girls today caring about Betsy? But I didn't have to worry. I was swept into Betsy's life the way I had been years ago. And by the time I read the final page of the last book, I was crying so hard my husband thought something terrible had happened. I explained it wasn't sadness that was making me cry—it was finding friends I thought I'd lost.

A whole generation of girls my age came to feel that Betsy was their friend. It's comforting to know that no matter how many years go by, no matter how different things are today, what's inside us is still the same. And what makes a good book hasn't changed either. Some characters become your friends for life. That's how it was for me with Betsy and Tacy.

—JUDY BLUME

Hills were higher then

—Hugh Mac Nair Kahler

1

Getting to Be Ten

BETSY, TACY, AND TIB were nine years old, and they were very anxious to be ten.

"You have two numbers in your age when you are ten. It's the beginning of growing up," Betsy would say.

Then the three of them felt solemn and important and pleased. They could hardly wait for their birthdays.

It was strange that Betsy and Tacy and Tib were in such a hurry to grow up, for they had so much fun being children. Betsy and Tacy lived on Hill Street which ran straight up into a green hill and stopped. The small yellow cottage where Betsy Ray lived was the last house on that side of the street, and the rambling white house opposite where Tacy Kelly lived was the last house on that side. They had the whole hill for a playground. And not just that one green slope. There were hills all around them. Hills like a half-opened fan rose in the east behind Betsy's house. Beyond the town and across the river where the sun set there were more hills. The name of the town was Deep Valley.

Tib didn't live on Hill Street. To get to Tib's house from the place where Betsy and Tacy lived, you went one block down and one block over. (The second block was through a vacant lot.) But Tib lived near enough to come to play with Betsy and Tacy. She came every day.

"They certainly have fun, those three," Betsy's mother used to say to Betsy's father.

They did, too.

Betsy's big sister Julia played with Tacy's sister Katie, but they didn't have so much fun as Betsy and Tacy and Tib had. They were too grown-up. They were twelve.

Betsy's little sister Margaret, Tacy's younger brother Paul, and Tib's yellow-headed brothers, Freddie and Hobbie, had fun all right, but not so much fun as Betsy and Tacy and Tib had. They were too little.

Going on ten seemed to be exactly the right age for having fun. But just the same Betsy and Tacy and Tib wanted to be ten years old.

They were getting near it now. Betsy and Tacy were growing tall, so that their mothers were kept busy lengthening their dresses. Tib wasn't as tiny as she used to be, but she was still tiny. She still looked like a picture-book fairy. The three girls had cut their hair when they were eight years old and didn't know any better, but it had grown out. Tib's curls once more made a yellow fluff around her little face. Tacy had her long red ringlets and Betsy had her braids again.

"When I'm ten," said Betsy, "I'm going to cross my braids in back and tie them with ribbons."

"I'm going to tie my hair at my neck with a big blue bow," Tacy replied.

"We can't put it up in pugs *quite* yet, I suppose," Betsy said.

"But pretty soon we can," said Tacy. "On top of our heads."

Tib did not make plans like that. She never did.

"I only hope," she said, "that when I get to be ten years old people will stop taking me for a baby."

For people always thought that Tib was younger than she was. And she didn't like it a bit.

Tacy got to be ten first because her birthday came in January. They didn't have many birthday parties at Tacy's house. There were too many children in the family. Mrs. Kelly would have been giving birthday parties every month in the year, almost, if every child at the Kelly house had had a party every birthday. But when Tacy was ten, Betsy and Tib were invited to supper. There was a cake with candles on it.

Tacy didn't look any different or feel any different.

But she knew why that was. Betsy and Tib weren't ten yet.

"We'll all have to get to be ten before it really counts, I suppose," Tacy said.

Tib got to be ten next because her birthday came in March. Tib didn't have a birthday party; she had the grippe instead. But she was given a bicycle, and her mother sent pieces of birthday cake over to Betsy and Tacy.

And Tib didn't look any different or feel any different. But she didn't expect much change until Betsy got to be ten. And Betsy's birthday didn't come until April.

Tacy and Tib didn't say very much about being ten. They were too polite. They talked about presents and birthday cakes, but they didn't mention having two numbers in their age. They didn't talk about beginning to grow up until the afternoon before Betsy's birthday.

That afternoon after school they all went up on the Big Hill hunting for violets. It was one of those April days on which it seemed that summer had already come, although the ground was still muddy and brown. The sun was shining so warmly that Betsy, Tacy, and Tib pulled off their stocking caps and unbuttoned their coats. Birds in the bare trees were singing with all their might, and Betsy,

Tacy, and Tib sang too as they climbed the Big
Hill.

They sang to the tune of "Mine eyes have seen
the glory," but they made up the words themselves:

> *"Oh, Betsy's ten tomorrow,*
> *And then all of us are ten,*
> *We will all grow up tomorrow,*
> *We will all be ladies then. . . ."*

They marched in a row and sang.

The Ekstroms, whose white house stood at the
top of the hill, were out making a garden. It made

them laugh to see Betsy, Tacy, and Tib marching along and singing. Betsy, Tacy, and Tib liked to make the Ekstroms laugh. They marched straighter and sang louder than ever.

Marching and singing, they turned to the right and went through the twin row of beeches which they called their Secret Lane, and past the foundations of that house which had never been finished which they called the Mystery House. Still marching and singing, they went down through a fold of the hills and up again. But now they had sung until they were hoarse, and they burst out laughing and fell down on top of each other.

When they were rested Tib stood up.

"We'd better get those violets," she said.

But Tacy cried out, "Look! We've come farther than we ever came before."

Sure enough, they stood on a part of the hill which was new to them. Climbing a little higher, they left the trees behind and came out on a high rocky ridge. Below, spread out in the sunlight, was a strange wide beautiful valley. In the center were one big brick house and a row of tiny houses.

"That looks like Little Syria," said Tib.

"It can't be!" cried Betsy and Tacy together, for Little Syria was a place they went to with their fathers and mothers when out buggy riding on a summer evening. It was not a place one saw when one went walking.

Yet this was certainly Little Syria.

"That big brick house is the Meecham Mansion," Tib said.

It certainly was.

Mr. Meecham had built it many years before, according to the story which Betsy and Tacy and Tib had often heard their fathers tell. He had come from the East and had bought all the land in this valley, calling it Meecham's Addition. He had tried to sell lots there, but none of his American neighbors had wished to live so far from the center of town. At last he had sold his lots to a colony of Syrians, strange dark people who spoke broken English and came to Hill Street sometimes peddling garden stuff and laces and embroidered cloths.

Angry and disappointed, Mr. Meecham lived on in his mansion among the humble houses of the Syrians. So did his wife until she died. And so did his middle-aged daughter. He was a tall old man with a flowing white beard and a proud scornful bearing. His team of white horses was the finest in the county; and it was driven by a coachman. Mr. Meecham and his daughter came to town in style, when they came, which was not often.

Little Syria belonged to Deep Valley but it seemed

as foreign as though it were across the ocean.

And now here it lay, at the very feet of Betsy, Tacy, and Tib.

The three of them stared down at it, and Betsy was thinking hard.

"Well, I'm surprised!" said Tacy. "I never knew we could walk to Little Syria."

"I'm not surprised," said Betsy.

"You're not?" asked Tacy.

"No," said Betsy. "Remember I'll be ten tomorrow. It's the sort of thing we'll be doing often from now on."

"Going to other towns?" asked Tacy.

"Yes. Little Syria. Minneapolis. Chicago. New York."

"I'd love to go to New York and see the Flatiron Building," said Tacy.

Tib looked puzzled.

"But Little Syria," she said, "is just over our own hill. We didn't know that it was. But it is."

"Well, we certainly didn't find it out until today," said Betsy.

"We certainly never walked to it before," said Tacy.

"That's right," admitted Tib.

They gazed down on Little Syria in the center of the broad calm valley. Mr. Meecham's Mansion with the little houses in a row looked like a hen followed by chicks.

"Shall we go down?" asked Tib, dancing about. Tib liked to do things instead of talking about them.

It was a daring suggestion. There were tales of the Syrians fighting one another with knives. A man called Old Bushara had once chased a boy with a knife. The boy was in their grade at school.

"Remember Sam and Old Bushara?" Tacy asked now.

"Sam's a horrid boy," said Tib. "He yelled 'dago' at Old Bushara. He yells that at all the Syrians and it's not a nice thing to do. Shall we go down?" she persisted, hopping from foot to foot.

Betsy looked at Tacy.

"Not today," she said. "It's too late. But some day we'll go."

They walked back slowly, picking flowers as they went. They didn't find many violets, but they found bloodroots, and Dutchman's breeches, and hepaticas, rising from the damp brown mat which carpeted the ground. They didn't march or sing going home. When they passed the Ekstroms' house, the Ekstroms, who were making a bonfire now, called out to ask where the parade was.

"What parade?" asked Betsy. "Oh, that! We

won't be parading much more, I expect."

"Betsy will be ten years old tomorrow, Mrs. Ekstrom," Tacy said.

"And then we'll all be ten," said Tib.

"You don't·say!" Mrs. Ekstrom answered.

They started down the hill.

Before they were halfway down, the sun hid itself behind purple curtains. And the air which had been so summerlike grew suddenly remindful of winter. Betsy, Tacy, and Tib pulled on their stocking caps and buttoned their flapping coats.

"That was our last parade, I expect," said Betsy.

"Why?" asked Tib. "I think they're fun."

"We're getting too old for them," Tacy said.

"That's right," said Betsy. "Marching along and yelling will seem pretty childish after tomorrow."

"I suppose we'll start having tea parties," said Tacy.

"Yes. We'll crook our little fingers over the cups like *this*," answered Betsy, crooking her little finger in a very elegant way.

"We'll say 'indeed' to each other," said Tacy.

"And 'prefer,'" said Betsy.

"Will it be fun?" asked Tib. She sounded as though she didn't think it would be.

"Fun or not," said Betsy, "we have to grow up. Everyone does."

"And we're beginning tomorrow," said Tacy. "On Betsy's birthday."

They had reached Betsy's hitching block and Betsy wished she could say something more about her birthday. She wished she could invite Tacy and Tib to her birthday supper. But her mother hadn't said a word about inviting them. In fact, her mother did not seem to take much interest in this birthday. Betsy wondered if that was because she was growing up.

"See you tomorrow," she said, because there was nothing better to say, and she waved good-by and ran into the house. For the first time she had a queer feeling inside about getting to be ten years old.

She woke up in the night and had the feeling again. She lay very still in the bed she shared with Julia and thought about growing up. The window at the front of the little tent-roofed bedroom which looked across to Tacy's house showed squares of dismal gray.

"Maybe it's not so nice growing up. Maybe it's more fun being a child," thought Betsy. "Well, anyway, there's nothing I can do about it!"

She dropped off to sleep.

And next morning when she woke up she was ten years old.

Betsy, Tacy, and Tib were ten years old at last.

2

Ten Years Old

I N THE MORNING it seemed thrilling to be ten years old.

Betsy jumped out of bed and ran to the window. The lawn, the road, the branches of the trees, and Tacy's roof across the street were skimmed with snow. But she knew it could not last, in April.

"Happy birthday!" said Julia, struggling into her underwear beside the warm chimney which angled up from the hard coal heater downstairs. She spoke politely. She did not pound Betsy on the back as on other birthday mornings. But Betsy suspected that Julia was thinking more of the dignity of her own twelve years than of Betsy's ten.

Betsy answered carelessly, "That's right. It *is* my birthday."

She dressed and went humming carelessly down the stairs.

Her father pounded her plenty. And he held her while Margaret pounded. She was pounded and tickled and kissed. Of course it was hard to act careless during such a rumpus, but after it was over Betsy acted careless again. She crooked her finger when she lifted her milk glass, but just a little; she was afraid that Julia would notice.

"Don't you feel well, Betsy?" asked her mother.

"Why, yes," said Betsy. "I feel fine."

"She's very quiet," said her father. "It's the weight of her years."

Betsy was startled until she saw that her father was joking. Her father was a great one to joke.

The pounding and joking showed that her birthday was remembered but still nobody mentioned asking Tacy and Tib to supper. Betsy got ready for school slowly. When her father left for the shoe store, she was still dawdling over her coat and stocking cap, tangling her mitten strings, and losing her rubbers. She gave her mother plenty of chance to bring up the subject. But it didn't do any good.

At last Betsy said, "Hadn't I better ask Tacy and Tib over to supper, Mamma?"

"Not today," answered Mrs. Ray. She sounded for all the world as though any other day would do as well.

"Mamma's pretty busy today. You know Friday's cleaning day," Julia said importantly.

Cleaning day! Betsy could hardly believe her ears. She tried to act as though it didn't matter.

"When I was only nine I would have teased," she thought.

She kissed her mother good-by and went humming out the door and across the street to Tacy's.

Mrs. Kelly came to the door and said, "Isn't this your birthday, Betsy?"

"*Indeed* it is," said Betsy, stressing the "indeed" and looking hard at Tacy. Her manner was light and careless, very grown-up.

Mrs. Kelly did not seem to notice the grown-upness. She took Betsy's round red cheeks in her hands and said, "It's five years today that you and Tacy have been friends."

"Goodness!" said Betsy, forgetting to act old for a minute because she *felt* so old.

But she and Tacy acted old all the way down Hill Street, and even more so after they had cut through the vacant lot to Pleasant Street and called for Tib at her beautiful chocolate-colored house. It was fun to watch Tib's round blue eyes grow rounder as she listened to them talk.

"Will you both come to tea some day this week?" Betsy asked carelessly.

"Yes *indeed*," said Tacy. "I'd love to. Wouldn't you, Tib?"

"Um-hum," said Tib.

"When I get some money," said Betsy, "I'm going to buy some nail powder. I'm going to start buffing my nails. I think we all ought to."

"So do I," said Tacy. "I think my sister Mary would lend us a little nail powder, maybe."

"Do you really?" asked Betsy.

"Yes *indeed*," said Tacy. Tacy loved to say "indeed."

Tib didn't know how to talk in the new way. She hadn't learned yet. But she tried.

"I borrowed my mamma's nail powder once and I spilled it," she said.

Betsy and Tacy hurried over that.

"We must buy some hair pins too," said Betsy. "Of course we're not quite ready to put up our hair, but we shall be soon."

"I can hardly wait to get my skirts down," Tacy said. "Ankle length is what I *prefer*."

"What do you *prefer*, Tib?" asked Betsy.

"I don't know what '*prefer*' means, exactly," said Tib. "Betsy, do you think I still look like a baby?"

Betsy glanced at her and hastily glanced away.

"Not so much as you did yesterday," she said.

"Try to talk like us, Tib," Tacy advised. "It's easy when you get started."

They talked grown-up all the way to school; and they kept on doing it coming home from school at noon, and going back after dinner, and coming home again at three o'clock.

On that trip, when they reached the corner by Tib's house, Betsy felt a strong return of that queer feeling inside. The snow was melting and the ground was slushy and damp. It wasn't a good time for playing out. Today of all days, she should be asking Tacy and Tib to come to her house. And her mother had told her not to!

Tacy and Tib acted embarrassed. Tacy looked at Tib and Tib looked at Tacy and said, "Why don't you come into my house to play?"

"I'd like to. Wouldn't you, Betsy?" Tacy asked.

"There are some funny papers you haven't seen," said Tib. "Is it all right for us to look at them, now we are ten?"

"Of course," said Tacy hastily. "Lots of grown people read the funny papers. Don't they, Betsy?"

"Oh, of course!" Betsy said.

So they went into Tib's house where they always loved to go; it was so beautiful with a tower on the front and panes of colored glass in the front door. They sat on the window seat and looked at the funny papers, crooking their fingers when they turned the pages. Betsy began to feel better. She had an idea.

"I think we're too old," she said, "to call each other by our nicknames any more. I think we ought to start using our real names. For instance, you should call me Elizabeth."

"Yes," said Tacy. "And you should call me Anastacia."

"And you should call me Thelma," said Tib. "Hello, Anastacia! How-de-do, Elizabeth?"

The big names made them laugh. Whenever they said "Anastacia" they laughed so hard that they rolled on the window seat.

Matilda, the hired girl, came in from the kitchen.

"What's going on in here?" she asked, looking cross. Matilda almost always looked cross.

"Anastacia and Elizabeth are making me laugh," said Tib.

"No. It's Thelma acting silly," cried Betsy and Tacy.

"Where are all those folks?" asked Matilda, looking around. Betsy, Tacy, and Tib shouted at that.

They had such a good time that Betsy almost forgot how strange it was not to have Tacy and Tib come to supper on her most important birthday. But when the time came to go home she remembered.

"Tacy," she said, as they walked through the vacant lot, "people don't make as much fuss about birthdays after other people grow up. Have you noticed that?"

"Um—er," said Tacy. She acted embarrassed again.

"Not that it matters, of course," said Betsy. "It doesn't matter a bit."

It did, though.

It was dusk when she reached home but no lamps had been lighted except in the kitchen where Mrs. Ray was bustling about getting supper. She wore a brown velvet bow in her high red pompadour and a fresh brown checked apron tied around her slender waist.

Julia was scrubbing Margaret at the basin. And Julia too looked very spic and span.

"Clean up good for supper, Betsy," her mother said.

"Yes, ma'am," said Betsy.

"Mamma," said Julia, "don't you think Betsy ought to put on her new plaid hair ribbons?"

"Yes, that's a good idea," said Mrs. Ray.

"After all, it's her birthday," said Julia, and Margaret clapped her wet hand over her mouth and said, "Oh! Oh!" Margaret was only four years old.

"Probably she thinks Julia is giving something away. Probably she thinks I don't know we'll have a birthday cake," thought Betsy.. And then she thought, "Maybe we won't. Things get so different

as you get older." She felt gloomy.

But she scrubbed her face and hands. And Julia helped her braid her hair and even crossed the braids in back; they were just long enough to cross. Julia tied the plaid bows perkily over Betsy's ears.

When she was cleaned up, Betsy went into the back parlor. The fire was shining through the isinglass windows of the hard coal heater there. It looked cozy and she would have enjoyed sitting down beside it with a book. But her mother called out:

"Betsy, I borrowed an egg today from Mrs. Rivers. Will you return it for me, please?"

"Right now?" asked Betsy.

"Yes, please," her mother answered.

"Of all things!" said Betsy to herself.

It seemed to her that she might return the egg tomorrow. It seemed to her that Julia might do the errands on this particular day. It was a nuisance getting into outdoor clothes when she had just taken them off.

"What must I wear?" she asked, trying not to show she was cross because it was her birthday.

"You'll only need your coat and rubbers. Go out the back way," her mother said.

So Betsy put on her coat and rubbers and took an egg and went out the back way.

Mrs. Rivers lived next door, and she was very nice. She had a little girl just Margaret's age, and a still smaller girl, and a baby. The baby was sitting in a high chair eating his supper and Mrs. Rivers asked Betsy to stay a moment and watch him. He was just learning how to feed himself and he was funny.

Betsy stayed and watched him. And she said "indeed" and "prefer" to Mrs. Rivers and that cheered her up a little. Mrs. Rivers kept looking out of the window. At last she said:

"I'm afraid your mother will be expecting you now. Good-by, dear. Go out the back way."

So Betsy went out the back way and climbed the

little slope which led to her house. The ground was slippery, for the melted snow had frozen again. The stars above the hill were icy white.

She went into the house dejectedly. There was no one in the kitchen. The door which led to the dining room was closed.

"They've started supper without me. On my birthday!" Betsy thought. She felt like sitting down and crying.

She opened the dining room door and then stopped. No wonder she stopped! The room was crowded with children. They called, "Surprise! Surprise! Surprise on Betsy!"

Betsy's father stood there with his arm around Betsy's mother and both of them were smiling. Tacy and Tib rushed over to Betsy and began to pound her on the back, and Julia ran into the front parlor and started playing the piano. Everybody sang:

> "*Happy birthday to you!*
> *Happy birthday to you!*
> *Happy birthday, dear Betsy,*
> *Happy birthday to you!*"

"It's a surprise party," cried Margaret, red-faced from joyful suspense.

It was certainly a surprise.

There were ten little girls at the party because Betsy was ten years old. Ten little girls, that is, without Margaret who was too little to count. Betsy made one, and Julia made two, and Tacy made three, and Katie made four, and Tib made five, and a little girl named Alice who lived down on Pleasant Street made six, and Julia's and Katie's friend Dorothy who also lived down on Pleasant Street made seven, and three little girls from Betsy's class in school made eight, nine, and ten.

There were ten candles on the birthday cake, but before they had the birthday cake they had sandwiches and cocoa: and along with the birthday cake they had ice cream; and after the birthday cake they played games in the front and back parlors. Betsy's father played with them; Betsy's mother played the piano for Going to Jerusalem; and when Betsy's father was left without a chair how everybody laughed!

Betsy and Tacy and Tib played harder than anyone. They forgot to crook their fingers and to say "indeed" and "prefer." They forgot to call one another Elizabeth and Anastacia and Thelma. In fact, after that day, they never did these things again.

But just the same, in the midst of the excitement, Betsy realized that she was practically grown-up.

Flushed and panting from Blind Man's Buff, her

braids loose, and her best hair ribbons untied, she found her mother.

"Mamma," she said, "this is the first party I ever had at night."

"That's right," her mother answered. "The children are staying until nine o'clock, and Papa is taking them home."

"Is it because I'm ten years old?" asked Betsy.

"Of course it is," her mother answered.

Betsy rushed to find Tacy and Tib. She drew them into a corner.

"You notice," she whispered proudly, "that we're having this party at night."

"What about it?" asked Tib.

"What about it?" repeated Betsy. "Why, it's a grown-up party."

"It's practically a ball," said Tacy.

"Oh," said Tib.

"Of course," she pointed out after a moment, "tomorrow isn't a school day."

Tib always mentioned things like that. But Betsy and Tacy liked her just the same.

3
The King of Spain

THE FIRST THING Betsy and Tacy and Tib did after they were ten years old was to fall in love. They all fell in love at once . . . with the same person too.

It happened this way.

Betsy was eating her supper. She was hurrying in order to get out to play, for on May evenings all the children of Hill Street gathered in the street to play. They played Run-Sheep-Run and Prisoners' Base and Pom-Pom-Pullaway and many other games, until the sun finally set behind Tacy's house and the first stars appeared in the sky. Betsy loved this wild hour of play and she usually thought about it all through supper, but tonight her attention was caught by something her father was saying.

"Sixteen years old. It's pretty young to be a king."

"Has he had his birthday yet?" Betsy's mother asked.

"Not yet. But they're making great preparations. You see, he comes to the throne that day." Mr. Ray folded the paper and handed it to his wife. "There's his picture. Handsome boy, isn't he?"

Julia and Betsy jumped up and looked over their mother's shoulder. They saw the picture of a slim dark boy on horseback. The line beneath the picture read:

"Alphonso the Thirteenth."

"Do you mean he's living some place? Right now?" asked Betsy.

"Yes," her mother answered. "He lives in Spain."

"That country we had the war with," said Julia. "It's your turn to wipe the dishes, Betsy."

"It is not," said Betsy. "I wiped them last night."

"But that was making up for the night before, when I did them for you, while you and Tacy practiced the 'Cat Duet.'"

Betsy could not deny it.

"And tonight," said Julia, "I have to practice my recitation."

There was lots of practicing going on, for there was to be a big Entertainment on the Last Day of School.

"All right," said Betsy. She didn't mind staying in to wipe dishes as much as usual. It was a chance to ask her mother about the King of Spain.

She had known, of course, that there were kings and queens outside of fairy tales and histories. But she had never thought much about them before. It was strange to think now of a real live boy being a king.

She listened eagerly while her mother told her all she knew about him.

His father had died many years before; his mother, the Queen, had been acting as regent; but on May seventeenth he would be sixteen years old, and then he would ascend the throne and rule the country himself.

"Madrid . . . that's the capital of Spain . . . is turned inside out with excitement," Betsy's mother said.

Betsy felt turned inside out with excitement too.

After the towels had been hung to dry, she ran into the back parlor to find the newspaper. Fortunately her father had finished with it; he had gone to work in the garden. Clutching the paper, Betsy ran outdoors.

Games had begun but Tacy was not playing. She was sitting on the hitching block waiting for Betsy. The sun was low and the new leaves on the trees shimmered in a golden light.

"Tacy!" cried Betsy. "Did you know there was a king in Europe . . . alive and everything . . . only fifteen years old?"

"I've heard about him," Tacy said.

"Here's a picture of him," said Betsy. She sat down beside Tacy on the hitching block and they looked at the picture together.

"Just think!" said Betsy. "We're sitting here on the hitching block and at this very minute he's *somewhere*, doing *something*."

"Maybe he's eating his supper," Tacy said.

"Maybe he's out horseback riding, like he was when this picture was taken."

"Maybe he's saying his prayers."

"Maybe he's blowing his nose."

"It seems queer to have him blowing his nose," said Tacy, looking displeased.

"Oh, probably he has an embroidered handkerchief," said Betsy. "I imagine he does."

They looked at the picture again.

"Tacy," said Betsy. "Do you know what?"

"What?" asked Tacy.

"I'm in love with him," said Betsy. "It's the first time I've ever been in love."

"Do you want to marry him?" asked Tacy.

"Yes," said Betsy. "I do. Do you?"

"I certainly do," Tacy said.

The games on the street were going full swing now, but neither Betsy nor Tacy cared about joining in. They sat looking at the King of Spain's picture which was gilded by the sunset light.

Just then Tib ran up, breathless.

"My mamma . . ." she began.

"Tib," said Betsy, interrupting. "Did you know there was a king in Europe, not sixteen years old yet?"

"Is there?" asked Tib.

"Here's his picture," said Tacy. "Betsy and I are in love with him."

"We want to marry him," said Betsy. "We'll be queen if we do."

"Could you both be queen?" asked Tib, staring.

"No, just one of us," said Betsy. "And it had better be Tacy because of her ringlets. She'd look nice in a crown."

"Tib would make a nice queen," said Tacy. Tacy

was shy. She didn't like the idea of being a queen very well.

"My mamma," said Tib, "is making me a white accordion-pleated dress. For the Entertainment. To dance my Baby Dance in. I was hurrying to tell you."

"A white accordion-pleated dress would be fine for a queen," said Tacy. "Don't you think Tib had better be queen, Betsy?"

"If she's in love with him," said Betsy.

Tib could see it was a kind of game.

"If you and Tacy are, I am," she said. "Let's play Pom-Pom-Pullaway now. They're choosing sides."

So they all played Pom-Pom-Pullaway until the golden light on Hill Street changed to soft gray and mothers began calling from the porches. Betsy, Tacy, and Tib didn't talk any more that night about the King of Spain. But they talked about him every night for a long time afterward.

The newspapers were full of news of the young King Alphonso as his sixteenth birthday drew near. Every night when her father had finished with the paper, Betsy took it outdoors. She and Tacy and Tib went up to that bench which stood at the end of Hill Street and there they pored over the printed columns together.

Madrid was a whirlpool of gaiety, they read. The

city was planning a Battle of Flowers. The buildings were hung with tapestries and carpets and with red and yellow cloth.

"Red and yellow must be his colors," Betsy remarked thoughtfully.

"We ought to wear them then, like badges," Tacy said. "After all, we're in love with him. We're expecting to marry him. At least, Tib is."

"If we could find some red and yellow cloth, I would make us some badges," Tib said.

Tib could sew.

Betsy and Tacy ran into their houses and rummaged

in their mothers' scrap bags. Betsy found some red cambric and Tacy found some yellow ribbon, and Tib took these materials home. The next evening she appeared wearing a red and yellow rosette, and when they had climbed the hill to their bench she pinned one on Betsy and one on Tacy. They felt very solemn.

"Now we've got a lodge," said Betsy. "My father belongs to a lodge. It's like a club only more important and very secret."

"Well, this has certainly got to be a secret," Tib said. "Julia and Katie would tease us plenty if they knew we were in love."

"They wouldn't understand being in love with a king," said Betsy. "At least Julia wouldn't. She likes just plain boys. Ordinary boys who walk home from school with her and carry her books, like Ben Williams."

"Katie would think the whole thing was silly," Tacy said.

"That just shows how little she knows about it," said Betsy.

Tib acted embarrassed. She wasn't so much in love as Betsy and Tacy were; she just liked to do whatever they did.

"What is the name of our lodge?" she asked, to change the subject.

"How would K.O.S. be? For King of Spain?" suggested Betsy.

They all thought that was fine.

After that, whenever anyone mentioned "Love" or "Marriage" in their presence, Betsy and Tacy and Tib said "K.O.S." They sighed and rolled their eyes. They wore their red and yellow rosettes faithfully, changing them from one dress to another.

What is more, they wore pictures of the King of Spain, cut from the newspapers, pinned to their underwaists. Betsy had the one in which he sat on a horse. Tacy had one that showed him in hunting costume, with a shawl thrown over one shoulder, a wide hat, and a gun. In Tib's picture he wore a white nautical-looking cap. Betsy and Tacy had a hard time concealing their pictures from Julia and Katie when they undressed at night. That made their secret all the more exciting.

They did not join in the games after dinner any more. Instead they walked up to their bench, and there in the cool spring twilight they read about King Alphonso. His birthday now was drawing very near. In fact, it would come next Saturday.

Peasants, the newspapers said, were flocking into Madrid, wearing the picturesque national costume. Great ladies draped in black lace mantillas sat on balconies.

"What are mantillas?" Tib wanted to know.

"They're shawls," answered Betsy, who had asked her mother.

"I think we ought to have some shawls then," said Tib. "But the only shawl my mamma's got is her old paisley shawl."

"My mamma's got that heavy brown one we play house with," Betsy said.

"My mamma's got a gray wool one," Tacy said. "She'd let me wear it, I think. We all ought to wear them next Saturday, the day he's crowned."

Betsy and Tib thought so too.

So on Saturday, the seventeenth of May, they wore shawls all day long except at mealtime. It happened that the weather turned very warm that day. The little leaves on the trees seemed to grow bigger by the minute and dandelions on the fresh green lawn almost popped up while you watched them. All up and down Hill Street children put off caps and jackets. But Betsy and Tacy and Tib went around wrapped up in heavy shawls.

The lilacs had come into bloom by Betsy's kitchen door. They picked a bouquet of fragrant purple clusters. Then they spread a blanket on the lawn and put the bouquet in the middle and they all sat down.

"Whatever are you wearing those shawls for?" asked Julia.

"And those rosettes?" asked Katie.

"K.O.S.," answered Betsy and Tacy, rolling their eyes.

"K.O.S.," answered Tib, trying not to laugh.

Julia and Katie went away.

"This is really a birthday party, isn't it?" asked Tib.

"Yes, it is," said Tacy. "And we ought to have a birthday cake."

"I can't very well ask my mamma for a birthday cake," said Betsy. "But I can ask for cookies and we can pretend they're cake."

That was what they did; and while they munched cookies they tried to imagine what was happening

in Spain where the young Alphonso was ascending his throne.

"The newspapers tomorrow will have it all in," said Tacy from the depths of her shawl.

Tib put out a small perspiring face.

"But we ought to read them together," she said. "On account of our lodge. And we're never together on Sunday."

That was true. They attended different churches, and on Sunday afternoon they often went riding or visiting with their parents.

"Well, let's not look at the newspapers tomorrow," Betsy proposed. "And when our fathers have finished with them, let's save them."

"Then Monday, after school, let's take a picnic up on the Big Hill," suggested Tacy.

"Let's go to that place we went to before, where we can see Little Syria. It's the farthest from home of any place we know. There won't be anybody around to disturb us and Betsy can read the papers out loud," said Tib. "This mantilla's hot," she added.

"If you're going to be Queen of Spain," said Betsy, "you've got to get used to a mantilla. And so have Tacy and I, because we'll be your ladies-in-waiting, I suppose."

"Oh, of course," said Tib.

It was difficult next day not to look at the Sunday

newspapers strewn so invitingly about. But they did not even peek; and when evening came they managed to hide away all the crumpled sheets.

Monday after school, carrying a picnic basket and a fat bundle of papers, they climbed the Big Hill.

They turned right at the Ekstroms' house, calling "hello" to their friend, Mrs. Ekstrom, who was weeding her garden. They went through the Secret Lane and past the Mystery House, down through a fold of the hills and up again. Then, leaving the thick-growing trees behind, they came out on a high rocky ridge just as they had done before.

Tib took the ends of her skirt into her hands. Holding them wide, as she did when she danced her Baby Dance, she ran to the edge of the ridge. Betsy and Tacy followed, and the three of them looked down over their discovered valley.

The hillside was freshly green now. The gardens of the Syrians made dark brown patches behind their little houses. Behind Mr. Meecham's Mansion an apple orchard made a patch of grayish pink. Everywhere wild plums, in dazzling white bloom, were perfuming the air.

"It's just a perfect place," said Betsy, "to read about his birthday."

Tacy and Tib thought so too.

They tucked the picnic basket into a cleft of the rocks behind them. Usually they ate their lunch as soon as they reached the place to which they were going, but today they were too anxious to read about the King of Spain.

Tib perched on a high boulder. Tacy sat down in the flower-sprinkled grass with her knees drawn into her arms. Betsy unfolded the newspapers and spread them on her lap. She leaned against a wall of rock and read:

"'Eight grooms on horseback led the procession. The King rode in the royal coach with his mother, the Queen, and his youngest sister, the Infanta Maria Teresa. He was pale but perfectly cool.'"

"I wish we could have seen him," Tacy interrupted.

She gave a long, romantic sigh and looked at Tib. Taking the hint Tib sighed too.

"'The King ascended the throne,'" read Betsy. "'He bore himself with manliness. Smilingly he acknowledged the ovations of the crowd.'"

"What's 'ovations'?" asked Tib.

"It's cheering and clapping."

"We'd have clapped good and hard if we'd been there," Tacy said. "It's terrible that we weren't there."

Betsy read on: "'He wore a dark blue uniform with gold facings, a steel helmet with a white plume, and a red silk waist-band from which hung a sword.'"

"He must have looked stylish," Tacy said.

"Isn't there a picture?" Tib asked.

"Plenty of them. Here's a picture of the Palace. This is where you'll live, Tib," said Betsy.

"It looks like our post office, only bigger," Tib remarked.

"It's sure to be nice inside," said Tacy. "You'll like living there."

"'Speculation,'" continued Betsy, "'is rife in the capitals of Europe as to whom he will choose as a bride. . . .'" She paused and her gaze ran down the column.

"Don't read to yourself!"

"What is it?"

Betsy did not seem to hear. She gave a small squeak of dismay.

"Oh dear, dear, dear!"

"What *is* it?" cried Tacy and Tib.

"Tib can't marry him after all! None of us can!"

"Why not?"

"Because," wailed Betsy, "we're not of the blood royal."

"What does that mean?" Tib demanded.

"It means we're commoners."

"It means we're not princesses," Tacy explained.

"He can only marry a princess."

"That's the silliest thing I ever heard of," said Tib. "Oh well! It doesn't matter. I'll wear my accordion-pleated dress when I dance my Baby Dance."

Betsy and Tacy looked at each other. Their eyes said, "Isn't that just like Tib?"

"But now we'll never see him!" cried Tacy in a tragic voice.

"Let's go over to Spain anyhow," said Betsy. "Let's be servants in the Palace if we can't be queen."

"You and Tacy wouldn't be any good as servants," said Tib. "You can't cook. I can cook, but I don't think it's worth while to go way over there just to cook."

They sat in a flat silence.

"It doesn't seem right," Tacy burst out, "that he doesn't know a thing about us. He ought to know there are such people as us, and that we have a lodge and wear his colors and pin his pictures to our underwaists."

"He certainly ought," Betsy agreed. An idea popped up in her head like a dandelion on a lawn.

"Let's write him a letter and tell him!"

"Betsy!" cried Tacy. "You wouldn't dare!"

"Do people write letters to kings?" asked Tib.

"If they want to they do. We do," Betsy said.

Tacy's blue eyes began to shine.

"We'd better do it right now," she said, "while Julia and Katie aren't around to catch on what we're doing."

"But we haven't any paper and pencil," said Tib.

"You can run to Mrs. Ekstrom's house and borrow some," said Betsy. "Tacy and I will wait right here."

Tib didn't mind going. She ran lots of errands for Betsy and Tacy. She was off now almost as swiftly as one of the little yellow birds which were flying in and out of the blooming wild plum trees.

When she was gone, Tacy said, "I certainly feel sorry about Tib's not being queen."

"So do I," said Betsy. "It's too bad we're not of the blood royal."

"She'd have made a nice queen," said Tacy, "in that accordion-pleated dress. And I've got kind of interested in queens. I wish we could think up another queen game so that Tib could be queen."

"Maybe we can," said Betsy. "There's a poem about Queen o' the May. Julia's reciting it for the School Entertainment. Maybe we can get an idea out of that."

They talked about it until Tib came back from Mrs. Ekstrom's.

She had a pencil and a tablet of paper, and an envelope too.

"I told Mrs. Ekstrom we were writing a letter. But I didn't say who to," she explained.

She sat down on one side of Betsy and Tacy sat down on the other. Betsy wrote the heading and the salutation just as she had been taught to do in school. Then she started the letter proper and when she couldn't think what to say next Tacy or Tib told her. When the letter was finished, it read like this:

Deep Valley, Minn.
May 19, 1902.

King Alphonso the Thirteenth,
Royal Palace,
Madrid,
Spain,
Europe.

Dear Sir,—

We are three little American girls. Our names are
Betsy, Tacy, and Tib. We are all in love with you and
would like to marry you but we can't, because we're
not of the blood royal. Tib especially would like
to marry you because she has a white accordion-
pleated dress that she's going to wear when she
dances the Baby Dance. She looks just like a
princess. So we're sorry. But we're glad you got to
be king. Three cheers for King Alphonso of Spain.

Yours truly,
Betsy Ray,
Tacy Kelly,
Tib Muller.

"That's a fine letter," said Tib.
"Tomorrow after school," planned Tacy, "we'll
walk to the post office and mail it."

❧ 323 ❧

"We'll have to take some money out of our banks," said Betsy. "It will cost quite a lot of money, I imagine, to send a letter to Spain."

They put the letter into the envelope and sealed it and addressed it to the King in his Palace, Madrid, Spain, Europe.

When they had finished they were suddenly very hungry.

"I'm famished," said Betsy.

"I could eat nails," said Tacy.

"Let's have our picnic," said Tib. And they scrambled over the rocks to that cleft in a big rock where they had left their basket.

But when they reached the cleft they stared with eyes of wonder and dismay.

The picnic basket was gone!

4
Naifi

ETSY, TACY, AND TIB all had the same thought . . . in the same instant too.

"Julia and Katie!"

"They were here! They were listening!"

"They heard us talking about the King of Spain."

It was a dark thought that sent a shadow over the golden afternoon. They looked at one another in horror, thinking how they would be teased. It would sound queer, said out loud in public, that they were in love with the King of Spain.

Tib bounded toward the path.

"Shall we chase them?"

"It wouldn't do any good," said Tacy.

"The sooner we don't see them the better, I think," said Betsy gloomily. "Gee whiz!" she added. Betsy very seldom said "Gee whiz!" She was too religious. But it was all she could think of to express her feelings now.

"Gee whiz!" repeated Tacy. "Gee whitakers!"

"Double darn!" said Betsy.

"We could get our lunch back anyway," said Tib. But neither Betsy nor Tacy paid any attention.

Tib bounced up and down.

"Let's look around," she said. "Maybe it wasn't them at all. Maybe it was a dog. . . ." She broke off in a squeal. "Look! Look! It is a dog, or something."

She dashed down the hill.

Betsy and Tacy ran around the rock. Halfway down the slope, worrying a basket, there was certainly a shaggy creature, the size of a large dog. But it wasn't a dog. It had horns.

"It's a wild animal, a jungle animal most likely," Betsy cried.

"Tib! Come back!" shouted Tacy.

But Tib continued to run headlong.

"It's a goat," she called back. "And he has our basket."

Betsy and Tacy weren't afraid of a goat. Besides, relief that Julia and Katie did not know their secret brought back their appetites. They ran after Tib who ran fiercely after the goat which bounded on small fleet hoofs over the tussocks of grass. The basket came unfastened, and a red and white fringed cloth flew out like a banner. Sandwiches, cookies, and hard-boiled eggs scattered in all directions.

"Oh! Oh! Oh!" panted Betsy and Tacy, pausing to pick them up. Tib did not pause. She chased the goat around some scrub oak trees, behind a clump of the white wild plum. Then. . . .

"Betsy! Tacy! Betsy! Tacy!" came Tib's voice, with something in it which caused Betsy and Tacy to drop the sandwiches again and run to find her.

They found her standing face to face with a little girl so strange that she seemed to have stepped out of one of Betsy's stories. Her dress had a long skirt, like a woman's, very full, made of faded flowered cloth. She wore earrings like a woman's too. A scarf was tied over her head. From a rosy-brown face very bright brown eyes darted from Tib to Betsy and Tacy.

Waving a stick in her hand, she began to talk excitedly. Not Betsy nor Tacy nor Tib could understand a word she said. She ran to the goat which had come to a standstill near by and shook her stick at it. She ran to the basket which he had dropped and then to some sandwiches which lay on the grass and began to pick them up swiftly. When she turned her back, Betsy, Tacy, and Tib could see that her hair hung in long black braids tied in red at the ends. Her shoes were red too, and under her dress she wore bloomers down to her ankles.

All this time she continued to pour forth a torrent of loud, strange words. Betsy, Tacy, and Tib could not understand one of them but they knew what the little girl was trying to say. She was trying to tell them she was sorry that her goat had spilled their basket.

"It doesn't matter," said Betsy.

"We don't care a bit," said Tacy.

"We don't mind sandwiches being a little mussed. We often eat them that way," Tib explained.

The little girl kept right on saying loudly . . . they didn't know what.

She kept on picking up sandwiches and cookies and hard-boiled eggs, and finally Betsy and Tacy and Tib did the same. At last the lunch was restored to the basket, except one sandwich which the goat had gulped.

The goat now was as meek as Grandpa Williams' cow, nibbling the grass and paying no attention to them. The little girl pointed from the goat to the basket and shook her head until her braids swung out.

"She's the excitedest person I ever saw," said Betsy.

"She can't speak any English," Tacy said.

"Or understand it," said Tib.

All three stared at her, and unexpectedly she smiled. She showed white teeth, and dimples flashed in her round rosy-brown face.

"Isn't she darling?" cried Betsy. "Let's invite her to our picnic."

"How can we," asked Tib, "when she can't understand our language?"

"I know," said Tacy.

She shook out the red and white fringed cloth which she had just rescued and spread it on the grass. Betsy and Tacy took sandwiches and cookies and hard-boiled eggs and arranged them invitingly upon it. Then all three sat down, leaving one side of the

cloth empty; and all three pointed from the little girl to the vacant place and back to the little girl again.

"Have a sandwich," said Tib, picking up the cleanest one she could find (it wasn't very clean) and offering it.

The little girl's smile gleamed whiter, her dimples flashed deeper than ever. She shook her head. Reaching into her girdle she brought out a chunk of cheese and a piece of a flat round loaf of bread. She sat down at the vacant place, her wide skirts billowing about her.

They had a picnic.

Betsy and Tacy had started picnicking when they were five years old, and Tib joined them soon after. They were all ten now, and they had had scores of picnics in the years between. But this was the most adventurous, the strangest, the funniest one they had ever had.

Trying to find a way to talk with their visitor, Betsy, Tacy, and Tib pointed to the goat.

"Goat," they said. "Goat. Goat."

The little girl pointed to the goat. She said one word too, and they knew it meant "goat" in her language.

Betsy, Tacy, and Tib pointed to their sandwiches and to the thin loaf the little girl was eating.

"Bread," they said. "Bread. Bread."

The little girl pointed to their bread and hers. She

said, they were sure, her word for bread.

A little yellow bird flew out of the white plum blossoms.

"Bird," said Betsy, Tacy, and Tib. "Bird. Bird."

The little girl said her word for bird. She laughed out loud, and they all laughed. They kept on saying words for a long time.

"Now we'll try something hard," said Betsy. And she jumped up. She pointed to herself. "Betsy," she said.

Tacy jumped up and pointed to *her*self.

"Tacy," she said.

Tib jumped up and pointed to *her*self.

"Tib," she said.

They did this two or three times.

Then the little girl got up. She bobbed a small bow. She pointed to *her*self, and her teeth and dimples flashed.

"Naifi," she said. Perhaps Betsy and Tacy and Tib were getting used to the sound of her strange language, but they understood the word. "Naifi," she repeated. They knew it was her name.

"Hello, Naifi," cried Betsy.

"Hello, Naifi," cried Tacy, clapping her hands.

"Hello, Naifi," cried Tib, jumping up and down.

"Hel-lo?" said the little girl, as though she were asking a question. She repeated the word several times. "Hel-lo? Hel-lo?"

Betsy pointed to herself.

"Say, 'Hello, Betsy.'"

"Say, hel-lo, Bett-see," Naifi said.

Betsy shook her head. She tried again.

"Hello, Betsy," she said, leaving out the "say."

This time Naifi got it right.

"Hel-lo, Bett-see," she repeated.

Tacy pointed to *her*self.

"Hello, Tacy."

"Hel-lo, Ta-cee," Naifi said.

"Hello, Tib," cried Tib.

"Hel-lo, Tib," said Naifi, looking very much pleased with herself.

Betsy and Tacy and Tib shouted, "That's fine!" And "Good for you, Naifi!"

"Hel-lo, hel-lo, hel-lo," said Naifi, as though she were practicing.

They had a lovely time, but at last Naifi sprang up, shaking out her skirts. She pointed to the goat and to the valley, with a stream of her strange, loud words.

"She means she must go home," said Betsy. "And we must too. Goodness! Look at the sun!"

While they were picnicking, the sun had gone halfway down the sky. That meant they must hurry for they were not allowed to stay up on the Big Hill after dark.

Naifi bobbed her little bob, showing her white

teeth and dimples. She picked up her stick and waved it and called to her goat.

"Hel-lo," she called in farewell.

"You mean 'good-by,'" cried Betsy.

"Good-by!" "Good-by!" cried Tacy and Tib.

They stuffed the red and white fringed cloth hurriedly into their basket and started up the hill, talking about Naifi.

"Is she a Syrian?" asked Tib.

"She must be," said Betsy. "She lives in Little Syria."

"She must have just come to America," said Tacy. "The other Syrians all know a little English and they don't dress like that."

"The women wear scarves on their heads when they come selling lace, though," Betsy said.

"Did you see her earrings?"

"And her red shoes?"

"They were beautiful."

"Why doesn't she come to our school, I wonder," Betsy asked.

"The Syrian children go to the Catholic School at the other end of town," Tacy replied.

They turned for a last look at the small gay figure, dimmed now by distance. A shadow lay on the valley. Mr. Meecham's Mansion led the row of little houses like a mother hen leading her chicks . . . safe home at dusk.

"We've got to *hurry*," said Tib. They started climbing again. And presently something drove Naifi out of their minds.

Fluttering down the hill to meet them came a multitude of newspapers. They came like tumbleweed, blowing lightly about in all directions. With a shock Betsy and Tacy and Tib remembered the King of Spain.

Again they all had the same thought in the same instant.

"Our letter!"

"What became of it?"

"What did we do with it when we ran after the goat?"

Nobody remembered. Running up to the rocks, they began to search frantically but they could not find the envelope. Their high ridge had been swept bare by the wind.

"It was all addressed. Maybe someone will find it and mail it," Betsy suggested hopefully.

"It didn't have a stamp on it, though," said Tib. "And you said it cost a lot of money to send a letter to Spain."

"That's right," said Betsy. She stopped still. "Gee whiz!" she said.

"What's the matter?" asked Tacy.

"I hope the wind won't blow that letter where

Julia and Katie can find it."

"We'd certainly never hear the last of it," said Tib.

Again dread like a cloud darkened the day.

It was darkening too from other causes. The sun, already low in the west, had dropped into a cloud-made pocket. The hilltop was windy and cold.

"I've got to get home," said Tib. "I get scolded if I'm not home on time."

"I get a pretty hard talking to," said Betsy.

"So do I," said Tacy.

They ran down the Secret Lane.

Halfway through it, they met Mrs. Ekstrom with an apron thrown over her head.

"I was looking for you," she said. "I was sure I hadn't seen you come past. Don't you know it's time you went home?"

"We're hurrying, Mrs. Ekstrom," Betsy said.

As they jogged down the Big Hill, they talked again about Naifi.

"Let's keep her a secret," Betsy said.

"Let's," said Tacy.

"And let's take the King of Spain's pictures out of our underwaists," said Tib, "as long as I can't be queen."

"You can't be *his* queen, but you're going to be a queen," said Betsy. "Tacy and I are planning it; aren't we, Tacy? Good-by," she panted, as their road met the path which led down to her home.

She raced past the barn and buggy shed where her father was unharnessing Old Mag. She darted among slim young fruit trees which looked chilly now in their pale pink and white finery, and skipped down the brown path dividing the kitchen garden. In the woodshed she paused to catch her breath.

She went into the kitchen softly, hoping that her late return would go unnoticed. As a matter of fact, it did. Her mother was busy, frying potatoes and listening to Julia rehearse the piece she was going to

recite at the School Entertainment.

Julia loved to recite. Her loose dark hair scattered on her shoulders, her face glowing, she went through her piece as though she were standing on a stage. She even made gestures.

Betsy sat down on the edge of a chair and listened. Secretly she admired Julia's reciting. It sent an icy trickle down her spine when Julia recited "Little Orphan Annie" and "The Raggedy Man." This new piece was different; it wasn't scary; but for Betsy it had a special value. Thinking of Tib she listened with pricked ears:

> "You must wake and call me early,
>   call me early, Mother dear,
> Tomorrow'll be the happiest time of all the
>   glad New-year,
> Of all the glad New-year, Mother,
>   the maddest merriest day,
> For I'm to be Queen o' the May, Mother,
>   I'm to be Queen o' the May!"

5
The School Entertainment

BEFORE THE day of the School Entertainment it turned cold again. For a week rains drenched the hills, the terraced lawns, the sloping road of Hill Street. After the rains stopped, the skies were still overcast. It was pleasanter indoors than out and this was just as well, for everyone was busy getting ready for the School Entertainment.

Julia went about murmuring sweetly:

"For I'm to be Queen o' the May, Mother,
I'm to be Queen o' the May."

Julia could hardly wait for the great day. Her feet loved a platform as Betsy's loved a grassy hill. Whether she was playing the piano, singing, or reciting, Julia was happy so long as she had an audience.

She was different in this from Katie who despised performing. For the Entertainment Katie was reciting Lincoln's Gettysburg Address. She knew every word of it; she could be depended upon not to make a single mistake. But she would not put in *expression*, no matter how much the teacher urged or coaxed.

Betsy and Tacy were singing a duet made up entirely of "meows." They were going to wear cat costumes cut from shiny black cambric, with cat ears and tails. Mrs. Ray and Mrs. Kelly were busy making the costumes and Mrs. Ray was busy too rehearsing Betsy and Tacy. They ran into difficulties for Betsy was singing alto. It was altogether too easy for her to slide up into the soprano part and sing along with Tacy.

When she did that, Tacy gave her a nudge which meant, "Get back to your alto!" Betsy's mother sounded the right note hard and Betsy got back to her alto as quickly as she could.

At almost any time or place Tib might practice her Baby Dance. She would pick her skirt up by the edges and run and make a pirouette. This was the opening of her dance. There were five different steps and she did each one thirty-two times . . . a slide, a kick, a double slide, a jump step, and then a Russian step which was done in a squatting position kicking out first one foot and then the other. It was hard but Tib could do it.

Betsy and Tacy had seen her practice her dance on hill, lawn, and sidewalk, but they had not yet seen the accordion-pleated dress.

"It's done," said Tib, the day before the Entertainment. "I'll be wearing it tomorrow when you call for me."

"We'll be there early," Betsy and Tacy said.

And next morning early they stopped at Tib's back door carrying their cat costumes in big cardboard boxes.

They wiped their feet hard on the mat and Matilda let them in. They ran into the back parlor and there stood Tib in her accordion-pleated dress. It was made of fine white organdie trimmed with rows of insertion and lace. A sash of pale blue satin was tied high in princess style. She wore a soft blue bow on her yellow curls.

Mrs. Muller, looking proud, turned her about for Betsy and Tacy to see.

"How do you like it?" she asked.

"It's beautiful," said Betsy.

Tacy only gazed, but with luminous eyes.

Tib lifted her skirt by the edges. She could hold it out wide because of the accordion pleats. She ran and made a pirouette.

"It's fine for my dance," she said, looking pleased.

"You can't put your grubby jacket on over that dress," Mrs. Muller said. "I'll let you wear my cape." And she left the room and came back with her best cape which was made of black lace trimmed with ribbons and rosebuds. "Take good care of it," she said, "and of the dress too. I'll see you at the Entertainment."

Betsy, Tacy, and Tib walked to school proudly. Betsy walked on one side of Tib and Tacy on the other.

The sun had come out in honor of the day. Snowball bushes nodded from the lawns, pansies and tulips in gardens looked festive with the sunshine on them, as though they knew about the Entertainment. The school steps were full of boys and girls looking unusually clean and dressed up. The upper grades were giving the Entertainment in the Seventh Grade Room, which was the largest in the building. But all the rooms were open and ready for visiting mothers.

Betsy, Tacy, and Tib went first into their own Fourth Grade Room. It looked as dressed up as themselves. On Miss Dooley's desk was a bouquet of lady's slippers which one of the boys had brought. Samples of the children's work were pinned up on the walls. There were arithmetic papers and spelling papers, maps, charcoal drawings of cups and saucers, and paintings of oranges and apples.

Miss Dooley looked as dressed up as the room. Instead of her usual shirt waist and skirt, she wore a flowing purple dress with large bell sleeves. Her hair was curled and her face was bright and anxious.

The class stayed in the Fourth Grade Room only long enough for prayer and roll call. Then Miss Dooley's bell tapped.

"Position! Rise! Turn! March!"

Someone was playing a march on the piano out in the hall. The Fourth Graders joined the other grades and they all marched into the Seventh Grade Room.

It was crowded but that made the occasion all the gayer. Children sat double in the seats. Folding chairs had been brought in and mothers sat or stood around the walls. Betsy found her own mother sitting among the others. Betsy glanced at her, trying not to smile, and glanced away quickly, trying to act busy and important. Tacy and Tib were looking at their mothers and trying not to smile, too. All the mothers were dressed up and looked nice.

To open the Entertainment, all the children sang together. They sang "Men of Harlech" and it was fine. Then there was a play, and then Julia gave her recitation. Her recitation was different from other children's recitations; it always was. She did not seem like Julia at all as she stood up in front of the room. She looked frail and wistful, with her long hair full of flowers. She smiled and yet she seemed ready to cry. Her hands moved appealingly. Her voice was like spring rain:

> *"Tomorrow'll be of all the year*
> *the maddest merriest day,*
> *For I'm to be Queen o' the May, Mother,*
> *I'm to be Queen o' the May."*

"That child is certainly going to be an actress," Betsy heard one of the visiting mothers say to another visiting mother.

Betsy felt embarrassed and proud.

Soon after came Katie's turn. Square on her sturdy feet, her face scornful, she rattled without a mistake through the Gettysburg Address. She walked back to her seat and sat down hard. When she had to take bad medicine, Katie knew how to take it.

About that time Betsy and Tacy sneaked out to the cloak room. Betsy's mother came too. While some other children sang songs and spoke pieces and the boy named Tom played a solo on his violin, Betsy and Tacy put on their cat costumes. Mrs. Ray tied perky red bows behind their tall cat ears.

Tom's solo ended and two large black cats jumped out on the stage. Betsy's mother began to play the piano and Betsy and Tacy began to sing:

"Mee-ee-ow! Mee-ee-ee-ow!"

Like a kettle boiling over, the room foamed with laughter.

And the louder the children laughed, the louder Betsy and Tacy made their caterwauls, the more they wiggled their ears and swished their tails. Sometimes Betsy slid up to the soprano and sang along with Tacy, but nobody cared. Tacy forgot to nudge her and Mrs. Ray forgot to pound the right note hard. When the Cat Duet ended, the children clapped and stamped. Mothers wiped tears of laughter from their eyes and Miss Dooley said:

"Betsy and Tacy will have to sing the Cat Duet again for us next year."

And so they did. In fact they sang it every year until they graduated from high school.

At the end of the program, Tib danced the Baby Dance. She ran out on the platform holding the accordion-pleated dress outstretched very wide. When she whirled, she looked like a butterfly. She did the first four steps, thirty-two times each, and when she began the Russian step, the hard one, squatting down and kicking out right and left, the audience began to clap. She went off the stage doing that step and the people clapped so hard that she had to come back to bow, holding the skirt out wide.

"She'll certainly make a good queen," Betsy whispered to Tacy as they clapped tired hands until they could clap no more.

The children marched back to their rooms after that. Mothers came visiting; it was like a big party. When the mothers left, the children returned to their desks briefly. Then Miss Dooley tapped her bell.

"Position! Rise! Turn! March!"

They marched out of the room and down the stairs.

On the front steps Betsy and Tacy took their places on either side of Tib. Still flushed from her dance, her eyes as blue as the soft blue bow which tied her curls, she looked pretty. But the accordion-pleated dress, alas, was covered up by the cape.

"Don't wear your cape home," said Betsy.

"I'll carry it for you," offered Tacy.

"Or I will," said Betsy.

Tib laughed.

"It seems funny to have *you* waiting on *me*," she said. "Usually *I* wait on *you*." It was true, and it was just like Tib to mention it.

Tib didn't feel any different or act any different because she looked so pretty and had danced so well.

"My mamma said I should take good care of this cape," she remarked, slipping it off.

"I'll take good care of it," promised Tacy. She

folded it over her arm. Betsy took the cardboard boxes containing the cat costumes. They all walked proudly down the steps.

They skirted the sandy lot known as the boys' yard. At the corner where it met the street a crowd of boys had gathered. Although they were dressed in their best clothes, they were acting very badly. They were bouncing in a circle, yelling.

"They're teasing somebody," said Betsy.

"Mean things!" said Tacy.

"I wonder who," said Tib.

Coming nearer they could hear what the boys were yelling. It was a singsong:

"Dago! Dago!"

"That's what they yell at the people from Little Syria sometimes," said Tib.

"They yell it at Old Bushara and he chases them with a knife."

"Maybe it's Old Bushara in there now."

"Let's look! I've never seen him."

None of them had. They pushed into the crowd.

The victim they discovered was not Old Bushara. It was a little girl, a lone little girl, looking fearfully from face to face around the cruel circle. She wore a scarf tied closely around her rosy face, a wide long flowered skirt. . . .

"It's Naifi," cried Betsy and Tacy and Tib in one horrified breath.

Naifi saw them; she recognized them. Her eyes widened with hope.

"Hel-lo, hel-lo, hel-lo," she cried in agonized appeal.

Someone began to mimic her.

"Hel-lo, hel-lo."

"Oh dear!" cried Betsy, tears clouding her eyes.

The boy named Sam who had been chased by Old Bushara jumped out of the circle. He was in Fourth Grade along with Betsy, Tacy, and Tib, but he was old enough to be in Seventh. He was big and rough. He snatched the scarf from Naifi's head and waved it. He pulled her long black braids.

Tacy struggled forward. She was shy but she wasn't shy enough to keep still now.

"You stop that!" she cried.

No one paid any attention to Tacy, except one boy who shouted, "Red-headed woodpecker!" because of her red curls.

Like a small shining comet Tib flashed into the ring.

"You let her go! You let her *be*!" she cried, pushing herself between Sam and Naifi. Sam pushed her back.

There was a singing sound. The accordion-pleated

dress ripped smartly in his hand.

There was a scuffle then. Heedless of her dress, Tib pushed Naifi through a break in the circle. Tacy ran to help; someone pulled her back; and Mrs. Muller's cape fell to the ground. Betsy couldn't let Tacy and Tib be so much braver than she was. She fought her way forward but she dropped the cardboard boxes. The two cat costumes, red ribbons and all, tumbled out.

With a shout Sam picked them up. Maybe he thought it would be fun to put on a cat costume. Maybe he was ashamed of himself and wanted an excuse to stop teasing Naifi. Certainly some of the other boys seemed ashamed.

Betsy, Tacy, and Tib surrounded Naifi and pushed her to the sidewalk.

"Run!" they whispered.

With one deep look of thankfulness, Naifi ran. A flash of blue bloomers, a gleam of red shoes, and she was gone.

Sam and another boy had put on the cat costumes. "Mee-ow! Mee-ow!" they cried, prancing about.

A third boy was strutting up and down in Tib's mother's cape. Tib looked from that to her torn dress and her face went from red to white.

Betsy and Tacy started to cry, but they remembered they were ten years old and didn't. It was hard not to, though. And just at that moment who should come running but Julia and Katie. Big sisters arrive handily sometimes.

"You leave my little sister alone!" Betsy heard Julia shouting.

"Give me those costumes and that cape and be quick about it!" Katie said.

Everyone always minded Katie . . . even big boys . . . even Sam. Sam threw down the cat costumes and another boy tossed Tib's mother's cape into the air and ran. They all ran except a few of the boys who had looked ashamed. These helped to pick up the black costumes, the red ribbons, and the cape. Then they ran, too.

When they were alone, Betsy, Tacy, and Tib told Julia and Katie what had happened. But they did not tell them that they knew Naifi. Upset as they were, they remembered to guard their secret.

Katie shook out Tib's mother's cape.

"It looks as good as ever," she said.

"And we'll go home with you, Tib," said Julia, "to explain about your dress."

"I wish you would," said Tib.

She looked forlorn with her blue hair ribbon missing, her sash untied, and the torn skirt dragging on the ground.

Julia and Katie, Betsy, Tacy, and Tib walked

slowly to the chocolate-colored house.

Julia explained the whole thing to Mrs. Muller. She talked her prettiest, almost as though she were reciting; and she made Mrs. Muller understand.

"It's all right," said Mrs. Muller. "I'm glad Tib stood up for the little Syrian girl. Foreign people should not be treated like that. America is made up of foreign people. Both of Tib's grandmothers came from the other side. Perhaps when they got off the boat they looked a little strange too."

Tib looked at Betsy and Tacy. She breathed a long sigh of relief.

"But my dress, Mamma!" she said. "Can it be mended?"

"Certainly it can be mended," Mrs. Muller answered.

"You'll have it to be queen in," Betsy and Tacy whispered.

For as soon as school was over, they intended to plan that game in which Tib would be queen.

6

A Quarrel

HE QUEEN GAME had an unexpected result. It led to a quarrel with Julia and Katie. Not an ordinary quarrel. Not one of the kind which arose all the time from Julia and Katie being bossy and Betsy and Tacy and Tib making nuisances of themselves. Those quarrels didn't amount to much. They were always made up at bedtime with a pillow fight or a peace offering. Once when Julia had been mean, she bought Betsy a candy fried egg in a little tin pan . . . one cent at Mrs. Chubbock's store . . . to show she was sorry.

This quarrel was different. It lasted for days. Their fathers and mothers knew about it; the whole neighborhood knew about it. And while it was exciting at first, it made Julia and Katie and Betsy and Tacy and Tib all feel bad before it was ended. Julia and Katie were good big sisters, as big sisters go, and Betsy and Tacy were no more exasperating than other little sisters. Everyone liked Tib, and Tib despised quarrels. Yet Tib was the very center of this bitter feud.

The plan for a queen game lagged, after school ended. Betsy, Tacy, and Tib were busy enjoying not having to go to school. They climbed hills and trees, ate picnics, lay on green lawns and talked.

But they did not forget about queens. They could not. For Julia kept reminding them.

Julia kept on reciting:

> "For I'm to be Queen o' the May, Mother,
> I'm to be Queen o' the May."

She recited it at the school picnic; she recited it for the High Fly Whist Club to which her father and mother belonged; she recited it for the Masons and the Eastern Stars; she recited it for all the neighbors. Julia was a great reciter.

Betsy, Tacy, and Tib had queens on their minds, all right. But they did not do much about their plan for making Tib a queen, until they were jolted into it by Julia and Katie.

For several days Julia and Katie had been whispering together. And one hot noon at dinnertime, Julia asked permission to go down to Front Street with Katie. After dinner she shook all the pennies out of her pig bank, put on her hat, and borrowed her mother's parasol. She and Katie started down Hill Street looking superior.

"They've got something up their sleeves," Betsy and Tacy agreed as they sat with Tib beside Tacy's pump, washing carrots and eating them. The carrots were small and tender; they came from Tacy's garden. Washed in the cold well water, they made refreshing eating.

"Let's think up something ourselves," suggested Tacy. "What about that queen business . . . you know . . . making Tib queen of something?"

"That's just the thing," said Betsy.

"But what can I be queen of?" asked Tib. "I can't be queen of the May because it isn't May any more."

"Minnesota is too cold for May queens anyhow,"

said Tacy. "Look how cold it was last month."

"You can be a June queen," said Betsy. "I'll find out how they make May queens, and then we'll do just the same things only we'll do them in June. I'll go ask Mamma about May queens now," she added, jumping up. She ran across the street to her home.

It was a good time to talk to her mother. Not only because Julia was out of the house, but because her mother was not busy. Mrs. Ray did her house work in the morning. After dinner she took a little rest, and after that she put on a fresh dress and sat down in the parlor. Sometimes ladies came to call.

No lady was calling today. Mrs. Ray rocked near a window from which she could look down Hill Street. She was keeping cool and embroidering the head of a Gibson Girl upon a pillow when Betsy burst into the room.

"Mamma," said Betsy. "Tell me about May queens." Mrs. Ray laughed.

"Queens! Queens! Queens!" she said.

Betsy thought that was a strange remark, but she persisted.

"How do people happen to have May queens?" she asked. "What do they do when they have them?"

"It's an English custom," answered Mrs. Ray, working her needle skillfully in and out of the Gibson Girl's hair. "On May Day people used to go to the wood and bring back flowers. They called it 'going a Maying.' Then they put up a Maypole with garlands running from the top and danced around it. And they chose a pretty girl and crowned her with a wreath of flowers."

It sounded enchanting!

"I suppose," said Betsy eagerly, "people could 'go a Juning' and then crown a Queen of June."

"Of course they could," answered Mrs. Ray. "But I *believe* that Julia and Katie have decided on a Queen of Summer."

Betsy jumped as though the needle in her mother's hand had pricked her.

"Haven't they?" asked Mrs. Ray, looking up.

Betsy did not answer. She stared at her mother with horrified eyes.

Mrs. Ray put down her needle. She looked worried.

"You knew what they were planning, didn't you?" she asked. "If you didn't, I'm sorry. But you'd have known soon anyway. Julia is going to be queen. Katie and Dorothy and some of the rest of their friends are going to be maids of honor. And you and Tacy and Tib and Margaret are all going to be in it."

"We are, are we!" muttered Betsy.

"Tacy and I," she burst out, "are planning the same thing. We've been planning it for weeks and weeks. Only we're going to have Tib for our queen."

She jumped up, blazing. "Julia and Katie must have found out about it somehow. They're just copycats, that's what they are."

"I'm sure they're not," answered Mrs. Ray. "It all came from Julia's saying, 'I'm to be Queen o' the May' so much. She got the idea . . . or Katie did . . . that she ought to be queen of something."

She looked reprovingly at Betsy's dark face.

"I don't see why you feel so badly about it," she said. "Julia and Katie are spending all their money to buy crepe paper and ribbons. You can all go in together and have a fine celebration."

Betsy did not answer. After looking blankly in her mother's face she rushed out of the room. She bounded over terrace, road, and lawn.

"Tacy! Tib! Tacy! Tib!" she shouted wildly.

Tacy and Tib, who had been lying on their backs munching carrots, shot upright.

"I know something awful! Terrible!" Betsy cried. "Julia and Katie are planning a queen."

"A queen!"

"And Julia is going to be it!"

"The copycats!" cried Tacy. "However did they find out our idea?"

"I don't know. But they've gone downtown to buy crepe paper and ribbons. They're going to have a Maypole and Dorothy and the rest of the big girls are going to help them."

"We'll make ours just as nice," said Tacy stoutly. But in their hearts they doubted that they could. Big girls knew how to put on such shows better than younger girls did.

Their dismay was mixed with chagrin. They had had the idea of a queen for weeks and weeks. But they had not done anything about it. And while they were dawdling, Julia and Katie had made this lovely plan. They had even taken money from their banks and gone downtown to buy crepe paper.

"They're planning to let us do some little thing," said Betsy bitterly, "along with Margaret and Paul and the rest of the babies."

"That's kind of them," said Tacy.

Tib looked from one to the other.

"Why not let Julia be queen if she wants to be?" she asked.

That was just like Tib! Betsy and Tacy would have none of such weakness.

"Has Julia got yellow hair?" demanded Betsy.

"Or an accordion-pleated dress?" Tacy wanted to know.

"Did she almost marry the King of Spain?" asked Betsy.

"No, sir," said Tacy. "You're the right one for queen."

Tib was silenced.

"We won't give in to those old copycats!" cried Betsy. And jumping up, she began to pump herself some water angrily. She made up a song as she pumped.

> "*Copycats, copycats,*
> *Having a queen,*
> *Copycats, copycats,*
> *Just to be mean.*"

Tacy and Tib learned it and sang it with her. And the louder they sang, the angrier they grew. The warmer they grew too, and that helped to make them angrier. Even in the shade by the pump, bare legged and bare footed, they were very hot.

Julia and Katie looked extremely hot when they came toiling up Hill Street, laden with packages, under Betsy's mother's parasol. Betsy, Tacy, and Tib ran to meet them, singing at the tops of their voices:

> "Copycats, copycats,
> Having a queen,
> Copycats, copycats,
> Just to be mean."

"What under the sun are you yelling about?" asked Julia and Katie.

Betsy, Tacy, and Tib danced around them wrathfully.

"You know perfectly well what!"

"Tib's going to be queen!"

"Tib! Tib! Tib! And nobody can stop her!"

Julia and Katie looked at each other; they shook their heads sadly.

"Well, talk about copycats!" said Julia. "Getting up a queen just because we're getting up a queen."

"We thought of it first!" shrieked Betsy, Tacy, and Tib.

"We've been planning it," said Katie, speaking slowly and reasonably, "ever since Julia began reciting her piece."

"So have we! So have we!"

Julia and Katie looked at each other again. Their eyes seemed to ask, "Is that likely?"

This time Julia spoke, using that tone of gentle patience which Betsy, Tacy, and Tib found particularly maddening.

"We were going to ask you in, you know. Just as soon as we got things planned. We were going to ask you to be flower girls."

Flower girls! That was the last straw.

In a rage Betsy snatched at the long roll of crepe paper under Julia's arm. She shouldn't have done it, but she did. Julia pushed her back, and Tacy snatched at Julia. Katie snatched at Tacy; and Tib, head first, butted in.

Margaret and Paul and the Rivers children came running. Mrs. Kelly and Mrs. Ray appeared on their porches. And just then Betsy's father came driving up the street. He said, "Whoa!" to Old Mag and stopped the buggy.

"See here! What's up?" he asked.

Betsy was crying and Julia was waving torn paper. Katie was boxing Tacy's ears, and Tib, very red in the face, was jumping up and down.

Mr. Ray wound the lines around the whip. He got out of the buggy and Old Mag found her own way up the little driveway that led to her barn.

Gripping Julia in one hand and Betsy in the other, Mr. Ray asked, "What's the matter?"

"Queen! Queen! Queen!" was all he could make out of their jumbled answers.

"Come along, all of you," he said; and, followed by the other children, he and Julia and Betsy went up to the front porch. He sat down there and loosened his collar. Mrs. Ray brought him some ice water.

"It's the most awful misunderstanding," she said.

"I'll clear it up," said Mr. Ray and he took a long

drink of the ice water. "Now," he said. "What's it all about?"

Both sides told their stories.

Julia spoke last and she was near to weeping.

"Ordinarily," she said, "Katie and I would give in. We always do. But we've asked Dorothy and some other girls. What would they think? And we've spent all our money for crepe paper."

"Which maybe is spoiled," muttered Katie.

Betsy could see from her father's expression that this was a telling point.

"Well, Tacy and Tib and I can't give in," she wailed.

"We've been planning this since May seventeenth."

"May seventeenth?" asked Mr. Ray. "Why May seventeenth?"

"It just was May seventeenth," Betsy replied.

"Yes it was, Mr. Ray," Tacy and Tib added.

That was a good point too, remembering the day.

Mr. Ray thought for a long time. Mrs. Ray stood in the doorway looking worried, and there was a smell of biscuits baking. (For shortcake, probably.)

"It seems clear," said Mr. Ray at last, "that each side thinks his side is right."

Mrs. Ray nodded.

"And certainly," he continued, "there must be just one queen. Rival queens would never do."

He paused while the children stood in silence and Mrs. Ray waited in the doorway.

"I have it," he said. "We'll settle this in the good old American way."

"How?" all the children asked together.

"By the vote. By the ballot," answered Mr. Ray.

"But Papa," said Julia. "That wouldn't do. Katie and I would vote for me, and Betsy and Tacy and Tib would vote for Tib."

"Let your friends vote," answered Mr. Ray. "Let the neighborhood vote."

He warmed to his idea.

"Take two sheets of foolscap," he went on, while

sniffs lessened and eyes brightened. "At the top of one write, 'We, the undersigned, want Tib Muller for queen.' And at the top of the other one write, 'We, the undersigned, want Julia Ray for queen.' Then tomorrow morning go out after votes. Take your papers up and down Hill Street. And may the best man win!"

It was a wonderful idea.

"Of course," said Mr. Ray, "you must be good sports. You must all agree to abide by the result of the vote. If Tib wins, Julia and Katie must pitch in and make a success of her coronation. And if Julia wins, Betsy and Tacy and Tib must be her loyal subjects. All right?" he asked.

"All right," everyone agreed.

"It's settled then," said Mr. Ray. He got to his feet. "Old Mag wants her supper and I do too."

"You're a perfect Solomon," said Mrs. Ray.

Katie and Tacy ran across the street and Tib skipped down Hill Street and home. Julia and Betsy and Margaret went into the house for supper, and there was strawberry shortcake.

At bedtime Mrs. Ray suggested to Betsy that she tell Julia she was sorry she had torn the crepe paper. Betsy told her, and Julia said it was perfectly all right.

Everyone thought that the quarrel was over. But it wasn't, somehow.

7
Out for Votes

ON THE RAYS' hitching block next morning Betsy, Tacy, and Tib made out their petition. They printed at the top of a piece of foolscap:

"We, the undersigned, want Tib Muller for queen."

Across the street, on the Kellys' hitching block, Julia and Katie were printing on a sheet of foolscap too. Margaret and the Rivers children ran from group to group. Paul waited on the Kellys' porch with the dinner bell in his hand.

Katie called across the street, "Are families allowed to sign?"

"No! No!" whispered Tacy, nudging Betsy to remind her that Julia and Katie were on the Kelly side of the street; they could get to the Kelly house first and there were lots of people in the Kelly family.

"No," called Betsy. "Of course not." She and Tacy and Tib had finished. They jumped to their feet.

"No fair starting 'til the signal!" warned Julia. It had been agreed in advance that no one was to begin until Paul rang the dinner bell.

Betsy, Tacy, and Tib rocked impatiently on their toes; Julia and Katie jumped up.

"Ready?" cried Paul. "One, two, three, go!"

He rang the bell vigorously, and the race for votes was on.

With excited whoops both sides started running down the sloping sun-dappled street. Julia and Katie ran on the Kellys' side; Betsy, Tacy, and Tib, on the Rays' side.

Betsy, Tacy, and Tib paused to sign up the oldest Rivers child. She hadn't started to school yet but she could print her name. They ran into the Riverses' house and Mrs. Rivers signed. They ran down the terrace to the next house.

In that house lived a deaf and dumb family. That is, the father and mother were deaf and dumb. The baby cried as loudly as any other baby. Their name was Hunt. Mrs. Hunt had taught Betsy and Tacy the alphabet in sign language. So they asked her in sign language to vote for Tib for queen. They showed her the petition too, and pointed to Tib and said, "Vote!" Mrs. Hunt smiled and wrote her name.

Betsy, Tacy, and Tib bounded down the terrace to the Williamses' blue frame house. They called there sometimes to borrow the Horatio Alger books. These belonged to Ben who walked home from school with Julia. His sister, Miss Williams, was Julia's music teacher.

Ben said that he was too busy to vote. He looked cross. Miss Williams wouldn't sign either. She exclaimed, "Why, Julia has been planning for weeks on being the queen!" Mrs. Williams signed though, and Grandpa Williams signed. So they came out even.

Across the street Julia and Katie could be seen at Mrs. Benson's door.

"She won't sign, I'll bet. She'll wait for us," said Tacy as she and Betsy and Tib leaped down another terrace to the Grangers' house.

This was a neat light tan house with brown trimmings. No children lived there; the Granger daughters were grown-up. But Betsy and Tacy knew the house well, for here they often borrowed *Little Women*. They had borrowed it almost to tatters.

Mrs. Granger signed and so did the woman in the house below. She had two small children . . . not old enough to print their names.

In the last house of the block lived a family with many children. All of them signed.

Betsy, Tacy, and Tib paused, panting and triumphant. Julia and Katie emerged from the last house in the block on their side and ran into the vacant lot which led to Pleasant Street.

Here both parties sighted the familiar stocky figure of Mr. Goode, the postman.

Mr. Goode had been bringing the mail to Hill Street for years. He was the children's friend. Julia and Katie, Betsy, Tacy, and Tib ran toward him as though running for a prize. They all fell upon him at once.

Mr. Goode read both petitions.

"I'll sign both or none," he said. So they let him sign both. But when he had passed on up Hill Street they decided not to let anyone else sign both petitions.

"It would mix things up," Katie explained. "We wouldn't know at the end who had won."

Betsy and Tacy and Tib agreed.

"Ta, ta," said Julia and Katie, and they cut through

the vacant lot to Pleasant Street. One of their best friends lived on Pleasant Street. She was the Dorothy whom they had included in their plans for a queen celebration. Her father and mother played with Betsy's father and mother in the High Fly Whist Club.

Julia and Katie were certainly heading for her house.

"Let's fool them," said Betsy. "Let's us go to Pleasant Street too. We'll go the other way."

So they raced back up Hill Street and went to Pleasant Street by the road which led down the Big Hill past Tacy's house. At that corner lived the little girl named Alice. She was an earnest little girl with fat yellow braids.

"I'll come along and help," she said.

"Come along," said Betsy, Tacy, and Tib.

They started down Pleasant Street with Alice.

And, just as they had expected, they found Julia and Katie at Dorothy's door.

"Ya, ya! Fooled you!" yelled Betsy, Tacy, and Tib.

"Copycats!" yelled Julia and Katie.

"Copycats!" echoed Dorothy. She was one of the little girls' favorite big girls, with brown curls and eyes and a very sweet voice. But she was their enemy now.

They were all having fun, though.

"How many votes have you got?" yelled Betsy.

"Show us your list and we'll show you ours," yelled Julia and Katie.

They met in the middle of the road and compared lists. Julia had fifteen votes for queen, but Tib had sixteen.

"It's certainly close," said Alice.

The two parties separated and ran from door to door.

They both rushed at the baker's boy when they saw him coming out of a house with his tray full of jelly rolls and doughnuts. He was a fat boy with red cheeks; they knew him well.

Like the postman he wanted to sign both lists.
But they wouldn't allow it.

He looked from Julia with her loose brown hair
on her shoulders to Tib with her crown of yellow
curls.

"By golly!" he said. "This is fierce!"

After a moment he signed Julia's list.

"But I'll give you a doughnut," he said to Tib.

She divided it with Betsy, Tacy, and Alice.

The two parties made rushes also at the grocer's
boy, the butcher's boy, the iceman, and the milkman. Up and down Pleasant Street they went. They
were amazed when the whistles blew loudly for
noon. They ran home in great good humor and
Julia and Betsy told their adventures at the dinner
table.

Mr. Ray winked at Mrs. Ray.

"See!" his wink seemed to say, "I straightened
everything out!"

"You must be almost ready to stop and count
votes," he said.

"Oh no, Papa!" cried Betsy.

"But you must have called on everyone you
know?"

"Why, Papa!" said Julia. "We haven't been to
School Street yet. Some of my best friends live on
School Street."

"Well, I don't want you to go too far away," said Mrs. Ray. "How far do you think they should be allowed to go, Bob?"

"Not beyond Lincoln Park," said Mr. Ray.

Lincoln Park was a pie-shaped wedge of lawn with a giant elm tree and a fountain on it. Hill Street turned into Broad Street there. It was the end of the neighborhood.

"Lincoln Park, then," said Mrs. Ray. "But before you start out, I want you to wash and wipe the dishes. I have to frost the cake I'm sending to the Ice Cream Social."

Julia's eyes widened.

"Where is the Social, Mamma?"

"It's on the Humphreys' lawn," said Mrs. Ray. "They're raising money for the Ladies Aid."

She had made a layer cake with lemon filling, and she frosted it with thick white frosting while Julia and Betsy washed the dishes. By the time they were finished, Katie and Tacy and Tib were yoo-hooing from the hitching block.

The two parties started out again.

Unlike Julia and Katie, Betsy, Tacy, and Tib had no friends on School Street, but they went there just the same. They wanted to keep Julia and Katie in sight. They could see them, on the opposite side of the street, running busily from house to house.

Betsy, Tacy, and Tib went from house to house too. And this was a different business from calling at the houses on Hill Street. It was fascinating, delicious, to knock at the doors of houses whose outsides they had known for years but whose insides were unknown and mysterious.

There was the red brick house with limestone trimmings where they had always imagined very wealthy people lived; there was the house with pebbles·set in plaster above the door; the house with an iron deer on the lawn; the house where bleeding hearts grew in the spring.

Some of these houses they had always loved; some they had almost feared. They had never expected such luck as to see inside them all. Opening doors gave glimpses of strange faces, of banisters leading mysteriously upstairs, of an organ, of a hired girl in a cap.

A few ladies slammed doors or said they were busy, but most of them signed the paper, voting for Tib. One told the children to wait and brought cookies. Another, a plump young woman, said she had just made fudge; she gave them some.

"I like going out for votes," said Tib, happily eating her fudge.

They were enjoying themselves so much that they did not notice when Julia and Katie dropped out of sight. But all at once they realized that their rivals were nowhere to be seen.

"They've cut through lots somewhere," said Betsy.

"They've lost us on purpose, I'll bet," Tacy said. "Where do you suppose they've gone?"

"I don't know," said Betsy. "But I think we'd better go around this corner and keep on as far as Lincoln Park."

That was what they did. But now the ladies in the houses at which they called said that Julia and Katie had been there.

"May we sign your list too?" they asked.

"No, ma'am. We have an agreement."

They were growing warm. They were a little tired too, and more than a little dirty.

Lincoln Park came into sight, cool and green under its elm, the waters of its fountain sparkling.

"Let's stop and rest before we go home," said Betsy.

"Look there!" Tib cried. "What's going on at the Humphreys' house?"

"It must be a wedding or a funeral," said Tacy.

Betsy remembered.

"It's the Ice Cream Social. They're raising money for the Ladies Aid. Mamma baked a cake for them."

They stared at the Humphreys' house, a large yellow stone house that overlooked the Park. The road before it was crowded with carriages and the lawn was crowded with tables. Ladies in light summer dresses trailed over the grass.

"It looks pretty," said Betsy.

"I wish we had money to buy some ice cream," said Tacy.

It was Tib this time who had an idea.

"We could get votes there," she said. "Lots and lots of votes. Enough to win."

Betsy and Tacy paid her idea the tribute of enraptured silence.

"Just pass the paper around," Tib explained, thinking that they did not understand.

"Tib!" cried Betsy then. "That's a wonderful plan!"

"Julia and Katie will be frantic," Tacy cried.

"You're the one to do it, Tib," said Betsy. "You're so little and cute."

"I'm dirty though," said Tib. And she certainly was. There was chocolate on her face, chocolate on her hands, and chocolate on the front of her dress.

"We'll go over to the Park," said Betsy, "and you can wash up in the fountain."

They ran across the street to Lincoln Park, and Tib washed her face and hands in the fountain. Betsy and Tacy picked a bouquet of clovers and pinned it over the chocolate spot on the front of her dress.

"Now," they said. "You look fine."

Tib took the paper and pencil and ran lightly across to the Social.

She was pleased to be going. People made a fuss over Tib because she was little and cute. She wasn't conceited about it but she liked it. She was certain now, and so were Betsy and Tacy, that she would come back with the signature of every single person at the Social.

Betsy and Tacy lay down beneath the elm. They stretched their tired bodies on the turf and gazed into the remote green branches. They did not speak, but they shared a great content.

This was shattered almost immediately and most unexpectedly by Tib's return. She arrived at a run, very red of face.

"You come with me!" she said. "Just come with me!"

Betsy and Tacy jumped to their feet and followed her back across the street.

"Look there!" said Tib, pointing to the Humphreys' lawn.

They followed her indignant finger.

A nearby table was covered with a snowy cloth. There was a big bouquet of roses in the center. Sitting at the table looking very grown-up, eating ice cream and helping themselves freely to cake, were Julia and Katie.

Their paper and pencil lay on the table between them.

Catching sight of Betsy, Tacy, and Tib, Julia lifted the paper and waved it.

"Don't bother to come in," she said. "We've got all the names."

"And Mrs. Humphreys just insisted," said Katie, "that we have some ice cream."

"Oh! Oh! Oh!" cried Betsy, Tacy, and Tib. They rushed furiously away.

They did not return to the Park. That cool greenness did not suit their rising temper. They began the long hot plod up Hill Street, raging.

"That's why they ducked us."

"I knew they were trying to."

"Julia asked Mamma this noon where the Social was going to be held."

"She was planning it then."

"It's the meanest thing I ever heard of."

"Of course," said Tib, "we were going to do the same thing ourselves."

Betsy and Tacy closed their ears to that remark. (It was just like Tib to make it.)

"They must have gotten a hundred names," said Betsy.

"We can never, never, never catch up."

"Gee whiz! Gee whitakers! We've got to."

"But there aren't any more names to get. We can't go beyond Lincoln Park," Tib reminded.

This time Betsy had the idea. She stopped still, planting her feet hard.

"We can't go beyond Lincoln Park," she said. "All right! We'll turn around and go back. And we'll just keep on going."

"But Betsy," said Tib. "There's no sense in that. We'll come to the hills."

"And we'll just keep on going," Betsy repeated.

Tacy did not speak at once. Her eyes began to sparkle.

Tib tried to puzzle it out.

"Of course there's the Ekstroms' house, up on the Big Hill. But there wouldn't be many votes there."

"You mean we should go to Little Syria!" said Tacy.

"Little Syria?" cried Tib.

Betsy nodded, her face tight with glee.

"I've always wanted to go there," Tib cried joyfully. "I'm not afraid of Old Bushara."

"We'll see Naifi too."

"And think of the votes! I'll bet there are more votes in Little Syria than there are at any old Ice Cream Social."

"It will serve Julia and Katie just right."

"We'll have to keep it a secret from them that we're going though."

"We'd better keep it a secret from everybody," said Betsy. "Of course we've never been forbidden to go. But then, nobody ever thought we *would* go."

"We'd better just go," said Tib. "Tomorrow morning! Take a picnic!"

They walked briskly, smiling, up Hill Street.

That night at supper Mr. Ray asked who was ahead in the queen-race.

"Julia, I think," said Betsy, as though it didn't matter much.

"Are you ready to count votes and decide?" asked Mr. Ray.

"Not quite," said Betsy. "But Julia's certainly ahead. She's got a big long list."

Mr. Ray looked at Mrs. Ray proudly. His lips formed the words, "Good sport!"

Julia looked at Betsy sharply. Betsy's face was innocently bright.

8

Little Syria

WHEN BETSY, TACY, AND TIB started out next morning, Julia and Katie were sitting on the Rays' side lawn making streamers. It was a shining morning. The rose bush under the dining-room window was covered with yellow roses which gave out a spicy smell. Julia and Katie were having a good time, twisting pink and green paper and making plans for Julia's coronation. They were very good natured for they were sure that Julia had won.

"Going for a picnic?" Julia called kindly as Betsy, Tacy, and Tib went past with their basket.

"Might as well," Betsy answered, trying to sound glum.

"You can get the Ekstroms' votes while you're up on the Big Hill," reminded Katie.

"That's so," Tacy replied.

"Try to make your backs look discouraged!" Betsy whispered. And she and Tacy and Tib all let their shoulders sag. Tib gave a loud sniff as though she were crying. Tacy put her arm around Tib's shoulder.

Julia and Katie looked after the three forlorn figures, and suspicion arose in their faces.

"They're up to something," Katie said firmly.

"Never mind," said Julia. "They couldn't get enough votes. Nobody lives up on the Big Hill except the Ekstroms."

"That's right," Katie said.

She and Julia went back to twisting streamers.

Betsy, Tacy, and Tib trudged on up the hill.

Their backs drooped in sadness, but their faces were wide with smiles.

"They'll be plenty surprised when we come

home," said Tacy as they climbed past the ridge where wild roses were in bloom. The air was freshly sweet with the smell of these blossoms. Flat, pink and golden-centered they clambered everywhere.

The grass was full of country cousins of the flowers down in Hill Street gardens. There were wild geraniums and wild sweet peas and wild morning glories. Betsy, Tacy, and Tib picked bouquets and gave them to Mrs. Ekstrom when they offered her their petition.

Mrs. Ekstrom put on her spectacles to read it.

"Queens, eh?" she said. "How do you get so interested in kings and queens? I thought we left kings and queens behind in the old country."

But in spite of her teasing, she signed her name. She signed it with pen and ink.

Betsy, Tacy, and Tib went on, through the shadowy Secret Lane, past the Mystery House, down through a fold in the hills and up again. They came out as usual on the high rocky point which overlooked the now familiar valley.

They felt as though it belonged to them, this wide green hammock stretching from sky to sky. They gazed on it with pride for never had it looked so lovely as it looked now clothed in summer green. Thickly leaved trees almost concealed Mr. Meecham's Mansion and the row of little houses. But the rooftops were visible.

Tib counted them.

"There are thirteen," she said. "Is our paper long enough, Betsy, for all the names we'll get?"

"I brought an extra sheet," said Betsy. "Just to be sure."

They ate their picnic quickly, tucked their petition and pencil into the empty basket, and started down the slope.

They descended boldly, yet with fast-beating hearts. Well they knew they were not supposed to be going to Little Syria, alone, on foot! They passed the clump of wild plum trees where they had picnicked with Naifi and looked about for the goat, but it was nowhere to be seen.

"I'm glad Naifi lives there," said Tacy. It was good to think of a friend awaiting them in the strange place to which they were going.

"I wonder whether she's learned to speak English yet," said Tib.

"Probably a little by this time," said Betsy. "Papa says it's wonderful how the Syrians get ahead."

Their feet were now on the path leading down to the settlement. It was just a row of small houses facing that eastern hill which Betsy, Tacy, and Tib were cautiously descending. They were ramshackle houses, much in need of paint. Here were no well-tended lawns or flower gardens as on Hill Street.

Just sun-baked dirt yards, and morning glories twining over a few of the porches.

There were vegetable gardens, however. People were working in them, and their voices rose, loud and harsh, speaking in a foreign tongue.

"I wonder which house Old Bushara lives in," said Tacy nervously.

"Let's go first to Mr. Meecham's. He can speak English," Betsy said.

They left the path and walked along the hillside parallel to the street. Mr. Meecham's Mansion faced west, so they came upon it from the rear.

It did not look hospitable. The buildings and grounds were enclosed in a high iron fence with spikes along the top. Moreover it was studded with signs which said bluntly, "No trespassing!" "Keep out!"

The fence was freshly painted and in excellent repair. Inside it, however, everything looked shabby and untidy. The big white barn with lightning rod atop, the carriage house, and woodshed needed paint as badly as the Syrian houses did. A broken wagon and some rusted tools lay in the barnyard.

"Mr. Meecham doesn't seem to take much interest in anything but his fence," said Tib, peeking through the narrow iron bars.

"I wish we could see his white horses," said Tacy.

"I don't believe they're there," said Betsy. "The carriage-house door is open and there's no carriage inside."

"Let's go around to the front gate," said Tib.

They followed the high iron fence around to the street.

The empty sunlit valley stretched away to the south. And the dusty street of little houses stretched away to the north. No one was in sight except some children playing and a young man who was chopping wood near the small house opposite.

Betsy, Tacy, and Tib stared at Mr. Meecham's gate. It was closed and looked forbidding. Within, through a weedy overgrown lawn, an avenue of evergreen trees led the way to the house.

"Those evergreens," said Tacy, "remind me of a cemetery."

"Maybe we shouldn't bother with Mr. Meecham's vote," suggested Betsy.

"Why not?" asked Tib.

"Well, there are some more of those 'No Trespassing' signs."

"We're not trespassers. We're callers," said Tib. And swinging her body lightly, as she did when she was gathering courage, she lifted the latch. It opened, and she stepped inside. Betsy and Tacy followed. But none of them liked it when the gate with a loud clang shut behind them.

The avenue of evergreen trees was like a tunnel. As Betsy, Tacy, and Tib walked slowly into its aromatic darkness they seemed to leave behind all the brightness of the sweet June day.

"I wonder," said Tacy, "whether Mr. Meecham really cares who's queen."

"Probably," said Betsy, "he doesn't care a bit."

"Well, *we* care," said Tib.

They kept on going forward.

The gray brick house had tall arched windows which looked like suspicious eyes. It was shabby and unkempt. Ragged clumps of honeysuckle fell over the doorway but its penetrating sweetness seemed to be wasted. The windows were all closed and the shades pulled down.

Betsy and Tacy looked at each other, but before either one could think of an excuse for turning back, Tib had tripped up to the door. She pulled the rusty iron bell. A peal resounded hollowly within.

"Nobody's home. We might as well go away," said Betsy after a quarter of a second.

"Maybe somebody's home," said Tib, and pulled the bell again.

"Don't bother to ring," said Tacy hastily. "I'm sure nobody's home."

But somebody *was* at home.

At that moment a large, dirty, ugly-looking dog swept around the house. Barking furiously, he took his stand in the driveway.

Even Tib looked dismayed for a moment. Tacy stepped forward, for she liked dogs and they usually liked her.

"Here, doggie! Good doggie! Nice doggie!" said Tacy. But the dog did not seem to like being called doggie. He stood on stiff angry legs, his head outthrust, looking as big as a horse. He showed his fangs and barked louder than ever.

"We'd better run," said Tib.

They took to their heels and the dog ran in pursuit. Never had sunlight looked so welcome as that bright arch which showed the end of the avenue of evergreens.

Rushing ahead of Tib the dog reached the gate first. He barked so angrily that Tib did not dare to touch the latch.

"Climb!" she cried, heading for the fence at the left of the gate. She was carrying the basket and she threw it over. Then she caught at the crosswise bar and pulled herself up.

Betsy and Tacy tried to do the same. They did it! They got to the top with the dog at their heels and slid down the outer side. But Betsy's dress and petticoats caught on the spikes. She hung like a scarecrow.

Tacy and Tib would have rescued her in time but they did not have to try. The man who had been chopping wood ran across the street. He lifted her down in a twinkling and set her on the ground. Tacy and Tib helped to smooth down her skirts. They were not too badly torn.

"Th-th-thank you!" said Betsy.

"You're welcome. Don't mention it," the young man answered. His speech had a foreign twist but they could understand him. He had thick black hair like a cap, and a dark merry face.

"What are you three little girls doing here?" he asked.

"We're out for votes," said Tib.

"Votes? For what?"

"For queen," said Tib. She found the basket, pulled out the list and handed it to him.

The young man looked perplexed. He glanced at the paper.

"Tib?" he said. "Which one is Tib?"

"I am," said Tib, looking at him with a smile.

"And is one of you Bett-see? And one Ta-cee?" he asked.

"Yes. How did you know?"

Striding across the narrow street, he called loudly, "Naifi!" He turned back, smiling. "I am Naifi's father," he said. "And I am very glad to meet the three little girls who were so kind to her."

Betsy, Tacy, and Tib were gladder than he was.

A little girl ran out of the house. At first they did not think it was Naifi, for she wore quite an ordinary short dress like their own and ordinary shoes and stockings. But she had Naifi's earrings, and her long dancing braids, and her dancing eyes, and her dimples.

Naifi stood smiling at them, and they at her. Her father had never stopped smiling. The place where they stood in the road was warm with smiles.

Naifi's father spoke first in Syrian, then in English. "These are your friends, my heart, my eyes?" he ended.

Naifi answered in Syrian.

"Speak English," he said. "You know you can speak it a little. And you are learning fast.

"She is now a little American girl," he said to Betsy, Tacy, and Tib. "She does not wear any more the old country clothes to be teased by bad boys. If she had a mother, she might have changed them quicker. But I am only a father. I am stupid. When her mother died, I came here from Syria and left Naifi behind. I and my father came, and Naifi stayed with my mother. But this year when we earned money enough, we sent for them."

Pushing Naifi gently he said, "Take your friends

inside to your grandmother, my little love, my eyes."

Betsy whispered to Tacy, "'My eyes!' Isn't that a funny pet name?"

"Well," said Tacy thoughtfully, "there is nothing more important than your eyes. And I guess that's what he means when he gives that pet name to Naifi."

They followed Naifi across the narrow porch and entered the parlor of her house. It had chairs, a table, a carpet, and a lamp hanging by chains from the ceiling. It was almost like any other parlor. And yet not quite.

A low bench with pillows on it ran around the walls. And a bony old man, wearing a round red cap with a tassel, sat on the floor, cross-legged, smoking

a pipe. It was a curious looking pipe. It stood on the floor, more than a foot high; a long tube led away from it, ending in the old man's mouth.

"That is a *narghile*," said Naifi's father, noticing their interest. "He draws the smoke through water, and it makes the sound you hear. You Americans call it a hubble-bubble pipe."

It was, in fact, making a sound like hubble bubble.

"He is Naifi's grandfather," Naifi's father said.

The old man took his pipe out of his mouth and said, "How you do?" and smiled. He had strong white teeth, as though he were not old at all.

Naifi led them on to the kitchen which was just behind the parlor. And here an old lady was sitting on the floor! She was sitting in front of a hollowed-out block of marble in which she was pounding something with a mallet.

"She is making *kibbee*," explained Naifi's father. "That is meat she is pounding; it is good lean lamb. She is Naifi's grandmother," he said.

He spoke to the grandmother in Syrian, and she got to her feet. She was a tiny old lady with a brown withered face like a nut. She wore earrings, and the same sort of long full-skirted dress that Naifi had worn the first time they saw her. She could not say even "How you do?" in English, but she made them welcome with excited gestures.

Betsy, Tacy, and Tib looked with all their eyes.

Naifi led them out of the kitchen into the sunny back yard. The goat was tethered there.

"Goat!" said Naifi. "Goat! Goat!"

She laughed, and they all laughed, remembering the English lesson. The goat looked at them with wise, mischievous eyes. He seemed to remember he had stolen their basket.

The grandmother came hurrying out with a glass jar in her hand. She opened it and passed it about. Betsy, Tacy, and Tib helped themselves to raisins.

"Raisin," said Naifi, holding one aloft.

Then the grandfather appeared. Standing, he was even more amazing than sitting, for he was very tall. He wore full trousers, gathered at the ankles, and he had not doffed his red be-tasseled cap. He shouted loudly, and the grandmother ran into the house. She came back with a second glass jar which she opened and passed. This one was full of dried figs.

"Figs," said Naifi proudly, smiling.

The grandfather looked pleased, and so did the grandmother. So did Naifi's father who joined them, and so did Naifi. When they had finished eating raisins and figs Naifi's father said, "Now tell me about this paper you have brought. What is it you want?"

Betsy explained about the election, and he listened seriously.

"I do not think," he said, "that queens are good to have. But Tib is my Naifi's friend. If she wants my vote, here it is."

Taking the pencil he wrote his name carefully. He wrote from right to left.

He explained the matter in Syrian to the grandfather, the grandmother and Naifi. And the grandfather signed the list; the grandmother signed the list; and Naifi signed the list. They all wrote from right to left.

Afterward Naifi's father talked a long time in Syrian. He talked in a loud harsh voice, but not an angry one, waving his arms. The grandfather, the grandmother, and Naifi all talked too. All of them waved their arms and acted excited.

There was a pause; then Naifi's father smiled at Betsy, Tacy, and Tib and said in English, "Naifi will take you to all our friends and neighbors. All of them will sign . . . those who can write. You three little girls were kind to my little girl, and the Syrians will sign your paper."

It was an adventure, getting the votes. With Naifi guiding them, Betsy, Tacy, and Tib went to every one of the little Syrian houses. They went into parlors, kitchens, gardens. They saw people drinking coffee, poured from long-handled copper pots into tiny cups. They saw women baking flat round loaves of bread such as Naifi had eaten the day they picnicked together, and other women making embroidery, and men playing cards. They saw a boy playing a long reed flute . . . a *munjaira*, Naifi said it was. They saw everything there was to be seen and they met everyone and everyone signed. Most of them wrote from right to left.

"I wonder why they write from right to left," said Tib.

"That is Arabic writing," one of the Syrians explained. "The Syrian language is Arabic."

Most of them spoke and understood English, but some of them did not. There was much loud harsh talk, but now Betsy and Tacy and Tib understood that that was just the sound of the Syrian language. There was much excited gesturing, stamping, and running about, but now they understood that that was only the Syrian way.

The houses were crowded, for sometimes more than one family lived in a house. There were many children in every family too. The paper was soon filled with names. They had to use the extra paper. Betsy was glad she had brought it.

At last all the people in the settlement had signed. It was time to go home.

Betsy and Tacy and Tib were ready to start. They had said good-by to Naifi's tall grandfather and her tiny wrinkled grandmother, to her merry father with his black hair like a cap, to Naifi and the goat. They had said "thank you" for the raisins and figs and were just stepping off the porch when they heard cries up the street.

Looking in that direction they saw Syrian children scrambling out of the road. They saw a cloud of dust and heard the thud of hoofs. A team of glossy white horses flashed into view. They were driven by a coachman who wore a plug hat like a coachman in a parade. A glittering open carriage swayed along the narrow street. Betsy, Tacy, and Tib glimpsed a white beard . . . a black veil. Here were Mr. Meecham and his daughter!

The carriage stopped at Mr. Meecham's gate, and the coachman sprang down. He unlatched the gate and was about to ascend to his seat when Tib darted forward.

"Please, Mr. Meecham," she said, "will you sign my petition so I can be queen?"

"Eh? What?" asked Mr. Meecham. He sounded as though he could not believe his ears.

His bearded face was stern and scornful. His daughter did not lift her veil, but she leaned forward curiously.

Tib stood in the road beside the carriage, the sun on her yellow curls.

"I want to be queen," she said, handing him the paper.

Mr. Meecham read the petition. He looked at Tib, and at Betsy and Tacy; and above the snowy Niagara of his beard a smile began to form.

Mr. Meecham took out a gold pencil.

"I'll sign with the greatest of pleasure," he said.

And he signed. And so did his daughter. And so did his coachman.

Betsy, Tacy, and Tib climbed the hill in a glow of satisfaction.

"Wasn't it lovely!" Betsy sighed.

"Wasn't it nice!" said Tacy.

"I like Little Syria," said Tib. "I always said I . . ."

She stopped without finishing her sentence. She whirled around and looked toward the valley.

"Where," she demanded, "was Old Bushara?"

Where, indeed!

They looked down on the thirteen rooftops over which the sun of afternoon was extending long golden arms. They had been in every one of those thirteen little houses and had met with nothing but gaiety and kindness. They had not seen a sign of Old Bushara and his knife.

"He must live in a den somewhere," said Betsy.

"I wonder where," said Tacy, looking behind her.

"He must have been out peddling," said Tib. "That's what most of the Syrians do for a living. They go out with horses and buggies or take satchels on their backs."

Of course that was where he was!

"Oh well," said Tib, "we have votes enough already."

"Votes enough!" said Betsy. "If you're not queen, I'd like to know the reason why."

"Won't Julia and Katie be mad!" said Tacy.

They climbed triumphantly, thinking how mad Julia and Katie would be.

9

The Quarrel Again

JULIA AND KATIE were mad all right.

It was now that the quarrel began to get so serious that all of them were sorry it had started. They wanted to end it, but they didn't know how. It was just as if the five of them were piled in a cart which was rattling down Hill Street lickety split, and no one could stop it. It was the worst quarrel they had ever had, and they never had another like it.

When Betsy, Tacy, and Tib came down the Big Hill, Julia and Katie were still sitting on the Rays' side lawn, working on their decorations. They had worked all day, just stopping for dinner. They were tired, but they looked happy.

They had decided not to have a Maypole since it wasn't May any more, but they were going to decorate one of the side lawn maples. They were going to twist it with green and pink streamers up to the lowest branch, and from there they were going to stretch ribbons and garlands to either side of the throne. Of course they were not putting up these decorations yet, for fear it might rain before the celebration, but they had them ready.

Tired and triumphant, Betsy, Tacy, and Tib came down through the orchard and kitchen garden. When they saw the beautiful streamers piled around Julia and Katie, they felt queer for a moment.

Tib said quickly, "We've got the most votes. Let's give in. I can wear my accordion-pleated dress and be a flower girl."

Tacy looked at Betsy, but Betsy got stubborn sometimes. And when Betsy got stubborn, Tacy was stubborn too because she didn't like to go back on Betsy.

"No, sir," Betsy said.

"We planned it first," said Tacy.

They walked down the side lawn where Julia and Katie were sitting.

"Lookee here, lookee here, lookee here," they cried, waving their petition.

Julia and Katie looked up and amazement spread over their faces. They could see at once that the petition had two pages. They could see that it was black with names.

"Where have you been?" asked Katie sharply.

"Don't you wish you knew!"

"There aren't *that* many Ekstroms up on the Big Hill," Julia cried.

Betsy, Tacy, and Tib danced about, acting exasperating.

But they couldn't resist telling where they had been, so in just a minute they shouted, "We've been to Little Syria, that's where!"

"You haven't!" cried Julia and Katie in dazed unbelief.

"How did you get there?"

"We walked there."

"But you're not allowed . . ."

"No one ever told us not to. And it's not on the other side of Lincoln Park either. So don't say it is."

Julia and Katie did not try to say it was.

They looked at each other, and their great disappointment seemed to fill the air. But Katie spoke in a matter-of-fact tone.

"There's no need to fight. We'll count votes like we said we would. Where's our list, Julia?"

They got out the list and Betsy, Tacy, and Tib flung their list down beside it. Betsy, Tacy, and Tib knew that they had the most votes, but they didn't enjoy having them as much as they had expected.

Julia and Katie began grimly to read.

In a moment anger flared out like a flame from gray ashes.

"What's this?" cried Julia.

"What under the sun!" cried Katie. "You don't expect us to count this gibberish, I hope."

"What gibberish?" demanded Betsy.

"This!"

Julia and Katie pointed with trembling furious fingers to that writing which ran from right to left.

"It's all right," said Betsy. "It's Arabic."

"Arabic!" cried Julia and Katie.

"You might have just scrawled it yourselves for all we know," said Julia.

"You might have let a chicken run over the paper," said Katie.

"Well, we didn't!" said Betsy indignantly. "Every single one is a name."

"Every single one of what?" asked Julia.

When Betsy looked she wasn't sure herself. You

couldn't tell where one word stopped and another began. Only Mr. Meecham's signature, and his daughter's, and his coachman's looked right.

"I know how you can count it," said Tib. "There were thirteen houses down there, and about ten people in a family . . ."

"As if we could count that way!" scoffed Katie.

"No, sir! You have to throw out these names that aren't in English."

"We won't!"

"You must!"

"We won't!"

"You've got to!"

"We won't!"

Their voices were so loud now that Margaret came scrambling up the terrace from the Riverses' lawn where she had been playing with the Rivers children. The Rivers children came too; and Paul and Freddie who had been playing on the Kellys' lawn; and Paul's dog and some other dogs and children.

The quarrel began to get bad. In a moment the Rays' side lawn looked as though a cyclone had struck it. Arms and legs were flying in all directions, and lists were flying, and pink and green streamers were flying. Margaret was shouting and Paul's dog was barking.

Mrs. Ray came to the kitchen door.

"What's this? What's this?" she asked.

"They won't count our Arabic votes!" cried Betsy, leaping frantically about.

"Your what?"

"Our Arabic votes that we got in Little Syria."

"In Little Syria!" said Mrs. Ray. Her tone was so astounded that Betsy, Tacy, and Tib shrank into silence. Tacy sniffed back her tears and looked at Betsy. Tib looked at Betsy too. After all, this was Betsy's mother, standing so tall and stern.

"Have you three been to Little Syria?" asked Mrs. Ray.

"Yes, ma'am," said Betsy.

"Who said you could go there?"

"Nobody. But nobody said we couldn't."

"Papa told you not to go beyond Lincoln Park."

"This isn't beyond Lincoln Park," said Betsy. "This is in the other direction."

Mrs. Ray looked nonplussed. But she was never nonplussed long. She spoke with vigor.

"Whether or not you did wrong to go to Little Syria can be decided later. But this quarreling must be stopped right now. Papa suggested a plan and you all agreed to it. You all agreed that the one who got the most votes should be queen. And you promised too that the losers would be good sports. So count your votes and let's decide the matter."

"But that's what we've been trying to do," cried Julia desperately.

"We can't read the names," said Katie. "Look at the writing, Mrs. Ray!"

She thrust the list with its strange scratchings into Mrs. Ray's hands.

"See?" said Julia. "They ought not to be allowed to count them."

"We will too count them!" shouted Betsy, Tacy, and Tib.

"You won't!"

"We will!"

"You won't!"

"We will!"

Julia burst out in a shaking voice, "Never mind! I wish I'd never thought about being a queen. Everything's spoiled! Everything! Everything!"

Her voice broke, and she bent to pick up streamers in order to conceal her quivering lips. She looked ready to cry, but Julia never cried, not even when she was spanked.

She didn't cry now, but Tib did. Tib cried good and hard.

"I wish I'd never thought about it too," wailed Tib.

Mrs. Ray knew how to be cross when children were naughty. But she wasn't cross now. She spoke gently.

"I won't try to settle this," she said. "It was Papa's plan. And he'll be at his lodge meeting tonight and won't be home until late. You children come over in the morning and we'll straighten everything out. Julia, Betsy, it's time to clean up for supper."

Katie and Tacy went home, but they didn't go together. Katie stalked ahead, and Tacy went behind with her face in her sleeve. Tib ran down the hill and her tears ran faster than her feet. All the children and dogs went home.

Julia and Betsy went into the house, with

Margaret following them. Margaret stared from one to the other with her round, black-lashed eyes. Margaret had never seen such a quarrel before. She was pretty surprised.

Betsy kept remembering how Julia had looked when she said, "Everything's spoiled! Everything! Everything!" Betsy didn't want to remember it. She couldn't help it.

She glanced guiltily toward Julia now, but Julia looked poised and icy. She had washed her face and combed her hair, and was reading a book. She didn't look at Betsy or speak to her. She acted as though Betsy weren't there.

Betsy washed her face and combed her hair too. She crossed her braids in back and tied the ribbons the best she could. (Usually Julia tied them.) She asked Margaret if she didn't want to play with blocks. And Margaret said she did. So Betsy made her a big block house and laughed and made jokes and looked at Julia now and then. But Julia did not look their way at all.

They had supper without their father, and that seemed odd. Julia talked to her mother in a cool grown-up way. Betsy talked to her too, and both of them talked to Margaret. But they didn't talk to each other.

When the games started in the street Julia didn't go outdoors. She kept on reading her book. Betsy went out, but the games weren't any fun. They weren't any fun at all that night.

"How's Katie?" asked Betsy. For Katie wasn't there. Neither was Tib.

"Bad," said Tacy. "She feels pretty bad."

"So does Julia," said Betsy. After a moment she said, "They ought to feel bad too. Not wanting to count our votes, after that long trip we took and everything."

"Um-hum," said Tacy. She sounded doubtful.

"I don't like to have Katie feel quite so bad though," she said. "She's pretty good to me sometimes."

"Julia's all right too," said Betsy.

She knew that Tacy was hoping she would say, "Let's give in." But she couldn't quite say it. Betsy was stubborn sometimes.

When she went into the house she glanced at Julia, but Julia didn't even look up. She kept on reading her book.

Their mother said it was bedtime and Julia and Betsy went upstairs. They undressed and put on their night gowns in silence. They said their prayers and climbed into bed and lay there without speaking.

Mrs. Ray came upstairs to tuck them in. She always did. She sat down beside them, looking worried.

"In this family," she said, "we have a rule. We never go to sleep angry. Sometimes during the day we get angry and do wrong things and say things we don't mean. Everyone does. But before we go to sleep we always say we are sorry. We always make up. Always."

After a moment Julia said stiffly, "I'm sorry, Betsy."

"I'm sorry," Betsy answered.

They kissed each other.

Their mother looked closely into their faces. She didn't seem satisfied. Maybe she thought they hadn't sounded sorry; at least, not sorry enough. But presently she leaned down and kissed them, first Julia and then Betsy. She took the lamp and went downstairs.

"Good night," she called.

"Good night," called Julia and Betsy.

But they didn't go to sleep.

The street lamp at the corner made a glow on the sloping walls. Sweet summer smells came in the open window with the loving chirping of birds. Betsy felt terrible. She could not forget that look on Julia's face when she had said, "Everything's spoiled." First she would remember how happy Julia had looked with her pink and green streamers piled around her; and then she would remember her pale strained face when she said, "Everything's spoiled."

Betsy lay still and thought about Julia. She thought how proud she was of her when she sang, and played, and gave her recitations. Julia was different from all the other children. There was nobody like her.

She thought how good Julia was to her sometimes. How she tied her hair ribbons. How she helped her with arithmetic. How she never would let anybody pick on her.

"You leave my little sister alone!" Julia always said.

She thought of the fun they had together when they went out on family picnics. She and Julia always sat in the back seat of the surrey and played games. She thought what fun they had on vacations at Uncle Edward's farm. Even when Julia was playing with Katie, and Betsy was playing with Tacy and Tib, they had fun. The quarrels had been fun up to now.

Betsy began to cry, but softly, so that Julia would not hear her. Julia on her side of the bed had not moved or stirred. Betsy was determined that Julia should not hear her cry. She cried too easily anyhow, and Julia never cried. Betsy pressed her fist against her mouth, but tears trickled down her cheeks and down her chin and even down her neck inside the collar of her night gown.

Then from the other side of the bed she heard a sound. It was a sob, a perfectly gigantic sob.

"Betsy!" cried Julia, and she came rolling over and hugged Betsy tight. "I'm sorry."

"I'm sorry too," Betsy wept.

"I don't want to be queen," Julia sobbed. "I want Tib to be queen."

"But Tib doesn't want to be queen," wept Betsy. "And Tacy doesn't want her to be queen, if it makes you and Katie feel bad. I'm the mean one. I'm the stubborn one."

"I'm meaner than you are," said Julia. "I always was."

She cried so that her tears ran down Betsy's face. Their wet cheeks pressed together.

"I've been feeling terrible," said Julia, "about your going down to Little Syria. It was mean of us to go to that Ice Cream Social and get so many votes. Why, I'm your big sister. I'm supposed to take care of you. And here I practically drove you down to Little Syria. You might have been killed. That awful place. . . ."

Betsy sat bolt upright.

"Why, Julia!" she cried. "It isn't awful at all. It's a lovely place."

"What do you mean?" asked Julia, blowing her nose.

"I mean just what I say. The people gave us raisins and figs. They're lovely people."

Julia gave Betsy her handkerchief, and Betsy blew her nose too. They both stopped crying, and Betsy told Julia all about the trip to Little Syria.

They talked and talked, but in whispers for they weren't supposed to be talking. They were supposed to be asleep. Betsy told her about the hubble-bubble pipe, the red cap with a tassel, the kibbee, the goat. Julia was fascinated.

They talked so late that their father came home

from his lodge meeting. They heard their mother talking with him; she was telling him about the quarrel. They heard their mother come upstairs to tuck in Margaret who slept in the back bedroom. She looked in on them too, but they pretended they were asleep. After that the house was very quiet.

"It's the latest we've ever been awake," said Julia.

"It's tomorrow, I imagine," Betsy said.

"I suppose," said Julia, "we'd better go to sleep."

And they kissed each other good night.

Julia rolled over, and Betsy tucked in cozily behind her. They didn't go to sleep right away, but they didn't talk any more.

Betsy felt happy, delicious, emptied of trouble. Only one small perplexity remained.

If Julia wouldn't be queen, and Tib wouldn't be queen, who would be queen?

"We just have to use those streamers," Betsy thought as she slipped through a gray mist into sleep.

10

A Princess

I N THE MORNING they were happy. They smiled at each other as they washed and dressed. Julia tied Betsy's hair ribbons. Then she hurried down to the kitchen.

"Mamma," she said. "I want Tib to be queen. I really mean it. I've told Betsy so."

Betsy was close behind her.

"No, sir," she said. "Julia's going to be queen. Tacy and Tib and I are going to be flower girls."

Mrs. Ray was making coffee. She put the coffee pot down and put her arms around them; they had a big hug. Mr. Ray was shaving at the kitchen basin. He looked around, with his face covered with lather, and smiled broadly.

"Katie and Tacy and Tib are out on the hitching block," he said. "Go and ask them what they have to say about all this. Then bring them in here because *I* have something to say. I have plenty to say."

Betsy wondered whether it concerned Little Syria. And Julia, evidently, had the same thought.

"It really wasn't Betsy's fault about Little Syria, Papa," she said. "Katie and I got so many votes at that Ice Cream Social that Betsy and Tacy and Tib just had to do something to catch up. And she says it's a very nice place. The people were lovely to them."

"Yes," said Mr. Ray, "I heard quite a lot about Little Syria yesterday. Mr. Meecham and his daughter came into the store to buy shoes."

"That's where they were coming from when we saw them!" Betsy thought. She wished her father would say more, but he didn't. Her mother spoke briskly.

"Run out to see what the children want," she said.

"Then bring them in here, so Papa can have his say."

Julia and Betsy ran out.

Katie was the first one off the hitching block.

"Julia," she said, "let's let Tib be queen. I sort of worried last night, thinking about those kids going down to Little Syria all alone."

Tib interrupted.

"But I've decided not to be queen," she said. "I want Julia to be queen."

"I'd just as soon let Julia be queen. Wouldn't you, Betsy?" asked Tacy.

"Yes, I would," said Betsy. "I was coming out to tell you."

"Well, I won't be!" said Julia. "I feel just as Katie does. I think Tib ought to be queen."

At the same moment all of them saw how funny it was to be talking that way, and they all began to laugh.

"Come in the house a minute," Julia said. "Papa has something he wants to say to us. But I warn you right now that I will not be queen."

"And neither will I," said Tib.

They marched into the kitchen where the coffee was bubbling, and Mrs. Ray was pouring glasses of milk and stirring oatmeal and turning sausage and making toast all at the same time. Mr. Ray had finished shaving. He had put on his collar and tie, and he looked nice. He was tying Margaret's napkin around her neck.

The five little girls came in, laughing.

"We're still fighting, Papa," said Julia. "But now it's not about being queen. It's about not being queen."

"Well, for Pete's sake!" said Mr. Ray.

"You see," said Julia, "I won't be queen. . . ."

"And neither will I," said Tib.

"No matter how many votes I have," continued Julia. "And I'm sure I don't have enough."

"But we'll throw out the Arabic votes," said Betsy.

"No you won't!" said Julia. "Syrian votes are just as good as any other votes."

"Where are their wings?" asked Mrs. Ray gaily. "Feel for their wings, Margaret. They're white feathery things and they crop out near shoulders."

Margaret jumped up and started feeling for wings. Everyone started feeling for wings, and it tickled, and things grew lively.

"Let's have the coronation soon," said Mrs. Ray, "while we're feeling so happy."

"And while the weather's so fine," said Mr. Ray.

"No telling how long it will last," said Mrs. Ray.

"The fine weather?" asked Mr. Ray, winking at her.

Julia and Katie, Betsy, Tacy, and Tib were bewildered by this talk.

"But Papa!" cried Julia. "How can we have a coronation without a queen?"

"That's what I have to talk to you about," said Mr. Ray. He sat down and crossed his legs and looked from one to another. "I heard something yesterday," he said, "that will interest you very much." He paused, then spoke impressively:

"There's a real princess in town."

"A real princess!" came an astonished chorus.

"A real princess," Mr. Ray repeated.

"Someone from the old country?" asked Tib.

"Someone from the old country."

"Is she of the blood royal?" asked Betsy.

"She's of the blood royal."

"Is she down at the Melborn Hotel?" asked Julia.

"No. She isn't. But she's here in Deep Valley. How would you like to go to see her and ask *her* to be queen?"

"Oh, we'd like it! We'd like it!" The kitchen resounded.

"Do you suppose she'll consent?" asked Julia.

"Where is she?" asked Katie.

"You never could guess, so I'll tell you. She's in Little Syria. Imagine," he said to Betsy, Tacy, and Tib, "having a princess right under your nose and not recognizing her!"

"Oh, I'm sure we didn't see her, Papa," cried Betsy.

And Tacy and Tib nodded vigorous agreement.

"Did you see the old man called Old Bushara?"

"No, we didn't. He was out peddling or something."

"Well, this girl is Old Bushara's granddaughter."

Old Bushara's granddaughter!

"And *she's* not away peddling, for Mr. Meecham saw her yesterday. Pour yourself some coffee, Jule," he said to Mrs. Ray, "and sit down while I'm telling the story.

"Mr. Meecham and I," he began, "started talking about his neighbors. He's interested in them, and no wonder. They come from a very interesting country. You can read about their country in the Bible. The Deep Valley Syrians are Christians, but most Syrians are Mohammedans. Syria is under the control of the Turks, and the Turks are Mohammedans too. A good many of the Christian Syrians are coming to America these days. And they come for much the same reason that our Pilgrim fathers came. They want to be free from oppression and religious persecution. We ought to honor them for it.

"Most of them come from the Lebanon district," Mr. Ray went on. "You've heard about Lebanon, I'm sure. King Solomon's temple was built from the cedars of Lebanon. Cedars still grow on those wild Lebanon hills; and in the ravines and valleys some brave groups of people still keep their loyalty to their native Syrian princes . . . in spite of the Turks. *Emeers*, these princes are called, and their daughters and granddaughters are *emeeras* or princesses. This Old Bushara is an emeer of Lebanon, and his granddaughter is an emeera."

"Mr. Ray," said Tib, "is that why Old Bushara gets so mad and chases boys when they yell 'dago' at him?"

"It probably is," said Mr. Ray. "An emeer of Lebanon is a very proud man, and he should be. He's an ancient prince of a very ancient race."

A dazzled silence filled the kitchen.

Mr. Ray looked from Betsy, to Tacy, to Tib.

"It was wrong of you to go to Little Syria yesterday without permission," he said. "But it's quite all right to go there *with* permission. If Mrs. Kelly and Mrs. Muller are willing, you and Julia and Katie may go there and ask Old Bushara's granddaughter to come and be your queen."

"Why don't you go today," suggested Mrs. Ray, "and have your coronation tomorrow?"

"Before the weather changes," put in Mr. Ray.

Mr. and Mrs. Ray smiled at each other.

Katie and Tacy and Tib ran home to breakfast, and they came back saying that they could go to Little Syria. So the five of them went that very afternoon.

Betsy, Tacy, and Tib led the way up the Big Hill. They stopped to invite Mrs. Ekstrom to the coronation.

"Kings and queens! Kings and queens!" said Mrs. Ekstrom, throwing up her hands.

"Oh, no, Mrs. Ekstrom," said Julia. "There isn't going to be a *king*."

"That's a wonder," Mrs. Ekstrom answered.

But she said she would come to the coronation. She wouldn't miss it, she said.

Betsy, Tacy, and Tib took Julia and Katie through the Secret Lane, and past the Mystery House, and down through a fold of the hill and up again. They stood hand in hand on the high rocky point looking down on their discovered valley. Betsy and Tacy and Tib pointed out and explained. Julia and Katie listened and asked questions. It was pleasant for Betsy and Tacy and Tib to know more than Julia and Katie knew, for once.

They went down the hill, running sometimes and walking sometimes, picking columbines and yellow bells and Jacks-in-the-pulpit and daisies to make a bouquet for the princess.

"I wonder why you didn't see her yesterday," said Julia.

"I suppose," said Betsy, "they sort of keep a princess hidden."

"I wonder which house she's in," said Tacy.

"Let's go straight to Naifi's and ask," Tib suggested. "Her father speaks English, you know."

They had reached the path which ran down to the settlement and the thirteen little ramshackle houses came into view. Loud harsh talk rose from the vegetable gardens, but no one felt nervous.

"That's just the way Syrians talk," Betsy explained.

They did not go around behind Mr. Meecham's house today. They skipped straight down the little dusty street, calling "hello" right and left to the many friends they had there.

They heard someone playing a flute.

"That's a munjaira," Tacy said off-handedly.

"And Naifi's grandfather," said Tib, "will likely be smoking a hubble-bubble pipe."

As a matter of fact, he was, when they entered Naifi's house.

The little grandmother answered their knock; and they knew from her smiling hospitable motions that she was inviting them in. They came in, and there sat the grandfather, cross-legged, smoking his pipe.

He took the pipe out of his mouth and smiled at them. And the grandmother ran to the back door and called loudly. Naifi's father and Naifi came

428

hurrying in from the garden.

"Today you are five," said Naifi's father merrily.

"Five," laughed Naifi.

"Five," chuckled the grandfather. He held five fingers up to the grandmother and pointed to the children and chuckled. She chuckled too.

Betsy introduced Julia and Katie.

"They are our sisters," she said. And the grandmother ran for the jars of raisins and figs. They all sat down on that low divan which ran around the room and ate raisins and figs.

Julia and Katie waited politely for Betsy or Tacy or Tib to state their errand. Tacy and Tib waited for Betsy. So after a moment Betsy said, "We came to ask you a question. Will you tell us, please, which is Bushara's house?"

"Bushara's house?" asked Naifi's father, looking startled.

"Where does Old Bushara live?" asked Tib.

"And his granddaughter?" added Tacy. Tacy was shy with people she didn't know very well. But she was so eager to find the princess that she forgot to be shy.

Naifi's father stared at them. He threw back his black head and laughed. He spoke rapidly in Syrian, and the grandfather, the grandmother, and Naifi all laughed too.

The visitors looked at one another in surprise. They could not imagine what had been said that was funny.

The old man stood up, tall in his red tasseled cap. He put his hand across his breast.

"Here, here is Bushara!" he said.

He flung his arms about.

"Bushara's house!" he cried.

He pointed to Naifi.

"Bushara's grand . . . daughter," he ended.

Julia and Katie, Betsy, Tacy, and Tib sat as if stunned.

Betsy, Tacy, and Tib turned timid faces toward Naifi. Naifi was the princess! Naifi with whom they had picnicked on the hill, Naifi with whom they had tramped from end to end of Little Syria, Naifi at whom rough boys had shouted "Dago!"

Seeing her sister struck dumb with amazement, Julia told Naifi's father why they had come. She talked prettily, just as though she were reciting. She told him that they had heard about the Syrian emeera; she told him that they were crowning a Queen of Summer tomorrow and wanted Naifi to be queen.

"We will come to get her, and my father will drive her home. Mr. Meecham can tell you all about us. We do hope she can come."

Julia talked so nicely that the children were surprised to see Naifi's father's merry face grow dark.

Naifi looked anxiously from the strange little girl to her father. She did not understand very much of what was being said, but she could see that her father did not like it. She listened attentively as he spoke in an earnest voice.

"It is true," he said, "that my father was an emeer of Lebanon. And that is an honor for which respect is due him, more respect than he receives sometimes, perhaps. But he is also an American. He is trying to get the citizenship and so am I. And that will be a greater honor, to be Americans.

"No, no," he continued, shaking his head, "I do not want my Naifi to play the Syrian emeera. She is forgetting about such things. She is an American now. Are you not, my heart, my eyes?"

Naifi nodded until her braids swung up and down. She stood very straight, and her eyes were bright.

"American!" she said.

"American!" said the emeer of Lebanon, striking his breast again.

"American!" said his wife. For even the old grandmother knew the word "American."

Something in the way they said "American" gave Betsy an idea. She jumped from her seat.

"Of course," she cried. "But this is to be an American celebration. It's an American queen we want Naifi to be."

"It is?" asked Naifi's father, looking puzzled.

Tacy followed Betsy's lead like lightning.

"We're going to have a big flag up, red, white, and blue, Mr. Bushara," she said.

Julia and Katie fell into line.

"I'm going to sing 'The Star Spangled Banner,'" said Julia. "And Katie maybe is going to recite Lincoln's Gettysburg Address."

"It's almost the Fourth of July, you know," Katie put in.

Tib looked from one to another in surprise. "When did you plan all this?" she began. But Betsy kicked her.

"It's lovely," Tib said hastily.

Naifi's father translated all they had said. He and his family talked in Syrian excitedly, waving their arms. Smiles broke over their faces, and Naifi's father put his hand on Naifi's head.

"She may go," he said. "I will bring her myself. I start tomorrow on a trip with my horse and buggy selling the linens and laces. But first I will bring her to your house, to be your American queen."

So it was decided! And Julia and Katie, Betsy, Tacy, and Tib were enormously elated. They didn't stay much longer. There was too much to be done on Hill Street for the morrow's celebration. But of course Julia and Katie took time to call on the goat.

The grandmother, meanwhile, was whispering to the grandfather, and giving him little nudges. Naifi started whispering to him too, and at last he rose as though offended and went into a room and shut the door.

Just as the visitors were ready to leave, he reappeared.

He had changed his garments and wore long flowing robes gathered slightly at the ankles. His

red fez was wound with folds of white which hung down to his shoulders, framing his brown seamed face. His manner was grave, his bearing was majestic. The children knew without being told that this was his garb of an emeer.

"It's wonderful, Mr. Bushara," said Julia. "Thank you for putting it on."

"Thank you," murmured the others, gazing with shining eyes.

Betsy whispered to Julia.

"Maybe," said Julia quickly, "Naifi could wear her emeera clothes tomorrow?"

Naifi's father smiled. He did not answer.

The old man was not listening. He was looking up at the hills, those green gentle slopes which rose around the valley in which he had found a new home.

"Those hills," he said haltingly, "they not the hills of Lebanon. And Bushara, not an emeer of Lebanon. Not now. Not any longer. Bushara, an American now."

Julia and Katie, Betsy, Tacy, and Tib said good-by and started toward home. After they had climbed awhile without speaking, Julia said soberly, "They think a lot of being Americans; don't they?"

"They certainly do," Katie answered.

"Boys like Sam ought to know more about

them," said Tib. Tib sometimes said very sensible things.

"Let's give Naifi a fine celebration," said Betsy.

"A real American celebration," said Tacy, and everyone agreed.

All the way home they made plans for crowning an American queen.

11

A Queen

NAIFI WAS CROWNED queen next day.
She was crowned on the Rays' side lawn
under one of the two young maples which
Betsy's father had set out; it was just the right size.

Pink and green streamers were wound around the
tree up to the lowest branch, and from that point
chains of flowers ran to either side of Mr. Ray's

armchair. It was a big leather armchair. It made a fine throne.

A large American flag overhung all, and small American flags were stuck into the ground in a half circle behind the throne. Flags which were ordinarily stored away in closets and brought out only on patriotic holidays had been produced by dozens to make Naifi's coronation strictly American.

Paul and Freddie borrowed flags all up and down Hill Street while Margaret and Hobbie and the Rivers children picked flowers on the hill and Betsy and Tacy and Tib wove garlands and Julia and Katie decorated. Everything was done without the smallest disagreement. Everyone was kind to everyone else. And the mothers were so pleased that Mrs. Ray made lemonade, and Mrs. Kelly baked a cake, and Matilda baked cookies. Even a coronation needs refreshments.

When the decorating was finished, the children went out to invite people. Julia and Katie, Betsy, Tacy, and Tib skipped down to Pleasant Street to tell Dorothy and Alice what time to come. All the neighbors were invited, and many of them came. By half past two o'clock the lawn was full of people.

Mrs. Ekstrom came all the way down the Big Hill. And Mrs. Benson came, and Mrs. Rivers and the children. Mrs. Hunt who was deaf and dumb came, bringing her crowing baby. Mrs. Granger came, and Miss Williams, and Ben, and the boy named Tom.

Julia and Betsy and Margaret and Katie and Tacy all wore their best Sunday dresses. When they stood together they made a bouquet of light summer tints. Tib wore the accordion-pleated dress. Dorothy, who had dark curls, wore a red dress; it was silk. And Alice's dress was blue, of thin nun's veiling.

Grown-ups sat on the lawn in chairs but the children kept racing to the Rays' front steps to look down Hill Street. They were pretty worked up about a princess coming. At last they saw an unfamiliar horse, a buggy loaded with satchels. It was Mr. Bushara, bringing Naifi.

He stopped at the hitching block and jumped out and pulled off his hat. The sun shone on his glistening cap of hair. He lifted Naifi out of the buggy, and his face was as proud as it was merry.

"Look at that, my heart!" he said, pointing to the big American flag.

The children swooped down upon them.

Naifi was a princess out of the Arabian Nights. Betsy could not have invented one more lovely. A cloud of chiffon floated about her face. Her mouth was hidden, but her dark eyes were sparkling. They were rimmed with sooty black.

Her dress was long and full-skirted, like the one

she had worn the day they saw her first. But this one was of soft rich cashmere, purple in color and embroidered in gold. The short jacket was gold-embroidered too. Bloomers were tied at her ankles above little slippers of gold.

She was laden with jewelry . . . bracelets, rings, earrings. . . .

"Naifi! You're wonderful! You're beautiful!" cried the children.

"Hel-lo," said Naifi. "Hel-lo, hel-lo, hel-lo."

Mrs. Ray asked her father to stay, but he said that he had to go. He returned to his buggy and drove down Hill Street with a proud smiling face.

The children hurried Naifi into the Rays' parlor. There the parade assembled. Mrs. Ray was going to play the piano for it; Tom was going to play the violin.

On the lawn the other mothers and the guests waited expectantly. The sun shone down, and the air smelled of roses.

"No more queens, I hope," Mrs. Muller said to Mrs. Kelly.

"It will be something else next week," Mrs. Kelly answered.

Mrs. Ray played a rousing march. It was named "Pomp and Circumstance." She played it with spirit and Tom played it with her on his violin. The procession streamed out of the door to the porch,

down the porch steps, and over the lawn.

First came Margaret and Hobbie waving flags. They waved them in time to the music.

Next came Paul and Freddie in their best suits. They were pages. Pages walked straight and tried not to smile.

Then came Betsy and Tacy, Tib and Alice. They scattered flowers as gracefully as they knew how. They scattered the flowers picked that morning on the hill, columbines and daisies and the scarlet Indian paintbrush.

Treading on the flowers came Naifi, dimples flashing. And just behind walked Dorothy, holding the edge of Naifi's dress. Julia and Katie came last of all, bearing a pillow with a crown upon it.

Betsy's mother played three or four crashing chords. Naifi seated herself on the throne. Two of the royal party darted indoors. The rest seated themselves on the grass.

Dorothy rose and swept her brown curls almost to the ground in a curtsey.

"Your majesty," she said in her sweet voice, "we will now endeavor to entertain you."

Mrs. Ray began to play the Baby Dance. Tib jumped up, picked her skirt up by the edges and made a pirouette.

After the Baby Dance, which was loudly

applauded, two black cats capered out on the lawn. Mrs. Ray played the Cat Duet and Betsy and Tacy sang it. They were loudly applauded too.

Katie recited the Gettysburg Address. She despised reciting but she was too patriotic to refuse. When she had finished, she and Julia knelt before the Queen. They held the cushion high and Dorothy lifted the crown.

As she put it on Naifi's head, Mrs. Ray, inside the house, began to play "Hearts and Flowers."

Julia went up and stood on the porch steps, looking solemn. Paul and Freddie handed out flags. Mrs. Ray switched to "The Star Spangled Banner." Everyone stood up, of course, and Julia sang.

She sang as only Julia could. Betsy thought about George Washington. She thought about Abraham Lincoln. She thought about Theodore Roosevelt, the President. She thought about Old Bushara saying that he was an American now.

At the end of a verse Julia smiled suddenly and asked everyone to sing. Everyone sang "The Star Spangled Banner" and waved flags. Naifi's eyes were something to watch then. Bright as diamonds, they looked about the lawn at the tossing banners.

After that it was just a party with plenty of lemonade, cookies, and cake.

In the midst of all the gaiety no one noticed

Mr. Goode, the postman. He had trudged up Hill Street on his usual afternoon round and arrived at the Rays' front steps. He paused to look around, holding a letter in his hand.

"Hey, there!" he said to Mrs. Ray who was passing a tray full of glasses.

She stopped and came toward him.

"Hello, Mr. Goode. Won't you have some lemonade?"

"Don't care if I do," he said. He slipped off his bag to rest his shoulder, but still he held the letter in his hand.

"Something for us?" asked Mrs. Ray.

"For Betsy and Tacy and Tib."

"All three of them?"

"All three of them. And if you ask me," he said, "it's pretty important." He handed it to her.

The envelope was large and square. It bore an unfamiliar stamp. Turning it over, Mrs. Ray saw an official-looking seal.

"Betsy! Tacy! Tib! Come here!" she said. And Betsy, Tacy, and Tib came running, for there was something compelling in her voice. Other children crowded behind them, grown-ups too.

"It's a letter from Spain," said Mr. Goode. "Do you know anybody in Spain?"

Betsy and Tacy and Tib felt for one another's hands. They didn't speak for a moment.

Tib whispered desperately to Betsy, "What shall I do if he wants to marry me? I don't want to marry him. I want to be an American like Naifi."

Tacy whispered to Betsy too. "Do you suppose it's against the law to write to a king?"

Mrs. Ray noticed the whispers, the frightened faces.

"Do you want me to open it?" she asked. "I can't imagine what it can be, but it's certainly nothing to be afraid of."

Betsy swallowed a burr in her throat.

"Yes. Open it," she said.

She knew that Julia and Katie were there; she could see their curious faces. There was a crowd of people, and teasing could be very hard. But this was serious. If it was against the law to write to kings and they were going to be sent to jail, their mothers might as well know it. Their fathers would have to get them out.

Betsy and Tacy and Tib waited in frozen panic.

Mrs. Ray opened the envelope. She unfolded a rich creamy paper.

"Heavens and earth!" she said. And then, "Children! Children!"

Betsy and Tacy and Tib did not speak. They squeezed one another's hands.

"What did you do?" demanded Betsy's mother.

They did not answer.

"This letter," said Mrs. Ray, "comes from the King of Spain. At least it comes from his Palace. It seems to be written by a secretary. I can't pronounce his name."

"What does he say?" asked Tib in a trembling voice.

"He says that His Majesty thanks you for the sentiments expressed in your letter."

"Is that all?"

"That's all. Isn't it enough?"

It was quite enough.

With a common impulse Betsy, Tacy, and Tib flung their arms about each other. They jumped up and down shouting in a glad release from fear.

"How did you happen to write to him?" asked three mothers at once.

"Oh," said Betsy vaguely. "It was his birthday."

Tacy remembered something.

"But how did our letter get mailed?"

"That's so," said Tib. "We lost it."

They looked around the agitated circle. One face stood out above all others. It was red from suppressed laughter.

"On the hill you lost it," Mrs. Ekstrom said.

Mrs. Ekstrom had mailed it!

The letter passed from hand to hand. And Betsy, Tacy, and Tib felt mighty proud now that they knew they hadn't done anything wrong or stepped into trouble.

Getting a letter from a king was a perfect ending to an afternoon in which a queen was crowned.

The fathers came home in time for some remnants of cake and to see Naifi's regal costume. Betsy's father took Naifi home. She left with many smiles and nods of thanks. Everyone went home . . . the grown-ups, the children . . . except Tacy and Tib. They sat on the hitching block with Betsy in the long golden rays of the sun.

"I was scared when that letter came," said Tib.

"So was I," said Tacy. "I'm certainly glad none of us had to marry him."

"So am I," said Betsy. She thought about Old Bushara. "Why I wouldn't not be an American for a million dollars."

"Neither would I," said Tacy. "Not for ten million."

"Neither would I," said Tib. "I should say not!"

"It was fun," said Betsy, "playing kings and queens like this. But I don't think we'll do it any more."

"What will we do?" asked Tib.

"Oh, American things. Patriotic things."

Betsy had an idea.

"I'll tell you what we'll do," she said. "We'll write to Ethel Roosevelt."

Ethel Roosevelt was the President's daughter. She was just their age.

"We'll offer to come and see her in the White House," Tacy cried.

"I could dance my Baby Dance," said Tib.

"We could sing the Cat Duet," said Betsy. "We'll write the first thing in the morning."

And they did. But if Ethel Roosevelt ever received their letter, which is doubtful, she never got around to answering it. And so the plan to dance and sing in the White House came to nothing.

It didn't matter though. Betsy and Tacy and Tib found plenty of things to do. They soon stopped being ten years old. But whatever age they were seemed to be exactly the right age for having fun.

Betsy and Tacy
Go Downtown

FOR HELEN
and the other inheritors
of Hill Street

Contents

Foreword

One Saturday morning when I was about twelve years old, I woke with a wonderful plan. The evening before, I had finished rereading my very favorite library book. It was *Downtown* (later retitled by the publisher as *Betsy and Tacy Go Downtown*) by Maud Hart Lovelace. It was the third time I had borrowed the book from the library, and when the two-week lending period was over, I would have to part with this treasured book once again. Hence my plan: I would copy the words of the story for myself.

This was the era before inexpensive paperback editions of popular books for children. And this was the era before the existence of photocopy machines (and laws forbidding the copying of entire books). My father was an ardent bibliophile, and so I suppose I might have thought to ask for my own copy of *Downtown*. But my father's idea of going to a bookstore was browsing in dimly lit and dusty secondhand shops. I often went with him and had the thrill of buying one or two old books for a nickel or dime each. Yet, somehow, I could not imagine a copy of *Downtown* in one of those shops.

So I took a large notebook and a freshly sharpened pencil, and carefully, in my best cursive writing, I began. The second paragraph that I wrote was less neat than the first. By the time I completed copying only the first page, my hand was very tired. I looked at my smudged paper and compared it to the clear print of the real book. I realized that even if I ever finished this monumental task which I had set for myself, it would not truly resemble the bound book I held in my hand. Nor would there be any of the charming drawings by Lois Lenski to accompany the text.

I tore the page from my notebook and gave up. I would just have to wait my turn and continue to borrow *Downtown* from the library whenever I could find it on the shelf.

Downtown was not my only favorite book. I loved the entire series about Betsy-Tacy. I had discovered them by chance on the library shelves and at once had fallen in love with Betsy (who was just like me!) and her friends. Betsy's friends were not like mine. My friends squabbled constantly. Three was not a good number for best friends in the Bronx where I grew up. In fact, very little in the Bronx resembled the idyllic community of Deep Valley. Betsy's parents never lectured her about the dangers of speaking to strangers. In fact, some of Betsy's best adventures took place when she spoke to strangers. *She even went inside their homes.* But more than the refreshing vacation from my own city tenement life, the books offered me a new best friend who was myself and yet not myself.

At twelve, I already knew that I wanted to be a writer—just like Betsy. At twelve, I entertained my friends with original stories that I wrote out and tried submitting to magazines—just like Betsy. I didn't have freckles and my teeth weren't parted in the middle, but I was chunkily built like Betsy and I think I had her "perky smiling face." That forty years separated my childhood from hers seemed immaterial. We were just alike in every important way.

I read the Betsy-Tacy books in order as they were published—with one important omission. The New York Public Library did not own *Heaven to Betsy* when I was growing up. This I later learned (when I was a children's librarian, working for NYPL myself) was because the matter of Betsy and her sister Julia changing religions was considered too controversial at that time.

I was in college and employed part time in the public library when the last book in the series was published. I happened to be browsing in the children's room when I discovered *Betsy's Wedding*. I stopped, stunned at the news. If my own sister had gotten married without telling me, I could not have been more surprised (or delighted). I grabbed the book from the library shelf and checked it out. If the children's librarian was amazed to see someone of my advanced age borrowing the book, she didn't say. Probably it happened all the time, anyhow.

The bond I felt with Betsy and Maud Hart Lovelace, her creator and alter ego, was strengthened by personal contacts over the years. In 1949, shortly after my eleventh birthday, I wrote a letter to Mrs. Lovelace. Writing letters to authors was not a classroom assignment in those days, and I don't remember how I figured out that if I wrote to her in care of her publisher, she might in time receive my letter. In any event, she did, and her response, written in her own hand, made me feel, more than ever, that we were personal friends. In time, I received several other handwritten notes from her.

Our bond was reinforced one evening when I was glancing at the newspaper. The *New York World Telegram*, a paper for which my father wrote, had recently merged with the *New York Sun*. I noticed an article written by Delos Lovelace. I recognized the name immediately because in the front of all the Betsy-Tacy books was a listing of other books by the author, including a couple which she co-authored with Delos Lovelace, her husband. I ran to my father to show him this wonderful new link with my favorite author.

He reported to his new colleague about my recognition of his name. And that year, at holiday time, I received a gift-wrapped and autographed copy of Maud Hart Lovelace's newest book, *Emily of Deep Valley*. I never found out if Mrs. Lovelace sent the book to me via my father or if my father purchased the book and asked her husband to have it signed for me. I think I preferred not knowing so I could pretend to myself that it was the former.

Growing up in an era when creativity was not praised or fostered in schools, I know that Betsy/Maud was the mentor I needed to encourage me to continue writing. There must be hundreds of writers who can point to the Betsy-Tacy books as a source of inspiration. But it is not just writers who owe a debt to Maud Hart Lovelace. What about the librarians and teachers who grew up reading these books and went on to become as important to the young people they worked with as the librarian and teachers who encouraged Betsy and her friends? And what about the parents who aimed to make their homes as open, warm, and hospitable as that of the Rays? These books gave us goals, consciously and unconsciously.

Let me mention one last thing: as an adult, I bought myself a copy of *Betsy and Tacy Go Downtown*.

—JOHANNA HURWITZ

"I stepped from plank to plank
So slow and cautiously;
The stars about my head I felt
About my feet the sea."

—The Poems of EMILY DICKINSON

1

The Maple Tree

ETSY WAS SITTING in the backyard maple, high among spreading branches that were clothed in rich green except at their tips where they wore the first gold of September. Three branches forked to make a seat, one of them even providing a prop for her back. To her right, within easy reach, was another smaller crotch into which a cigar box had been nailed. This was closed and showed on the cover a plump coquettish lady wearing a Spanish shawl.

From this lofty retreat Betsy had a splendid view. It did not look toward the Big Hill where she and her friends Tacy and Tib had had so many adventurous picnics. It looked toward the town. Strictly speaking, her leaf-framed vista was of rooftops going down Hill Street like steps. But Betsy knew whither those steps led.

Sitting in her maple, she was aware of the town, spread out below, of Front Street where the stores were, of streets lined with the houses of people she did not know, of the Opera House, the Melborn

Hotel, the skeleton of the new Carnegie Library, and the High School that her sister Julia and Tacy's sister Katie now attended. She was aware of the river winding through its spacious valley and of a world, yet unexplored, lying beyond.

Lifting the lid of the cigar box, Betsy took out a small tablet. It said on the cover, "Ray's Shoe Store. Wear Queen Quality Shoes." She took out a pencil, short and well tooth-marked, and chewed it thoughtfully. Then opening the tablet she wrote:

The Repentance of Lady Clinton

by Betsy Warrington Ray
Author of *Her Secret Marriage, The Mystery of the Butternut Tree, A Tress of Golden Hair, Hardly More than a Child.* Etc. Etc.

Chapter One
Lord Patterson's Ball

She had progressed no further when a scratching sound caused her to look down. A red ringleted head was rising toward her. The visitor was Tacy who lived across the street and had been her dear friend for many years. Seven, to be exact, for Betsy and Tacy had started to be friends at Betsy's fifth birthday party, and now they were both twelve.

Tacy paused on a limb just below.

"Is it all right for me to come up?" she asked.

The perch in the maple tree was Betsy's private office. Here she thought out stories and poems and wrote them down. Here she kept what she had written in the cigar box that her mother had given her and Tacy had helped her nail to its present place.

"Of course," said Betsy. "Why weren't you in school this afternoon? Why couldn't you come out to play?"

"Something awful, something terrible has happened," Tacy said. She hoisted herself into a crotch near the one in which Betsy was sitting.

Tacy's large blue eyes swam with tears. Her lids were red, her freckled cheeks were wet. Betsy put her tablet and pencil into the cigar box and closed the lid with the Spanish lady on it.

"What's the matter?" she asked.

Tacy wiped her eyes on a wet ball of handkerchief.

"You remember," she said, "Rena loaned me *Lady Audley's Secret.*"

Betsy nodded.

"Well . . . Papa found it."

"What happened?"

Tacy's eyes overflowed.

"I had hidden it under the bed. And this noon while we were eating dinner, Mamma told Papa she thought there was a mousehole in our room, and

Papa went looking for it, and he found the book.

"He was furious, but he never dreamed it was mine. He marched down to the table and asked Mary whether she'd been reading it, and she said 'no.' And he asked Celia, and she said 'no.' And he asked Katie, and she said 'no.' And then he came to me and I had to say 'yes.'"

Tacy began to sob.

"Papa said he was amazed and astounded. He said he thought he had brought us up to appreciate good literature. He said there was a set of Dickens in the house, and Shakespeare, and Father Finn, and how did a child of his happen to be reading trash? Then he went out to the kitchen range and lifted the lid and threw it in . . ."

"Tacy!"

"Yes, he did!" wept Tacy. "And now what am I going to tell Rena?"

What, indeed!

Looking down from the maple, Betsy could see Rena contentedly stringing beans on the back doorstep, unconscious of her loss. Rena had come from a farm to help Mrs. Ray. She was young and good-natured, not like Tib's mother's hired girl, Matilda, who was old and cross. But even Rena got mad sometimes, and her paper-backed novels were her dearest treasures. She kept them locked in her trunk, and Betsy read them out loud to her evenings when Mr. and Mrs. Ray happened to be out—at their High Fly Whist Club or a lodge dance or prayer meeting. Prompted by the same instinct that had caused Tacy to hide *Lady Audley's Secret* under her bed, Betsy had never mentioned these readings to her father and mother. But she had told all the stories to Tacy and Tib and had even persuaded Rena to lend them the books. And now *Lady Audley's Secret* had perished in the flames!

"We'll have to buy her another one," said Betsy. "They have those paper-backed books at Cook's Book Store. I've seen them."

"But they cost a dime," answered Tacy through her tears.

That was true. And a dime, ten cents, was hard to come by, especially when one could not tell for what one needed it.

"We'll earn it," said Betsy stoutly.

"How?" asked Tacy.

"Somehow. You'll see."

"Betsy! Tacy!" came a voice from below.

"It's Tib," said Betsy. "Come on up," she called. And in half a minute a fluff of yellow hair rose into view. Tib swung herself lightly to a seat on a neighboring branch.

Tib had been friends with Betsy and Tacy almost

as long as they had been friends with each other. She lived two blocks away on Pleasant Street in a large chocolate-colored house. Betsy's house faced Tacy's at the end of Hill Street. The town ended and the country began there, on a green tree-covered hill that made a beautiful playground for all the neighborhood children. There was hardly a day when Tib did not come to play with Betsy and Tacy.

She looked anxiously now at Tacy's tear-stained face.

"What's the matter?" she asked.

"Tacy's father found *Lady Audley's Secret* under her bed."

"And he threw it in the kitchen stove," said Tacy. "He said it was trash."

"Trash!" cried Betsy. "I'm trying to write books just like it."

Tib's round blue eyes grew rounder.

"What are you going to tell Rena?" she asked.

"We're not going to tell her anything," said Betsy, "until we have a dime to buy her another book."

"How are you going to get a dime?" asked Tib.

"We're going to earn it," said Betsy. "But we haven't quite decided how."

The screen door creaked, and they looked down to see Rena with the pan of beans under her arm going into the kitchen. At the same moment they saw something else . . . Julia, with a boy beside her, walking up Hill Street.

Julia was fourteen. Her skirt came down to the tops of her shoes. A braid with a curl on the end hung down her back, past her slender, belted waist. She wore a big hat.

The boy, who wore the uniform of a military school, was carrying her books.

"It's a good thing," said Betsy sarcastically, "that she has Jerry to carry those heavy books."

"They'd break her back practically," said Tacy, "if she had to carry them herself."

"Look at him help her up the steps!" jeered Betsy. "It's too bad she's so weak."

"This going around with boys makes me sick," said Tacy.

"I like Herbert Humphreys," said Tib.

It was just like Tib to like a boy and say so.

"Oh, if you have to have a boy around, it might as well be Herbert," said Betsy, who liked him too.

"He wears cute clothes," said Tacy, blushing.

Herbert Humphreys, who had come to Deep Valley from St. Paul, wore knickerbockers. The other boys in their grade wore plain short pants.

"Why does Jerry wear a uniform?" asked Tib, peering down.

"He goes away to school. To Cox Military. It hasn't opened yet. And every day he walks up to the high school to walk home with Julia. Silly!" Betsy gave a sniff. "But he's nice. I'll say that much. He's mighty nice to me. Always giving me money for candy . . . Tacy!" She broke off in a shout. "Money! A dime! Ten cents!"

"Of course," cried Tacy, a smile breaking over her face.

"What is it? What are you talking about?" asked Tib in bewilderment.

"We need money, don't we?" asked Betsy. "Well, here's our chance to earn some."

"But how?" demanded Tib, as Betsy swung downward.

"By being nuisances," cried Tacy, following.

"Do you get *paid* for being nuisances?"

"For not being nuisances."

"I don't understand."

Betsy hung to a limb to explain.

"Jerry likes to talk to Julia without us sticking around. So sometimes he gives us money to go to the store for candy."

"Oh," said Tib, and slid nimbly to the ground.

Down on the ground, Tib did not look to be ten, much less her actual age of twelve. She was dainty and small. With her short yellow hair, round eyes and rosebud mouth, she looked like a doll. She wore a long-waisted pink lawn dress and a pink bow in her hair. Betsy and Tacy wore sailor suits.

Betsy was not so tall as Tacy but she was taller than she had been at ten. She wore her brown braids crossed in back and tied with perky ribbons which somehow matched her perky smiling face.

Tacy was slim and long of limb. Her face was still crowded with freckles, but they didn't matter when she shook back her curls and looked out shyly with blue Irish eyes.

All three were barefoot.

Single file they padded softly around the corner of the yellow cottage. A vine was turning red over the small front porch. Julia sat in the hammock there and Jerry sat on the railing staring into her slim wistful face.

"Why does he look at her like that? She's only Julia," Tacy whispered.

"Don't ask *me*," answered Betsy in disgust.

"Why does Julia look so sad?" asked Tib.

"She's just putting that look on. Thinks it's pretty," Betsy said. Scornfully she led the way to the porch.

Jerry turned around and smiled. He had a friendly, toothy smile in a brown pleasant face.

"Hello, kids," he said.

"Hello, children," said Julia languidly.

"*Kids! Children!*" said Betsy, not quite under her breath.

"Hello," said Tacy.

"Hello," said Tib.

They sat down in a row on the steps.

Conversation on the porch lagged. Julia unpinned her hat and fluffed her dark pompadour. She wore a big bow on the top of her head and another at the top of her braid.

"Remember, Jerry," she said at last, "you promised to help me with my algebra."

"Glad to," Jerry said.

"Betsy," said Julia. "I think Mamma is looking for you."

"She can't be," said Betsy. "She's taken Margaret downtown to get an English bob."

"Maybe Rena is looking for you then," said Julia pointedly.

"Nobody's looking for me," said Betsy.

"Or me either," said Tacy.

"Or me either," said Tib.

They sat like lumps.

"Algebra," said Julia, "is hard. Jerry can't explain it with so many around. He can't concentrate."

"That's right," said Jerry. He turned around to smile at them again. Betsy liked him when he smiled.

But she hardened her heart and didn't budge.

"Oh, well," said Julia. "Let's let the arithmetic go. Come on in the house, Jerry, and sing a while. I have some of the music from *Robin Hood*. Did you hear it?"

"Yes, I did."

"Wasn't it good? I went with Papa and Mamma. They decided I was old enough to start going to the theatre and they thought *Robin Hood* was a good thing to begin on. I loved it. I'm sure I'll like grand opera better, though."

Betsy writhed. It was her sorest grievance that she had not seen *Robin Hood*. She had never even been inside the Opera House.

Chatting in a grown-up way, Julia went into the house and Jerry followed. Betsy and Tacy and Tib followed too. They sat down in the largest, most comfortable chairs. They said nothing.

Julia went to the piano stool and ran her white fingers trippingly over the keys. She fluttered the music on the rack.

"Here's that good baritone solo. Sing it for me, Jerry."

"Well, gosh!" said Jerry, bending to look at it. "I'd like to. But I'm no De Wolf Hopper."

"Please, Jerry! You've sung for me before."

"But we were alone."

Julia turned the piano stool about.

"Why don't you three run over to the Kellys' to play?" she asked pleadingly.

"Paul's got the stomach ache," said Tacy. "Too many green apples."

"Mamma's got company," said Tib, after being nudged.

"I'm afraid we've got to stay right here," said Betsy. "Of course," she added cautiously after a moment, "we could go to Mrs. Chubbock's store for candy . . . if we had any money."

"We haven't any though," said Tacy. "At least I haven't."

"Neither have I," said Tib.

"Neither have I," said Betsy. "Not a cent."

Jerry dived into his pocket.

"Here, take this," he said, pulling out a dime.

Betsy looked from the dime to Tacy. And Tacy looked from the dime to Betsy. And Tib looked from the dime to Betsy and Tacy. What they were thinking, of course, was, "Of all the luck!" But Jerry misunderstood.

"Maybe a dime isn't enough," he said, "for three of you. Of course it isn't! You need a nickel apiece."

And he drew out a nickel.

This time Betsy and Tacy and Tib did not hesitate. With shouted thanks they grabbed and ran. They ran to Tacy's hitching block.

"There's enough for the book and *still* some for candy!"

"A nickel's worth of jaw-breakers!"

"Let's go downtown right now," suggested Betsy. "We can go to Cook's Book Store and buy the book. Get some jaw-breakers on the way. Of course, we'll have to ask."

"Mamma will let us go, I think," said Tacy. "She feels sorry for me, on account of how hard I cried. Wait here while I ask."

She ran into the house.

She was slow in returning, but when she came it was with a sparkling face.

"We may go if we put on shoes and stockings. I've put mine on."

"Mine are underneath the maple," said Tib, darting off.

"I'll get mine," Betsy said.

She raced into the house and upstairs to the little front bedroom. She and Julia shared it with Margaret now. Rena slept in the little back bedroom that had once been Margaret's. The house was getting crowded, Mr. Ray said.

Rena was baking gingerbread. Betsy could tell by the smell rising from the kitchen. In the parlor Jerry was singing a song about *Brown October Ale.*

Betsy and Tacy and Tib started down Hill Street. They were pleased and excited because they were going downtown. But they did not suspect what marvel they would see before they returned.

2

The Horseless Carriage

THE WALK downtown was uneventful . . . as uneventful as a walk downtown could be. It always seemed important to go beyond Lincoln Park, that pie-shaped wedge of lawn with an elm tree and a fountain on it which marked the end of the neighborhood.

Ahead stretched Broad Street where fine houses sat on wide, tree-shaded streets. Wooden sidewalks changed to cement ones here. Church steeples loomed ahead, and the shiny framework of the new Carnegie Library.

"When that library is finished," Betsy remarked, "we won't need to borrow our novels from Rena."

Parallel with Broad Street to the right were other streets rising one above another on the bluff. The High School that Julia and Katie attended lifted its tower there.

Parallel with Broad Street to the left was Second Street with more houses, churches, livery stables, and the Opera House. Beyond that, Front Street lay along the river. But the river could not be seen except in glimpses between stores and shops, the Depot, the Big Mill, and Mr. Melborn Poppy's splendid Melborn Hotel.

September lay upon Front Street in pale golden light. Horses were drowsing at hitching rings and poles. In front of the Lion Department Store a bronze lion stood guard over a drinking trough. The thoroughfare was quiet, except for the occasional clop clop of horses on the paving and the whir of passing bicycles.

"Let's get our jaw-breakers first," said Tib, so they went into Schulte's Grocery Store and bought a nickel's worth of jaw-breakers. They divided them equally and went on to Cook's Book Store.

"A copy of *Lady Audley's Secret*, please," said Betsy, putting down their dime.

Mr. Cook looked at them sharply out of very bright blue eyes. He was tall and thin and wore a toupee, thick and silky, parted in the middle.

"That is a strange book for three little girls to be buying," he remarked.

"We're buying it for my mother's hired girl," said Betsy. "She likes those ten-cent books."

"It's a fine story, Mr. Cook," volunteered Tib, and Betsy and Tacy both nudged her. They didn't think it was such a good idea to let Mr. Cook know that they read Rena's novels. But he accepted their dime.

It was when they came out of the store, with *Lady Audley's Secret* under Tacy's arm, that they had their first hint of the marvel which was to make the day forever memorable.

Front Street was suddenly full of people. People seemed to have sprung up from nowhere, and all were rushing in one direction as though blown by a great wind. Shoppers; clerks from stores, wearing alpaca jackets; hatless women, untying aprons as they went; dozens and dozens of children.

"Whatever can it be? What's happened?"

Betsy, Tacy, and Tib started to run.

They sighted Winona Root, pedaling by on her bicycle. She was a classmate who lived on School Street in a white-painted brick house with a terrace and a beautiful garden. Her father was the editor of the *Deep Valley Sun*.

Winona had black hair that hung in long straight locks on either side of a somewhat sallow face. She had gleaming black eyes and very white teeth which she showed almost constantly in a teasing smile. She always wore bright dresses of red, purple or yellow. She was wearing a purple one now.

"Winona! Stop! Tell us what's the matter!"

"Don't you know?"

"If we did, we wouldn't ask you."

Winona grinned.

"Don't you wish you *did* know?"

"Of course. Please tell us, Winona."

Winona stopped pedaling. She rested on long legs.

"Well," she said, drawing out the suspense. "It came this noon but he's just got it to going."

"Who is 'he' and what is 'it'?"

"*He* is Mr. Poppy who owns the Melborn Hotel and runs the Opera House. *It* is down by the Opera House now."

"But what *is* 'it'? Winona Root, you tell us. You might as well! We'll follow the crowd and find out."

"All right," said Winona, not wanting to be cheated of the pleasure of delivering the news. "It's a horseless carriage."

A horseless carriage! Betsy, Tacy, and Tib were stunned into silence.

There had been rumors for some time of a marvelous invention called the horseless carriage, a vehicle that ran without being pushed or pulled . . . even uphill. They had seen pictures of it. *The Ladies' Home Journal* had shown Miss Julia Marlowe, the actress, sitting in one. And some Deep Valley people had gone to the Twin Cities, as Minneapolis and St. Paul are called in Minnesota, to view the wonder. But this was the first automobile to reach Deep Valley.

Winona took their silence for skepticism.

"Come on, if you don't believe me. My father's going to have a ride in it, so's he can write a piece for the paper. I'll be the first kid in town to get a ride, I imagine."

She probably would be, Betsy thought gloomily. Winona Root did everything first. Just because her father was an editor, she had complimentary tickets—"comps," they were called—to the circus, to the Dog and Pony Show, to the glass blowers, to the lantern slide performances, to all the matinees that played at the Opera House.

"Maybe you won't be," said Tib.

"Betcha I will," Winona answered.

She jumped on her bicycle and started pedaling

with long agile legs. Betsy, Tacy, and Tib raced along behind her.

"I don't even want to be," panted Tacy as she ran.

"Want to be what?"

"The first to get a ride. I'd be scared."

"What of?" asked Tib.

"The horseless carriage. It sounds crazy to me. If there isn't a horse to say 'whoa!' to, how do you stop the thing?"

"That's what I wonder," said Betsy. "How does it know when Mr. Poppy is ready to stop?"

"It might keep right on going."

"Up one street and down another."

"Into the slough, maybe."

"Or into the river."

"Are you scared too?" Tib asked Betsy.

"Well . . . Winona Root can have the first ride for all of me."

"I'm not scared," said Tib. "I'd like to be the first to ride."

They ran past the office in which Tacy's father sold sewing machines; it was closed. Past Ray's Shoe Store; that was closed too. Store after store was closed and empty. They reached the Melborn Hotel and turned the corner and ran to the Opera House.

There, where the crowd was thickest, they could see what looked like an open carriage . . . only without any shafts and without a horse hitched to it. Near by stood Mr. Root and Winona, the Mayor and other notables, and, of course, the Poppys.

Mr. and Mrs. Poppy were worth looking at themselves when there wasn't a horseless carriage about. He weighed over three hundred pounds and his wife, two-thirds as much. Today they looked even larger than usual, for they wore the loose linen dusters fashionable for automobiling. Mr. Poppy wore a leather cap that had flaps tied over his ears and enormous froglike goggles. Mrs. Poppy's hat was tied down with yards and yards of veiling.

The Poppys were always models of elegance. They were city people; they had come from Minneapolis, and no one in town knew them very well. They lived in the hotel; Mrs. Poppy did not keep house as other Deep Valley wives did. Blonde and radiant, she was said to look like the famous beauty and actress, Lillian Russell . . . except that she was stouter, of course. Before her marriage, she had been an actress herself.

She and her husband went to the Twin Cities often, to see plays. But they saw plays in Deep Valley too. When Mr. Poppy built the Opera House, he had two special seats made for Mrs. Poppy and himself. Extra wide, extra deep, and extra comfortable, designed for extra-stout people. Betsy had heard about them often.

She and Tacy and Tib squirmed through the crowd until they were near the Poppys. A sweet scent floated from Mrs. Poppy, and whenever she moved there was silken rustle beneath the linen duster. She looked down to smile at Tib. Tib always drew a flattering smile even from strangers; and today in the long-waisted pink lawn dress, she looked even prettier than usual.

A man in overalls lay underneath the horseless carriage. Wrenches and other tools were scattered in the dust.

"Two hours' work for one hour's riding is the average, I hear," the Mayor remarked jocularly to Mr. Poppy.

"Oh, come now! It isn't that bad," answered Mr. Poppy, smiling too, although his round red face with its garlands of chins looked hot and flustered. "How you coming, Jim?" he called to the man underneath the carriage.

The man crawled out. He was Sunny Jim who worked in the livery stable next door to the Opera House. Everyone called him Sunny Jim because of his resemblance to the smiling figure in the Force advertisements.

"It'll go this time, sir. No doubt about it."

Mr. Poppy turned with a courtly bow to his wife.

"First ride for Mrs. Poppy. And then you gentlemen must try it out."

Winona took her father's hand.

"May I go along, father?" she asked.

"We'll see," her father answered indulgently.

Winona grinned wickedly at Tib.

There was a spreading circle of perfume and a swishing sound of silken petticoats as Mr. Poppy handed Mrs. Poppy into the back seat. Settling herself comfortably, she almost filled it. Under her veil-tied hat, her face glowed with pleasure.

"You show commendable courage, Mrs. Poppy," said Winona's father, leaning forward.

"Oh, I adore automobiling," Mrs. Poppy answered. She smiled at the crowd, and her smile lingered on the group of children. She and Mr. Poppy were very fond of children although they had none of their own. Tib waved at her, and Mrs. Poppy waved gloved fingers in response.

"Steady now," Mr. Poppy said.

He walked to the back of the vehicle and turned a crank. With Sunny Jim at his elbow and the crowd waiting intently, he turned it again . . . and again. He turned it once again, and there was an explosive chugging noise. The carriage began to shake.

"Good!" cried Mr. Poppy, and he ran around and climbed into the front seat where the children now observed a wheel at the right side. He took this into his hands with firm determination. The carriage continued to shake convulsively. An evil smell crept into the air.

Sunny Jim rushed to Mr. Poppy's side. He shouted excited directions. Mr. Poppy turned keys, pressed pedals, pulled levers. The carriage was shaking so hard now that Mrs. Poppy vibrated like jelly, but she continued to smile.

"Got it, Mr. Poppy?" Sunny Jim shouted.

"Got it."

"Off, sir?"

"Well, practically."

And at that sovereign moment, Tib danced forward.

"Please, Mr. Poppy," she called. "May I have a ride?"

Betsy gasped, and Tacy gulped. They had not dreamed that Tib had this in mind. It would be an inconceivable glory to get the first ride. What a triumph over Winona Root!

But Mr. Poppy was too busy turning keys, pressing pedals, and pulling levers even to glance at Tib.

"Some other time, little girl! Some other time!" he answered absently.

Winona Root flashed Betsy and Tacy a smile of good-natured scorn.

Mrs. Poppy leaned forward to touch her husband's shoulder.

"Give her a ride, Mel. She can sit here with me and won't be a bit of trouble."

"All right . . . if you want her."

"Come along, dear. Jump up!"

Mrs. Poppy moved heavily over, drawing aside her billowing fragrant skirts. Tib jumped.

"Father!" Winona Root called urgently. "Can't I . . ."

But it was too late. With a burst of vapor and a clanking that drowned out her voice, the horseless carriage moved. It actually moved. It went ahead without pushing or pulling. It ran right along behind nothing.

The crowd sent up a tremendous cheer. Betsy and Tacy yelled at the tops of their voices. Nestled beneath Mrs. Poppy's bosom, Tib waved frantically to Betsy and Tacy who waved frantically back.

Horses reared, and drivers all around pulled at their reins. The crowd ran along beside the uncannily moving vehicle. Betsy caught a glimpse of her father . . . he was throwing his hat into the air. For just a moment he did not look like her father; he looked like a boy. She saw Tacy's father, too; and Tib's. And Herbert Humphreys, wearing his knickerbockers. And Tom Slade. And ever so many of their schoolmates. All were running madly beside the horseless carriage.

But it gained speed. It left them behind. Clanking,

rattling, spitting, it turned the corner and vanished from sight.

Betsy and Tacy jumped up and down and screamed a while. Then they raced back to the Opera House. In the milling crowd they found Winona Root, standing under one of the two billboards that flanked the entrance doors. Her teeth gleamed in her indomitable smile.

"Yah! Yah!" yelled Betsy and Tacy. "Tib got the first ride!"

"What of it?"

"What of it?" shouted Betsy indignantly. "You said *you* were going to be the first. That's what!"

Winona flipped a careless arm toward the advertisement above her.

"See that? *Uncle Tom's Cabin* or *Life Among the Lowly*. They're giving a matinee next Saturday. I'm going."

"What of it?" Tacy remembered to retort. But Betsy's gaze wandered to the billboard and clung there fascinated.

"I've read the book," said Betsy slowly.

"'Foremost American drama and the nation's pride,'" Winona read aloud. "'Dear to Americans as the Declaration of Independence. Struck the death knell of slavery.'"

"Pooh!" said Tacy.

"'Presenting America's most talented and beautiful child actress, Miss Evelyn Montmorency, in the role of Little Eva,'" chanted Winona. "'Don't miss her ascension to the heavenly gates, nor the grand brilliant spectacular transformation scene.'"

"She dies and goes to Heaven," Betsy said.

"'See the ferocious pack of man-eating Siberian bloodhounds. See them chase Eliza in the most thrilling scene ever depicted!'"

"They chase her over the ice," Betsy explained. "She jumps from block to block."

"'Hear the plantation singers! See the comical

Topsy do her famous breakdown dance! See the heart-breaking, tear-wringing death of Uncle Tom . . .'"

"I've heard that on the graphophone!" Tacy interrupted excitedly. "You've heard it, Betsy! The flogging scene . . ."

Winona Root looked from one to the other, smiling exultantly. Reaching into her pocket, she pulled out four pieces of pasteboard, and held them above her head.

"'Comps!'" she said. "Four of them! I asked my father for them and I got them, just a minute ago. I can take three kids but I haven't quite decided which ones I will take."

With an impish grin, Winona sprang to her bicycle.

A clanking and rattling was heard up the street.

"Here it comes!" "Here it comes!" "Here's the horseless carriage back again!"

The crowd shouted, and Betsy and Tacy shouted louder than anyone. But Winona did not wait to see Tib's triumph. Flourishing her tickets in an upflung arm, guiding herself with one jaunty hand, she pedaled off toward home.

The horseless carriage drew to a stop exactly in front of the Opera House.

"You see," Betsy said. "Mr. Poppy knows how to stop it."

Tib stepped out, smiling.

"Thank you, Mr. Poppy. Thank you, Mrs. Poppy," she said politely. She flung a glance toward Herbert Humphreys, who was staring in admiration, and danced away to join Betsy and Tacy.

Tib was modest about her sensational ride; Tib was always modest. But as they walked up Front Street, up Broad Street, up Hill Street, going home with Rena's book, she told them exactly how it felt to ride in a horseless carriage.

"It's grand," she said. "No old horse in front to block your view. You simply sail along. And you can go so *fast*. Twelve miles in an hour, Mr. Poppy said. Of course, we only went ten today, because we were in town and the horses were so scared."

"Were *you* scared?" Tacy asked.

"Not a bit."

Then Betsy and Tacy told her about the coming of *Uncle Tom's Cabin*. They told her about Little Eva and Topsy, the transformation scene and the flogging scene and Eliza crossing the ice. They told her about Winona's tickets to the Saturday matinee.

"Gee whiz!" said Betsy. "We've just *got* to be the ones she takes."

"I'd certainly like to see those man-eating blood-hounds," said Tib.

"I'd have to keep my eyes closed while they flogged Uncle Tom though," said Tacy, the tender-hearted.

"I want to see Little Eva go up to Heaven. She goes right up while you're watching her, and sits on a pink cloud. It's spiffy," Betsy said. "How *can* we make her ask us?"

"We've got to manage it somehow."

"We've just *got* to!"

But before they thought of a way to inveigle an invitation out of Winona Root, they met Jerry. He was walking down Hill Street whistling the song about *Brown October Ale*.

"There's a horseless carriage in town!" Betsy, Tacy, and Tib shouted together.

"I rode in it!"

"Tib rode in it!"

"No!" Jerry cried. "Whose is it? Where is it? Gosh, I'm crazy to see one." He set off at a run downtown.

And Betsy, Tacy, and Tib savored again the triumph of Tib's ride. They progressed up Hill Street slowly, pausing at every house to shout the news. They collected a crowd of envious children, of agitated women.

"It's grand," Tib repeated over and over again. "You sail right along behind nothing."

3
Winona's Tickets

NEXT MORNING on the way to school they held an earnest consultation on the matter of getting Winona Root to invite them to *Uncle Tom's Cabin*.

The evening had gone with much jubilant talk of Tib's ride in the horseless carriage. At the Ray supper table, at the Kelly supper table, at the Muller supper table, in Rena's and Matilda's kitchens and, later, on the Rays' hitching block surrounded by spellbound children in the smoky September dusk, Betsy, Tacy, and Tib had told and retold the afternoon's adventure. Even modest Tib had swaggered a little as she tripped down Hill Street on her homeward way.

In the morning, however, she was the one to suggest that hereafter they should belittle her achievement.

"We mustn't brag in front of Winona. She'd give those tickets away right in front of our face and eyes."

"That's right, Tib. You're smart to think of that."

"Well, we've bragged plenty anyway," Betsy said contentedly. "Even Julia was just knocked over by your ride."

"So was Katie," Tacy said. "And my big brothers! They made me tell them every single thing you said, Tib."

With a long satisfied sigh, Tib dismissed her honors.

"Let's plan now how to go after those tickets. I've got an idea."

Tib's idea was a practical one, of course. Tib was always practical. She proposed to bribe Winona Root with a combined gift of all their treasures. Betsy's agate marble, Tacy's copy of a Gibson Girl, her own Schlitz beer calendar, sent by her uncle in Milwaukee.

"She'd be sure to take us in return for all that," Tib said.

Betsy, however, favored acting as though they didn't want to go.

"She's so contrary. She's most apt to invite us if we act as though we didn't care a thing about it."

Tacy disagreed.

"I think we ought to be extra nice to her. Ask her to play at recess. Ask her to come home to play after school. Mamma bakes today, and she'd give us some bread right out of the oven, with honey on it. You could let her ride your bicycle, Tib. And Betsy could let her use the telephone."

Mr. Ray had just installed a telephone; it was a novelty to Hill Street.

"She's got a telephone herself," said Betsy. "They had the first one in town."

"Well, she can telephone her mother then."

But Betsy shook her head.

"It would be just like her to let us do all that, and then give the tickets to somebody else."

Tacy and Tib knew that this was true. All of them could visualize Winona's mocking smile.

They had reached Mrs. Chubbock's candy store beside the school grounds when Tacy stopped suddenly and clutched an arm of either friend.

"I've got it! We'll hypnotize her!"

"Hypnotize her!"

"You remember the hypnotist who came to the Opera House last year? Mary and Celia saw him. He could make anyone do anything he wanted to, just by thinking about it. Let's us think toward Winona, '*Take* us to *Uncle Tom's Cabin*. *Take* us to *Uncle Tom's Cabin*.'"

"Tacy Kelly, that's wonderful!" cried Betsy.

But Tib was doubtful.

"Don't you remember," she asked, "that just after the hypnotist came, we tried to hypnotize our fathers? We tried to make them give us a dollar. We thought about it at every meal. I stared at Papa just like you told me to and thought, 'Give me a dollar. Give me a dollar.' You all did the same thing, but not one of us got a dollar."

It was just like Tib to dig up this unsuccessful venture.

"Tib," said Betsy. "You forget. There was just one of us thinking toward each father. Besides, a dollar is a lot of money. If we'd made it a nickel or a penny, we'd probably have got it. All three of us will be thinking toward Winona Root, and she can't help but feel it. It will be powerful. It will be terrific."

"We can try it," Tib said glumly.

"We'll all think the same thing," said Tacy. " '*Take* us to *Uncle Tom's Cabin. Take* us. *Take* us. *Take* us.' "

"I like that," said Betsy. "It sounds like a poem. Let's practice it now."

They put their arms around one another's shoulders and bent their heads together.

"*Take* us to *Uncle Tom's Cabin. Take* us. *Take* us. *Take* us."

It did sound like a poem. It sounded weird and mysterious.

"We'll stare at her while we think it," said Betsy.

"That's what the hypnotist did," Tacy explained.

The school bell rang noisily, and Betsy, Tacy, and

Tib ran across the sandy boys' yard and up the long flight of steps leading to the school door. They went up to the second floor and into their room.

Miss Paxton was their teacher. She had a gray pompadour and wore shirt-waist suits in which her stock was always very high and her belt very trim. The room was sunny and large. There was a bouquet of purple asters, goldenrod, and sumac leaves on Miss Paxton's tidy desk.

Betsy, Tacy, and Tib took their seats, which were not close together. Every year they sought for adjoining seats and every year the teacher foiled their plan and placed them as far apart as possible. Betsy and Tacy sat toward the back of the room, one at the far right and one at the far left. Tib sat near the front. Winona Root sat halfway back in the very center of the room.

With the second bell she dashed in, wearing a red dress. Her black eyes went at once to Tib. Tib was staring at her. Winona seated herself with a breezy flipping of skirts. Tib turned around and continued to stare with eyes like round moons.

Winona looked surprised. She had expected bragging, boasting, taunts, perhaps. But not this . . . whatever it was. Slightly uncomfortable, she turned to the left, only to find Tacy's Irish eyes fixed on her dreamily. She turned to the right and encountered

Betsy's piercing hazel gaze.

Winona tossed her head.

Miss Paxton called for "Position." She smiled at Tib.

"You may pick the opening song, Thelma," she said. "That is, if you will turn around and face the front."

Tib picked, *Onward Christian Soldiers*. And she turned around and faced the front, but only for a moment. When the singing began, she twisted about to stare at Winona. Betsy and Tacy were staring at her too. Betsy was not singing the right words of the hymn. She was singing (but softly, so that no one could hear):

> "Take *us*, take *us*, take *us*,
> *Take us to the show,*
> Take *us*, take *us*, take *us*,
> *To Uncle Tom, you know.*"

After the hymn came the prayer. Betsy and Tacy consulted with their eyes as to whether it would be sinful to hypnotize while praying. Deciding that it wouldn't be, they put their hands over their eyes reverently but stared through their fingers at their victim. Tib, when she saw what they were doing, did the same.

After the prayer came physical exercises. Tom

was asked to open all the windows, and the boys and girls stood and jerked their arms up and down, out and back, in time to Miss Paxton's "*One*, two. *One*, two."

Betsy jerked her arms in time to, "*Take* us. *Take* us." She mouthed the words to Tacy who began to say them too. Both of them stared unceasingly at Winona. Tib turned around to stare.

"Face *front*, Thelma," Miss Paxton interrupted her counting to cry.

Reluctantly Tib faced front.

When the class sat down, Miss Paxton folded her hands on the desk. She looked around brightly.

"I heard some interesting news this morning," she said. "A member of our class, Thelma Muller, had a ride in the new automobile that reached town yesterday."

She smiled at Tib. But Tib looked blank.

"Did you enjoy it?" Miss Paxton asked.

"It was all right," said Tib.

"Would you like to come up front and tell us about it?"

"There's nothing to tell, Miss Paxton," Tib replied.

Miss Paxton looked crestfallen, and also surprised. Tib was anything but shy. Usually she enjoyed an opportunity to appear before the class. Winona looked mystified too, and Betsy and Tacy, whom Miss Paxton had expected to see puffed up with pride, were yawning.

"In that case," said Miss Paxton, to end an awkward pause, "we will study geography."

With a series of thuds and bangs, the big geography books were brought out and opened. Quiet descended on the room. Stealthily, Tib took a sideways pose again. Instead of looking at the New England states, she looked at Winona.

Tacy sat turned to the right. Her face framed by her long red curls, she gazed fervently at Winona. Betsy sat turned to the left. Leaning on one elbow, she stared at Winona too.

Winona shifted uneasily. She looked around once or twice.

"Now," said Miss Paxton, "you may close your books. Betsy, will you name the New England states?"

Betsy jumped up.

"*Take* us. *Take* us. *Take* us," she began.

"What did you say?" Miss Paxton asked sharply.

"Excuse me, Miss Paxton. That was a mistake. Maine, New Hampshire, Vermont . . ."

Next they studied arithmetic. Again Tib studied half turned around.

"Thelma," said Miss Paxton, "I don't know what's got into you today. Please face the front and look at your book instead of at Winona."

Tib flung Betsy and Tacy a pleading look. She turned to the front. Betsy and Tacy kept on staring. Winona was like a mouse between two cats.

At recess Betsy and Tacy and Tib sat with their backs to the high board fence that marked off the girls' yard. Their legs were stuck out stiff and straight in front of them. They sat motionless, staring at Winona.

She was playing Prisoners' Base, and whenever she flashed past them on long jaunty legs, she glanced quickly to see whether they were staring. They always were.

The bell rang and the children crowded into line. Winona pulled four tickets from the pocket of her dress.

"'Comps,'" she said, tossing her black locks. "They're for *Uncle Tom's Cabin*. I've got three to give away."

She turned around to see whether Betsy and Tacy and Tib were listening. They were. They were listening, and they were staring with marble-like eyes. Their lips were moving soundlessly.

After recess came the reading lesson. While the others, in turn, droned through *The Courtship of Miles Standish*, Betsy, Tacy, and Tib stared at Winona.

"Thelma Muller, you are to look toward the *front*," Miss Paxton said.

"Tacy Kelly. Please sit straight in your seat. You aren't looking toward the front either."

"Betsy Ray. Look toward the *front*. What ails you three today?"

Beneath her desk, Winona got out the tickets. She spread them into a fan; she built a little house with them; she showed them to the boy in front of her and to the girl behind. Now and then she glanced at Betsy, Tacy, and Tib with nervous bravado.

At last the bell announced that it was time for the noon departure. Miss Paxton rapped on her desk.

"Position! Rise! Turn! March!"

The grade formed into two lines and marched into the hall, but even in this orderly procession Tib turned around to stare. Betsy leaned out from her place in line to stare, and so did Tacy. Glances like bullets shot toward Winona.

Winona brought out her tickets again. She flourished them defiantly.

"'Comps,'" she called to Herbert Humphreys in the boys' line. "For *Uncle Tom's Cabin*. Don't you wish you were me?"

"Who're you taking, Winona?" Herbert Humphreys asked.

"I haven't decided," said Winona. Her teeth gleamed wickedly. She looked down the line toward Betsy and up the line toward Tib.

They were staring of course. They were staring harder than they had ever stared before. Their eyes were almost popping from their heads with their agonized concentration.

"I know who I *won't* take," Winona said loudly.

"Who?" Herbert Humphreys asked.

"People who stare at me all the time," Winona said.

She put the tickets back into her pocket.

4
More about Winona's Tickets

BETSY, TACY, and Tib scarcely spoke, going home at noon.

"It didn't work," Tib said, blaming no one, just stating a fact.

"No. It didn't work," admitted Tacy.

"We won't try to hypnotize her any more," said Betsy.

That was all they said. They parted with unhappy nods.

After dinner they walked back to school still unsmiling. During the afternoon they were quiet and subdued. Tib faced toward the front, and none of them looked at Winona. Even when she counted her tickets and made a little pack of them and flipped it in all directions, they did not look at her except out of the corners of their eyes.

After school they went to Tacy's house because Mrs. Kelly was baking. It was a sight to see the plump loaves of golden brown bread pulled from the oven and buttered. Mrs. Kelly took the loaves out of their pans and set them on a clean cloth to butter them. Betsy's mouth watered when the butter melted and ran in rich streams down the nutlike crusts of the loaves. When the bread was cool enough to cut, Mrs. Kelly gave a soft piece to each of them. She gave one to Paul who ran in from the bonfire he was tending. And she gave one to Katie who was helping her as usual. Katie always helped her mother after school these days. Mary and Celia were typewriter girls now and away from home all day. Katie was as cheerful about work as though it were play. She seemed to like helping her mother with the bread.

Betsy and Tacy and Tib began to feel better when they had buttered their bread and spread honey on it and gone out to the pump in Tacy's back yard.

This was a favorite place with them. The wooden platform made a comfortable seat, and they could look up at the encircling hills where the softwood trees were turning red and yellow, making bright bouquets against the green. Smoke from Paul's bonfire scented the air that was as warm and golden as their bread.

Betsy had been thinking deeply about *Uncle Tom's Cabin*. Her heart yearned toward the play as it had never yearned toward anything before. The longing was a little like what she felt when she saw rows and rows of books in other people's bookcases. (She had read all the books in the bookcase at home.) But this feeling was stronger and more violent. She *had* to go to *Uncle Tom's Cabin*! She *had* to!

It was more than possible that if she asked her father, he would let her go. But then, what about Tacy? Tacy's father ruled his kingdom of children with a kindly but inflexible justice. What one child had, all of them had, or its equivalent. What one child did, all of them did. He would not send Tacy to a matinee at the Opera House unless he could afford to send Katie and Paul too. As for Tib, she might not be allowed to go. Tib's mother was strict. And for Betsy to see *Uncle Tom's Cabin* without Tacy or Tib would be a hollow joy.

If all three were invited to go as Winona's guests,

the situation would be different. That would be a party; they could accept, of course. Somehow the three of them had to be invited. But Betsy was empty of ideas.

Tib was hopeful that the matter could be arranged.

"Let's try my plan," she said, "of telling her we want to go and offering her presents."

"No," said Betsy. "At least, let's not say right out that we want to go. If we do that, and she doesn't take us, she can laugh at us. We might give her the presents though, in a careless kind of way."

"Let's do what I suggested," said Tacy. "Ask her to play after school. And while we're being nice to her, just hand out a few presents."

"All right," Betsy said. "I certainly hope it works."

They jumped up then to help Paul with the bonfire. Tib's brothers, Freddie and Hobbie, and Margaret and the Rivers children were helping him too. Paul's black and brown mongrel dog, Gyp, was rushing about through the leaves. The children threw sticks which he retrieved with happy snorts. They had a good time, but through it all Betsy thought with longing about *Uncle Tom's Cabin*.

At recess the next day she said to Winona, "Come on and play with us."

"Let's play statues," said Tacy. "I always think you're good at statues, Winona."

"You can make such awful faces," said Tib.

Winona looked suspicious but flattered.

"All right," she said, and they played statues. When Tacy flung Winona, she called out "Cross schoolteacher!" And Winona's scowling face between locks of black hair, her fiercely upraised finger were pronounced magnificent.

"You're practically an actress, Winona," Betsy said. "It's probably because you go to so many plays."

"You're certainly lucky," said Tacy.

"I should say you are," said Tib.

The bell rang, and Betsy said, "Why don't you come home with us after school? You've never been to see us. We could have lots of fun."

Winona's eyes glittered with dawning comprehension.

"All right," she replied. "I'd just as soon."

Winona enjoyed herself that afternoon. They went to Betsy's house first and urged Winona to telephone her mother over the Rays' new telephone. It was fixed into the wall beside the dining-room door. Winona had to climb on a stool to reach it. She rang the bell, lifted the receiver and said "Hello Central" with an assurance that her companions envied. Her mother was surprised to hear from her.

Afterwards they played a game of Ping-Pong. (Winona's side won, of course.) They took her out in the kitchen and introduced her to Rena, red cheeked and pretty with ribbons woven into the braid that was knotted behind her pompadour. Rena gave them some rocks she had baked that morning. These were little cakes full of raisins and nuts and were very good.

Betsy put the agate marble secretly into her pocket. They crossed the street to Tacy's house.

There they made Gyp do his tricks for Winona. He fetched and carried willingly. They showed Winona Tacy's father's violin. And Mrs. Kelly, who did not know that they had had rocks over at the Rays', gave them some fat ginger cookies. Tacy slipped upstairs for her Gibson Girl picture. She had traced it and colored it and framed it in passe-partout. She put it under her skirt, and they all went on to Tib's house.

Tib offered Winona a ride on her bicycle. Winona had a bicycle of her own, of course, but she enjoyed riding Tib's. They took her all over Tib's beautiful house. As they came down the curving front stairs, Betsy pointed out the panes of colored glass in the entrance door. They went into the front parlor that was round because it was a tower room, and through blue velvet draperies into the back parlor where the window seat was, and through the red and gold dining room into the kitchen.

Matilda did not know they had had rocks to eat at the Rays' and ginger cookies at the Kellys'. She gave them some apple cake, and they took it out to the knoll.

While the others were eating under the oak tree, Tib skipped into the house and upstairs to her room. She came back bearing the Schlitz beer calendar that her uncle had sent her from Milwaukee. It had a picture on it of a pretty girl skating. It said, "The beer that made Milwaukee famous."

Tib looked with raised questioning eyebrows at Betsy who signaled to Tacy who nodded. Simultaneously the Schlitz beer calendar, the Gibson Girl picture, and the agate marble were thrown into Winona's lap.

"Some presents for you, Winona," Betsy said.

For just a moment Winona looked startled.

"It isn't my birthday," she said.

"Oh, we just thought you might like them," said Betsy.

"You don't come to see us very often, so we thought we'd give you some presents," said Tacy.

"That's the only reason," said Tib. "Really it is."

Winona's eyes shone now with full understanding.

"Oh," she said. "Thanks. This is a spiffy calendar.

Gee, this is a good copy of a Gibson Girl. I haven't got a marble like that."

Then she jumped up.

"Well," she said. "I guess I'll have to be going."

Betsy, Tacy, and Tib looked at one another.

"Come over again," said Tib.

"What are you doing Saturday?" asked Betsy.

"Saturday?" repeated Winona. "Saturday? Oh, I remember! I'm going to *Uncle Tom's Cabin*."

"Decided who you're going to take?" asked Tacy.

"No," said Winona. "Quite a lot of people want to go. Well, good-by!"

"Good-by," said Betsy and Tacy and Tib.

They watched glumly while Winona skipped off with heartless jauntiness bearing the agate marble, the Gibson Girl picture, and the Schlitz beer calendar.

The situation was getting really desperate. This was Wednesday. Tomorrow would be Thursday. Friday was the last day before the matinee.

"Tomorrow," said Betsy. "We'll try my plan. We won't pay a bit of attention to her. Just snub her good and hard."

Tacy and Tib agreed reluctantly.

"It seems awfully dangerous," said Tacy. "Can we risk it?"

"We've got to," Betsy answered.

So the next day they snubbed Winona all day

long. But it didn't help, because she didn't even notice it; she was too busy having a good time with other children who wanted to go to *Uncle Tom's Cabin*. She was decked with a thorn apple necklace that Alice had made. And she was letting everybody listen to a seashell that Herbert Humphreys' aunt had sent him from Boston, and she wore someone's gift of a peacock feather in her long black hair. When she ran at recess it floated out behind her. It suited her somehow.

She barely glanced at Betsy and Tacy and Tib. When she did look their way, it was only to see whether they were noticing her triumphs. They were.

Tib forgot her pride to ask with pretended casualness: "Decided who you're going to take to the matinee, Winona?"

"Haven't thought about it," Winona said.

She called Alice and pulled out Betsy's agate marble.

"Want to trade?" she asked.

Betsy and Tacy and Tib conferred after school in the depths of discouragement. Beside Tacy's pump they lay on their backs and looked up sadly at the glory of the hills.

"We might as well give up," said Betsy. Then in a fierce resentment of the disappointment that filled her body like an ache, she sat suddenly upright. "I know what let's do! Let's give a play ourselves."

"We often do that," said Tib. "It's fun, but it isn't like going to a play with bloodhounds in it."

"We can put bloodhounds in our play," cried Betsy. "At least we can put a dog in it. We can put Gyp in it!" Gyp heard his name and came running, leaping and barking as though stage struck.

"What play shall we give?" asked Tacy, brightening.

"I'll turn my novel into a play."

"*The Repentance of Lady Clinton?*"

"*The Repentance of Lady Clinton*. It will make a spiffy play. Before she repents, Lady Clinton gets chased by this dog. Across some chunks of ice, maybe. I haven't decided."

"If there was a girl like Topsy doing a dance," said Tib. "I could black my face and dance."

"There *is* a girl like Topsy, but I think Tacy had better play that part, because we need you for another part. There's a girl like Little Eva in it too, and she dies and goes to Heaven. We'll have to pull her up to the ceiling, and you'll be light to pull."

"How'll we manage it?"

"We'll manage. And I'll ask my mother if we can use the costumes out of Uncle Keith's trunk."

"Where shall we give this play?" asked Tib.

"Let's ask your mother if we can give it at your house. We could draw the curtains between the front and back parlors, and use the parlor for the audience to sit in, and the back parlor for the stage. We could use the dining room for a dressing room; close the sliding doors. It would be perfect."

"Do you think she'll let us?"

"We can ask her," said Tib. "Let's all go ask her now."

They bounced off the pump platform and ran down Hill Street and through the vacant lot to Tib's house.

Mrs. Muller gave her consent with surprising readiness.

"Go ahead," she said. "Matilda and I haven't housecleaned downstairs yet. You may get those rooms good and dirty before we go to work. When do you want to give your play?"

"As soon as we can get it ready."

"The sooner, the better," Mrs. Muller said.

They raced back to the Ray house and asked Mrs. Ray whether they might use the costumes from Uncle Keith's trunk.

Uncle Keith was Mrs. Ray's brother, and no one knew where he was. Betsy had never seen him, but she had heard about him all her life.

He had run away to go on the stage when he was

only seventeen. Like his sister, Betsy's mother, he was redheaded, spirited, and gay, and he had quarreled with their stepfather, a grim man who had not approved of the boy's lightheartedness. He had gone with a *Pinafore* company and had never come back. When the Spanish-American War broke out, he must have enlisted; at any rate, at just that time, his trunk came unexpectedly to Betsy's mother's house. Years had passed, but it had never been called for. And Keith had never come home.

Mrs. Ray's face shadowed when Betsy asked to use the costumes. But after a moment she smiled.

"Why not?" she said. "I can't imagine Keith objecting. And it would do the things good to be aired."

She went to the little garret off Rena's bedroom, and Rena and the children helped her pull out a flat-topped, foursquare trunk.

"A real theatrical trunk," said Mrs. Ray as she unlocked it and threw back the lid.

A smell of camphor greeted twitching noses.

Betsy had seen the trunk opened before. It was always opened spring and fall at housecleaning time. But she never ceased to thrill to the depths of her being when she touched the big plumed hats, the wigs, the velvet coats.

Mrs. Ray's eyes filled with tears as she lifted out the gay trappings, but she winked and kept on smiling.

"There!" she said. "You may help me put them on the line, and after you've used them I'll pack them away again. When do you plan to give your play?"

"Next week probably," Betsy replied.

She and Tacy and Tib were so enchanted with the costumes that they almost forgot about *Uncle Tom's Cabin*. The next day, Friday, they hardly spoke to Winona. They were too busy making plans with one another. And Betsy was busy writing. She carried one of those notebooks that said on the cover: "Ray's Shoe Store. Wear Queen Quality Shoes." She wrote in it all through recess.

Winona glanced at her curiously once or twice, and at last she came close.

"How do you happen to be studying at recess?"

"I'm not studying," said Betsy.

"She's writing a play," said Tacy.

"*The Repentance of Lady Clinton*," said Tib. "We're giving it in my parlor."

"Pooh!" said Winona. "I'm going to a real play tomorrow."

"It isn't any realer than this one is," said Betsy. "We're not charging any old pin admission, I can tell you that. We're charging five and ten cents. Ten cents for the reserved seats . . . the rocking chairs. We're going to have velvet draperies for curtains, and we're going to wear real actors' costumes."

"Where you going to get them?"

"Out of a theatrical trunk. My uncle was an actor, and we've got his trunk at home. It has tights in it, and wigs, and coats with gold braid."

Other children paused to listen. Now Betsy, Tacy, Tib, and Winona were the center of a crowd.

"Pooh!" said Winona again. "I guess you haven't any bloodhounds."

"I guess we have," said Betsy. "We're going to use Gyp . . . you saw him . . . for a bloodhound. He's going to chase Lady Clinton over cakes of ice in Tib's back parlor."

Tib shuddered. She did not know how her mother would like cakes of ice on the back-parlor carpet.

"*Is* he?" Winona demanded, turning to Tib.

"Pay a nickel, and you'll find out," Tacy cut in quickly, knowing how regrettably honest Tib was.

"That's right. If you don't believe us, just come to the show," said Tib, much relieved.

"I'm going to black my face," said Tacy, "and do my hair in pigtails."

"And I'm going to die and go to Heaven right on the stage," said Tib.

"It sounds to me," cried Winona angrily, "as though you were just copying me and having *Uncle Tom's Cabin*."

"Well," replied Betsy. "We're not. This is a play we made up ourselves. It's called *The Repentance of Lady Clinton*."

"Who's going to be Lady Clinton?" Winona asked.

Tib started to say, "Betsy," but at that moment she got two pokes, one from each side, one from Betsy and one from Tacy.

Betsy and Tacy had seen in Winona's face something that gave them a glimmer of hope. Inspired by the pokes, Tib looked and saw it too.

Winona was more interested in this play than she was in *Uncle Tom's Cabin*. After all, she went to plays at the Opera House often.

"Who's going to be Lady Clinton?" she repeated in an urgent voice.

Betsy looked at Tacy, and Tacy looked at Betsy.

"We haven't decided," said Tacy carelessly.

"We've got to be careful whom we pick," said Betsy. "It's a very important part. She's got to be dark. Lady Clinton is a whopping villainess, you know. And all villainesses are dark."

"She needs long black hair."

"And black eyes."

"And white teeth," said Tib, staring at Winona.

Winona laughed.

"Sounds sort of like me," she said, tossing her head.

"Oh, but it couldn't be you," said Betsy. "Because we're giving it Saturday afternoon."

"No, Betsy," broke in Tib.

"Why, yes we are," said Tacy, jabbing Tib violently. "Don't you remember?"

"Why do you have to give it Saturday?" asked Winona mistrustfully.

"Mrs. Muller wants us to give it before she housecleans downstairs. 'The sooner, the better,' she said. And we can get it up tomorrow if we hurry. I must get this finished, though." Betsy licked her pencil industriously. "The first scene is at Lord Patterson's ball."

At noon Betsy, Tacy, and Tib left the schoolhouse arm in arm. Winona joined them.

"Talking about your play?" she asked.

"Yes," said Betsy. "We're planning how we'll get Tib up to Heaven. If they get Little Eva up to Heaven at the Opera House, we ought to be able to do it with Tib in her back parlor. Do you know how they do it at the Opera House, Winona?"

"I can find out Saturday."

"That will be too late to do us any good," Betsy said regretfully.

"We could tie a rope to the gas chandelier," suggested Tacy. "When Tib dies, she could just shinny up."

"That doesn't seem very dignified," said Betsy.

"Besides," said Tib. "I don't think Papa would like it. I might pull the chandelier down."

"She could climb up a ladder and sit there," Winona said. "You could decorate the ladder with pink tissue paper and make it look just like Heaven."

"That's a marvelous idea!" cried Betsy. "We could draw angels and cut them out and pin them to the ladder."

"And doves."

"And harps."

They looked at Winona with spontaneous admiration.

At recess that afternoon Betsy wrote on her play again.

"How's it coming?" asked Winona, prancing by.

"Gee whiz!" said Betsy. "The *trouble* this Lady Clinton has!"

"Going to get it done for tomorrow?"

"You bet!"

Betsy scribbled furiously.

After school Winona approached the three friends.

"Can't you come to my house to play?"

"I'm sorry," Betsy said. "We just can't. The play's done, and we've got to rehearse it. But I don't know *who* we'll get for Lady Clinton. In the ballroom scene she wears a velvet dress with a train and carries a peacock feather fan."

"I've got a peacock feather," Winona said. "And my mother's got a yellow velvet dress with a train. She'd let me wear it, I think."

"That would be peachy!"

"If you only could!"

There was an expectant pause.

"But do you suppose you'd know how to repent?" asked Betsy. "It's pretty hard. You have to carry on, I tell you."

She broke away from the rest, and clasped one hand to her forehead, the other to her heart beneath her sailor-suit pocket.

"'Oh, my children!'" she cried in a deep vibrant voice. "'Forgive me! Forgive me! I can ask you now for I am dying! I am on my death bed! My brow is damp! . . .' You'd have to weep real tears," said Betsy, resuming her normal tone.

Winona blinked.

"I could," she said. "You said yourself when we were playing statues that I was a regular actress."

"That's right," said Tacy.

"Well, it doesn't matter anyhow," said Betsy. "For you'll be busy tomorrow. You'll be at *Uncle Tom's Cabin*."

Winona was thinking deeply.

"Can't that play possibly be postponed?" she asked.

"Why should it be?" Betsy replied. "We haven't anything else to do tomorrow."

"We'd sort of like to have something nice to do when *Uncle Tom's Cabin* is in town," Tacy admitted.

"Then we won't feel so bad about missing it," Tib said.

They could go no further.

They looked at Winona fixedly, in silence. There was a trapped look in her black eyes. But after a moment she grinned nonchalantly.

"Well, good-by," she said. She skipped jauntily away.

Betsy, Tacy, and Tib walked home on dragging feet. They did not even mention rehearsing for their play. All their interest in Lady Clinton, her sins and her repenting, had vanished.

At first it had been real. They had not planned to use their play as a device for attracting Winona. But her interest in it had raised ecstatic hopes which now were dashed to the ground.

They went to Tacy's house and sat by the pump again, but it was dreary there today. The weather was changing. Clouds dimmed the sky. A cold wind scurried the dead leaves.

Gyp ran up barking as though to ask merrily, "What about the play?" But they did not speak to him. They did not even throw a stick for him to retrieve.

"Come over to play after supper?" asked Betsy when the Big Mill whistles blew.

"I suppose so."

"I suppose we've got to rehearse."

"Sure."

But in their hearts they knew that they would not rehearse. They would not give their play. It was as dead as the leaves blowing down from the hill.

Tomorrow in the Opera House the great painted curtain would rise on the glories of *Uncle Tom's Cabin* . . . with them not there to see. Bloodhounds chasing Eliza, Topsy dancing, Little Eva dying and going to Heaven . . . and the three of them sitting at home. It was almost too much to bear.

"I wish we could have made her invite us," said Tib. Tears moistened her round blue eyes.

Betsy and Tacy did not look at each other. They were not accustomed to failure.

Julia came out on the front porch of the Ray house.

"Betsy," she called, sounding surprised. "Somebody wants to talk to you . . . over the telephone."

"The *telephone*!"

Betsy could hardly believe her ears. She was never called to the telephone. She had spoken over it, of course, talking to her father down at his shoe store to test the miracle. But she had never received a call before. No one she knew had a telephone.

At that point in her thoughts she remembered that someone she knew had a telephone, someone very important. Winona Root had a telephone.

As though her feet had sprouted wings, Betsy leaped up the steps and into the house. Tacy and Tib flew after. She ran to the telephone, jumped up on the stool and took the dangling receiver into her hand.

"Hello."

"Hello. Is this you, Betsy? This is Winona Root."

"Hello, Winona."

"Hello. Can you hear me?"

"Yes, I can hear you."

"How are you?"

"Fine."

After a pause, Winona said: "You know those 'comps' I've got for *Uncle Tom's Cabin*?"

"Yes."

"Four of them."

"Yes."

"Well, I want you and Tacy and Tib to go with me."

"Oh, do you?" Betsy said.

"Yes. I did all the time. I asked my father for four 'comps' just so's I could take you."

Betsy could not answer.

"We're going to sit in a box," Winona said.

Still Betsy was speechless with delight.

"Will you be at my house at twelve o'clock sharp?" Winona asked. "The matinee begins at two-thirty, and I like to get there early. I like to be out in front of the Opera House before the doors open, even."

Betsy felt a warmth of affectionate understanding, a warmth of fellowship. She had never been to a play before but she knew that she loved them just as Winona did.

"We'll be there," she said. "At your house. At twelve."

She put the receiver reverently into its hook.

529

5
Uncle Tom's Cabin

ND SO BETSY, Tacy, and Tib went with Winona Root to see *Uncle Tom's Cabin*.

Instead of calling for Winona at noon, they called for her at half-past eleven. Since early morning all of them had been in a fever of impatience. They had started to get ready right after breakfast and had clamored for their dinners at ten o'clock. Their mothers were exhausted by the time the three girls, well scrubbed and wearing their Sunday best, rang the Root doorbell.

Winona was waiting, as impatient as themselves. Shortly after noon the expectant four stood under the canopy of the Opera House. While they waited for the doors to open, Winona entertained them by describing the inside of the building. Betsy, Tacy, and Tib hung on every word.

Outside, the Opera House was a large brick structure. It was a fine theatre for a town the size of Deep Valley. But Deep Valley was what is known as a good show town. It was a thriving county seat, and theatrical productions, passing from the Twin

Cities to Omaha, found it a convenient and profitable one-night-stand.

Winona finished her eloquent description. Children by the dozens had joined them. She rehearsed the stories of all the plays she had seen; still the big doors did not open. Out of the jostling crowd two boys came into view, climbing one of the pillars that supported the canopy. The girls recognized Tom Slade and Herbert Humphreys. At the same moment, the boys saw them.

"So *that's* who you took," Herbert shouted to Winona, pointing at Betsy, Tacy, and Tib. He and Tom slid down the pillars and pushed their way through the crowd.

"You certainly were hard up for someone to take," said Tom.

"*We* wouldn't have gone with you, even if you'd asked us," said Herbert.

"Like fun you wouldn't," answered Winona, tossing her head.

Winona liked Herbert, just as Betsy, Tacy, and Tib did. He had attractions other than his knickerbockers. He was a handsome boy with thick blond hair, a rosy skin, and lively blue eyes. Tom was dark with shaggy hair. Ever since Herbert came to Deep Valley, the two had been friends.

"We're going to sit up in the peanut heaven and

eat peanuts," said Tom.

"And throw the shells at people in the boxes."

"Spitballs too, at the people who have 'comps.'"

"Don't you dare!" Winona said.

They weren't quarreling. The boys thought it was fun to be talking to the girls. And the girls felt as old as Julia and Katie. They joked and laughed . . . except Tacy who blushed and didn't say much. Tacy wasn't bashful with Tom because she had known him all her life but she was bashful with the glorious Herbert Humphreys.

Herbert offered them peanuts and Tom pointed to a billboard picture that showed Eliza running across the ice with the bloodhounds almost at her throat.

"I saw those dogs," he said. "A man had them out walking this morning. He let me pet them."

"*Pet* them!"

"Yes, but they're plenty wild, he says. He says Buffalo Bill would give a fortune for them. He's offered it, even, but the manager won't sell."

"Did you see Miss Evelyn Montmorency?"

"Who's she?"

"Just America's most talented and beautiful child actress, that's all."

"Is that so, smarty?"

"Who cares about her?" asked Herbert, hurling a

peanut shell at the billboard where Little Eva was ascending into Heaven on the back of a milk-white dove.

There was a rattle at the big entrance doors. They swung open, showing Sunny Jim's smiling face. Children stampeded inside, toward the ticket window. Winona ignored the ticket window. With Betsy, Tacy, and Tib following her proudly, her 'comps' in her hand, she swaggered toward the inner door.

"Hello, Mr. Kendall."

"Hello, Winona."

Winona and Betsy and Tacy and Tib were the first ones inside the house.

They did not go at once to their box. First they raced all over the auditorium. It was elegant beyond even Winona's descriptions and Betsy's wildest dreams. A giant chandelier hung with glittering crystal drops was suspended from the ceiling. The seats were upholstered in red velvet. The boxes were hung with red velvet tied back with golden cords.

"Isn't it beautiful?" Winona asked, enjoying their stupefaction.

"Oh, Winona! It's wonderful! It's grand!"

"Didn't I tell you?" Winona acted as proud as though she and not Mr. Poppy had built it.

She raced up to the balcony, Betsy, Tacy, and Tib running after her. They all ran down the aisle and leaned over the railing. Tib leaned so far that Betsy and Tacy held on to her skirts.

Behind the balcony was the gallery where Tom and Herbert would sit.

"Those seats are the cheapest. Ten cents. This show is a ten, twent, thirt. The balcony costs twenty. The dress circle costs twenty, too, and the parquet, thirty."

Dress circle! Parquet! What were they?

They pelted back downstairs, and Winona pointed out the dress circle under the balcony. A low railing separated it from the parquet, down front. Where the dress circle met the parquet, in the very center of the house, were two wide, well-padded seats.

"Those are Mr. and Mrs. Poppy's seats. But they probably won't be here this afternoon. They'll come to the night show."

In this opinion Winona was mistaken. When she and her party reached their upper front box and, having explored its delights, seated themselves in the frail chairs overlooking the auditorium and stage, they saw Mrs. Poppy settling herself in one of the two spacious seats. She took out hatpins and lifted off a big plumed hat. Her hair shone like gold.

"There's Mrs. Poppy after all," Betsy cried. "For such a fat lady, Mrs. Poppy's pretty."

"Yes, she is. She's nice too," said Tib.

Leaning out of the box, with Betsy and Tacy holding her skirts again, Tib waved. Mrs. Poppy did not see her at first, but having been poked by children in adjoining seats, she looked up. Then her smile was as bright as the diamonds in her ears. She waved happily back.

There was a great deal of waving, calling, and whistling going on. Tom and Herbert whistled through their fingers and threw peanut shells as they had promised until the girls in the box stopped turning around.

Betsy stopped turning around because somewhere down in the bowels of the Opera House violins were being tuned. She sat back rapturously and read her program through. Then she gave her attention to the curtain on which a gentleman in a sedan chair and beautiful ladies in hoop skirts were transfixed in a gay romantic moment. There was a flower booth behind them. There were some hens scratching at the front.

A workman came out and crossed the stage. The audience clapped vociferously. Men filed into the orchestra pit. The children clapped some more. The boys in the gallery whistled and gave cat calls. Mrs. Poppy looked up at the box and put her hands over her ears for a joke. Winona, Betsy, Tacy, and Tib clapped harder than ever, laughing down at Mrs. Poppy.

The orchestra started to play. It played sad tunes. *Old Kentucky Home. Swanee River, Massa's in de Cold Cold Ground.* All over the house the lights went low. There were rainbow colors in the crystals of the great chandelier as the lights faded away. Then . . . oh, magic moment! . . . the curtain started to rise. Slowly, slowly, while the music kept on playing and the rainbow in the chandelier flickered out, forgotten, the curtain lifted. Betsy reached out for Tacy's hand and squeezed it. She wanted to share this rapturous moment of the curtain going up.

Sympathetically Tacy squeezed back. By now the full stage was revealed. They saw a Negro cabin. The slave Eliza sitting with her child . . .

Betsy and Tacy still clasped hands but they forgot each other and everything but the play.

The story unfolded in dramatic scenes which kept the four girls in a front upper box rigid with excitement. George, Eliza's husband, ran away. Eliza, hearing that her child was to be sold, ran away too. She reached the icy river.

"Better sink beneath its cold waters with my child locked in my arms than have him torn from me and sold into bondage!"

The ferocious pack of man-eating Siberian bloodhounds leaped into view. (There were two in the pack.) Eliza took to the ice.

"Courage, my child! We will be free . . . or perish!"

Miraculously she escaped, and the party in the box relaxed, but only for a moment.

Presently they were in the elegant St. Clare parlor. The languid Marie lay on the couch. Little Eva ran in, her yellow curls flowing about her.

"Mamma!" she cried in a sweet piping voice.

"Take care! Don't make my head ache."

St. Clare came in, and good old Uncle Tom, and funny Aunt Ophelia with her corkscrew curls, and the comical Topsy.

The audience laughed uproariously at Topsy.

"I 'spect I growed," she said. "Don't think nobody never made me."

She sang a song about it.

> "*Oh, white folks I was neber born,*
> *Aunt Sue, she raised me in de corn . . .*"

She danced her breakdown, and Tib poked Betsy. "I could do that," she said.

The waits between the acts of the play did not break the spell. A black-faced quartette sang plantation melodies, told jokes, and cakewalked. The girls did not talk very much. They waited for that moment of unfailing rapture when the curtain would go up.

Little Eva hung garlands of flowers around the neck of Uncle Tom. She told him she was going to die.

"They come to me in my sleep, those spirits bright. Uncle Tom, I'm going there."

"Where, Miss Eva?"

"I'm going *there*, to the spirits bright. Tom, I'm going before long."

And in the next scene she expired, breathing, "O love, O joy, O peace." Sad music played, and she was glimpsed in Heaven.

Tacy's weeping almost shook the box. Betsy joined her tears to Tacy's, and Tib put her head into Betsy's lap to cry. Even Winona cried, big brilliant tears that glittered in her eyes after the curtain went down.

But there was worse to come.

St. Clare died without signing the freedom papers for Uncle Tom. Uncle Tom was sold down the river. He was flogged by Simon Legree. Tacy kept her eyes shut tight, but that could not keep out the dreadful crack of the lash.

At the end the scene showed sunset clouds. Little Eva, robed in white, sat upon a milk-white dove. Her hands were extended over St. Clare, her father, and Uncle Tom, kneeling below. The music was stately. The curtain went slowly down.

There was an uproar of applause and the curtain went up and down again, not once but many times. All the actors came out to bow, even those who had died in the play, which was very consoling.

Uncle Tom came, and Tacy wiped her eyes and sniffed. St. Clare came, looking very handsome. And his wife, Marie, not lazy and complaining now, but smiling and happy.

Aunt Ophelia came. And Topsy. And Simon Legree. When Simon Legree appeared the boys in the gallery hissed and booed, and Simon Legree laughed, and cracked his big whip.

Little Eva, of course, came again and again, still wearing her heavenly robes, her yellow curls shining. She came with the entire cast, and she came with Uncle Tom, and with her father, and mother, and Topsy. She bowed to them and to the audience and smiled and kissed her hands.

Betsy, Tacy, Tib, and Winona clapped and cheered and pounded. At last the curtain came down to stay down. The play was over.

"Didn't I tell you it was good?" Winona asked. She seemed to feel that she had written the play and acted every part.

Betsy didn't mind. She felt warm inside toward Winona. Winona had given her this wonderful gift of the play. And Winona loved it just as she did.

Reluctantly they put on their hats and jackets. Even as they had been the first to enter, they were the last to leave the Opera House. Everyone knew Winona . . . the ushers, the cleaning women. They greeted her cordially and she greeted them. Betsy, Tacy, and Tib were awed and proud.

"If you like," said Winona grandly as they went through the big front doors, "we can go around in back and see Little Eva come out."

"Winona! Can we really?"

Betsy, Tacy, and Tib were almost overwhelmed with the magnificence of this idea.

"Of course. I do it often," Winona said nonchalantly.

She led them around the side of the Opera House. A small crowd of children had preceded them. Herbert and Tom were there, but now they did not joke with the girls. Their eyes were burning; their talk was all of the show.

"Gosh darn, those bloodhounds were fierce!"

"And to think I *touched* them today!"

"Did you see their jaws drip?"

"Golly, yes! Do you think they'll come out, Winona?"

"I don't think so. You see, there's a show tonight. They'll probably be fed inside."

They all stared expectantly at the stage door that said in big white letters, "Private. Keep out."

It swung open and a man in a silk hat emerged. Swinging a cane, he walked briskly down the alley.

"Was that St. Clare?"

"Naw! Too old."

"It was too St. Clare. I recognized him."

The door swung open again, and again. More silk toppers, canes, and fancy vests with watch chains draped across them. Large dashing hats, short pleated jackets, sweeping skirts, pocket books dangling from chains. Men and women looking remotely like the characters in the play came out by ones and twos. Some looked tired; others were fresh and gay; many showed traces of burned cork.

"Is that Uncle Tom?" "Is that Topsy?" "There comes Simon Legree!"

Most of the stage folk smiled when they heard

the whispers. Simon Legree cracked an imaginary whip.

At last a woman came out with a little girl, unmistakably Little Eva. The rosy cheeks she had had in the play were gone; she was pale. But the shining light curls were the same. Her bonnet and coat were of blue velveteen. She wore white kid gloves and carried a small purse on a chain.

She and the woman (who looked ever so faintly like Eliza), walked up the alley and over to Front Street. Betsy and Tacy, Tib, and Winona followed at a respectful distance behind. Tom and Herbert followed too, still burning-eyed. Now and then the little girl turned around. Her eyes were large and blue.

To the surprise of all, the woman did not stop at the fine big Melborn Hotel. She and Little Eva proceeded up Front Street to the Deep Valley House. This was the place farmers stayed when they came to town. There was a hitching shed for horses behind the low wooden structure.

"If I was Evelyn Montmorency," said Tib, "I'd stay at the Melborn Hotel."

It was just like Tib to mention that. Betsy and Tacy and Winona all spoke quickly.

"She could stay there if she wanted to."

"I should say she could! The most beautiful and talented child actress in America!"

"Probably it just didn't pay them. They're leaving town so soon."

At the door of the Deep Valley House, the little girl turned around again. She smiled at the children, not radiantly as she had smiled on the stage, but shyly.

"Good-by," she said.

"Good-by," shouted Betsy, Tacy, Tib, and Winona.

"Good-by," said Herbert and Tom.

Unexpectedly, they pulled off their caps, staring in adoration.

Little Eva went into the Deep Valley House and the door closed behind her. The children did not see her again. But none of them was ever to forget her.

6
Betsy's Desk

BETSY, TACY, and Tib did not give *The Repentance of Lady Clinton.* Winona understood. She understood so well that she never even mentioned it. They gave plenty of plays that year, and Winona was in them, but they did not give that one.

Mrs. Muller cleaned her downstairs without the satisfaction of having it mussed up first. Uncle Keith's costumes were aired and put away without having had their hour on the boards. Betsy helped her mother fold the garments and lay them in the flat-topped trunk. As they worked she asked questions, for since seeing *Uncle Tom's Cabin* she had a new interest in her actor-uncle.

"He'll come home sometime," Mrs. Ray said. "He must want to see me again, just as I want to see him. He was awfully hurt and angry when he left. And he doesn't know that our stepfather has gone out to California with mother."

"Do you think he's still an actor, Mamma?"

"Yes, I do. Of course he went into the Spanish

War. But if anything had happened to him the government would have told us. He must be just trouping, waiting for the big success he wanted to have before he came home.

"'I'll come home, Jule, when I have a feather in my cap.' That's what he said when he said good-by to me." Betsy's mother paused in folding a Roman toga, and her face grew sad with the old sad memory of the night Keith ran away.

"What did he look like, Mamma?" asked Betsy, although she had heard a hundred times.

"He looked like me," Mrs. Ray answered. "That is, he was tall and thin with a pompadour of red wavy hair. His eyes were brighter than mine, so full of fun and mischief. And he had the gayest smile I ever saw. None of you children look like him. You look like your father and his sisters. You get plenty of talents from your Uncle Keith, though."

Mrs. Ray's voice lifted proudly. She finished folding the Roman toga and laid it into the trunk.

"Does Julia get her reciting from him?" asked Betsy, knowing the answer well.

"Yes, she does. And her beautiful singing voice. And her gift at the piano. How Keith could make the piano keys fly, though he never had a lesson in his life! He could play and sing as well as act and he could draw and paint and model and write . . ."

"Write!" cried Betsy. She always loved to hear about the writing part.

"Yes, write. He wrote poems, plays, stories, everything. He was always scribbling, just as you are. And that reminds me, Betsy. Isn't it getting pretty cold to write up in the maple tree?"

Mrs. Ray knew all about the office in the maple tree. She had given Betsy the cigar box. Betsy's mother was a great believer in people having private places.

"Yes, it is," said Betsy. "I haven't been writing lately."

"You must bring your papers indoors then. Your father and I are very proud of your writing. We want you to keep at it. You ought to have a desk but we can't afford one yet. I'll find a place for your things, though."

Mrs. Ray smoothed the last costume into place and closed the trunk.

"Rena will help me lift this into the garret," she said. "Come on into your room, Betsy."

Betsy followed her mother into the front bedroom. It was a small room with low tentlike walls. There was a single window at the front looking across to Tacy's house and the trees and the sunsets behind it. The big bed for Julia and Betsy, the small bed for Margaret, the chest of drawers, and the commode for wash bowl and pitcher filled the room.

Mrs. Ray pulled out the drawers in the chest. They were all crammed full. She looked around in some perplexity.

"I could make a place for your things in the back parlor," she said. "But I've noticed that you like to get away by yourself when you write."

"Yes, I do," said Betsy.

"It's got to be here then," Mrs. Ray answered. She tapped her lips thoughtfully.

"I have it!" she cried after a moment, her eyes flashing as brightly as she had said that Uncle Keith's used to flash.

"What?" asked Betsy.

"The trunk. Uncle Keith's trunk. You may have that for a desk. It can fit here under the window out of the way. It's just the thing."

She ran back into Rena's room and Betsy followed. They opened the trunk again. Swiftly her mother stowed the articles filling the tray into the bottom compartment.

"You can have the tray for your papers," she told Betsy happily. "Just wait until I get it fixed up!"

Mrs. Ray loved to fix things up around her house. And when she got started, Mr. Ray often said, she didn't let any grass grow under her feet.

She called down the stairs to Rena.

"Will you come up, please? Bring some shelf

paper with scalloped edging. And my old brown shawl. And a couple of pillows."

"What are the shawl and pillows for?" asked Betsy, dancing about with excitement.

"They're to make a little window seat out of the trunk when you're not writing. When you feel like writing, you'll put the pillows on the floor and sit on them and open your desk. It's much nicer than an ordinary desk, because it's a real theatrical trunk."

Betsy thought so too.

Rena came up the stairs on a run. She was used to Mrs. Ray's lightning ideas. They carried the trunk into the front bedroom and placed it beneath the window. Mrs. Ray started papering the tray.

"I'll go out to get my things," said Betsy joyfully.

She ran down the stairs and out the door and waded through golden leaves to the backyard maple.

When she reached the crotch where the cigar box was nailed, she looked out on a scene rivaling Little Eva's Heaven. The maples of Hill Street were golden clouds; and the encircling hillside made a backdrop of more clouds, copper colored, wine-red and crimson. The sky was brightly blue.

It was a sight to make one catch one's breath, but there was a chill in the air. Betsy brushed the dead leaves off the cigar box and opened it. A squirrel had already entered claim to possession. Six butternuts were there.

Hurriedly Betsy gathered up her belongings. Those tablets marked "Ray's Shoe Store. Wear Queen Quality Shoes," in which her novels were written. Two stubby pencils. An eraser. Some odds and ends of paper on which she had made verses. Leaving the Spanish lady to guard the butternuts, she wriggled down the tree.

She rushed eagerly into the kitchen and started up the stairs two at a time. Halfway up, she slowed her pace a little. It occurred to her to wonder whether her mother would notice the titles of her books.

Her mother did not read Betsy's writing without express permission. And she did not allow anyone else to do so. She was very particular about it. But these titles were printed out so big and bold. She could hardly help seeing them. And if she did, she would know that Betsy had been reading Rena's novels.

Betsy walked slowly with a suddenly flushed face into the front bedroom.

"It's all ready," her mother called cheerfully. Rena, Betsy saw, was gone. "I've finished papering it. Doesn't it look pretty?"

It did.

"Here is a case for your pencils. I'll ask Papa to

bring you fresh ones, and an eraser, and a little ten-cent dictionary. Perhaps you would like to put in a book or two? The Bible and Longfellow?"

"Yes, I would," said Betsy. Her mother noticed her changed voice. She looked up quickly and saw that Betsy was hugging her tablets secretively to her breast.

"You can put the tablets right into this corner," Mrs. Ray said. "Don't think I might ask to read them, dear. I won't. Keith was just like you about that. He never wanted anyone to read what he was writing until he was through with it, and sometimes not then. Whenever you show anything you've written to Papa or me, we're interested and proud. But never feel that you have to."

Betsy threw the tablets roughly into the trunk.

"I don't care if you read them."

"But I don't want to read them," said her mother, looking troubled, "unless you want me to. The whole idea of this desk is to give you privacy. There is even a key to it, you know."

"Read them," said Betsy crossly. She turned away and scowled.

Mrs. Ray gathered up the tablets. The titles flashed past. *Lady Gwendolyn's Sin. The Tall Dark Stranger. Hardly More than a Child.*

For quite a while she did not say a word. She did not open the books. She just stacked them into a pile which she shaped with her hands, thoughtfully.

Betsy stole a glance at her mother's profile, fine and straight like George Washington's. It did not look angry, but it looked serious, grave.

"I think," said Mrs. Ray at last, "that Rena must have been sharing her dime novels with you."

Betsy did not answer.

"Betsy, it's a mistake for you to read that stuff. There's no great harm in it, but if you're going to be a writer you need to read good books. They train you to write, build up your mind. We have good books in the bookcase downstairs. Why don't you read them?"

"I've read them all," said Betsy.

"Of course," said her mother. "I never thought of that."

She took her hands away from the neat pile. The tray of the trunk, with its lining of scalloped blue paper looked fresh and inviting. Betsy felt ashamed.

"I'll throw those stories away if you want me to," she said.

"No," answered her mother. "Not until *you* want to." She still looked thoughtful. Then her face lighted up as it had when she thought of using Uncle Keith's trunk for a desk.

"I have a plan," she said. "A splendid plan. But I have to talk it over with Papa."

"When will I know about it?"

"Tonight, maybe. Yes, I think you will know tonight before you go to bed."

Smiling, Mrs. Ray jumped up and closed the trunk. She and Betsy arranged the brown shawl and the pillows.

"It's almost like a cozy-corner," Mrs. Ray said.

She and Betsy ran downstairs and told Julia and Margaret about the new desk. Betsy ran outdoors to find Tacy and Tib and tell them. She brought them in to see it, and they liked it very much.

She kept wondering what the plan was. And after supper she found out. She had been playing games out in the street with the neighborhood children. Julia and Katie didn't play out any more. They were too grown up or too busy or had too many lessons or something. Margaret and the Rivers children played, and Paul and Freddie and Hobbie, and somehow the street seemed to belong to them even more than it did to Betsy, Tacy, and Tib.

When Margaret and Betsy went into the house, Julia was writing to Jerry. Their father and mother were reading beside the back-parlor lamp. Their father was reading a newspaper and their mother was reading a novel. It wasn't a paper-backed novel like Rena's. It was called *When Knighthood Was in Flower*.

Margaret climbed up on her father's lap and he put down his newspaper. Mrs. Ray put down her novel. She smiled at her husband.

"Papa has that plan all worked out," she said. "Tell her about it, Bob."

Mr. Ray crossed his legs, hoisted Margaret to a comfortable position and began.

"Well, Betsy," he said, "your mother tells me that you are going to use Uncle Keith's trunk for a desk. That's fine. You need a desk. I've often noticed how much you like to write. The way you eat up those advertising tablets from the store! I never saw anything like it. I can't understand it though. I never write anything but checks myself."

"Bob!" said Mrs. Ray. "You wrote the most wonderful letters to me before we were married. I still have them, a big bundle of them. Every time I clean house I read them over and cry."

"Cry, eh?" said Mr. Ray, grinning. "In spite of what your mother says, Betsy, if you have any talent for writing, it comes from her family. Her

brother Keith was mighty talented, and maybe you are too. Maybe you're going to be a writer."

Betsy was silent, agreeably abashed.

"But if you're going to be a writer," he went on, "you've got to read. Good books. Great books. The classics. And fortunately . . . that's what I'm driving at . . . Deep Valley has a new Carnegie Library, almost ready to open. White marble building, sunny, spick and span, just full of books."

"I know," Betsy said.

"That library," her father continued, "is going to be just what you need. And your mother and I want you to get acquainted with it. Of course it's way downtown, but you're old enough now to go downtown alone. Julia goes down to her music lessons, since the Williamses moved away, and this is just as important."

He shifted his position, and his hand went into his pocket.

"As I understand it," he said, "you can keep a book two weeks. So, after the library opens, why don't you start going down . . . every other Saturday, say . . . and get some books? And don't hurry home. Stay a while. Browse around among the books. Every time you go, you can take fifteen cents." He gave her two coins. "At noon go over to Bierbauer's Bakery for a sandwich and milk and ice cream.

Would you like that?"

"Oh, Papa!" said Betsy. She could hardly speak.

She thought of the library, so shining white and new; the rows and rows of unread books; the bliss of unhurried sojourns there and of going out to a restaurant, alone, to eat.

"I'd like it," she said in a choked voice. "I'd like it a lot."

Julia was as happy as Betsy was, almost. One nice thing about Julia was that she rejoiced in other people's luck.

"It's wonderful plan, Papa," she cried. "I've thought for ages that Betsy was going to be a writer."

"I thought Betsy learned to write a long time ago," said Margaret, staring out of her new English bob.

Everyone laughed, and Mrs. Ray explained to Margaret what kind of writer Betsy might come to be.

Betsy was so full of joy that she had to be alone. She ran upstairs to her bedroom and sat down on Uncle Keith's trunk. Behind Tacy's house the sun had set. A wind had sprung up and the trees, their color dimmed, moved under a brooding sky. All the stories she had told Tacy and Tib seemed to be dancing in those trees, along with all the stories she planned to write some day and all the stories she would read at the library. Good stories. Great stories. The classics. Not like Rena's novels.

She pulled off the pillows and shawl and opened her desk. She took out the pile of little tablets and ran with them down to the kitchen and lifted the lid of the stove and shoved them in. Then she walked into the back parlor, dusting off her hands.

"Papa," she said, "will you bring me some more tablets? Quite a lot of them, please."

7
A Trip to the Library

EARLY IN NOVEMBER Betsy made her first expedition to the library.

It was a windy day. Gray clouds like battleships moved across a purplish sea of sky. It looked like snow, Mrs. Ray remarked as she and Julia stood on the front porch seeing Betsy off. She looked a little doubtfully at Betsy's Sunday hat, a flowered brim that left her ears perilously exposed.

"Oughtn't you to wear your hood, Betsy?"

"Mamma! Not when I'm going downtown to the new Carnegie Library!"

"You'd better put on leggins and overshoes though."

"There isn't a speck of snow on the ground."

Mrs. Ray looked at the thick woolen stockings, the stout high shoes.

"All right. Just button your coat. But if it snows, walk over to the store and ride home with Papa."

"I will," Betsy promised.

She tried to act as though it were nothing to go to the library alone. But her happiness betrayed her.

Her smile could not be restrained, and it spread from her tightly pressed mouth, to her round cheeks, almost to the hair ribbons tied in perky bows over her ears.

Julia had loaned her a pocket book to hold her fifteen cents. It dangled elegantly from a chain over Betsy's mittened hand. Betsy opened it and looked inside to see that her money was safe. She closed it again and took the chain firmly into her grasp.

"Good-by," she said, kissing her mother and Julia.

"Good-by," she waved to Rena, who was smiling through the window.

"Good-by," she called to Margaret, who was playing on the hill as the small girls of Hill Street did on a Saturday morning. Betsy could remember well when she used to do it herself. (It was only last Saturday.)

Tacy ran across the street to walk to the corner with her. It was a little hard, parting from Tacy. They were so used to doing everything together.

"I wish you were coming too," Betsy said.

"I'll be all right. I'm going to play with Tib."

"Some Saturday soon you'll be coming."

"Sure I will."

In spite of her brave words Tacy sounded forlorn. She looked forlorn, bareheaded, the wind pulling her curls.

But at the corner she hugged Betsy's arm. She

looked into Betsy's eyes with her deep blue eyes that were always so loving and kind.

"I *want* you to go," she said. "Why, I've always known you were going to be a writer. I knew it ahead of everyone."

Betsy felt all right about going then. She kissed Tacy and went off at a run.

The big elm in Lincoln Park, bare and austere, pointed the way downtown. She entered Broad Street, passing big houses cloaked in withered vines against November cold. She passed the corner where she usually turned off to go to her father's store and kept briskly on until she reached the library.

This small white marble temple was glittering with newness. Betsy went up the immaculate steps, pulled open the shining door.

She entered a bit self-consciously, never having been in a library before. She saw an open space with a big cage in the center, a cage such as they had in the bank, with windows in it. Behind rose an orderly forest of bookcases, tall and dark, with aisles between.

Betsy advanced to the cage and the young lady sitting inside smiled at her. She had a cozy little face, with half a dozen tiny moles. Her eyes were black and dancing. Her hair was black too, curly and untidy.

"Are you looking for the Children's Room?" she asked.

Betsy beamed in response.

"Well, not exactly. That is, I'd like to see it. But I may not want to read just in the Children's Room."

"You don't think so?" asked the young lady, sounding surprised.

"No. You see," explained Betsy, "I want to read the classics."

"You do?"

"Yes. All of them. I hope I'm going to like them."

The young lady looked at her with a bright intensity. She got down off her stool.

"I know a few you'll like," she said. "And they happen to be in the Children's Room. Come on. I'll show you."

The Children's Room was exactly right for children. The tables and chairs were low. Low bookshelves lined the walls, and tempting-looking books with plenty of illustrations were open on the tables. There was a big fireplace in the room, with a fire throwing up flames and making crackling noises. Above it was the painting of a rocky island with a temple on it, called *The Isle of Delos*.

"That's one of the Greek islands," said Miss Sparrow. Miss Sparrow was the young lady's name; she had told Betsy so. "There's nothing more classic than Greece," she said. "Do you know Greek mythology? No? Then let's begin on that."

She went to the shelves and returned with a book.

"*Tanglewood Tales*, by Nathaniel Hawthorne. Mythology. Classic," she said.

She went back to the shelves and returned with an armful of books. She handed them to Betsy one by one.

"*Tales from Shakespeare*, by Charles and Mary Lamb. Classic. *Don Quixote*, by Miguel de Cervantes.

Classic. *Gulliver's Travels,* by Jonathan Swift. Classic. *Tom Sawyer,* by Mark Twain. Classic, going-to-be."

She was laughing, and so was Betsy.

"You don't need to read them all today," Miss Sparrow said.

"May I get a card and take some home?"

"You may have a card, but you'll have to get it signed before you draw out books. You may stay here and read though, as long as you like."

"Thank you," Betsy said.

Miss Sparrow went away.

Betsy took off her hat and coat. She was the only child in the room. Others came in shortly, but now she was all alone.

She seated herself in the chair nearest the fire, piled the books beside her and opened *Tanglewood Tales*. But she did not start to read at once. Before she began she smiled at the fire, she smiled at her books, she smiled broadly all around the room.

When the Big Mill whistle blew for twelve o'clock, she was surprised. She got up and put on her things.

"Did you have a good time?" Miss Sparrow asked, as Betsy passed the desk.

"Yes. I did."

"Be sure to come again."

"Oh," said Betsy, "I'll be back just as soon as I eat."

"But I thought you lived way up on Hill Street?"

"I do. But I'm eating at Bierbauer's Bakery. My father gave me fifteen cents. I'm going to eat there every time I come to the library," Betsy explained. "It's so I can take my time here, browse around among the books."

Miss Sparrow regarded her with the brightly intent look that Betsy had observed before.

"What a beautiful plan!" Miss Sparrow said.

Eating at Bierbauer's Bakery was almost as much fun as reading before the fire. It was warm in the bakery, and there was a delicious smell. Betsy bought a bologna sandwich, made of thick slices of freshly baked bread. She had a glass of milk too, and ice cream for dessert. But she decided that she wouldn't always have ice cream for dessert. Sometimes she would have jelly roll. It looked so good inside the glass counter.

Betsy couldn't help wondering if the other people in the bakery weren't surprised to see a girl her age eating there all alone. Whenever anyone looked at her she smiled. She was smiling most of the time.

On the way back to the library she looked eagerly for snow. She hoped she would have to call for her father. She loved visiting the store, riding the movable ladders from which he took boxes from the highest shelves, helping herself to the advertising tablets, talking to customers. But there wasn't a flake in the air. The battleships had changed to feather beds, hanging dark and low in the purplish sky.

Betsy returned to her chair, took off her coat and hat, opened her book and forgot the world again.

She looked up suddenly from *The Miraculous Pitcher* to see flakes coming past the window. They were coming thick and fast. She ran to look outdoors and saw that they had been coming for some time. Roofs and branches and the once brown lawns were already drenched in white.

"Now I've got to go to the store," she thought with satisfaction. She hurried into her wraps, said good-by to Miss Sparrow.

"It's too bad," said Miss Sparrow, "to take that pretty hat out into the snow."

"I haven't far to go," said Betsy. "I'm going to the store to ride home with my father. I'll see you in two weeks."

"Good-by," Miss Sparrow said.

Betsy's shoes made black tracks on the sidewalk. But the snow covered them at once. Filmy flakes settled on her coat and mittens. Soon she was cloaked in white. The air was filled with flakes, coming ever thicker and faster. Betsy ran and slid and slid again. She longed for Tacy and Tib. It was the first snow of the winter and demanded company.

She was soon to have it.

At the Opera House she paused to stare up at the posters. She wondered if there were a matinee coming. Winona would take them if there were. Then she noticed Mr. Poppy's horseless carriage, standing in front of the livery stable, blanketed in snow. She had not seen it since the day Tib took her ride, and she ran to inspect it.

A soft ball hit the back of her head. She whirled around. It was the worst thing she could have done. A snowball broke in her face.

She stooped blindly to mold a ball herself.

"All dressed up in her Sunday hat," somebody yelled.

A volley hit her hat, knocking it off. Snow oozed down the collar of her coat.

Her assailants were boys she had never seen before. She was one to three or four, and never any good at snowballs. Besides, she was handicapped by holding Julia's pocket book. She grabbed her hat and started to run.

She slipped on the soft snow. Swish! her feet went up!

Bang! she clattered down.

Yelling fiendishly, the boys ran away.

A little man came out of the livery stable and helped her to her feet. Behind him came a very large

lady whose fur coat breathed a sweet perfume. Sunny Jim and Mrs. Poppy helped Betsy to her feet.

"Did you hurt yourself?" asked Mrs. Poppy.

"No ma'am. Not a bit." Betsy winked back the tears of which she was ashamed.

"They were bad boys."

"If I knew who they were," said Betsy, shaking off snow, "I'd bring Tacy and Tib and come back. Tib would fix them. She can throw snowballs better than any boy."

"Tib?" asked Mrs. Poppy. "My little friend Tib?"

"That's right. We waved to you from the box at *Uncle Tom's Cabin*. Tib and Tacy and Winona and me."

"Of course. I know you. But I don't know your name."

"Betsy Ray."

"Her pa runs Ray's Shoe Store," said Sunny Jim. "I know him well."

"I'm on my way to the shoe store now," said Betsy. "To ride home with my father." She shook the snow from her hat and put it on her head, grasped Julia's pocket book firmly. "Thank you for helping me," she said.

Mrs. Poppy was looking down at Betsy's feet.

"Speaking of shoes," she said, "yours are very wet, and your stockings are sopping. Why don't you come over to the hotel and dry out? I can telephone your father."

"Why . . . why . . . I'd love to," said Betsy.

"We'll have some hot chocolate with whipped cream," said Mrs. Poppy. She spoke fast and eagerly, like a child planning a party.

Her face alight, she turned to Sunny Jim.

"Just tell Mr. Poppy I won't wait. Tell him I've gone on home. It's just a step."

"Yes, Mrs. Poppy," said Sunny Jim respectfully.

Mrs. Poppy took Betsy's hand. They started

toward Front Street through waving curtains of snow. The visit to the Carnegie Library raced into Betsy's past before a future which held hot chocolate at the Melborn Hotel.

8
Mrs. Poppy

WHAT AN ADVENTURE to tell Tacy and Tib! thought Betsy, as she waited for Mrs. Poppy in the big lobby that smelled of cigars and of the fat red leather chairs.

Winona too would have to hear about it. Winona had been in the Melborn Hotel, of course. But Betsy doubted that she had ever had hot chocolate in Mrs. Poppy's rooms; she doubted that Winona had ever come in as she had, hurrying gaily through the swinging door with Mrs. Poppy herself.

Mrs. Poppy was large and elegant in her black sealskin coat. Beneath the matching cap shone her yellow hair and the diamonds in her ears. Her face too shone with pleasure as she came back from the telephone behind the big desk.

"Your father says you may stay. I'm going to take you to the store at five o'clock. There's time for a real party," Mrs. Poppy exclaimed.

She held Betsy's hand and looked around the lobby.

"Which would you rather do?" she asked. "Take the elevator, or walk up the stairs?"

Betsy hesitated. She had never ridden in an elevator. But she looked at the grand staircase rising at the end of the lobby. It was richly carpeted, and there was a statue on the landing.

"The stairs," she said. "And the elevator coming down."

They climbed slowly. The sealskin coat was soft and cold when Betsy brushed against it. It smelled sweetly of Mrs. Poppy, and her silken skirts swished in Betsy's ears.

Betsy looked around often to get a view of the lobby which stretched impressively to the large plate glass windows, veiled now by snowflakes.

The statue on the landing had no head. It was the statue of a woman, or an angel . . .

"It's called the *Winged Victory*. It's Greek," said Mrs. Poppy.

"Greek!" said Betsy. "It's probably a goddess then." She walked around it, staring. Her reading of the day illumined the triumphant figure.

At the top of the stairs stretched the hotel dining room. It was two stories high and overlooked the river. Here Deep Valley gave its fashionable parties, its dances and cotillions, with an orchestra playing behind potted palms and those guests who did not care to dance amusing themselves with whist and euchre in the luxurious parlors. Betsy had read all about it many times in the society columns of Winona's father's paper.

She looked about her eagerly as Mrs. Poppy paused to speak to a maid in a white cap.

"Will you send in some hot chocolate?" she asked. "Plenty of whipped cream, please, and a plate of cakes."

"Yes, Mrs. Poppy," answered the maid, smiling at Betsy.

Mrs. Poppy tripped down a corridor, carpeted so

deeply that their footfalls could not be heard. At the end she paused, took a key out of her bag and opened a door. They were greeted by a burst of warmth and of Mrs. Poppy's perfume.

"This is my little house," she said, leading the way inside.

It was indeed like a little house, a doll's house. (But Mrs. Poppy was a pretty big doll.) There were parlor, den, bedroom and bath; no dining room or kitchen.

"We eat in the big dining room, or else have our meals sent in here," Mrs. Poppy explained.

They went first into the bedroom which was blue, blue, blue. Blue flowers climbed up the walls and blue flowers bloomed on the carpet. Blue draped the windows, the bed, the bureau and the chiffonier. The bathroom where Mrs. Poppy asked Betsy to take off her shoes and stockings was blue too.

Mrs. Poppy brought out a pair of bedroom slippers lined with white fur. Into these Betsy thrust her feet, while Mrs. Poppy took off her own wraps. Her dress was very modish with braid appliquéd on the blousy waist, the baggy sleeves, the trailing skirts. There was a fresh white bow at her neck.

Although she was so large, Mrs. Poppy looked young after her hat was removed. Her blonde hair was dressed in a high pompadour with a figure eight down her neck. Her skin was freshly pink, and her dark-lashed blue eyes brimmed with smiles.

Beside the bed was a small rocking chair with a doll in it.

"Was this your doll when you were a little girl?" Betsy asked.

"No," said Mrs. Poppy. "That doll belonged to our little girl, our Minnie. She died, and that's why I like to borrow other people's little girls sometimes."

"Oh," said Betsy. She was sorry. She wished she knew how to say she was sorry; Julia would have known. But Mrs. Poppy seemed to understand. She took Betsy's hand and squeezed it.

"Come on," she said. "Let me show you my little house."

They swished through leather portieres into the den. It was almost filled by a sofa piled with burned-leather pillows. The walls were crowded with Gibson Girls and Remington cowboys. There was a plate-rack full of beer steins, and on a table beside a capacious Morris chair was Mr. Poppy's collection of pipes.

"When Mr. Poppy is in here, there isn't room for me," Mrs. Poppy said laughing.

They swished through bead portieres into the parlor. Pink ribbons tied back long lace curtains that fell to the mossily carpeted floor. More pink ribbons were woven through wicker chairs and tables. A full-length mirror, framed in gold, stood between the windows reflecting the pictures on the walls, the great horn of a graphophone and a piano covered with velvet drapery and loaded with photographs.

While Mrs. Poppy opened a table underneath one of the windows and spread it with a white embroidered cloth, Betsy sat on the piano stool and looked at the music. There were popular songs . . . *Hiawatha*, *Bluebell*; there were the books of musical comedies . . . *The Prince of Pilsen*, *The Silver Slipper*, *The Belle of New York*; there were albums of piano pieces and the same Czerny that Julia was forever practicing.

"Do you play the piano?" asked Mrs. Poppy as she put cups and saucers, hand painted with roses, out on the table.

"No. But my sister Julia does. She plays and sings and speaks pieces and everything. You ought to hear her speak 'Editha's Burglar,'" Betsy said. She often bragged about Julia when Julia wasn't around.

"Have you any other brothers and sisters?"

"Yes. A little sister, Margaret. She has an English bob. She's cute, and not so much trouble as she used to be. She goes to school now."

"Tell me about your friends Tacy and Tib," said Mrs. Poppy, laying out spoons.

Betsy told her gladly. She told her how long the three of them had been friends, and about the good times they had together. She told her how Winona had taken them to see *Uncle Tom's Cabin* and how they had liked it and how they had followed Little Eva to the Deep Valley House.

Betsy liked to talk. Her father always said she got it from her mother, and her mother always said she got it from her father. But whomever she got it from she was certainly a talker. Sitting on the piano stool, swung about to face a smiling Mrs. Poppy, Betsy talked so fast and hard that they were both surprised when the maid knocked at the door.

"There's our chocolate already," Mrs. Poppy said.

The maid brought in the pot of chocolate, a bowl of whipped cream, and a plate of cakes. Betsy and Mrs. Poppy sat down at the little table by the window. It had stopped snowing now.

Like the hotel dining room, Mrs. Poppy's parlor looked out on the river. Betsy had never realized before how near the river was. From here she could see it clearly, and the bridge that spanned it, and the high bank rising on the other side covered with its fresh cloak of snow.

"Is the river frozen yet?" asked Betsy.

"It's mushy," Mrs. Poppy answered. "It thaws out in the middle of the day, but soon it will freeze for the winter. I hate to have it do that."

"Why?" Betsy asked.

"I like to look out and see it moving." After a moment Mrs. Poppy explained. "You see, I know that it's moving toward St. Paul, and that it joins the Mississippi there and keeps on going down to St. Louis and Memphis and New Orleans."

Betsy was surprised to hear that. Their own river! In which, beyond the town, they fished and bathed in summer and on which they skated in the winter. She had never thought of it going traveling. She told Mrs. Poppy so.

"It travels!" said Mrs. Poppy. "Like I used to do."

"You used to be an actress, didn't you?" asked Betsy.

"Yes. I sang in musical comedy."

"Why did you stop?"

"I stopped to marry Melborn Poppy and I've never regretted it."

"Do you like living in Deep Valley?"

"Yes," said Mrs. Poppy, but she said it slowly and without conviction. "I'm not acquainted here yet, of course. Living in a hotel you don't get acquainted easily. You don't have neighbors." She added the explanation quickly as though she had made it often to herself.

Betsy looked down at the melting mountain of whipped cream on her chocolate. She had a sudden sure knowledge of an amazing fact. Mrs. Poppy was lonesome. Lonesome in Deep Valley!

"Won't you have another cake?" Mrs. Poppy asked abruptly, gaily. "There are two frosted in chocolate, and two in pink, and two in vanilla. That means, we must have three apiece."

"I ate eighteen pancakes once," said Betsy, taking another cake. She looked out at the river and thought of Mrs. Poppy, an actress, traveling.

"I have an uncle who's an actor," she said.

Mrs. Poppy was much interested.

"Really? What's his name?"

"Keith Warrington. He's my mother's brother. He ran away from home because he didn't like his step-father and he never came back."

She told Mrs. Poppy all she knew of Uncle Keith's story. Mrs. Poppy listened attentively.

"Keith Warrington!" she said. "I've never heard of him, although I have many friends in the profession. But do you know, Betsy, that if he's still an actor he's very likely to come to Deep Valley some day? Almost all the companies get here one time or another."

"That would be wonderful!" cried Betsy. "But I don't believe," she added thoughtfully, "that he would come to see us. You see, he doesn't know that Grandpa and Grandma have gone to California."

"We'll have to watch the programs. Keith Warrington," Mrs. Poppy said.

When they had finished their chocolate, Betsy and Mrs. Poppy looked over the magazines on Mrs. Poppy's table. They were all about the theatre with pictures in them of actors and actresses, and scenes from plays. Maude Adams in *The Little Minister*. E. H. Sothern in *An Enemy to the King*. James K. Hackett and Charlotte Walker in *The Crisis*, the

Anna Held who took milk baths, and the matchless Lillian Russell.

Betsy and Mrs. Poppy were having such a good time that they were indignant when the cuckoo clock struck five.

"Oh dear me!" cried Mrs. Poppy. "I must take you to your father's. And I was going to show you my album, and play the graphophone. You'll have to come again.

"I know what we'll do," she said rapidly. "We'll have a party, a Christmas party here. You bring your friends Tacy and Tib and Winona. Do you think you could?"

"Of course!" cried Betsy. Her face shone.

"I'll write a note to your mother," Mrs. Poppy said. "For one day in Christmas vacation."

They planned about the party while Betsy took off the fur-lined white slippers and put on her dry stockings and shoes. Mrs. Poppy put on her coat and cap and the two of them hurried out of the apartment and down the hall to the elevator.

Betsy liked going down in the elevator, although when it sank downward she seemed to be turned into liquid and flowing upward. She laughed out loud, and Mrs. Poppy said:

"If it weren't so late, we'd ride up and down two or three times."

But it was late. Lights had been lighted in the lobby. Outdoors the new snow gleamed in the radiance of Front Street.

Mrs. Poppy sniffed the cold fresh-smelling air.

"Feels like sleighs and sleighbells."

"Will you put sleighbells on the horseless carriage?"

"I'm afraid not," Mrs. Poppy laughed.

"We'll be coasting down the Big Hill soon," Betsy said. "I'm big enough to coast at night, on bobsleds now."

They talked busily all the way to the shoe store.

At home the story of Betsy's afternoon created much excitement.

"It was very kind of Mrs. Poppy," Mrs. Ray said. But there was something doubtful in her voice.

"Think of getting acquainted with a real live actress! Is she nice?" Julia asked.

"Yes," answered Betsy. "Very nice."

After a pause she addressed her mother.

"Mamma," she said. "Why don't you go down and call on Mrs. Poppy? Take your card case and drive down in the carriage and call, like you do on other ladies."

"She wouldn't care to have me, Betsy," Mrs. Ray said.

"Why not?" asked Betsy.

"Oh, she's different from us. It's sweet of her to take such an interest in you children, but she's different from us really. She's rich. And she lives in a hotel. And she's an actress," Mrs. Ray said.

Betsy remembered the feeling she had had that Mrs. Poppy was lonesome. She wished she could put that feeling into words, but any words, she feared, would sound absurd. She might have mentioned the doll in the rocking chair and Mrs. Poppy's little girl. But Mrs. Ray jumped up from the supper table and everyone got up. Julia went to the piano and Betsy helped Rena with the dishes. It was her turn.

9
The Pink Stationery

THE FIRST SNOW melted. But the next one stayed on the ground. Another snow came, and another, and another, until everyone lost count. Snow loaded the bare arms of the maples; it lodged in the green crevices of firs; it threw sparkling shawls over the bare brown bushes shivering on Hill Street lawns.

The lawns themselves were billowing drifts, and so were the terraces, and so were the sidewalks. Men and boys came out with shovels to make Indian trails that children might follow to school. Along with the scraping of shovels came the frosty tinkle of sleighbells, as runners replaced wheels on the baker's wagon, cutters replaced carriages and buggies, and farm wagons creaked into town on runners. To steal a ride on those broad runners, or to hitch a sled thereto, was a delightful practice, shocking to parents.

Skates were sharpened; and down on the river, snow was swept from the ice. Up on Hill Street, in the Kelly front lawn, Paul was busy with a giant snowman. Freddie and Hobbie were building an Ice Palace in which they proposed to spend the winter . . . eat, sleep and everything, they said. Margaret and the Rivers children got out their small sleds, painted brightly with pictures of flowers, dogs, and horses, and adventured harmlessly down the friendly slope of Hill Street.

Betsy, Tacy, and Tib got out their sleds, too. But with less enthusiasm than in previous years. It was fun to slide on the little sleds, yes; but what about bobsleds? Long, low, reckless, the bobsleds flew from the top of the Big Hill along a hard-packed frozen track in a thrilling sweep, almost to the slough. What about going out on bobsleds after supper, as Julia and Katie and their friends did?

"Please! You said last year we could."

"Please! We're old enough now."

"Please! All the kids our age stay up and go bobsled riding."

The same entreaties fell in the yellow Ray cottage and the rambling white Kelly house and the chocolate-colored house where Tib lived. It was a joint attack of exceptional vigor.

Jerry, home for Thanksgiving, helped them. Strange to say, he liked Betsy, Tacy, and Tib in spite of the nickels and dimes they had cost him. He had a fine big bob, and he and his friend Pin were taking Julia and Katie out coasting the night after Thanksgiving night.

"Let the kids come too," he urged Mrs. Ray. "Gosh, I'll be careful! There's a moon and the road is perfect."

"All right," said Mrs. Ray. "If you'll come in early."

When the other mothers heard that Mrs. Ray had given in, they gave in too.

Margaret watched, big-eyed, as Julia and Betsy put on their multitude of wraps. Mrs. Ray had two fur pieces that she let them wear over their coats. As a finishing touch, over Betsy's hood and Julia's Tam o' Shanter, they wound bright knitted scarves called fascinators. These were stretched over their foreheads, crossed in back and tied around their necks.

Katie and Tacy and Tib arrived, as stiff with clothing as Julia and Betsy were.

"Gosh! Are you girls or mummies?" asked Jerry when he came in with Pin. Pin was called Pin because he was tall and thin. He was an expert on bobsleds.

Mr. and Mrs. Ray and Margaret went to the door to see them off.

"Come in early, so there'll be time to pop corn," Mrs. Ray said. If she mentioned popping corn, they always came in early. So she usually mentioned it.

They went out into the icy night.

The wastes of snow on the hill were ghostly in the moonlight. The stars were piercingly bright. They all helped pull the bobsled. It was a long way to the top of the Big Hill.

At the very top, near the Ekstroms' house, they stood looking out over the snowy roofs, the silent, snow-embedded town.

"It looks like something out of Whittier's 'Snowbound,'" Julia said.

Julia could always think of things like that to say.

They took their places on the bob. Jerry at the front with his feet on the steering bar, his knees hunched high and his firm hands grasping the rope that was first wound around his arms and wrists.

The rest sat one behind the other, with arms around the waist of the one in front. Pin waited at the end.

"Feet up?"

"Hold tight, everybody."

"Ready?"

"Ready, go!"

Pin pushed off and leaped to his place.

Down, down, down, they sped. The bob was like an arrow flying an icy path. The stars sang overhead. The cold air slashed their faces. Down, down, down.

Past Betsy's house. The yellow windows blurred. Past Tacy's. But now the wind was so cold that their eyes were shut fast. Down, down, down. Block after block. Almost to the slough.

Like slow chords ending a piece of music the bob slackened speed, dragged to a stop.

The run down was worth the climb up, although that was long and cold. As they climbed they made jokes and called out to other coasting parties. The hill was well populated now. Julia and Katie waved to their friend Dorothy. Betsy, Tacy, and Tib saw Tom Slade and Herbert Humphreys. They were pleased to have Tom and Herbert see them out coasting after supper. Passing Tacy's house, and Betsy's, they waved to Paul and Margaret in the windows. At last for the second time they topped the Big Hill.

They went down twice, a third time . . .

On the third trip the bob tipped over. It wasn't a real accident, just a spill into snow. But when Betsy tried to stand up afterward, her ankle hurt. It was twisted, Jerry decided.

"Sit on the bobsled, Betsy," he said. "We'll haul you home."

Her ankle didn't hurt much, and Betsy felt important, especially when Jerry began to worry about facing her mother.

"Gosh!" he said. "The next time I ask you to go coasting she'll tell me to go way back and sit down."

"No, she won't," Julia answered. "She'll know it wasn't your fault."

Julia was right. Mrs. Ray was reassuring when Jerry burst in with his explanations and apologies and Betsy followed, limping, on Pin's arm.

"Don't worry," she said. "It isn't a bobsled party without a spill or two."

Her tone was cheerful. But her eyes were a little anxious. The truth was, Mrs. Ray didn't like bobsled parties. None of the mothers did.

After Mr. Ray had bandaged Betsy's ankle and pronounced it a trifling sprain, Mrs. Ray was as gay as a bird. She was so thankful that nothing worse had happened.

"Come on! Pop your corn," she said. "There are apples to roast, too."

Julia and Katie, Jerry and Pin repaired to the kitchen. Laughter rose above the sound of popcorn bouncing in a shaker. Tacy and Tib put apples to roast on the back of the hard-coal heater that sat like a rosy smiling god in a corner of the back parlor.

Betsy sat on the back-parlor sofa with her foot on a pillow. Jerry came in often to see how she felt.

"Gosh, she was a good soldier, Mrs. Ray!" he kept saying.

Betsy felt heroic.

The big pan of fluffy buttered popcorn was brought in and passed. Julia went to the piano, and everybody sang. They sang *Navajo* and *Hiawatha* and *Bedelia*, and Jerry and Julia sang a duet called, "Tell me, pretty maiden."

Mr. Ray smoked his pipe and looked pleased. He liked people to have a good time at his house.

At last Mrs. Ray played the piano, and Julia and Jerry, Katie and Pin danced a waltz. They pushed back the dining-room table and had a Virginia Reel. Mr. Ray joined in, and so did Tacy, and Tib, and Rena who came in smiling from the kitchen. The blue plates on the plate rail danced, too. Only Betsy could not dance because of her foot. But she had a good time anyway, feeling heroic.

"As soon as I get back to Cox," Jerry told her when he said good-by, "I'm going to send you a present. What would you like? A postcard album?"

A postcard album! It was just what she had been wanting.

Betsy was out of school for a week, but she didn't mind very much. It was pleasant to snuggle down in bed when she heard the hard-coal heater being shaken down in the morning. Julia and Margaret had to get up; they hurried into their clothes over the open register that brought heat into their bedroom. Betsy didn't need to hurry.

She hobbled downstairs late and spent most of the day on the back-parlor sofa. She liked to watch the red flames flickering behind the isinglass windows of the stove. After the postcard album came (for Jerry sent it! It had leather covers and the seal of Cox School on it.) she enjoyed putting in her collection of postcards. Postcards from her grandmother in California and from various uncles and aunts, from her father that time he went to St. Paul and from Tib when she went to visit in Milwaukee.

She had two new books to read for she had been to the library just the Saturday before the bobsled party. Miss Sparrow had picked them out for her. *The Water Babies* by Charles Kingsley and

Pickwick Papers by Charles Dickens.

When she grew tired of reading she played paper dolls.

Betsy hardly ever played with her paper dolls any more. Yet she loved them; she didn't want to throw them away. And when she was sick, or kept indoors for any reason, she got them out and played with them.

At last, however, she grew sick of paper dolls, too.

Her mother was going out that day. She and Margaret were going to the high school to hear Julia sing at the Literary Society program. It was Rena's afternoon off.

"I'm glad Tacy and Tib always come in after school," Mrs. Ray said. "You won't be alone very long."

She put out a plate of cookies to be ready for Tacy and Tib, and she and Margaret kissed Betsy and went out. Old Mag, hitched to the cutter, was waiting in front of the house. Mr. Ray had left her there at noon.

Betsy waved from the back-parlor window, and when the cutter had vanished down Hill Street and the sound of the sleighbells had died, she kept on staring out of doors. The street was empty. There was nothing to see but snow glistening in the sunshine.

Betsy stared a long time. Then she hobbled upstairs to her desk and brought down one of those tablets marked "Ray's Shoe Store. Wear Queen Quality Shoes."

When Tacy and Tib came in after school, they found her on the sofa, scribbling furiously. Her braids had come loose, her cheeks were red, and there was a smudge on her nose.

"I'm just finishing a story," she said. "Would you like to hear it?"

"You bet. Swell," said Tacy and Tib.

"It'll be done in a jiff."

Tacy and Tib took off their wraps and stowed them away in the closet. They helped themselves to cookies and sat down in comfortable chairs.

By that time Betsy was ready. She sat up and cleared her throat.

"It's a very good story," she said.

She announced the title sonorously.

"*Flossie's Accident.*"

Betsy liked to read her stories aloud and she read them like an actress. She made her voice low and thrillingly deep. She made it shake with emotion. She laughed mockingly and sobbed wildly when the occasion required.

And she was right about this story. It was a good one. Tacy soon stopped munching cookies and leaned forward in excitement. Tib cried real tears. She always cried real tears in the most flattering manner when Betsy's stories were sad.

Flossie's Accident was very, very sad.

It was about a girl named Flossie who was hurt in a bobsled accident. The accident was something like Betsy's, but Flossie didn't look like Betsy. She had long black ringlets, and big black eyes, and a dead white skin with lips as red as blood. She was dressed all in fluffy white fur, white coat and cap, mittens, boots and everything. She was white as a snowdrift and very beautiful.

When the bobsled turned over, her head was broken off. She was still alive and beautiful, but she didn't have a head.

Her father and mother didn't like the way she looked.

"You are no child of ours," they said, and cruelly shut the door in her face.

Bad boys and girls threw snowballs at her. They laughed at her and chased her.

Holding her head by its long black ringlets, she ran along the frozen river.

"Could she see with it?" Tib interrupted.

"Oh, yes. She could see. She held it up like a lantern."

"Could she hear?"

"Yes. She could hear too. She couldn't eat though. It wouldn't have been practical for her to eat."

"I should think she'd have starved to death," said Tib.

Betsy did not answer.

Flossie followed the river as far as St. Paul. It met the Mississippi there. She followed it to St. Louis, to Memphis, to New Orleans. Forlorn and outcast she wandered everywhere.

She shunned towns and cities, for the people in them laughed at her; or worse still, they ran from her in terror. But after dark she liked to look in at the windows of houses where happy families lived.

Sometimes she saw good things to eat on the tables. Baked beans and brown bread. Or stewed chicken with dumplings. Or pancakes with maple syrup. She looked at them longingly, for she was very hungry.

She saw children romping beside the hard-coal heaters and husbands kissing their wives.

Flossie's heart almost broke when she saw scenes like that. She couldn't ever get married without a head. She couldn't have children. In fact, there was nothing Flossie could do. She couldn't teach school. She couldn't clerk in a store. She couldn't do anything but wander.

So she kept on wandering.

"Did she wear her fur coat all the time?" Tib wanted to know.

"Yes," answered Betsy. "She wore it year in and year out."

"It must have been pretty hot in the summer time."

"Sweltering. There was one good thing about that coat though. It never got dirty. Wherever she went or whatever she did, it stayed as white as snow."

Flossie wandered and wandered, as the story ran on and on. Her adventures were many and excruciatingly sad. At last she hid in a ship and crossed the ocean. When she got off, she was in Greece.

She was walking along a road there (carrying her head, of course), when she met a handsome youth. He had blond hair and blue eyes and tanned rosy cheeks.

"He reminds me of Herbert Humphreys," said Tib.

"His name," said Betsy, "was Chauncey."

Chauncey did not laugh and jeer at Flossie as other people did. He stopped and asked her kindly what her trouble was.

"You look like the *Winged Victory*," he said.

She did, too, although she did not have wings.

Flossie told him her story.

"Come with me," said Chauncey.

Taking her by the hand, he led her to the top of a mountain. They looked down on olive groves and the blue Mediterranean Sea.

He built a fire of cedar boughs and when smoke began to rise he said a prayer to the gods and goddesses. He was sort of a god himself. He took Flossie's head by its ringlets and swung it back and forth in the smoke from his fire. Then he clapped it on her swanlike neck, and it fastened there at once. She was just as beautiful as she had been before the bobsled accident. They got married and went to live on the Island of Delos, and they had ten children, five boys and five girls.

"That's the end of the story," said Betsy, closing the tablet.

"Betsy! It's wonderful!" cried Tacy.

"It's the best story you ever wrote," said Tib.

"It's the best story I ever heard in my life."

"That poor Flossie!"

Tacy jumped to her feet.

"Betsy," she said, excitedly, yet earnestly, "your stories ought to be published. I've been thinking that for a long time although I never mentioned it before."

Betsy looked at Tacy deeply. It was strange, she thought, that Tacy should say that for she had been thinking the very thing herself.

"They're just as good as the stories in the *Ladies' Home Journal*," said Tacy. "Don't you think so, Tib?"

"Better," Tib said.

"How do people get stories published, do you suppose?"

"I think," said Betsy, "they just send them to the magazines."

"Why don't you send this one then?"

"Maybe I will," said Betsy. Her heart leaped up like a little fish in a bowl. "I haven't any good paper though."

"My sister Mary has some," said Tacy. "A box of lovely pink stationery. Got it for her birthday. She'd give me some, I think. And since she isn't at home, I'll just take it."

"You mean . . . right now?"

"Right now. We'll copy that story and get it off."

"I'll print it for you," cried Tib. Tib was famous for her printing.

Tacy seized her coat and overshoes and ran out of the house. Tib opened the bookcase desk and spread Betsy's tablet on it. She took Betsy's pencil out to the kitchen and sharpened it to an exquisite point. Betsy waited, feeling queer inside.

Tacy came back breathless with the pink stationery.

"I didn't dare take more than one sheet. Do you think you can get the story on, Tib?"

"I think so," said Tib. "I'll print small."

She set to work with painstaking care. While she labored, Betsy and Tacy made plans.

"Betsy," said Tacy solemnly, "you're going to be famous after that story is published."

"How much do you suppose I'll be paid for it?" Betsy asked.

"Oh, probably a hundred dollars."

"What shall we spend it for?"

"Let's see! What!"

They decided to buy silk dresses with hats to match. A blue one for Tacy (because she had red hair). A pink one for Betsy and a yellow one for Tib.

"We'll wear them to Mrs. Poppy's party," said Betsy.

"We'll wear them to the next matinee Winona takes us to. They'll look fine in a box," Tacy said.

"See here," said Tib, sounding worried. "It's going to be hard to squeeze this story on."

"Oh, you can squeeze it on," said Betsy.

"I'll have to print awfully small."

"It doesn't matter," said Tacy. "They'll be so anxious to know how that story's coming out that they'll use a microscope on it, if they have to."

So Tib persisted, and by printing very, very, very small she got all the story on the sheet of pink stationery, down to the last word.

"I saw the Lord's Prayer printed on a dime one time," said Betsy. "It looked a good deal like that."

They put the pink stationery into an envelope and addressed it to the *Ladies' Home Journal*, Independence Square, Philadelphia, Pa. Betsy found a stamp and stuck it on.

"I'll put it in the mailbox on my way home," said Tib, sighing with content.

They all sat on the sofa then, while the sky, behind brown tree trunks, took on the tint of mother-of-pearl, matching the tint of the snow. They planned about the silk dresses and hats.

Betsy and Tacy and Tib were twelve years old now, and when they made plans like that they didn't quite believe them. But they liked to make them anyhow.

10

Christmas Shopping

"HOW LONG does it take a letter to go to Philadelphia?" Betsy asked her father that night at supper.

"Two or three days," he replied.

"Whom do you know in Philadelphia?" asked Julia, stressing the "whom."

"Never mind," said Betsy. "Someone important."

"The King of Spain maybe," said her father. He was teasing. For when Betsy and Tacy and Tib were only ten years old and didn't know any better, they had written a letter to the King of Spain. They had received an answer, too.

Betsy laughed at her father's joke, but underneath the table she was counting on her fingers.

Three days for the story to go, a day for the editor to read it, three days for his letter and the hundred dollar bill to return.

The transaction could be completed in a week, she told Tacy and Tib next day. But a week passed, and another, without any word about Flossie.

Betsy was back in school, of course. At the end of

the second week, school closed for the Christmas vacation. That meant that Betsy, Tacy, and Tib had an important engagement. For years on the first day of Christmas vacation they had gone shopping together.

"Let's take Winona this year," Tib suggested.

Winona had come to be quite a friend of theirs. They often stopped after school to slide down her terrace, a particularly steep and hazardous one, or to play show in her dining room. Winona loved to play show; she was always the villainess.

"I'd like to take her," said Tacy. "She'd be pretty surprised, I guess, at the way we shop."

"She certainly would be," said Betsy, and all of them laughed.

"You see," Betsy explained to Winona when they invited her, "we usually make our Christmas presents, or else our mothers buy them for us . . . the ones we give away, I mean."

"Then why do you go shopping?" Winona asked.

"We go shopping to shop," said Tacy.

The three of them smiled. Winona looked mystified.

"We've done it the same way ever since we were children," said Betsy. "We always take ten cents apiece, and we always buy just the same things."

"What do you buy?"

"You'll see," said Betsy, "if you want to come along."

They liked to tease Winona because she was such a tease herself.

Winona's black eyes snapped.

"I'll come," she said.

They made plans to meet the next day at a quarter after two. Betsy didn't want to leave home until the mail came. (She and Tacy and Tib were watching every mail for her hundred dollars.)

Every day they changed their minds about how they would spend it. First they had decided on the silk dresses and hats. Then they changed to a Shetland pony, and now it was a trip to Niagara Falls.

They were planning the trip to the Falls with great enthusiasm when Mr. Goode, the postman, came into sight.

They swooped down upon him, three abreast. (They had been waiting on Betsy's hitching block.)

"I haven't a blessed thing for any of you," he said. "What are you looking for, anyway? Another letter from a king?"

He was like Betsy's father; he couldn't forget that letter from the King of Spain.

"This is a business letter, Mr. Goode," Betsy said.

"Money in it, too," said Tib. "A hundred dollars, we expect."

"I'll be careful with it when it comes," said Mr. Goode.

They hurried down to call for Winona, running and sliding in the icy street.

Winona was waiting in front of her house wearing a crimson coat and hat. She looked like a rakish cardinal against the snow.

"Does it matter," she asked, swinging her pocket book, "if I take more than ten cents?"

"Of course it matters. It isn't allowed." Betsy, Tacy, and Tib were noisily indignant.

"That's all I've got anyway," Winona grinned. "Just asked for fun."

"You go way back and sit down," Tacy said.

They started off downtown.

The fluffy white drifts had packed into hard ramparts guarding the sidewalks. The four had to keep to the sidewalks after they passed Lincoln Park. The streets were crowded with sleighs and cutters. Chiming bells added to the Christmassy feeling in the air.

Front Street was very Christmassy. Evergreen boughs and holly wreaths, red bells and mistletoe sprays surrounded displays of tempting merchandise in all the store windows. In one window a life-sized Santa Claus with a brimming pack on his back was halfway into a papier-mâché chimney.

"Look here!" said Winona, stopping to admire. "This will tickle the little kids."

"The *little* kids?"

"The ones that believe in Santa Claus."

"Gee whiz!" said Betsy. "I didn't think we were *little* kids any more. I thought we were twelve years old; didn't you, Tacy?"

"I was under that impression," said Tacy.

"Why, we are! What do you mean?" asked Tib.

Winona knew what they meant.

"Are you trying to tell me," she asked, "that you believe in Santa Claus?"

"Certainly, we do!"

"Well, of all . . ." began Winona. She stopped, words failing her, and looked at them with a scorn which changed to suspicion as she viewed their broadly smiling faces.

"I expect to believe in Santa Claus when I'm in high school," said Tacy.

"I expect to believe in him when I'm grown up and married," said Betsy. "I hear him on the roof every year; don't you, Tacy?"

"Sure I do. And I've seen the reindeer go past the bedroom window, lots of times."

"You see," explained Tib, "we've made an agreement about him. We've crossed our hearts and even signed a paper."

"You three take the cake!" said Winona. "All right. I believe in him too."

They came to Cook's Book Store.

"We start here," said Betsy.

"Is that where we spend our dimes?" asked Winona.

"Mercy, no! We don't spend them for hours yet. We just shop. Choose a present."

"I know what I'm going to choose," said Betsy. "*Little Men*. I got *Little Women* last year."

They went in and said hello to Mr. Cook. His bright eyes looked out sharply under his silky toupee.

"You never pass me up, do you?" he said. He said it good naturedly though.

"This year we brought Winona Root. She's another customer for you, Mr. Cook," said Tib.

"Customer!" said Mr. Cook. "Customer! Oh well, look around."

They looked around. They looked around thoroughly. They read snatches in the Christmas books. They studied the directions on all the games. Tacy chose a pencil set, and Tib chose colored crayons.

"Choose! Go ahead and choose! Choose whatever you like," they urged Winona hospitably.

Winona chose a book about Indians.

They went next door to the harness and saddle

maker's shop. There wasn't much to choose here, just whips and buggy robes. Getting into the spirit of the game, Winona cracked a dozen whips before she chose one. Betsy and Tacy chose robes, with landscapes printed on them.

There was a tall wooden horse standing in the window. It was almost seven feet tall, dapple gray, with flashing glass eyes and springy mane and tail. Every year the harness and saddle maker let Tib sit on the horse.

He looked at her sadly now as she put her foot in a stirrup and swung nimbly upward.

"If the horseless carriages keep coming to town, I'll have to take that fellow down," he said.

That gave Tib an idea.

"*I* know what *I'll* choose then," she cried. "I'll choose this horse. I'll put him up in our back yard and all of us can ride him."

"Tib! What fun!"

"I wish I'd thought to choose him."

"It's a spiffy idea, Tib!" Betsy cried.

Winona had an idea even spiffier.

"Let's go choose horseless carriages," she suggested nonchalantly. "The hardware-store man sells them."

For a moment Betsy, Tacy, and Tib were dazzled by this brilliant plan. Then Tib scrambled down from the horse. Saying good-by to the melancholy harness and saddle maker, they raced to the hardware store.

Sure enough, there was a horseless carriage on display there. They inspected it from every angle, and the curly-haired hardware-store man let them sit in it for awhile. He was very obliging. All four of them chose it, and while they were in the store they looked at skates and bicycles.

"I could use a new sled," said Winona.

So they looked at sleds too.

At the Lion Department store they shopped even

more extensively. There were many departments, and they visited them all. The busy clerks paid little attention to them. They wandered happily about.

They chose rhinestone side combs, jeweled hat pins, gay pompadour pouffs. They chose fluffy collars and belts and pocket books. They chose black lace stockings and taffeta petticoats and embroidered corset covers.

It was hard to tear themselves away but they did so at last. They went to the drug store where they sniffed assiduously. They sniffed every kind of perfume in the store before they chose, finally, rose and lilac and violet, and new-mown hay.

"I want new-mown hay because it's the kind Mrs. Poppy uses," Betsy said.

"Mrs. Poppy!" exclaimed Tacy. "That reminds me of her party. We'd better go to the jewelry store and choose some jewels."

"Goodness, yes!" said Betsy. "I need a diamond ring to wear to that party."

They hurried to the jewelry store. The clerks there weren't very helpful, however. They wouldn't let them try on diamond rings, or necklaces, or bracelets. They wouldn't even let them handle the fat gold watches, with doves engraved on the sides, which looked so fashionable pinned to a shirtwaist.

"They act this way every year," said Betsy to

Winona. "Let's go to the toy shop. That's the nicest, anyhow."

The toy shop was what they had all been waiting for. They had been holding it off in order to have it still ahead of them. But the time for it had come at last.

At the toy shop it was difficult to choose. In blissful indecision they circled the table of dolls. Yellow-haired dolls with blue dresses, black-haired dolls with pink dresses, baby dolls, boy dolls, black dolls.

Betsy, Tacy, Tib, and Winona had stopped playing with dolls, except on days when they were sick, perhaps, or when stormy weather kept them indoors. Yet choosing dolls was the most fun of all. They liked the dolls' appurtenances too.

They inspected doll dishes, doll stoves, sets of shiny doll tinware, doll parlor sets.

There was one magnificent doll house, complete even to the kitchen. Winona asked the price of it.

"Twenty-five dollars? Hmm! Well, it's worth it," said Winona thoughtfully, swinging her pocket book.

When they were through with the dolls they began on the other toys. Trains of cars, jumping jacks, woolly animals on wheels.

"Gee!" said Winona at last. "I'm getting tired. When do we spend our dimes?"

"Dimes!" said the clerk who had told her the price of the doll's house. "Dimes!" She settled her eye glasses on the thin ridge of her nose and looked at the four severely.

When she had turned away, Betsy whispered, "Right now!"

"I hope," said Winona, "we spend them for something to eat."

"We don't. But after we've spent them, we go to call on our fathers. And you can't call on four fathers, without being invited out to Heinz's Restaurant for ice cream."

"I suppose not," Winona agreed. "Well, what do we buy then?"

Betsy turned and led the way to the far end of the store.

There on a long table Christmas tree ornaments were set out for sale. There were boxes and boxes full of them, their colors mingling in bewildering iridescence. There were large fragile balls of vivid hues, there were gold and silver balls; there were tinsel angels, shining harps and trumpets, gleaming stars.

"Here," said Betsy, "here we buy."

She looked at Winona, bright-eyed, and Winona looked from her to the resplendent table.

"Nothing," Tacy tried to explain, "is so much like Christmas as a Christmas-tree ornament."

"You get a lot for ten cents," said Tib.

They gave themselves then with abandon to the sweet delight of choosing. It was almost pain to choose. Each fragile bauble was gayer, more enchanting than the last. And now they were not only choosing, they were buying. What each one chose she would take home; she would see it on the Christmas tree; she would see it year after year, if she were lucky and it did not break.

They walked around and around the table, touching softly with mittened hands.

Betsy at last chose a large red ball. Tacy chose an angel. Tib chose a rosy Santa Claus. Winona chose a silver trumpet.

They yielded their dimes and the lady with the eye glasses wrapped up four packages. Betsy, Tacy, Tib, and Winona went out into the street. The afternoon was drawing to a pallid close. Soon the street lamps would be lighted.

"Which father shall we call on first?" Winona asked.

"Mine is nearest Heinz's Restaurant," said Betsy. They walked to Ray's Shoe Store, smiling, holding Christmas in their hands.

11

Mrs. Poppy's Party

TO GO FROM Before Christmas to After Christmas was like climbing and descending a high glittering peak. Christmas, of course, sat at the top. The trip down was usually more abrupt and far less pleasurable than the long climb up, but not this year. For this year, the After Christmas held Mrs. Poppy's party.

Before Christmas started with the shopping expedition. Or even earlier, with the school Christmas Entertainment. The carols, the pungent evergreens, made their first appearance there. The Sunday School Christmas Entertainment followed, with speaking pieces and presents.

After the shopping trip one climbed through mists of secrecy . . . at the Ray house, one did. There was whispering and giggling. Doors were slammed when one approached. Rena was working with crepe paper in her bedroom; Julia kept whisking her sewing bag out of sight. Everyone cautioned everyone else not to look here or look there.

"Betsy, don't open the lowest sideboard drawer."

"Don't look in the right-hand upper drawer of my bureau."

"Keep out of the downstairs closet!"

Betsy knew so many secrets that she was afraid to speak for fear one would pop out like the jack-in-the-box she had seen in the toy shop.

What if she should accidentally mention the silver cake basket her father was giving to her mother? Or the burned wood handkerchief box Julia was making for her father? Or, above all, Margaret's talking doll? Everyone was waiting to see Margaret's eyes when the doll said "mamma" on Christmas morning.

Margaret's eyes were big in her little serious face. The long black lashes seemed not so much to shade them as to make them bigger and brighter. They were big and bright enough the night her father brought the tree home. It was a feathery hemlock and smelled deliciously when Betsy and Margaret visited it in the woodshed.

On Christmas Eve it was brought indoors. It was set up in a corner of the dining room and a star was fixed on its crest. Strings of popcorn and cranberries were woven through its branches that were hung with colored balls.

Betsy put on the red ball she had bought on this year's Christmas shopping trip. She looked for the harp she had bought last year, and the angel from the year before. When all was ready, the candles were lighted. Bits of live flame danced all over the tree.

Betsy's mother went to the piano then. They all sang together. *Oh, Little Town of Bethlehem. It Came Upon the Midnight Clear.* And *Silent Night*, most beloved of all.

"Let's read about the Cratchits' Christmas dinner," Mr. Ray said. He always said it.

He crossed his legs and got out his pipe and Betsy went to the bookcase for Dickens' *Christmas Carol*. Betsy read aloud about the Cratchits' goose, and Tiny Tim. Margaret pretended to read . . . (she knew it by heart) . . . *'Twas the Night Before Christmas*. Julia read the story of Jesus' birth out of the *Book of Luke*.

The stockings were hung around the hard-coal heater. Mr. and Mrs. Ray and Rena all hung stockings too. In some families, Betsy had heard, only children hung stockings. But it was not so in the Ray house. Mr. Ray complained loudly of the smallness of his sock.

The lamps were turned low and they scurried around in the dimness putting presents into one another's stockings. One could not avoid seeing knobby bundles being stuffed into one's own stocking.

"I don't peek; do I?" asked Margaret, trotting about.

"I should say you don't," Mrs. Ray replied.

"I'd be ashamed to, wouldn't I?" Margaret continued.

"You certainly would."

"I wouldn't," said Mr. Ray and pretended to make a dash for his sock. Margaret caught him around the knees. Julia and Betsy pinioned his arms, while Rena screamed and laughed at once.

"Lord-a-mercy! Lord-a-mercy!"

"Stop it! Stop it!" cried Mrs. Ray, pulling them apart. "Bob, you behave and go down cellar and get us some cider. These children must get to bed sometime tonight. We have to give Santa Claus a chance."

Santa Claus, of course!

After Julia and Betsy and Margaret went upstairs, when the lamp had been blown out, they looked out the window. They saw the snowy roof of Tacy's house, the snowy silent hill, the waiting stars.

"No Santa Claus yet," they said.

But after they got into bed they began to hear him.

"Margaret! Don't you hear something on the roof?"

"I think it's reindeer. Don't you, Betsy?"

"It can't be yet. Papa and Mamma haven't gone to bed."

"Julia, he's so fat and our chimney's so small, how can he get down?"

"He gets down. It's magic."

"What would he do . . ." Margaret breathed hard with daring, "if we ran downstairs and caught him?"

"Better not do that. He'd never come again."

"I won't." Margaret shivered in delighted apprehension. For the dozenth time she snuggled down in bed.

Mrs. Ray called upstairs.

"Children! Stop talking!"

"Children! Get some sleep! Remember tomorrow's Christmas."

Remember tomorrow's Christmas! As though they could forget it!

Margaret waked up first. It was the first year she had waked ahead of Betsy. In her little high-necked, long-sleeved flannel night gown, she pattered through Rena's bedroom, downstairs.

"Margaret! Go back to bed! It's only four."

On the second trip Betsy went with her. On the third trip Julia went too. It was still as black as night, but now the three of them jumped into the big bed with their mother.

They cuddled there, laughing and giggling, while

their father in his dressing gown shook down and filled the hard-coal heater.

"My! My! You ought to see what I see!" he called out over the sound of rattling coal.

"Has Santa Claus come?" Margaret's fingers were clutching Betsy's arm.

"Sure, he's come."

"Can we get up? When can we get up?"

"Not until the room gets warm."

Betsy's mother got up though. Rena was up already. The smell of coffee and sausages was drifting through the house. Julia got dressed. But Betsy and Margaret stayed in bed imagining things.

They did not imagine the glory of that moment when they opened the bedroom door and saw the stockings, around the glowing stove, swimming in Christmas-tree light!

Margaret stared at the yellow-haired doll peeping from her stocking. She walked toward it slowly.

"Take it out, Margaret," called her mother, while the others waited breathlessly.

She took it out.

"Squeeze it, Margaret."

She squeezed it, looking down with a grave face.

"Harder!"

She squeezed it harder, and the yellow-haired doll spoke.

"Mamma! Mamma!" said the doll in a light quick voice.

"Mamma! Mamma!" cried Margaret, her eyes like Christmas stars.

That was the sparkling summit of Christmas at the Ray house.

The descent was gay. Stockings were unpacked down to the orange and the dollar from Grandpa Ray that were always found at the bottom. There were presents for everyone, beautiful presents, and joke presents too.

Julia got a postage stamp (for a letter to Jerry) tastefully wrapped in a hat box. Margaret got one

butternut with a card signed "Squirrel, Esquire."
Betsy got one of her own much-chewed pencils "With
Sympathy from William Shakespeare." Mr. Ray got a
pan of burned biscuits. Rena had been saving them
ever since she burned them almost a week before.

Mr. Ray's antics with those biscuits made Rena
laugh until she cried. He acted as though he did
not know they were a joke; he acted as though he
thought he was expected to eat them. He chewed
and chewed, looking solemn and worried, while the
others rocked with mirth.

"Lord-a-mercy, I've got to get that turkey on!"
said Rena at last.

"And my pies!" cried Mrs. Ray jumping up lightly to kiss Mr. Ray for the silver cake basket.

Everyone kissed everyone else, saying "Thank You." And Betsy dressed and ran over to show Tacy *Little Men*. (Mr. Cook must have told her father she wanted it.)

The Kelly house was a happy bedlam. Betsy stayed there until the family went to church. Then she went on to Tib's to feast on Christmas cookies, cut in the shapes of stars and animals and frosted with colored sugar.

Dinner came at one o'clock sharp. Full of turkey and turkey dressing, gravy and cranberry sauce, mashed turnips, creamed onions, celery, rolls, and mince and pumpkin pie, people either took naps or went sliding. Betsy, Tacy, and Tib went sliding. So did Margaret and all the younger children.

Everyone out on the hill had something new. A new sled, or a new cap, or new red knitted mittens. They slid and slid until purple shadows fell across the snow. Betsy came in at last to read beside the fire. Turkey sandwiches, made by her father, ended the day.

Usually she went to bed on Christmas night feeling very much on the other side of the glorious holiday peak. But not this year. She was almost as excited as though it were Christmas Eve, for the next day came Mrs. Poppy's party.

The note of invitation had arrived several days before. It was written in a large childish handwriting on rich blue paper, heavily scented with new-mown hay perfume.

"Of course you may go. It's very nice of her." But Mrs. Ray's voice still held that note of reservation. Why was it? Betsy wondered. Mrs. Poppy wasn't any different from anybody else except that she was nicer than most.

"I wish," said Betsy slowly, "you were acquainted with Mrs. Poppy. I think she'd like to get acquainted with you."

"P'shaw!" said Mrs. Ray. "She isn't interested in anything here. She's in the Twin Cities, half the time. We haven't anything in common. If I thought she was lonesome, I'd go to see her, of course." Her tone added, "I'm sure she isn't though."

Julia broke into the conversation. She had just come in from skating with Jerry, at home for the Christmas vacation.

"I'm longing to meet her. Jerry says she was a very fine singer. She sang in *Erminie*. That lullaby you used to sing to us."

"Oh, really?" Mrs. Ray seemed interested in this. But when Betsy pressed her, asking, "*Will* you go to see her, Mamma?" she answered, "Maybe.

Sometime," in that tone which meant "Probably not."

Mrs. Kelly, Mrs. Muller, and Mrs. Root seemed to feel much as Mrs. Ray did. But fortunately Tacy and Tib and Winona were allowed to go to the party.

They were trig and trim down to their polished shoes when they pushed through the swinging door at the Melborn Hotel. They wore their best hats and big vivid hair ribbons; best dresses too, under their winter coats.

Betsy took the lead. It was hard to take the lead from Winona but she did it because she had visited Mrs. Poppy before.

"This is the *Winged Victory*," she said, pausing by the statue on the landing.

"The one Flossie looked like?" Tib asked, staring up.

"Yes. Only Flossie didn't have wings."

"Who was Flossie?"

"She's in a story I wrote," Betsy answered quickly. They hadn't told Winona about the pink stationery. They were afraid she would tease them if the hundred dollars didn't come. And it still hadn't come. They had stopped making plans about it.

Mrs. Poppy opened the door to them, smiling radiantly. She looked like a big peony in a peony-pink silk dress. She wore a sprig of holly pinned to her shoulder.

"Merry Christmas!" she cried.

"Merry Christmas!" cried Betsy, Tacy, Tib, and Winona. They surged into the hall.

They took off their wraps in the blue bedroom and Betsy shot a look at Minnie's doll. It looked faded and old in the little rocking chair beside Mrs. Poppy's bed. She wondered whether Minnie had been given that doll for a Christmas present and how long ago. She wondered whether Mr. and Mrs. Poppy had grown used to not having Minnie around on Christmas morning.

Suddenly she wished urgently that she had brought Mrs. Poppy a present. Why hadn't she thought of it? Why hadn't her mother, usually quick with such ideas, had this one? Or Mrs. Muller . . . she might have sent some Christmas cookies. She was always sending people boxes of her cookies. But no one had sent anything.

"We've got to do something about Mrs. Poppy," Betsy thought so vigorously that she found herself frowning into the mirror. She made herself smile, and presently she felt like smiling.

Mr. Poppy's den had a sprig of mistletoe over the door.

"I put it there," said Mrs. Poppy, looking roguish.

In the parlor there were wreaths at the windows. A fat glittering tree stood on a table.

"There are packages for all of you. They have

your names on," Mrs. Poppy said.

Her eyes brimmed with pleasure as they jostled one another, hunting for their gifts.

They all received perfume. Rose and lilac and violet and new-mown hay.

"You may exchange with one another," Mrs. Poppy said. "I knew you wanted those four scents, but I didn't know which wanted which."

"But how did you know we wanted perfume at all?" they cried, exchanging.

"The man at the drug store told me. I told him whom I was buying it for and he seemed to know all about you."

"He does! He does!" They went off into gales of laughter.

"It's the first perfume I ever had, Mrs. Poppy," Tacy said.

"Me too," said Tib, sniffing her beloved rose.

"I've had perfume, but never lilac," said Winona.

"Now I'll smell just like you," Betsy said.

Rapturously they doused themselves and each other. They played the graphophone; and Mrs. Poppy played the piano for them to sing. The first thing they knew they were giving a sort of entertainment. Betsy and Tacy sang their Cat Duet; it was a duet they often sang at school. Winona sang a very sad song about *The Baggage Car Ahead*. And Tib danced her Baby Dance.

She had danced her Baby Dance many times since she danced it first at a school entertainment. Betsy and Tacy knew the music so well they could sing it. They sang it now, for Tib to dance by in Mrs. Poppy's parlor.

Tib loved to dance, and Tib was like Julia . . . she loved to perform. Smilingly, she lifted her skirts by the edges, ran and made her pirouette. There were five different steps in the Baby Dance, each one to be done thirty-two times. She did them all triumphantly, and when her audience applauded at the end, she ran back to the center of the room to curtsey and kiss her hands, as she had seen Little Eva do.

Mrs. Poppy was enchanted with the Baby Dance.

"Thank you so much for doing it," she said, ruffling Tib's yellow curls.

"I like to do it," said Tib. "I'm getting a little tired of it though. I wish I knew a new dance."

"Do you?" Mrs. Poppy cried. "I could easily teach you one, if your mother would like me to. I know quite a lot of steps."

Winona played a tune, and Mrs. Poppy lifted her peony-pink skirts. Her feet were small and dainty in slippers the color of her dress. In spite of her weight Mrs. Poppy danced lightly, with a skill which fascinated Tib.

When the maid knocked, Mrs. Poppy cried, "Mercy me! I haven't even set the table."

They all helped her spread the white embroidered cloth and put out the hand-painted cups and saucers and plates. The maid came in smiling, and there was ice cream today, in addition to the frosted cakes and the pot of hot chocolate and the bowl of whipped cream.

They had a gay time eating the refreshments.

Mrs. Poppy asked them how the man in the drug store had happened to know what kinds of perfume they wanted. They told her about their Christmas shopping, and she laughed and laughed, and so did they. They told her all about their Christmases, too.

Now and then Betsy looked out to the river, white and still in its blanket of snow. She wondered whether Mrs. Poppy missed its restless journeying down to St. Paul to meet the Mississippi. She thought about Mrs. Poppy's journeyings and her acting and her singing. She thought about Uncle Keith.

She was glad when Mrs. Poppy sent Tacy and Tib and Winona out to ride in the elevator, and said in a lowered voice:

"Betsy, I want to talk with you a minute. I want you to know that I'm trying to find your uncle. I'm making inquiries and looking for his name in the casts of all the plays Mr. Poppy books. Don't mention it to your mother yet. I don't want her to be disappointed if I haven't any luck."

"Mrs. Poppy!" cried Betsy. "How kind of you! Mamma would be so glad."

She wished she could say that her mother was coming soon to get acquainted but she knew she couldn't. She did repeat, though, what Julia had said about wanting to meet her.

"She's the one who sings?" asked Mrs. Poppy with vivid interest. "Why, I'd love to have her come! Maybe I could help her."

Her blue eyes suddenly misted over.

"Wouldn't it be wonderful, Betsy," she said, "if I could *help* here in Deep Valley? Help children like

Tib and your sister with the things I know how to do? I've studied with good masters. I know how to dance, and something about music. It would make me feel I *belonged* if I could be of use here."

Betsy did not answer. She was a talker, her family always said, but sometimes when she most wanted to talk she couldn't say a word.

She looked out at the river, fixed in ice, bedded under snow. She looked at the brave gay Christmas tree, and thought of the doll beside Mrs. Poppy's bed.

She turned abruptly and gave Mrs. Poppy a big hug and a kiss.

Mrs. Poppy hugged her back. Betsy felt a wet cheek touching her own.

"Betsy!" cried Mrs. Poppy. "Betsy! Why, you've given me a Christmas present!"

And that was the very thing Betsy had wanted to do.

12

Three Telephone Calls

NE DAY soon after Mrs. Poppy's party, the telephone at the Ray house rang three times. The last time was the most important of all.

The first time it was for Julia.

She came into the back parlor where Mrs. Ray was sewing and Margaret was playing paper dolls and Betsy was reading *Huckleberry Finn*, a book that Miss Sparrow had picked out for her.

"Mamma," said Julia, looking very pleased. "It's Jerry. The play of *Rip Van Winkle* is coming to town. There's going to be a matinee next Saturday afternoon, and he wants me to go."

"I think that would be lovely," said Mrs. Ray. "That's a wonderful play. Papa and I saw Joseph Jefferson in it, years ago." She seemed as pleased as Julia.

Betsy closed her book, jumped up and went to the back-parlor closet where outdoor wraps were kept.

"Where are you going, Betsy?" asked Mrs. Ray as Julia returned to the telephone.

"To see Winona," said Betsy. "I think she'll want

to take Tacy and Tib and me to that matinee." She pulled on her coat with a determined air.

Margaret ran to her mother.

"I wish I could go too, Mamma," she said.

"Maybe you can," said Mrs. Ray. "I've half a notion," she added, "to ask Papa to take *me*. I've never forgotten that play."

Julia came back from the telephone, and while Betsy strapped on her overshoes and hunted for her mittens, Mrs. Ray told them about Rip Van Winkle. Julia and Betsy knew the story, of course; they had read it in school. But they liked hearing their mother tell about the lovable ne'er-do-well, who played at bowls with a strange ghostly crew in the Kaatskills, and drank from their flagon, and slept for twenty years.

Mrs. Ray was describing Rip's awakening to find his dog gone, his gun old and rusty and himself with a long white beard, when the telephone rang again. This time it was for Betsy. She returned to the back parlor, dancing.

"It's Winona," she cried. "And she *does* want us to go. Tacy and Tib and me. She has 'comps.'"

"That settles it," said Mrs. Ray to Margaret. "You and I are going too."

As soon as Betsy had finished talking to Winona, Mrs. Ray went to the telephone and gave Central the number of Ray's Shoe Store. Julia and Betsy and Margaret hugged and shouted.

Then Betsy ran out the front door and over to Tacy's. Mrs. Kelly said that Tacy could go; and Betsy and Tacy ran down Hill Street and through the snow-covered vacant lot to Tib's house. Mrs. Muller said that Tib could go; and they all ran on to Winona's.

It had started to snow now, and the whirling, dancing flakes seemed as happy as they were.

Winona had on her wraps when they arrived.

"Let's go look at the billboards," she said.

There were billboards at the end of School Street, a full half-block of them, concealing the slough. The children visited them often, to taste Deep Valley's dramatic fare. Many plays had come to the Opera House since *Uncle Tom's Cabin*, but this was the first matinee.

The bill poster had just finished pasting the large gaudy sheets which announced that the beautiful legendary drama of *Rip Van Winkle* would be shown at the Opera House on Saturday afternoon and evening. They showed pictures of Young Rip, tattered and smiling, with a troop of children at his heels, and Old Rip, waking in the Kaatskills with the white beard Betsy's mother had described; Young Rip with his little daughter, a wee girl wearing a quaint Dutch cap, and that same daughter grown to young womanhood, standing with her sailor lover.

"How can the same actress play first a little girl and then a young lady?" Tib wanted to know.

"A child plays one part, and a woman the other," Winona explained.

"Let's follow that little girl home from the Opera House like we did Little Eva," cried Tacy.

"Let's!" "Let's!"

They were reminded by this of the magic of the other matinee, and they talked about it all the way back to Winona's. It was snowing hard now, and too wet to play out, so they went into Winona's house and played a game of authors.

Tacy and Tib and Winona played; Betsy didn't want to. She asked Winona for a pencil and a piece of paper and sat in a window seat in Winona's father's library. The snow was a spotted veil, concealing trees and houses, but Betsy would not have seen trees and houses anyway. Looking out into the snowstorm, she saw the inside of the Opera House at that dim expectant moment when the curtain went up.

"I've written a poem," she said, returning to the parlor where the game of authors was in progress. "Want to hear it?"

"Sure," said Tacy. She and Tib and Winona were used to listening to what Betsy wrote.

"It's called, *The Curtain Goes Up*," said Betsy.

She read it in a dreamy singsong.

"*The lights are turned low,*
The violins sing,
A feeling of waiting is
On everything.
Winona and Tib,
And Tacy and me,
We sit very still
In the mystery.
The Opera House feels
Like a big empty cup,
And then something happens,
The curtain goes up.

The curtain goes up,
The curtain goes up,
It's a wonderful moment,
When the curtain goes up.
It's like Christmas morning,
Stealing down stairs,
It's like being frightened,
And saying your prayers,
It's like being hungry
And ready to sup,
It's a wonderful moment,
When the curtain goes up."

"Betsy!" cried Winona. "I like that poem."

Tacy and Tib said that they did too.

"The things you write ought to be published!" Winona declared.

Betsy and Tacy and Tib looked away from one another. The story Tib had printed so neatly on the sheet of pink stationery had never been heard from. As the days went by, they became sadly certain that it never would be heard from.

They were glad now that they had decided not to tell Winona about it.

"Some day they'll be published, maybe," said Betsy in a tone so lacking in her usual soaring confidence that Winona was moved to express unaccustomed praise.

"Some day, nothing!" she exclaimed. "That's as good as the poems in our school reader. I like the part about me. May I have a copy of it, Betsy?"

"You may have the whole thing," said Betsy. "Oh, kids! Isn't it grand about Saturday? Let's talk about Saturday."

Making a dive for the game of authors, she swept it to the carpet. They began to throw cards.

Winona's mother came in and asked them if they didn't want to make fudge. Perhaps she thought that was a good way to quiet them down. They made fudge, but it was slow hardening, and of course they had to wait for it to harden. Then they had to wait to eat the rich chocolatey squares. It was late when Betsy, Tacy, and Tib started for home.

Just as they left Winona's house they heard the telephone ring.

"That's Mamma wanting to know what's become of me," said Betsy.

She did not stop at Tacy's house or Tib's, but hurried through the snowy dark. When she reached home she saw that the dining-room lamp had been lighted. Her father was at home.

She pushed open the kitchen door. The smell of frying ham greeted her first. Right behind that delicious aroma came Margaret.

"Betsy! Betsy!" she cried. "Who do you think telephoned?"

"Wait, Margaret!" Mrs. Ray said. "I want to tell her. Unless you've heard already, Betsy, from Mrs. Muller or Mrs. Kelly?"

"I didn't see them," said Betsy. "What is it?"

"It's something wonderful," cried Julia. She seized Betsy and spun her around the room.

"Me and Margaret, we're going to be in the front row," cried Rena. "I wouldn't miss seeing you, Betsy . . ."

"Sh-sh, Rena," said Julia, and Margaret ran to put her hand over Rena's mouth.

"Of course," said Betsy's father, "I have to give my

consent." His eyes were twinkling as he stood with his hands in his pockets.

"Mamma! Julia! What is it?" cried Betsy. "Hurry and tell me, please!"

"It's this," said Mrs. Ray. "You and Tacy and Tib and Winona are all going to act in *Rip Van Winkle* Saturday. Both afternoon and evening. Tib will take the part of Meenie, Rip Van Winkle's little girl, and the rest of you are going to be village children."

"What?" cried Betsy. "On the stage?"

"On the stage," her mother answered. "Behind the footlights."

"You'll wear a costume, have grease paint on," babbled Julia.

"I'm taking Margaret," Rena explained.

"Papa and I are coming in the evening," Mrs. Ray added.

Betsy thought she must be dreaming. The kitchen was whirling. The lamp made a yellow track.

"But why? How did it happen?" she asked.

"Sit down, and I'll tell you," her mother said.

Mrs. Poppy, it developed, had telephoned that afternoon. She and Mr. Poppy had received a letter from Minneapolis where the *Rip Van Winkle* company was playing. The manager had said that the little girl who took the part of Meenie, Rip's daughter, had been called back to New York. She was leaving the company when it left the Twin Cities, and the new little Meenie would join them in Omaha.

For the Deep Valley engagement, the manager had asked Mrs. Poppy to find a Deep Valley child. Mrs. Poppy had thought at once of Tib who, although she was twelve years old, was small enough to look much younger.

"She knew Tib could do the part," Mrs. Ray said. "For her dancing has made her accustomed to performing on the stage."

"Oh, Tib will be darling!" cried Betsy. She thought of Tib with her fluffy yellow curls, wearing a little

Dutch cap like the child in the billboard picture. "But how do Tacy and Winona and I happen to be in it?"

"There are village children needed in the play," Mrs. Ray explained, "and it is the custom of the company to get local children for those parts. They haven't any lines to say; they just follow at Rip Van Winkle's heels."

"I know," said Betsy. "I saw us on the billboards."

"Mrs. Poppy thought it might be fun for you to do it."

Betsy felt a wave of love for Mrs. Poppy.

"Tib's part is quite hard," Mrs. Ray went on. "But Mrs. Poppy will teach her. I've talked with the mothers, and all of us think that you children will enjoy the experience."

The kitchen had stopped whirling now. The lamp was fast in its bracket, and its glow was no brighter than the glow on Betsy's face.

Before she ate supper, she telephoned to Winona. That telephone ring they had heard, Winona said, had been Betsy's mother telling the news.

After supper Betsy ran over to Tacy's. Tacy was blissfully scared. In view of the unusual circumstances, she and Betsy were allowed to pay an evening call on Tib.

Tib was calm at the prospect of playing a part on

the stage, but she was happy.

"I can do it," she said. "I'll like to do it."

Back at home Betsy sat in front of the hard-coal heater, her arms around her knees. Inside herself she was saying over and over her poem, *The Curtain Goes Up.*

> "The curtain goes up,
> The curtain goes up,
> It's a wonderful moment,
> When the curtain goes up . . ."

"When I wrote that poem," she thought, "I didn't know where I'd be when the curtain went up."

She had a vision of the great curtain rising, and herself with Tacy and Tib and Winona, looking out at the dark crowded house from the golden glory of the stage.

13
Rip Van Winkle

BETSY, TACY, and Tib made many trips downtown that winter but none equaled or even approached in excitement the one they made on Saturday to act in *Rip Van Winkle*.

They walked as far as Winona's house. From there they were driven down in Winona's father's cutter. It had been arranged that Mr. Root would drive them all down. After the matinee each father was to take charge of getting his own child home for supper and back to the Opera House for the evening performance.

Tib had been at the Opera House all morning, rehearsing with the cast. Mrs. Poppy had taught her the part in the several days preceding. New Years had come and gone almost unnoticed, so great was the agitation aroused by Tib's daily visit to the Melborn Hotel.

Tib was not what is called "a quick study"; on the contrary, she was slow. But having learned the part she would not forget it. There was no danger of stage fright or nervousness throwing her off. She would do exactly as she had been told, and Mr. Winter who played the part of Rip had been pleased, Tib said with satisfaction.

"What does he look like?" Winona asked, as the cutter slipped gaily along the polished streets.

"He wears a silk hat, and a diamond ring, and a big gold watch chain. He looks important, and he *is* important, too. I'm supposed to step back and let him cross in front of me. That's one thing I mustn't forget."

"It will seem strange," said Betsy, "to hang on to the coat tails of such an important person."

She and Winona had been told by Mrs. Poppy that they would make their entrance hanging to Rip's coat tails.

"Oh, he's kind," said Tib. "And he likes children. But he's important. Don't forget that."

"Did you try on your costume?" Winona asked.

"Yes. I'm wearing a little Dutch cap like the one we saw in the picture. You all are, I think. And our skirts come down to our ankles. Girls must have dressed that way in Colonial times.

"I ought to look nice," she added. "Mamma washed my hair. And they're going to paint my cheeks."

"We'll all be painted!" Betsy bounced with joy.

"All the kids in our class are coming," said

Winona. "Herbert . . . Tom . . ."

"I'm getting scared," said Tacy. Her cheeks didn't need any paint; they were flaming.

"You'll be all right," Betsy assured her. "Just stay close to me."

Mr. Root stopped his horse in front of the Melborn Hotel. They had planned to meet Mrs. Poppy in the lobby there. But she was waiting out in front, walking up and down, more nervous than they had ever seen her.

"I'm as worked up as though I were playing myself," she said when Mr. Root had wished them all luck and driven away.

She put her arm around Tib.

"Girls," she said, "you're going to be proud of Tib today."

"We know it!" shouted Betsy and Tacy. It wasn't the first time they had been proud of Tib.

Winona shouted too. They surrounded Tib like a loyal bodyguard on the walk to the Opera House.

Mrs. Poppy walked bulkily in their midst. She was wearing her sealskin coat and cap; and her yellow hair and the diamonds in her ears gleamed against the fur. She was smiling, but now and then she looked at Betsy with an urgent, almost worried look.

"I'm going to get along all right, Mrs. Poppy," said Betsy. "All of us are."

"Of course you are," said Mrs. Poppy. "It isn't that . . ."

She didn't say what it was.

Sunny Jim darted out of the garage to cheer them on their way. Outside the Opera House a crowd of children had already gathered; they cheered too. All of Deep Valley seemed to know that Betsy, Tacy, Tib, and Winona were acting in *Rip Van Winkle*.

They turned in at the alley that led to the stage door. This was the same door they had seen Little Eva come out of.

"How surprised we'd have been that day," said Betsy, "if we'd known how soon we'd be walking in here ourselves."

"I love to go in doors that say 'Private, Keep Out,'" said Winona.

Tacy said nothing. She hugged her arm through Betsy's as they left their own bright snowy world behind, and entered the theatre.

They found themselves in a dusty barnlike space. They knew it was the stage, because they could see the curtain, half-raised, and the dim empty house beyond. There were stacks of canvas scenery about, and piles of ropes, and an assortment of miscellaneous objects including a wash tub.

"Props," said Tib waving her hand.

Men in overalls were hurrying about.

"Scene shifters," said Tib.

A worried-looking man in a rumpled checked suit approached Mrs. Poppy.

"Mr. Drew, the stage manager," whispered Tib.

Mr. Drew leaned toward Mrs. Poppy. He spoke in a lowered voice, as though he were telling a secret, but his words were audible.

"It's all arranged, Mrs. Poppy," he said. "Mr. . . . er . . . Kee is to show the children their routine. They can dress first."

"Thank you, Mr. Drew," said Mrs. Poppy. "I'm very grateful. This way," she said to the girls and led them down some stairs into a damp-smelling cellar.

They followed a narrow corridor. The walls were covered with show bills. *The Old Homestead. The Silver Slipper. Flora Dora. Ben Hur.* The names, the half-seen brightly colored pictures flashed past in glamorous parade.

Rows of dressing rooms opened off the hall. Tib went into one of them. Betsy, Tacy, and Winona were ushered into another. It contained a cracked mirror, a bare, scratched dressing table, a wash bowl and pitcher, and three wooden chairs.

A small wrinkled old lady with beadlike eyes came in, carrying a bundle of clothing.

"Hello," she said. "I'm Mrs. Mulligan, the wardrobe mistress. These are the costumes for village children, and see that they fit you! I think nothing of snipping off an arm here or a leg there."

Mrs. Mulligan made jokes like that, but she was painstaking about the costumes. Mrs. Poppy came in to help her, and they pinned and fitted energetically.

The dresses were long like Tib's; and the girls wore quaint Dutch caps. Tacy's long red ringlets flowed out becomingly, and so did Winona's straight black locks. Betsy wanted to unbraid her hair, but Mrs. Poppy said "No." She arranged the pigtails so that they stuck out jauntily and tied ribbons on the ends.

Mrs. Poppy painted round red circles on their cheeks. She painted their lips red too. They looked in the mirror at themselves and looked at one another, anticipation bubbling up in laughter.

They ran in to see Tib. She was sitting in front of a mirror. Her yellow hair curled up babyishly around her cap; her cheeks and lips were red like theirs and her lashes were beaded with black.

She wasn't excited in the way the others were, but for Tib she was excited. Her eyes were shining. She looked pleased when they praised her, although she said only:

"Thank goodness I'm up in my part!"

She had learned that expression from Mrs. Poppy but she used it naturally. It didn't sound affected coming from Tib as it would have if one of the others had said it.

With Tacy's icy hand in hers and Winona prancing behind, Betsy followed Mrs. Poppy up the stairs. Now the front part of the stage was enclosed; the scenery had been run into place, and the curtain was lowered.

Mr. Drew was waiting in the wings with a tall thin young man who wore a brown wig, knee breeches and a long-tailed coat. Lines were painted on his face.

"Mrs. Poppy," said Mr. Drew. "This is Mr. . . . er . . . Kee. He plays the Vedders, first father, then son."

"And in between," said the young man lightly, "one of Hendrik Hudson's men."

"He understudies Mr. Winter too," said Mr. Drew.

"You sound like an important person," Mrs. Poppy smiled. She put out a white-gloved hand. "How do you do?" she said.

"How do you do?" answered Mr. Kee. He had dancing blue eyes that passed now from Mrs. Poppy to Winona, to Tacy, to Betsy.

"Hello, kids," he said. *Spricht deutsch?*

"They look as though they should . . . don't they?" Mrs. Poppy asked.

"They're perfect."

"I'd like them to have a very good time."

"So Mr. Drew explained. I'll take care of them,"
said Mr. Kee. He took Betsy's hand with a flashing
smile. "Come on, Braids," he said. "And you, Curls,
and Locks. I'll show you the Village of Falling Water
before the curtain goes up."

They went through the wings to the empty stage.

At the back rose the Kaatskill Mountains, brightly
purple. To the left stood a country inn with a swinging sign reading George III. To the right was a tumble-
down cottage.

"Rip Van Winkle's palace," Mr. Kee said. "That's
Dame Van Winkle's wash tub out in front."

"And there's the stool where Tib will be sitting when the curtain goes up," said Betsy.

"You know the play?"

"Yes. Mrs. Poppy told it to us. We don't know exactly what we're to do though."

Mr. Kee explained. They came on in the first act, he said. They would wait in the wings until the words: "Here he comes now, surrounded by all the dogs and children in the district. They cling around him like flies around a lump of sugar."

When they got that cue, they would come on stage, running behind Rip.

"Two of us carry his coat tails, Mrs. Poppy says."

"That's right, Braids. Which two shall it be?"

"She and I," said Winona. "Tacy doesn't want to."

"Braids and Locks at the coat tails then, with Curls bringing up the rear." Mr. Kee seemed amused with the names he had made up for them.

He explained further.

"Rip will be carrying a small boy pick-a-back, and another boy will be holding his gun. Those two boys, Tom and Jeff, belong to the company. They know exactly what to do, and you must do just as they do."

"Do we come on and go off when they do?"

"Yes. Stick close to them and you can't go wrong.

Don't wander down to the front of the stage or get in anyone's way."

He gave them a few more instructions, then told them that after the first act they would not appear until the fourth.

"You can sit in the wings and watch the play. I'll join you whenever I can. Any questions now?"

"No," said Betsy. "I'm sure we can do it. We give plays ourselves all the time. I'm sure I ought to know how to act," she added importantly. "My uncle is an actor."

"He is?" asked the young man. "What's his name?"

"Keith Warrington." Betsy pronounced it proudly.

"Keith Warrington?"

Mr. Kee sounded so surprised that Betsy asked quickly, "You don't happen to know him; do you?"

"Never heard of him."

The young man settled his wig with long flexible fingers and looked hard at Betsy with his bright blue eyes.

"How do you like that . . . having an uncle in the profession?"

"Oh, I like it," Betsy said.

"She has a trunk full of his costumes," said Winona.

"She uses it for a desk," Tacy put in shyly.

"Desk, eh?" said the young man. "You do your arithmetic there, I suppose?"

"Arithmetic!" said Betsy scornfully. "I write stories there, and poems, and plays."

At that moment two boys in Dutch costume came bounding on the stage.

"Hi, Tom and Jeff!" called the young man. "Come here and meet the 'supes.'" Betsy and Tacy and Winona were "supes," it appeared; that was short for "supernumeraries."

"These are the boys," Mr. Kee explained, "whom you follow through thick and thin."

He walked away.

Tom and Jeff took the girls in hand good-naturedly. They took them to the front of the stage and let them look through a peephole in the center of the curtain. It was bad luck, they explained, to peep from any other place. The girls looked out eagerly and saw the audience filing in, laughing and talking.

"There are Julia and Jerry."

"Katie and Pin are with them."

"I see my father and mother," said Winona.

"I see mine too," said Tacy. "And all the Mullers."

"Rena and Margaret are in the front row," cried Betsy. "Rena's wearing her best hat, with pansies on it."

Winona took another turn at the peephole.

"I can't be sure," she said, "but I *think* I see Tom and Herbert up in the peanut heaven."

There were plenty of boys and girls there to judge by the racket going on.

Through all the noise they could hear the violins being tuned. That thin insistent sound increased the turmoil in their breasts. There was a call for the stage to be cleared, and Tom and Jeff hurried the girls past the Inn of George III, around a canvas wall into the wings. They stood where they could look out on the stage, although they were them-selves unseen.

Dame Van Winkle strolled out and took her place at the wash tub. Tib passed by with Mrs. Poppy and sat down on the stool. Mrs. Poppy arranged Tib's cap, the fluffy curls, her skirts. Then Mrs. Poppy rustled off the stage and Tom and Jeff pulled the girls further back in the wings. The orchestra was playing a piece Julia played, Mendelssohn's *Spring Song*.

They could not see the stage now, but they knew what had happened from the hush that fell on every-thing. Winona leaned out and whispered to Betsy:

"The curtain goes up."

They waited tensely, and after a moment they heard Dame Van Winkle speaking. They heard Tib's voice, sweet and unafraid. They heard Hendrik Vedder, the boy who was little Meenie's friend. Mr. Kee, who was playing Hendrik's father now, would play the grown-up Hendrik later.

Presently Mr. Winter joined the children in the wings. He was dressed in Rip's old deerskin coat, ragged breeches and torn hat, but he did not look merry as Rip was supposed to look; he looked grave.

He warned the girls in a whisper to stay close to Tom. Unsmiling he hoisted Jeff to his back and handed Tom the gun. They waited together so silently they could almost hear their heart beats. Tacy reached for Betsy's hand.

They heard a voice. "Here he comes now. . . . They cling around him like flies around a lump of sugar."

Mr. Winter's expression changed; he began to laugh. All at once he was Rip, and Betsy and Winona picked up his coat tails, laughing too. Tacy smiled, although her teeth were chattering. With Jeff riding pick-a-back, they all trooped out into a blaze of light.

After a few minutes Betsy got used to the light. She was conscious of the hushed expectant darkness of the house. Intent only on staying close to Tom and Jeff, she scarcely listened as Rip talked and the Dame scolded, as Meenie and Hendrik and Hendrik's father and themselves went on and off the stage.

Tib did not glance toward her friends. She too was intent . . . upon saying her lines and doing exactly as she had been told. But in the dance that ended the act, she gave them a cloudless smile.

When the curtain went up after having gone down, and the principals went forward to receive their applause, Tib floated out. She held Rip's hand with one hand and with the other she lifted her skirt in the daintiest of curtseys. Beyond the footlights her family and friends and half of Deep Valley, it seemed, clapped and cheered approval of the play, and especially of Tib. Modest but pleased, she curtsied again and again. The curtain went down.

Betsy, Tacy, and Winona did not appear in the

second act. Mr. Kee placed chairs for them in the wings at a point where they could see the stage, and while they waited for the curtain to go up, he dropped casually down on a barrel.

He stretched his long arms and locked his hands behind his head.

"Tell me," he said to Betsy, "why you use a trunk for a desk."

"It's much nicer than an ordinary desk," said Betsy. "A real theatrical trunk!"

"How do you happen to have it at your house?"

Betsy, talkative as always, explained.

She told him how Uncle Keith had run away from home, and why; she told how his trunk had come back at the outset of the Spanish War, and had never been called for, and how no one knew where he was.

"But he'll come back some day," Betsy said. "He must want to see Mamma, just as she wants to see him."

"*Does* she want to see him?" asked the young man. But just then the bell rang as a warning that the act was about to begin. Without waiting for an answer, he jumped up and strode away.

"It's a good idea, Betsy," said Tacy, "to tell that actor about your Uncle Keith. Maybe he'll meet him some day."

"He seems so interested too," said Betsy.

"Hush now!" cried Winona. "There's the music."

The curtain rose slowly on the dimly lighted kitchen of Rip's house.

Meenie sat by the window, looking out at a raging storm. It would be interesting, Betsy thought, to run around in back and see how they made that storm . . . the rain, the frightful wind, the thunder, and the lightning flashes. But she could not bear to take her eyes from Tib.

As the act progressed, however, she forgot that Meenie was Tib. Lost in the drama, she looked and listened, while the boy Hendrik told Meenie tales of the spirits that played at nine pins in the mountains, while Rip and his wife quarreled and Dame Van Winkle turned the hapless fellow out into the torrent. She forgot it was Tib's treble saying:

"Oh mother, hark at the storm!"

Again Tib curtsied before the big curtain, holding Rip's hand.

Between the second and third acts, Mr. Kee came to talk with the girls again. He was dressed as one of Hendrik Hudson's ghostly crew, wearing a high-crowned hat and gray doublet and hose.

He dropped down on his barrel.

"I suppose," he said to Betsy, "your family is all here to see you act."

"Papa and Mamma are coming tonight," said Betsy. "But Rena and Margaret and Jerry and Julia are here."

"How many brothers and sisters do you have?" he exclaimed, sounding surprised.

"Only two," said Betsy. "Jerry is a friend of Julia's. He invited her to come and see the play. And Rena is our hired girl. She brought Margaret."

"Is Julia old enough to be coming to a play with a young man?" Mr. Kee seemed amazed.

"Of course," said Betsy. "Why shouldn't she be?"

"She's in high school," said Tacy.

"You ought to hear her sing, Mr. Kee," Winona said. "She sings and speaks pieces too."

Betsy explained.

"She takes after Uncle Keith."

"She . . . what?" The young man jumped up as though he had heard the bell. But he hadn't. Erect on his long legs, he stood still, staring at Betsy.

"Does she look like him?" he asked abruptly.

"No," said Betsy. "Julia and Margaret and I all have dark hair like our father's. Uncle Keith has red hair like our mother's. But Julia gets her talent for singing and acting from Uncle Keith, and I get my writing from him."

"You do?"

"That's what my mother says," answered Betsy

firmly. "And my father says so too."

The bell really did ring then, and in a few moments they were transported to a wild mountain glen. Rip played at nine pins with an eerie crew; he drank from their flagon.

As soon as the act ended, Mr. Kee appeared.

"Braids," he said. "Let's take a look through the curtain. If I were ever to meet this uncle of yours, I'd like to be able to tell him I'd seen his family."

"Mr. Kee," said Betsy. "That's a splendid idea."

They went to the peephole in the curtain.

Margaret was acting very ladylike. Every hair of the brown English bob was in place. She was turning her big eyes solemnly about.

Julia was chatting with Jerry, looking very grown-up, with a fluffy bow at the top of her pompadour and another at the back of her neck.

"Father and mother coming tonight, eh?" asked Mr. Kee.

"Yes," said Betsy. "Papa can't get away from the store in the afternoon."

"What about your grandparents?" Mr. Kee asked. "The peppery old gentleman you told me about? I don't suppose *he*'d come to see a play."

"He and Grandma live in California now," Betsy replied. "He isn't as peppery as he used to be. Mamma thinks he's sorry he made Uncle Keith run away."

"He didn't actually *make* him run away," said the young man.

"Oh, yes he did!" answered Betsy.

"Not in my opinion," said Mr. Kee. "The young man must have been plenty peppery himself. You told me he had red hair, you know. He certainly gave everyone plenty of worry, and now, probably, he's ashamed to come back."

"*Ashamed* to come *back*?" Betsy cried. The honest surprise in her voice made Mr. Kee start.

"Why, that's the silliest thing I ever heard in my life!" she cried. "Everyone is longing for him to come back. It would make my mother happier than anything else in the world. He ought to be ashamed of *not* coming back."

"Hmm! You think so? Hmm!" said Mr. Kee.

The last act was in several scenes. Rip woke from his twenty-year nap. Wrinkled and ancient, with his flowing white beard, he returned to the village to find George III replaced by George Washington on the Inn's swinging sign. Betsy, Tacy, and Winona were part of a crowd hooting cruelly at the old man's heels.

No one believed the story of his long sleep in the Kaatskills. His old friends were dead, his wife was married to someone else, and Meenie (now a young lady, and played by a young lady actress) was about to be forced into marriage with a villain.

Mr. Kee appeared in the very nick of time, as the dashing sailor, Hendrik Vedder, come home to claim his sweetheart. Rip was recognized; he got his wife back; he came into a fortune, and he gave Meenie to Hendrik.

Everything came out right, before Rip raised his glass.

"Here's to your good health, und to your family's, und may you all live long and prosper!"

No wonder the audience almost wore out its hands with clapping!

Again and again the company appeared before the curtain. Betsy, Tacy, and Winona went now, trying to curtsey like Tib, smiling broadly at their respective families. Their classmates in the peanut gallery shouted and whooped. It was glorious! Like all glorious things it had to end, but unlike most of them it was going to be repeated that night, right after supper.

The girls scampered down to the basement to get into their own clothes. They washed their faces but were careful to leave some actress-red on their cheeks. They rushed back up to the stage door where their families were gathered. Betsy saw Jerry and Julia, Rena and Margaret. Her father, she knew, would be out in the alley, holding Old Mag.

To her surprise and pleasure she recognized Mr. Kee in the crowd around the door. In street clothes, he was tall and slender with a sweep of dramatic red hair.

"Braids," he said to Betsy, coming forward, "what do you think your mother is having for supper?"

Betsy was surprised at the question.

"Why . . . fried potatoes, probably," she said.

"Just what I thought," the young man answered. "In that case, I'm going home with you."

"You're . . . coming . . . home with me?" Betsy was delighted and bewildered.

"The reason I'm coming home with you," Mr. Kee said confidentially, "is that your mother fries potatoes so extremely well."

He smiled at her, his bright eyes dancing. He had a smile like . . . like . . . like . . .

"Uncle Keith!" cried Betsy. She tumbled into his arms.

Echoes to her cry sprang up all around her.

"Uncle Keith!" cried Tacy.

"Uncle Keith!" cried Tib.

"Uncle Keith!" cried Winona, and Julia, and Margaret, and even Rena.

Mr. Ray, out in the alley, heard the cries; he left Old Mag standing alone and pushed his way in at the door and found the young man's hand.

Dancing about in delirious joy, Betsy saw Mrs. Poppy. She was standing a little distance away, watching them and smiling. Her eyes looked as though she were ready to cry.

14

The Curtain Goes Up

THE SLEIGH was crowded going home, but nobody minded. In the back seat Margaret sat on Rena's lap, and Julia and Betsy sat close together squeezing each other's hands. They did not talk much. The great adventure of the play was dimmed by the far greater adventure of finding Uncle Keith.

In the front seat Uncle Keith talked in a quick earnest voice. He sat with his arm along the back of the seat, his face turned to Mr. Ray's kindly and now serious face. Uncle Keith wore a fur coat and a broad-brimmed actorish hat. His deep voice ran on and on beneath the chime of sleigh bells and the beat of Old Mag's hoofs.

He seemed to be pouring out the story of his wanderings. He *had* been in the Spanish War, the girls heard him say. He had been at Santiago. As an actor he had not done too badly; he had had his ups and downs; all actors had. The present engagement was with a solid company. But it had not satisfied his pride; he had not been willing to make his presence known in his own home town . . . until he met Betsy.

He turned with his flashing smile.

Mr. Ray turned, too.

"We must plan quickly how we're going to surprise Mother."

There was a clamor of voices then, for everyone had an idea. Mr. Ray wanted Uncle Keith to rap at the kitchen door and pretend he was delivering groceries. Margaret thought he should go down the chimney like Santa Claus. Julia wanted him to stand underneath the window and sing a serenade.

Rena thought Mrs. Ray should be prepared.

"She might have an attack," said Rena. "Lord-a-mercy, it's the last thing in her mind to have her long-lost brother walking in."

"But she's never had an attack," said Mr. Ray. "She doesn't have attacks. What's your idea, Betsy?"

Betsy bounced beneath the buffalo robe.

"Let's take a scene out of the play," she cried. "You be Rip, Uncle Keith, and take Margaret on your back, and Julia and I will carry your coat tails, and all of us will prance through the kitchen door."

"Betsy has picked it," said Uncle Keith. "That's just what we will do."

They climbed out of the sleigh on the little road that led around to the barn.

"I'll be along to give you some supper," Mr. Ray

told Old Mag, slapping her bay rump.

Old Mag went on without a driver. The conspirators tiptoed over the snowy lawn and looked in at the kitchen window.

Sure enough, Mrs. Ray was frying potatoes. She was dressed for the theatre, in her green broadcloth dress . . . it was that shade of soft green which was most becoming to her. She wore a green bow in her high red pompadour. A fresh checkered apron was tied around her waist.

"Still as slim as a breeze," said Uncle Keith.

"She's a wonder," said Mr. Ray.

He pushed open the side kitchen door.

"Hi, Jule! Want to see a scene from the play?"

"Is my actress daughter in it?" Mrs. Ray asked, laughing.

"There are plenty of actors in it," said Mr. Ray.

"Well, hurry up with it. You're letting the cold in."

But he held the door open a minute.

Uncle Keith put his hat on the back of his head and shook his red hair into his eyes. He picked up Margaret and swung her to his back. Julia and Betsy took hold of his coat tails.

"We laugh and yell," Betsy explained.

Laughing and yelling, they all trooped into the kitchen.

The long-handled fork Mrs. Ray was holding clattered to the floor. She turned so pale that it looked for a moment as though Rena might have been right about that attack. But instantly a wave of color rushed back into her cheeks. Joyful tears filled her eyes, and she ran to Uncle Keith who flung his arms about her.

Julia and Betsy and Margaret stood silent and abashed. Rena wiped her eyes, saying "Lord-a-mercy!" "Lord-a-mercy!" over and over again. Mr. Ray's eyes looked dampish too.

"Now, now! There, there!" he kept saying, for Betsy's mother was crying hard. Uncle Keith was crying too, and presently Julia began to sniff, and then Betsy did, and then Margaret.

"Make some coffee, Rena," Mr. Ray said. "Come on, you idiots, and cry in the parlor, so that Rena can get supper on. I'm going out to feed Old Mag. She's got more sense than you have."

That made them all laugh, and Rena took off her coat and her best hat with pansies on it, and tied on an apron. When Mr. Ray came back from the barn the family was in the back parlor. The crying was over, and everyone was talking at once trying to explain to Mrs. Ray just what had happened.

"I didn't know he was Uncle Keith because his name was Mr. Kee," Betsy said.

"Mr. Kee?" Mrs. Ray asked.

"Yes," said Uncle Keith. "I act under two names usually, Waring Kee for the Nicholas Vedder part, and Keith Warrington for Hendrik. But I asked to be programmed only as Waring Kee in Deep Valley."

"Why did you do that, Keith?" Mrs. Ray asked, holding his hands. "Would you really have come to Deep Valley and gone away without seeing me?"

"I'm afraid I would have," said Uncle Keith, looking ashamed, "if Braids here hadn't told me you'd forgiven me."

"Then how lucky, how incredibly lucky, that you and Betsy happened to get acquainted!"

Uncle Keith smoothed back his red hair thoughtfully.

"That wasn't just luck," he said. "Somebody managed it. I felt there was something funny in the air when Drew, the stage manager, asked me to look after the 'supes.' That's never part of my job. He said it was a favor the theatre owner's wife had asked . . ."

"Mrs. Poppy," said Betsy. "I heard her thank Mr. Drew for arranging it."

"Mrs. Poppy!" exclaimed Mrs. Ray. "But how could she have known who he was?"

"I told her about Uncle Keith long ago," said Betsy. "She's been making inquiries about him. She asked me not to tell you, Mamma, because she didn't want you disappointed in case she didn't find him."

"She saw the name Kee Waring, no doubt, and thought that was an easy change from Keith Warrington," Mr. Ray said.

"Or she may have looked up a Minneapolis program. I was Keith Warrington there," said Uncle Keith.

As it came out later, both these things had happened. Mrs. Poppy had seen the name Kee Waring, and thinking it sounded like Keith Warrington had asked Mr. Poppy to get a Minneapolis program. She had received one just a few minutes before Betsy, Tacy, Tib, and Winona had found her pacing back and forth in front of the hotel.

Mrs. Ray's eyes grew soft as Mrs. Poppy's part in the affair became clear.

"How very very kind of her!" she said. "From now on, Betsy, Mrs. Poppy is my friend as well as yours."

"Will you call on her?" asked Betsy.

"With my card case and Old Mag, just as you asked me to," Mrs. Ray answered, smiling.

"Will you take me?" asked Julia. "Remember what Betsy said about her helping me with my singing."

"I'll take you too," Mrs. Ray promised.

Betsy knew then that Mrs. Poppy's wish was coming true.

All talking at once, they moved to the dining room, where Uncle Keith ate fried potatoes with one arm around Mrs. Ray and Margaret on his lap. He kept looking across the table at Julia and Betsy with his dancing bright blue eyes.

Rena had made a pot of coffee, good and strong. And she had stirred up some biscuits to go with the fried potatoes and cold meat. Without being told, she had opened some Damson plum preserves. It was a good supper, but only the children ate much.

Uncle Keith kept looking around the table at the faces under the hanging lamp as though he couldn't look at them enough.

After supper Betsy took him upstairs to see her desk.

"I suppose you'll want your trunk now," she said. "And that's all right. I can get another desk."

"Don't you dare!" he said. "Braids, some of the stories and poems I've always wanted to write are going to be written on this trunk."

Betsy liked to hear him say that. It made her feel better about the sheet of pink stationery that had gone to the *Ladies' Home Journal* and had never been heard from.

When they got down stairs, Uncle Keith asked Julia to sing for him. She sang a new song called *The Rosary*, and she sang it so well that Uncle Keith got up and kissed her.

Mr. Ray went out to the front porch and brought in the newspaper.

"Thought I'd see what the *Sun* had to say about your show," he remarked, unfolding it.

"Good gosh!" said Uncle Keith to Betsy, jumping up. "You and I have to get back to the theatre."

He looked around for his coat and hat, and Julia ran to get them for him. Betsy started putting on her wraps too.

"Can you come back here to stay tonight?" Betsy's mother asked.

"Yes, I can. Tomorrow's Sunday. I can take the train to Omaha tomorrow night."

"I'll bring Old Mag around right away," Mr. Ray said.

He delayed, though, to glance at the newspaper. And then he did not move.

"The notice of the play will be on the inside, dear," Mrs. Ray said, but Mr. Ray did not open the paper further. He stared at the front page.

"Well, bless my soul!" he said at last, in such an unbelieving tone that everyone started. Julia ran to look over his shoulder.

"Betsy!" she cried.

Dropping her overshoes, Betsy ran to look. She could hardly believe her eyes at what she saw.

There on the front page of Winona's father's paper, in the very center of the page, enclosed in a decorative box made of roses and doves, was a poem. The title was printed at the top and the author's name at the bottom.

The title was, *The Curtain Goes Up*.

The author's name was Betsy Warrington Ray.

"Why, Betsy, how did this happen?" her mother asked in an agitated voice.

"I don't know," said Betsy. "I've no idea."

"Did you send the poem to the paper?"

"No. But I gave it to Winona. She asked me for it. She liked it."

"Liked it!" said Mrs. Ray. "I should think she *would* like it. It's splendid! It's wonderful."

Mrs. Ray always thought that about her children's achievements.

"I love it!" cried Julia.

"Couldn't have done better myself," said Mr. Ray.

Rena came running from the kitchen to look, and Margaret took the paper into her chubby hands.

Uncle Keith was all ready to leave for the theatre. He had put on his fur coat, and his hat was in his hand. He was in a hurry, but he didn't act hurried.

Standing in the middle of the Ray front parlor, he read Betsy's poem aloud.

Betsy's father stood listening, trying not to look proud. Betsy's mother was crying for the second time that night. Margaret's face was shining as though it had been buttered. And Julia held Betsy's hand tight.

Uncle Keith read the poem aloud in his beautiful trained actor's voice. It wasn't as good as he made it sound; Betsy knew that. But it was good enough so that she felt as she listened that some day she could write something good. Some day in her maple or on Uncle Keith's trunk, she would write something good.

Tacy would be proud, and so would Tib. And so would Winona who had brought about the present golden moment. And so would Miss Sparrow who had helped her at the library. And so would dear Mrs. Poppy on whom her mother would call.

Thoughts are such fleet magic things. Betsy's thoughts swept a wide arc while Uncle Keith read her poem aloud. She thought of Julia learning to sing with Mrs. Poppy. She thought of Tib learning to dance. She thought of herself and Tacy and Tib going into their 'teens. She even thought of Tom and Herbert and of how, by and by, they would be carrying her books and Tacy's and Tib's up the hill from high school.

> *"The curtain goes up,*
> *The curtain goes up . . ."*

Uncle Keith read in his vibrant actor's voice.

THE END

Maud Hart Lovelace and Her World

Maud Palmer Hart circa 1906

Estate of Merian Kirchner

MAUD HART LOVELACE was born on April 25, 1892, in Mankato, Minnesota. Like Betsy, Maud followed her mother around the house at age five asking questions such as "How do you spell 'going down the street'?" for the stories she had already begun to write. Soon she was writing poems and plays. When Maud was ten, a booklet of her poems was printed; and by age eighteen, she had sold her first short story.

The Hart family left Mankato shortly after Maud's high school graduation in 1910 and settled in Minneapolis, where Maud attended the University of Minnesota. In 1917, she married Delos W. Lovelace, a newspaper reporter who later became a popular writer of short stories.

The Lovelaces' daughter, Merian, was born in 1931. Maud would tell her daughter bedtime stories about her childhood, and it was these stories that gave her the idea of writing the Betsy-Tacy books. Maud did not intend to write an entire series when *Betsy-Tacy*, the first book, was published in 1940, but readers asked for more stories. So Maud took Betsy through high school and beyond college to the "great world" and marriage. The final book in the series, *Betsy's Wedding*, was published in 1955.

The Betsy-Tacy books are based very closely on Maud's own life. "I could make it all up, but in these Betsy-Tacy stories, I love to work from real incidents," Maud wrote. "The Ray family is a true portrayal of the Hart family. Mr. Ray is like Tom Hart; Mrs. Ray like Stella Palmer Hart; Julia like Kathleen; Margaret like Helen; and Betsy is like me, except that, of course, I glamorized her to make her a proper heroine." Tacy and Tib are based on Maud's real-life best friends, Frances "Bick" Kenney and Marjorie "Midge" Gerlach, and Deep Valley is based on Mankato.

In fact, so much in the books was taken from real life that it is sometimes difficult to draw the line between fact and fiction. And through the years, Maud received a great deal of fan mail from readers who were fascinated by the question—what is true, and what is made up?

Maud Hart Lovelace died on March 11, 1980. But her legacy lives on in the beloved series she created and in her legions of fans, many of whom are members of the Betsy-Tacy Society and the Maud Hart Lovelace Society. For more information, write to:

The Betsy-Tacy Society
P.O. Box 94
Mankato, MN 56002-0094
www.betsy-tacysociety.org

The Maud Hart Lovelace Society
277 Hamline Avenue South
St. Paul, MN 55105
www.maudhartlovelacesociety.com

The original cover of Betsy-Tacy, ***illustrated by Lois Lenski.***

Thomas Y. Crowell Company, 1940

About Betsy-Tacy

IN THE SPRING OF 1897, Maud Hart and Frances "Bick" Kenney met at Maud's fifth birthday party and became lifelong friends—just like Betsy and Tacy. As Maud wrote to Bick Kenney's granddaughter in 1960, when she was sixty-eight years old, "Tacy certainly is your red-haired grandmother and has been my dearest friend ever since my fifth birthday."

In the story, Betsy thinks Tacy is calling names when she first introduces herself because her name is so unusual. (Maud first discovered the name "Tacy" in a colonial newspaper when she was doing research for another book.) We don't know if this happened in real life, but it's possible that a similar misunderstanding resulted when Bick told Maud *her* name, which is also a bit unusual. Bick Kenney's niece explained the origin of the nickname: "Frances Kenney had very red hair as a child and was called 'Brick.' Not being old enough to pronounce it properly, she called herself 'Bick.'" And Bick is the name she used throughout her life.

Maud seemed to recall the occasion of her fifth birthday very vividly, and much of the description

apple
tree

The Easter Egg
Tree

Maud Hart Lovelace

The
Little Hill

Road up the Big Hill

Tacy's
Home

*This map of the Hill Street neighborhood by Lois Lenski
was printed on the endpapers of early editions of the first
four Betsy-Tacy books.*

Maud's straight hair was curled for these photographs, taken for the occasion of her fifth birthday.

Maud Hart Lovelace Archives

Lois Lenski probably referred to the photos when she drew Betsy in her special party dress.

of the party in the book was based on her memories. For example, she remembered that she wore a "checked silk [dress] in tan, rose, and cream," like Betsy's. And Bick really did bring Maud a little glass pitcher as a birthday gift. Although its gold-painted rim has now worn away, the pitcher can be seen today in the Maud Hart Lovelace wing of the Minnesota Valley Regional Library in Mankato, Minnesota.

In fact, Betsy and Tacy's adventures throughout the book are based on Maud's real childhood experiences. In an interview, Maud described some of the games she and Bick used to play, which will sound very familiar: "We used to color sand and put it in bottles and have sand stores and sell it. We cut our paper dolls out of the magazines. We dressed up in our mothers' long skirts. We went on picnics."

In 1897, there really was a bench on the hill at the top of the street where Maud and Bick ate their suppers, although it was gone by 1906 or 1907. But readers may be pleased to know that a memorial bench was placed there in 1989, and it is still there today—a testimony to the powerful effect of Maud's writing, and in commemoration of a very special friendship.

Maud (right) and Bick (left) were lifelong friends— here they are at age ten.

The glass pitcher that Bick gave to Maud for her fifth birthday is now on display at the public library in Mankato.

Julie A. Schrader

Maud lived with her family in this little house at 333 Center Street.

The Ray house, at 333 Hill Street, closely resembles Maud's.

Maud's mother, Stella Palmer Hart, was a schoolteacher before her marriage to Tom Hart.

Kathleen and Helen Hart, Maud's sisters, the models for Julia and Margaret Ray.

*Maud and her friends attended Pleasant Grove School,
a redbrick building that was built in 1871.*

*Lois
Lenski's
drawing
of the
school-
house.*

Maud once spoke of "the fresh exciting world in which children live" and said, "I do think I remember that better than most grown-ups." Many generations of Betsy-Tacy fans would certainly agree!

The original cover of Betsy-Tacy and Tib, *illustrated by Lois Lenski.*

Thomas Y. Crowell Company, 1941

About Betsy-Tacy and Tib

BETSY AND TACY first meet Tib Muller at the end of *Betsy-Tacy*, when the girls are six years old. In real life, however, Maud knew Marjorie Gerlach—or "Midge," as she was called—before then, although they may not really have been friends yet, because they were so young. As Maud remarked: "I have heard from my mother that I had known [Midge] since we were in our baby carriages, for our mothers knew each other." So perhaps it wasn't until the girls were six that they first started to play together. But we do know that by the summer of 1900, when Maud, Bick, and Midge were eight years old, the three girls had become fast friends, just like their fictional counterparts at the beginning of *Betsy-Tacy and Tib*.

Maud and Bick were fascinated by Midge's house, just as Betsy and Tacy are by Tib's. Maud

Maud and Bick were fascinated with Midge's house, which stood at 503 Byron Street in Mankato.

once wrote: "Bick and I discovered [Midge's] chocolate-colored house with colored glass over the front door, which to us was a mansion of all glories." Midge's father, who was an architect, like Mr. Muller in the story, apparently designed the Gerlach house. But readers may be surprised to know that although Midge's house *was* brown, and really *did* have a pane of colored glass over the front door, it never had a tower. Instead, it was the house behind Midge's that had a tower, and it is

Although Midge's house didn't really have a tower, Maud may have gotten her inspiration from this house, which stood behind Midge's.

Lois Lenski's drawing of Tib's house

The Standard Historical and Pictorial Atlas and Gazetteer of Blue Earth County, MN, 1895

Henry Gerlach, Midge's father, was an architect, like Mr. Muller.

likely this tower that inspired Maud to invent one for Tib's house.

While Midge's house was a favorite place for indoor fun, the three girls loved to roam the Big Hill—which was really Prospect Heights—for outdoor fun. A Mankato neighbor once described Prospect Heights in much the same way Maud describes the Big Hill in the story: "It was a natural playground for all the children in our neighborhood. On the other side of the hill was a ravine with a small creek, and on the other side of the creek was Bunker Hill. On the hill and in the ravine, the wildflowers grew in abundance." And there really was a house on the hill, where Anna Asplund lived with her family. Mrs. Asplund was the inspiration for the character Mrs. Ekstrom, who offers sugar cookies to the three hungry beggars at her door.

Many of the episodes in the book, including the

Maud Hart Lovelace's Deep Valley by Julie A. Schrader

Midge's mother, Minnie Gerlach.

begging episode, were based on real-life incidents. While describing a Thanksgiving dinner reunion with Bick, Maud reminisced: "We talked about old days and laughed very hard about the time we made Everything Pudding and cut off one another's hair." And an old friend of Maud's remembered that "the street carnival was just as it is in the book, flying lady and all." Maud also recalled that Bick played the part of the Flying Lady on the end of a seesaw in the Hart woodshed. Even the mishaps—such as when Bick yelled that she was falling off—are accurately depicted in the book.

Of course, not everything in the book is based on real life. One interesting difference involves Midge's family. Although Midge's brothers, Henry and William, are fictionalized in the books as Freddie and Hobbie, her baby sister, Dorothy, never appears in the books at all. But Dorothy's nickname will be familiar to readers—Maud uses her name for the character Aunt Dolly, who first appears in *Betsy-Tacy and Tib*.

At the end of *Betsy-Tacy and Tib*, the girls wonder what it would be like to be ten. "We won't be going to balls, maybe," Betsy says to Tib. "But we'll have lots of fun, you and me and Tacy." And we can guess that Maud, Bick, and Midge did too.

About Betsy and Tacy
Go Over the Big Hill

BETSY AND TACY GO OVER THE BIG HILL was first published in 1942 by Thomas Y. Crowell Company. It was originally published as *Over the Big Hill*, but the publisher later decided to add the names "Betsy and Tacy" to the title so that it would appeal to fans of the previous books. But Maud had an entirely different title in mind at first, which the publisher didn't like. She wanted to call it "Betsy-Tacy and Tib are Ten." And the events in the story are based on Maud's life at around the time she and her friends really did turn ten, in 1902.

In writing about her childhood so many years later, Maud didn't depend on just her own memory to get the details right. She reread her diaries, wrote to friends in Mankato, and did a lot of other research to make sure that as much as possible was historically accurate. For example, not only did Maud, Bick, and Midge write to the King of Spain as Betsy, Tacy, and Tib do, but Alphonso the Thirteenth really *was* crowned the King of Spain on May 17, 1902, and it really *was* a Saturday, as it is

The original cover of Betsy and Tacy Go Over the Big Hill,
illustrated by Lois Lenski.

Thomas Y. Crowell Company, 1942

The illustrator, Lois Lenski, based many of her drawings on photographs—here, Tib looks just like the photo of Midge!

Midge Gerlach ("Tib") in her accordion-pleated dress.

Maud's older sister, Kathleen Hart, loved to perform just as much as Julia Ray does in the book.

in the book. It is this kind of attention to the very smallest detail that makes the books feel so true.

Readers may be curious to know if there really was a Syrian settlement in Mankato, Minnesota, at the turn of the last century. There was. It was called Tinkcomville after its founder, James Ray Tinkcom. Like Mr. Meecham in the story, Mr. Tinkcom came to Mankato from New York and in 1873 bought all the land in the valley. He called it Tinkcom's Addition and sold parcels of land to a group of immigrants in the 1890s. (Although the immigrants called themselves Syrians, they were actually of Lebanese descent. At the end of the last century, Lebanon was part of Syria; it became a country in its own right in 1948.) And just like Betsy, Tacy, and Tib, Maud and her friends enjoyed visiting the friendly community, which seemed exotic to them. Maud wrote: "From spring to fall we children picnicked and roamed on the hills. We loved to invade Tinkcomville, fascinated by the colorful Syrian colony. There was a rumor which used to enthrall us that one Syrian child was a princess."

Unfortunately, we can find no historical evidence of a Syrian princess in Mankato. So we don't know if Maud, Bick, and Midge really did meet a little Syrian girl on the Big Hill or if they really did fight with their older sisters over who would be the

The character of Mr. Meecham was based on James Ray Tinkcom.

Maud, Bick, and midge probably sighed over newspaper photos of the sixteen-year-old King of Spain like this one.

Queen of Summer. But in the summer of 1902, there was an event that may have provided a model for Naifi's patriotic coronation at the end of *Betsy and Tacy Go Over the Big Hill*. It was the fiftieth anniversary of the founding of Mankato, and as she so often did, Maud put a real-life event to good use in her fiction.

About Betsy and Tacy Go Downtown

BETSY AND TACY GO DOWNTOWN was published in 1943. Like *Betsy and Tacy Go Over the Big Hill*, it was first published under a different title, *Downtown*. The publisher later decided to add the names "Betsy and Tacy" to the title so readers would know it was part of the growing series. The book is based on things that happened in 1904 and 1905, when Maud, Bick, and Midge were twelve years old. Maud recalled, "As we grew older we made more trips downtown"—just as Betsy, Tacy, and Tib do in the book.

Downtown Deep Valley is a fictional version of Maud's hometown, Mankato. In the early 1900s, Mankato was "a thriving county seat" with a population of about eleven thousand people. Maud uses many of Mankato's actual street names in the book. Front Street, Broad Street, and Second Street are all described in exact detail, as are the Melborn Hotel (really the Saulpaugh Hotel), the new Carnegie Library, and the Opera House.

We are introduced to several new characters in *Downtown*. Not surprisingly, they are all based on

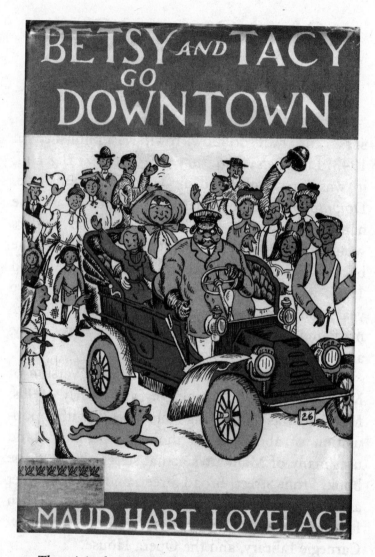

The original cover of Betsy and Tacy Go Downtown,
illustrated by Lois Lenski.

Thomas Y. Crowell Company, 1943

The "Melborn Hotel" was really the Saulpaugh Hotel, which once stood on the corner of Front Street at Main, in Mankato.

The Opera House

Blue Earth County Historical Society

Maud's friend Beulah Hunt was the model for Winona Root. Beulah is shown here with her dog, Peter.

Maud Hart Lovelace Archives

Frank Palmer ("Uncle Keith") with Stella Palmer Hart ("Mrs. Ray").

real people. Winona Root was based on Maud's friend Beulah Hunt. Her father, Frank W. Hunt, ran a newspaper, and as Maud remembers: "Sometimes, if we were lucky, we went to the matinee at the Opera House; on passes, since Beulah's father was the editor of the *Free Press*." Mr. and Mrs. Poppy were based on Clarence and Roma Saulpaugh, who ran the Saulpaugh Hotel. Midge got a ride in one of the first autos to reach Mankato, just like Tib, although we don't know if it was Mr. Saulpaugh's. While writing *Downtown*, Maud wrote to a Mankato friend: "I would like to bring in Mr. Bennett . . . or Mr. Saulpaugh's automobile . . . I feel sure it was about that date that Midge took her famous ride." And Uncle Keith was based on Frank Palmer, her mother's brother. He really did run away from home and join an opera troupe, but since Maud didn't meet him until she was grown up, the touching reunion scene at the end of the book never took place in real life.

Maud wrote many plays that she and her friends performed. She really did write one called *The Repentance of Lady Clinton*, which Maud and her friends performed in real life, although Betsy, Tacy, Tib, and Winona decide not to in the story. Maud remembers: "We gave *The Repentance of Lady Clinton* in Midge's back parlor. I repented so hard

The character of Mr. Poppy was based on Clarence Saulpaugh . . .

Maud Hart Lovelace's Deep Valley by Julie A. Schrader

Maud Hart Lovelace's Deep Valley by Julie A. Schrader

. . . and Mrs. Poppy was based on Roma Saulpaugh.

*The Saulpaughs
in their auto . . .*

*. . . and the
Poppys in their
auto.*

Mankato's Carnegie Library opened its doors in 1904.

Lois Lenski's drawing looks just like the photo.

and to such good effect that I made a little boy in the audience cry. We had to stop the show to soothe him."

Maud had always known what she wanted to do. "I cannot remember back to a year in which I did not consider myself to be a Writer, and the younger I was the bigger that capital 'W,'" she wrote. "Back in Mankato, I wrote stories in notebooks and illustrated them with pictures cut from magazines. When I was ten my father, I hope at not too great expense, had printed a booklet of my earliest rhymes." We don't know if Maud wrote a story similar to "Flossie's Accident," but she did submit one of her early efforts to a magazine. Like "Flossie's Accident," it was "written on a brilliant pink paper . . . [but] never heard from."

A prediction about Betsy appears on the last page of *Downtown*: "Some day in her maple or on Uncle Keith's trunk, she would write something good." Maud certainly did!

About Illustrator
Lois Lenski

Lois Lenski

The Lois Lenski Carey Foundation Inc.

LOIS LENSKI was born on October 14, 1893, in Springfield, Ohio, the fourth of five children to Lutheran minister Richard C. H. Lenski and his wife, Marietta. When Lois was six, the family moved to Anna, Ohio, a place Lois remembered fondly as a "perfect child's town. . . . The most familiar sounds were the whistles of a train passing through, the *clop-clop* of horses' hooves on the dirt streets, the barking of dogs, and the ringing of church bells"—a place very much like Betsy Ray's Deep Valley, Minnesota.

As a child, Lois enjoyed reading, sewing, and drawing. After graduating from high school, Lois entered Ohio State University, where she majored in education but used all of her electives for art courses. Upon completing her degree in 1915, Lois refused a teaching offer and instead traveled to New York City to study at the Art Students League in order to polish and perfect her technique. In the evenings, she worked at the School of Industrial Art as an assistant in the illustration class taught by artist and mural painter Arthur Covey. During this time, Lois worked on a set of nursery rhyme illustrations that were published by Platt and Munk as a children's coloring book.

In 1921, Lois married Covey, a widower, and became stepmother to his children, Margaret and Laird. Lois found her time consumed with household chores—taking care of a large house, garden, and children—yet she continued to make time for her art. Carrying a sketchbook wherever she went, Lois drew the faces and figures of people she saw, and submitted many of these sketches to publishers, hoping to get hired as a book illustrator. Helen Dean Fish, an editor at Stokes, suggested that Lois write her own stories. Lois's first book, *Skipping Village*, published by Stokes in 1927, was a fictionalized picture book of her own childhood.

After the birth of her son Stephen in 1929, Lois's family soon moved to a 113-acre farm in Harwinton, Connecticut, which they named Greenacres. A small wooden building on the top of a hill became Lois's studio, where she continued to write and illustrate picture books, the most popular of which was the Mr. Small series, including *The Little Train* and *The Little Auto*.

In the 1930s, Lois began to write longer historical fiction books for 8- to 12-year-old readers, such as *Puritan Adventure* and *Indian Captive*. Lois's knack for capturing children's expressions and movement, as well as her many collaborations with other authors, led to her being chosen to illustrate a new children's book series in 1940—the Betsy-Tacy books by Maud Hart Lovelace. Lois created the pictures of Betsy and Tacy using photographs from Maud's childhood. She also traveled to Mankato, Minnesota, to see the actual homes where Maud Hart and Frances Kenney had lived and drew a detailed map of the places in "Deep Valley," which was included in early editions of *Betsy-Tacy*.

Lois illustrated *Betsy-Tacy*, *Betsy-Tacy and Tib*, *Betsy and Tacy Go Over the Big Hill*, and *Betsy and Tacy Go Downtown*, which tell the stories of the girls' adventures from age five to twelve. Readers have their favorite Lenski illustrations of Betsy, Tacy, and Tib, including the piano box, Everything Pudding, and Betsy writing stories in the maple tree.

In 1944, Lois was approached by Crowell, the publisher, and offered the chance to illustrate the Betsy-Tacy high school books, beginning with *Heaven to Betsy*, which were aimed at teen readers. Lois declined to work on the new books, as she preferred to illustrate books for younger readers, and suggested artist Vera Neville for the position.

During the 1940s, Lois's family began to travel throughout the South. Lois observed the lifestyles and customs of children in the states they visited, and these sketchbooks led to her "Regionals" series for middle grade readers, including *Bayou Suzette* and *Texas Tomboy*. The second Regional, *Strawberry Girl*, won the 1946 Newbery Medal for outstanding work in children's literature.

In the 1950s, Lois suffered from pernicious anemia and was advised by her doctors to spend winters in Florida. Despite her illness, Lois continued to write and illustrate two books per year. In 1958, her husband, Arthur Covey, became ill and passed away in 1960. Lois sold the Connecticut farm, Greenacres, and made her permanent home in Tarpon Springs, Florida. From 1960 to 1971, she continued to write and illustrate her children's series, including Mr. Small, Davy, Roundabout, and Debbie. Her autobiography, *Journey into Childhood*, was published by Lippincott in 1972.

Lois Lenski passed away on September 11, 1974, at her Florida home. Her legacy includes the nearly one hundred books she wrote and illustrated as well as illustrations for more than fifty books by other authors, including the Betsy-Tacy childhood books.

—Teresa Musgrove Gibson

Sources: Lois Lenski,
Journey into Childhood (Lippincott, 1972);
Something About the Author,
vol. 26 (Gale, 1982)

THE BETSY-TACY SERIES BEGINS

BETSY-TACY

ISBN 978-0-06-440096-1 (paperback)

BETSY-TACY AND TIB
Foreword by Ann M. Martin

ISBN 978-0-06-440097-8 (paperback)

BETSY AND TACY GO OVER THE BIG HILL
Foreword by Judy Blume

ISBN 978-0-06-440099-2 (paperback)

BETSY AND TACY GO DOWNTOWN
Foreword by Johanna Hurwitz

ISBN 978-0-06-440098-5 (paperback)

THE BETSY-TACY HIGH SCHOOL YEARS AND BEYOND

HEAVEN TO BETSY AND BETSY IN SPITE OF HERSELF
Foreword by Laura Lippman

ISBN 978-0-06-179469-8 (paperback)

Heaven to Betsy: In the first of the high school books, Betsy is 14 and a freshman at Deep Valley High.

Betsy in Spite of Herself: It's Betsy's sophomore year and she takes a glamorous trip to Milwaukee to visit Tib.

BETSY WAS A JUNIOR AND BETSY AND JOE

Foreword by Meg Cabot

ISBN 978-0-06-179472-8 (paperback)

Betsy Was a Junior: Betsy (unwisely) introduces the idea of sororities to Deep Valley High.

Betsy and Joe: Betsy's senior year arrives and finally she is going with Joe!

BETSY AND THE GREAT WORLD AND BETSY'S WEDDING

Foreword by Anna Quindlen

ISBN 978-0-06-179513-8 (paperback)

Betsy and the Great World: Betsy sets off for a year-long tour of Europe to start her writing career.

Besty's Wedding: As WWI sweeps across Europe, Betsy hopes she and Joe find happines.

THE DEEP VALLEY BOOKS

EMILY OF DEEP VALLEY

Foreword by Mitali Perkins

ISBN 978-0-06-200330-0 (paperback)

Maud Hart Lovelace's only young adult stand-alone novel, *Emily of Deep Valley,* is considered by fans of her beloved Betsy-Tacy series to be one of the author's finest works.

CARNEY'S HOUSE PARTY AND WINONA'S PONY CART

Foreword by Melissa Wiley

ISBN 978-0-06-200329-4 (paperback)

Carney's House Party fills in the gaps in Lovelace's wildly popular high school Betsy-Tacy books, and *Winona's Pony Cart* revisits Betsy, Tacy and Tib as young girls.